Praise for
The Other Side of Darkness

"A moving and profound look into the world of obsessive-compulsive disorder, Melody Carlson's *The Other Side of Darkness* is a powerfully told tale of deception, redemption, and the true character of God. Your heart will break and heal again as this unlikely heroine discovers that God really isn't as she imagined and His love and grace are greater than her fears."

—MARLO SCHALESKY, author of *Beyond the Night*

"Melody Carlson's matchless insights into human character shine in *The Other Side of Darkness*. Every spiritual weakness, every flaw of the heart, every desire to be loved and accepted, Ms. Carlson understands, caresses, and clarifies. A powerful read."

—SUSAN MEISSNER, author of *The Shape of Mercy*

"*The Other Side of Darkness* is a frank and sometimes harrowing portrayal of mental illness tangled with spiritual disorder. Anyone with a heart can identify with Melody Carlson's fragile protagonist. This is a book that needed to be written, and it's a book that needs to be read. Despite its somber subject, I couldn't put it down. And I'm a better person for the experience."

—KATHRYN MACKEL, author of *Boost*

"Melody Carlson possesses a rare and riveting gift for seeing compassionately into the troubled soul and pointing with rich prose toward the real answers to mental illness found in Christ. *The Other Side of Darkness* captured my attention and stirred my heart from the first page to the wrenching conclusion. No matter how far along we may think we are in the Lord, a book like this will remind us—but for the grace of God, there go I!"

—JILL ELIZABETH NELSON, author of the
To Catch a Thief series

"Powerful. Chilling. Compelling. *The Other Side of Darkness* held me from the very first page. Anyone who has ever been in doubt about what being a Christian truly means should read this book. It not only explores the tragedy of obsessive-compulsive disorder, but it also shows the tragedy of innocent people being led astray. I highly recommend this book."

—LENORA WORTH, author of *Heart of the Night*

"Real and razor-sharp, *The Other Side of Darkness* is a startling look at mental illness and the toxicity of the church gone astray. A frightening reminder that true darkness does not wear the guise we most expect...but the most familiar of faces."

—TOSCA LEE, author of *Demon: A Memoir*
and *Havah: The Story of Eve*

the other side of DARKNESS

Books by Melody Carlson

ADULT FICTION
Finding Alice
Crystal Lies
All I Have to Give

TEEN FICTION
Diary of a Teenage Girl series
The Secret Life of Samantha McGregor series
Notes from a Spinning Planet series
True Colors series
The Carter House Girls series

NONFICTION
Piercing Proverbs
True

Melody Carlson

a novel

the other side of DARKNESS

MULTNOMAH
BOOKS

THE OTHER SIDE OF DARKNESS
PUBLISHED BY MULTNOMAH BOOKS
12265 Oracle Boulevard, Suite 200
Colorado Springs, Colorado 80921
A division of Random House Inc.

All Scripture quotations, unless otherwise noted, are taken from the New King James Version®. Copyright © 1982 by Thomas Nelson Inc. Used by permission. All rights reserved. The quotation of Proverbs 31:30 on page 17 and the paraphrase of 1 Corinthians 13 on page 44 are taken from the New American Standard Bible®. © Copyright The Lockman Foundation 1960, 1962, 1963, 1968, 1971, 1972, 1973, 1975, 1977, 1995. Used by permission. (www.Lockman.org).

The characters and events in this book are fictional, and any resemblance to actual persons or events is coincidental.

ISBN 978-1-4000-7081-7

Published in the United States by WaterBrook Multnomah, an imprint of The Doubleday Publishing Group, a division of Random House Inc., New York.

MULTNOMAH and its mountain colophon are registered trademarks of Random House Inc.

Library of Congress Cataloging-in-Publication Data
Carlson, Melody.
    The other side of darkness : a novel / Melody Carlson. — 1st ed.
        p. cm.
    ISBN 978-1-4000-7081-7
    1. Women—Fiction. 2. Obsessive-compulsive disorder—Fiction. 3. Cults—United States—Fiction. 4. Psychological fiction. I. Title.
    PS3553.A73257O84 2008
    813'.54—dc22

                                         2008023097

Printed in the United States of America
2008—First Edition

10 9 8 7 6 5 4 3 2 1

Author's Note

Most of my novels begin with a single question, some puzzling dilemma I need to resolve. *The Other Side of Darkness* is a perfect example. Except this story is filled with *many* questions. Questions like, What kind of person gets pulled into a pseudo-Christian cult? Does she simply wake up one morning and say, "I think I'll join some wacky church today"? And what kind of person becomes a leader in a church that's going sideways? Does a wolf in sheep's clothing intentionally set out to do evil from the start? Or is he just as deceived as his followers?

Research proves that some personality types are more susceptible to spiritual fraud than others. Some people, by nature, are more gullible, more needy, more emotionally fragile. And those are the ones whom cult leaders often prey upon—good-hearted and well-meaning people who can be controlled through fear and guilt and then bullied into submission. But how can we become more aware of this vulnerability in others—in ourselves? How do we help a sister or a brother who, though set on diligently serving God, is being steadily reeled in by a spiritual charlatan?

Sometimes fiction is the most direct way to convey hard-to-tell truths. In this based-on-fact but fictional story, we will journey with Ruth Jackson, unraveling her past to find clues as to why she has been lured into a cult. We will walk with her into the dark places of fear and guilt and torment. We will see her struggle against both real and imagined demonic powers. We will begin to understand how a chemical imbalance such as obsessive-compulsive disorder (OCD) can make a person exceptionally vulnerable to the deceptions of brain-washing. And we will witness her flawed thinking as she drags her own precious children along this perilous path, endangering both their emotional and physical lives.

As disturbing as parts of this story may seem, it is reality. It is happening today. And like other mental-health issues, OCD is not limited to any socioeconomic level, just as cult churches are not con-fined within any one denomination. Both are widespread. Not only that, but as biblical prophecy predicts and contemporary culture reveals, a whole generation of young people are extremely vulnerable right now, ripe for the picking for cults of all kinds. Maybe it's time to open our eyes—as well as our hearts.

For God has not given us a spirit of fear,
but of power and of love and of a sound mind.

—2 TIMOTHY 1:7, NKJV

Prologue

That's not good enough."

I scratch the mosquito bite on the back of my arm and adjust my thick-lens glasses to look up at my mom. Her eyes feel like two sharp prongs probing right into my forehead—as if she can read my thoughts. And maybe she can.

"Why not?" I say quietly, then glance away, wishing I'd kept quiet.

"Look at that carpet." Her index finger points down like an arrow at the new orange shag carpeting that goes wall to wall in our small, wood-paneled family room.

I look but see nothing other than carpet. Still, I know better than to state this as fact.

"Pull the vacuum back and forth in straight lines. Back and forth, back and forth, *like this*." She uses her hands to show me, as if I don't fully understand the concept of back and forth.

I stand with my shoulders hunched forward, staring dumbly down at the sea of orange at my feet.

"If you did it right, Ruth, I would see neat, even rows about six inches wide. Now, start in the corner by the fireplace, and do it again."

I frown and, although I know it's not only futile but stupid, say, "But it's clean, Mom. I vacuumed everything in here. The carpet is already *clean*."

The family room becomes very quiet now. With the Hoover off, I can hear the sounds of kids playing outside, enjoying their Saturday freedom like normal ten-year-olds, not that I mistake myself for normal. And then I hear the familiar hissing sound of my mother as she blows air like a jet stream through her nostrils.

"Ruth Anne!" She bends down and peers at me, those flaming blue eyes just inches from my own. "Are you talking back to me?"

I glance down at my faded blue Keds and mutely shake my head. I do not want to be slapped. Without looking at her, I turn the vacuum cleaner on again and drag its bulky, cavernous body over to the wall by the fireplace next to the big picture window, although I don't look out. I don't want to see my friends playing. Even worse, I don't want them to see me.

As I vacuum the rug all over again, I try not to think about my older sister, Lynette, the pretty one. I try not to imagine her at her ballet lesson just now, looking sleek and lovely in her black leotard and tights, doing a graceful arabesque with one hand on the barre, glimpsing her long straight back in the gleaming mirror behind her.

"You are not made for ballet," my mother had told me two years ago when I pleaded with her for lessons. "You're much too stout, and your arms and legs are too short and stubby. You take after your father's side of the family."

And I can't disagree with her when I examine myself in the bathroom mirror. With my dark hair and untamable curls and these muddy brown eyes, I definitely do not look like I belong in this particular family of blue-eyed, long-limbed blonds. Well, my mother isn't a true blonde. A monthly bottle of Lady Clairol helps her out, although no one is allowed to mention this fact, *ever,* and she takes care to purchase her "contraband" in a drugstore in the neighboring town where no one knows her. But she lets it be known that Lynette and my little brother, Jonathan, both get their silky blond locks from her side of the family—a respectable mix of English and Scandinavian.

Jonathan is four years younger than I am, but unlike me, he is *not* an accident. Plus he is a much-wanted boy, named after my father, Jonathan Francis Reynolds. Once while playing hide-and-seek at church, I was hiding behind the drapes in the fellowship room when I overheard my mother talking to a lady friend. The other woman commented on how Lynette and I look nothing alike. "Oh, Ruth wasn't planned, you know," my mother said in a hushed tone, causing my ears to perk up and actually listen for a change. "Good grief. My little Lynette was still in diapers, and suddenly I was pregnant again! Can you imagine? Well, I was completely devastated by the—"

Just then Jonathan raced over and threw himself around my mother's knees, complaining that he'd been left out of the childish game.

"Now, this one"—my mother spoke with pride as she ruffled his pale hair—"he was no mistake."

I t's all a mistake." I wash my hands again, perhaps for the seventeenth time in the last hour. Never mind that they are already red and chapped or that the skin on my knuckles cracks when I make a fist. "I will call Pastor Glenn first thing in the morning and tell him it's all just a stupid mistake."

But even as I speak these words aloud for no one to hear but myself, I know that's one phone call I will never make. Me stand up to a man in his position? Accuse him of error? Why, that would be like taking a stand against the Lord.

Or my mother.

I suck in a deep breath. Everything will be okay. Somehow I will make everything right again. I will pray for *three* hours tonight instead of two. That should help.

"Mommy?"

I turn to see my younger daughter standing in the hallway, her pale pink nightgown backlit by the hallway light so I can see her spindly legs trembling. "What's wrong, sweetie?"

"That dream," Sarah says in a shaky voice. "I had that dream again."

I gather her into my arms, carry her over to the sofa, and pull a woolly afghan around both of us. "Dear Jesus, please drive away the demons. Take them from us and throw them into your fiery pit. Send your angels to protect Sarah now. Take away those evil thoughts, and replace them with your good thoughts, O Lord…" I ramble on and on, just as I've been taught, until I finally hear Sarah's even breathing and I am assured that she is asleep. I sigh. Once again I have kept the demons at bay.

This is all my fault, I think as I tuck her back into bed. I glance over to make sure Mary is still asleep in the twin bed across from her little sister. Hopefully the demonic nightmares won't attack her as well.

Satisfied that both my daughters are safe, I tiptoe down the hallway and pause by Matthew's bedroom. I shake my head as I push open his partially shut door and see his floor strewn with castoff pieces of clothing—jeans in a heap right where he took them off, dirty socks in tight little wads next to his bed. How many times must I tell him to put his things away—that cleanliness truly is next to godliness? When will he get it? I consider going in there right now and doing it myself, but that would risk waking him. And right now Matthew is going through a difficult period.

Barely eighteen and just out of high school, he threatens on a regular basis to leave home. I can't believe he'd really go through with it though. His job at the bookstore would never support him, and besides, wouldn't he be scared out there—all on his own with so much evil lurking about? If he's not careful, if he continues this careless living, the demons will come into his life and take over. And then what will I do?

I must pray harder than ever tonight. It seems the spiritual safety of my entire household is at stake. Maybe it has something to do with the full moon. Or the fact that it's autumn, with Halloween only a few weeks away. Pastor Glenn says the demons are more active now. Especially up here in Oregon, where nighttime and darkness come quickly this time of year.

I bite my lip as I glance at the clock. Rick will be home from work in less than two hours. At first I hated his so-called promotion because of the new nighttime hours at the shipping company, but sometimes, like now, I'm thankful for his absence. And I cringe to think what he will say when he gets home and hears what I've done.

Perhaps I should keep this from him since it will only upset him. There must be some way to make up for this mistake. If it really is a mistake. Maybe it was meant to be, just a blessing in disguise that will unfold later. Whatever it is, I think I can keep this secret between the Lord and me—and, of course, Pastor Glenn.

I slowly kneel in front of the worn plaid sofa, my elbows digging into the familiar grooves in the center of the middle cushion. I bow my head and prepare myself for spiritual battle. I know I will be drained before this is over.

"What are you doing?"

I startle, surprised to find that I'm still on my knees, slumped over the sofa like a rag doll. I attempt to stand, but my legs are numb from lack of circulation, and the best I can do is to roll over in an ungraceful flop as I look up at my husband and try to read his expression. His brow is creased, but is it with anger or concern?

"I was praying. I must've fallen asleep."

"Why don't you pray in bed?" Rick sets his Thermos lunchbox on the coffee table in front of me with a tired sigh. "Then at least you could fall asleep there."

I just stare blankly at the blue and white insulated lunchbox. All I can think is, *That doesn't belong there.*

"Ruth!"

I look back up at him, then blink. "Huh?"

"I was talking to you."

"I guess I'm just sleepy."

"Or spacey." He reaches out to help me stand.

"Yeah…" I slowly get to my feet. "Sorry."

"I was just asking you if you made that deposit today."

"Sure, of course…"

"I tried to use my debit card at noon, and the ATM said we had insufficient funds."

"Oh, I didn't make it to the bank until after three. I ended up helping out at school again and—"

"Seems like you end up helping out there every other day." He runs his fingers through his scraggly brown hair, his sign of frustration and a reminder that he needs a haircut again.

"They were short-handed, and there's a lot to do for the Harvest Celebration."

"Well, then maybe they should just hire you. Better yet, just give us a discount or even a refund on the girls' tuition. You told me one of the benefits of getting them into a Christian school, well, aside from their *spiritual welfare,*"—he shakes his head—"was that it'd make it easier for you to focus on *other* things, things like managing the house and the bills, grocery shopping. You even said you might get a part-time job, Ruth. What happened to all those high aspirations?"

"I don't know…"

"And now you can't even make it to the bank on time?"

"Sorry."

"I told Leon that I'd pay him back that fifty today, and I ended up looking like a real jerk."

"Sorry."

"Yeah, whatever. Just give me some cash, and we'll call it good."

"I, uh, I didn't get any cash back."

"Why not?"

"I…I forgot."

He shakes his head dismally. "But you did remember to deposit the check, right?"

I nod.

"Okay, where's the checkbook?" He walks over to where my purse is hanging on its usual hook on the oak hall tree by the front door and begins to dig through it. "I'll just write Leon a check."

I can't hide this anymore. Once Rick sees the checkbook, he'll know what I did. It'll all be out in the open. *God, help me.*

He extracts the checkbook and trudges toward the kitchen. I pick up his lunchbox and follow, preparing myself for this next scene.

"What the—" Rick turns, holding the opened checkbook to the spot where I wrote Pastor Glenn that check today.

"Three hundred dollars?" He glares at me. "For Valley Bridge Fellowship? What's this for? We already paid up their tuition. We bought the girls their fancy-dancy uniforms and school supplies and God only knows what else. Another three hundred dollars? What in God's name for?"

I cringe at his careless use of our Lord's name. Rick knows better than to take it in vain. And he knows how painful it is for me to hear him talk like that.

"It was a misunderstanding. A mistake. I plan to take care of it—"

"A *mistake*?" He steps closer, holding the checkbook right

under my nose. "It looks like *your* handwriting, Ruth. How is this a mistake?"

I explain how Pastor Glenn told me he was collecting donations to get groceries and pay the electric bill for a family in need and how when I said I wanted to help, he somehow misunderstood me. "He thought I said that I wanted to cover the entire expense myself, but I didn't understand. And when it turned out that he needed three hundred dollars and he was so blessed by our generosity, well, I just didn't know how to explain that wasn't what I meant and that I'd only planned to give him twenty dollars…and the next thing I knew, I was writing out a check for the full three hundred."

"That's insane, Ruth."

I don't respond.

"You gave away *our* grocery and *our* bill-paying money to help a family in need, for Pete's sake. Now *we're* a family in need!"

"Don't talk like that, Rick!"

It's too late. Now he's swearing and slamming his lunchbox into the sink, and I slip away, going into the girls' room, where I lie on the floor between their two beds.

Dear Lord, I am so sorry. I am so sorry. I am so sorry. I say this sentence over and over. Like a scratched vinyl record, I am stuck on these four words. But I believe that they are the right words and that repeated enough times they will make things better. All I want is for things to get better. I am so sorry.

2

I wake up in the darkness, my back aching from the hard floor beneath the plush pink carpeting in my daughters' bedroom. According to the alarm clock on the maple dresser between their beds, it's only 4:56. Too early to wake them, and yet I don't want to return to my own bedroom. Even if Rick is asleep, which is likely, I'm not ready to be near him yet.

I stay where I am and use this time to pray for my girls—to pray that their day will be especially blessed and that their classes will go well and, perhaps most important, that they will finally start to feel like they fit in at their new school.

It's only their fourth week, but I expected they'd have made the adjustment by now. The fact that they're still struggling fills me with guilt and doubt. Was it a mistake to make this move? Mary would've started middle school this year, and I'd heard such bad things about the flawed and ungodly curriculum taught in public schools, the horrendous peer pressure, and even an increase in drug use among preteens. Really frightening.

Thankfully, Pastor Glenn does an excellent job of keeping his congregation informed. He often preaches on the serious problems facing public education these days and how our society will pay a high price for the low morals and values being taught to the younger generation. Of course, Rick says he only espouses these "opinions" in order to promote the church's Christian school because the school is steadily losing popularity as well as money. But I'm sure Rick is simply biased. More and more it seems that Rick is falling away from the church, falling away from the Lord. And I feel certain that Pastor Glenn, as our spiritual shepherd, only wants the best for his sheep.

But changing over to a private school hasn't been easy on the girls, and only yesterday Sarah complained about missing her old friends at Hampton Elementary. Then Mary chimed in by saying how the kids at Valley Bridge Fellowship still treat her like an outsider. "We'll never fit in there," she lamented as I drove them home. And I could see that Mary was holding back tears. Poor thing. I know it's not easy being twelve.

And it's not as if I can't relate to their misery. I always felt like a misfit as a child. Although I'm sure Mary will never go through the sort of pain I experienced. At least she gets to dress like her peers. No one can tease her about her clothes. It wasn't like that for me. For starters, even though all the other girls in my class had been wearing blue jeans to school since fourth grade, when the dress code changed, my mother would not allow us to wear jeans for anything besides chores and play.

"I want my daughters to look respectable," she had told us again and again, completely unaware that Lynette had been sneaking jeans to school since her first year in junior high, quickly changing in the bathroom before class started.

But I was never that brave. I settled for the mandatory skirts and sweaters, and if I wore pants, they were always "trousers," as Mom called them. Corduroy or twill and always neatly pressed. But besides dressing like a nerd, I always seemed to be worried about something or other, and I know this must've kept any potential friends at bay. But I just couldn't seem to help myself.

"Why do you put your shoes in a circle like that?" Marilyn Van Horn had asked me one afternoon when she surprised me by agreeing to come home with me after school. At first I'd been extremely nervous about her visit, imagining all the things my mom could do to embarrass me. But luckily for me, Mom had taken Jonathan to Cub Scouts that afternoon, and Lynette was off at ballet, so I had the house to myself.

"Oh, I just do that for fun," I told Marilyn, not willing to admit that I felt better when the toes of my shoes were all touching, connected.

"Your room is *so* neat and clean." She eyed my comb and brush and hair barrettes, all lined up meticulously along my spotless dresser top. "Do you guys have a maid or something?"

I laughed. "No. My mom just likes us to keep things picked up." And that wasn't a lie. It's just that I took cleanliness to a whole new level. This was partially to keep Mom off my back but also for my own sense of security. I believed life was under control when my room was in perfect order.

Marilyn continued walking around my room, examining everything. She reminded me of my aunt's terrier, Fritz, as she sniffed about searching, I felt certain, for oddities or perhaps even a dead rodent somewhere. And after just a few minutes, her presence started to make me very uncomfortable, and each time she touched any of my things, I wondered why I had allowed this girl into my world. I even hinted to her that maybe she should leave.

"You're a really weird girl, Ruth Reynolds." She rearranged my brush-and-comb set, probably just to bug me.

"Gee thanks." I tried to sound sarcastic, not wanting her to know that her words cut deeply.

"I mean, you're pretty smart and kinda fun to hang around with at school…sometimes. But you're not like the other kids. No offense, Ruth, but you're kinda uptight, you know? You sort of remind me of my grandma."

Well, I didn't know how to respond, and I can't remember exactly what we did after that or how long she stayed while making these unpleasant observations, but I do remember being hugely relieved when she finally told me it was time for her to go home. And I went around my room and systematically put everything she'd moved, whether intentionally or not, back in its proper place.

The next day Marilyn told some of the other girls in sixth grade about my unusually neat room and my "circle of shoes," and naturally I became the focus of their ridicule. Oh, I'm sure there were worse things than being called "Neat Freak" or hearing "Let the Circle (of Shoes) Be Unbroken" sung mercilessly for several days. And I learned to wear my "flat face." I imagined myself as an Etch A Sketch that had just been shaken to void it of all images. Likewise I would void my face of all emotion. It wasn't long before my classmates added "Miss Perfect" and "Weirdo" to my ever-growing list of labels, but I just continued wearing my flat face, determined not to let them know I cared. And I told myself that I didn't really need friends.

Throughout junior high I maintained a low profile, high grades, and probably the beginnings of an ulcer, because my stomachaches seemed to be almost constant by the time I was fourteen. By then I had accepted that I really was a freak. There seemed to be no disputing this fact. My only goal was to survive school and peers and even my family, who were also treating me as if I was some weirdo that had been dropped off from another planet. I used my imagination to get me through these hard times, convincing myself that someday I would actually have a life worth living. Looking back, I'm not even sure how I managed to do this, but I think television helped.

My mom didn't like for us kids to watch too much television, but Lynette was a master at getting her own way. As a result, I often got lost in shows like *Mary Tyler Moore,* where I imagined myself to be as cool as Mary Richards, living on my own in a big city and having *real* friends who were fun and interesting. Or else I was part of the *Happy Days* crowd, where everyone but Fonzie wore nerdy clothes and Joanie Cunningham and I were best friends, except that she would be upset if she knew I nurtured a secret crush on her boyfriend, Chachi.

It wasn't until the end of my sophomore year in high school that I finally got fed up with my lackluster little life. Tired of the Miss Perfect label and good-girl image, I made an effort to befriend Colleen Frazer. Two things about this totally out-of-character action still amaze me today—first, that I actually mustered the nerve to speak to this new girl who smoked and cussed and dressed like a Madonna wannabe and, second, that someone like her was willing to speak to someone as mousy and insignificant as me.

But it wasn't long before Colleen was teaching me all her tricks, including smoking cigarettes, swearing like a logger, and wearing underwear as outerwear while holding your head up. Naturally, I kept my new tough-chick image top secret from my mom. By then Lynette had gotten our parents to lighten up on some of Mom's restrictive dress-code rules, but she still had to sneak some of her makeup and certain clothing items to school. I simply followed her example…and then some.

Of course, it was the eighties, and everything about fashion was big and overblown. Big hair, bulky shoulder pads, fluffy layered skirts, and more layers of makeup—and for me it was like donning a costume as I put myself together at Colleen's house each morning before school. My exterior was something I could hide behind, allowing me to act however I liked. The only problem was, I did feel a little phony, and I was actually pretty scared a lot of the time. The idea of getting caught by my mother constantly nagged at me, keeping me from completely cutting loose and having the crazy kind of fun Colleen was capable of. Still, my new defiant image was far better than being Neat Freak or Miss Perfect.

Oh, my rebel years… I'm sure my feeble attempt at insurrection would make most people laugh. I never really learned to smoke right, not the way Colleen did, inhaling it deep into her lungs and holding it there before she slowly exhaled, but I was a pretty good faker and knew how to hold the cigarette just right. And I never really drank like she did, although I would take a few sips and pretend to be tipsy, just to fit in. And when we were at drinking parties, I always kept a tight rein on myself, constantly glancing out windows or down the road to make sure the party wasn't about to get busted. I was paralyzed by the fear of being dragged home by a cop.

But I did get pretty good at spewing out foul language that made even me cringe at times. I'd never admit it to anyone now, but I even used God's name in vain at times. It shames me to think of this. In fact, it's rather hard to believe that I, Ruth Anne Jackson, strong believer and faithful church member, ever managed to look and behave like such a tough girl during those high-school years. Although I suspect that some kids, like Marilyn Van Horn, knew it was all just an act. But the truth is, I was relieved when it was over and done with, and I would be completely humiliated if anyone at church besides Colleen, whom I've sworn to secrecy, knew anything about that old Ruth Reynolds. And I hope and pray that my children never find out.

Suddenly I notice there's a slit of pale morning light beneath the window shade, and the clock says it's almost seven. Not wanting to be caught sleeping on the floor of the girls' room when their alarm goes off, I roll over and quietly get onto my hands and knees and, feeling the stiffness in my bones, stand upright, then tiptoe out of their room and down the hall.

I take a few minutes to freshen up in the bathroom, but I'm sure anyone who looked closely would suspect that I slept on the floor last night. Dark shadows rest beneath my slightly bloodshot eyes, and my skin is pale and sallow. My brown hair is flat and dull, showing the tinges of gray that started appearing last year, and my usual stubborn curls look worn out.

I've heard people say that forty is the new thirty, but I'm thinking my forty looks more like fifty or maybe even sixty today. But the Lord doesn't want me to glory in my appearance, and the Bible says that "charm is deceitful and beauty is vain" and that the "silver-haired head is a crown of glory." So I rebuke myself for my vanity and head to the kitchen to prepare breakfast.

Today, like so many other days, it will be oatmeal. Not because we particularly like oatmeal but because I've been attempting to cut back on the food budget. Paying the girls' tuition last summer completely depleted our savings, and I've promised Rick that I'll do everything I can to make up for it. Of course, this reminds me of yesterday's "mistake," filling me with a deep sense of dread and shame. *Dear Lord, please help me fix this.*

As I stir the rolled oats into the boiling water, I wonder if I could place a stop payment on the three-hundred-dollar check this morning. Oh sure, it would be embarrassing, but at least it would pacify Rick and restore peace in our house for the time being. Perhaps I could create some believable excuse, maybe even tell Pastor Glenn that the check bounced because we were overdrawn since I hadn't deposited a check on time, which is actually the truth, sort of.

Unfortunately, I suspect that Pastor Glenn would see right through me. He's gifted that way. He has this uncanny ability to discern things that are hidden deep inside of people. Especially when it comes to sinful things. I was somewhat shocked the first time I witnessed our savvy pastor giving what he calls a "word of knowledge" right in front of the entire congregation at a Wednesday night service. With just a few words, he reduced Tom Finley, a respected real-estate broker, to a blubbering child when his sin of "material lust" was exposed for all to see. But Tom thanked him and begged forgiveness, and it was really quite amazing—and moving. Although, now that I think of it, I haven't seen any of the Finleys at church recently.

A few weeks ago at a Sunday morning service, Pastor Glenn did it again. This time he rebuked Paul Hendricks for having "adultery of the heart." When Paul stood up to Pastor Glenn, telling him that he was wrong, Pastor Glenn told Paul that he also had a "spirit of deception" and that he wouldn't be welcome in our fellowship until he publicly confessed these sins and repented. Naturally, this made Rick really mad since he and Paul have been friends for years.

"Pastor Glenn is going too far!" Rick said as we drove home after church.

"What happened?" Mary asked with typical preadolescent curiosity.

"Never mind." I tossed Rick a warning glance. "Not in front of the girls."

"Mom?"

I'm brought back to the present as I turn to see little Sarah coming into the kitchen. Her long honey-colored hair is still messy from sleep, but she's dressed in her navy and white uniform, although the little red tie is not properly tied, and she has on only one white kneesock. I help her with the tie and ask about the missing sock.

"I can't find any clean ones," she whispers, mindful of her daddy's recent change in schedule.

"Go look in the dryer." I turn off the burner beneath the oatmeal. I retrieve bowls from the cupboard and milk from the fridge, then look again to ensure that I really turned off the stove. I don't want to scorch our oatmeal.

Soon the girls are dressed and fed, snarls brushed out of hair, teeth brushed, and we are heading out to the car. But once again I go back to make sure I turned off the stove.

"It's off, Mom," Mary hisses at me in a loud whisper. "Why do you always do that?"

"I don't want to burn the house down while your brother and dad are sleeping in it," I tell her as we go out to the garage.

"Do you want to burn it down when no one's there?" She climbs into the minivan.

This makes me laugh, and then my girls are laughing, and we're all making jokes about burning down the house. And it feels good to make light of such things. But then I feel guilty. Are our jokes offensive to the Lord? Silently I repent as I pull in front of the church. And I remember the three-hundred-dollar check and wonder how I'm going to make that right.

My girls are just getting out of the van, telling me good-bye, when someone calls my name. I spot Cynthia Leman waving at me from the parking lot.

I halfheartedly wave back, and she hurries over to the car with a look of importance. Cynthia heads up the women's ministries in our church, and as much as I try to respect her, I also cringe when I see her coming my way since it usually means one of two things. Either she wants me to help with something, or I've done something wrong. Cynthia has a gift similar to Pastor Glenn's, and she often uses it in the women's ministries. So far I've managed to avoid it personally, but the idea of being pointed out for all to see, being the subject of a public rebuke…well, it's rather frightening.

"I'm so glad I caught you," she says through my now-open window.

"Hi, Cynthia." I force a smile.

"Are you feeling okay?" She leans down and peers at me with concern.

I shrug. "I guess I didn't sleep too well. Does it show?"

She nods with a grave expression. "I want to ask you something, Ruth."

Now I feel a mixture of relief and anxiety. On one hand, I'm thankful I'm not in trouble, but at the same time I know I won't be able to say no to this woman of influence. And while some women in our church tell Cynthia no with regularity, those same women wear an invisible black check mark by their names. They are considered the less spiritual in our church. "Immature, selfish, carnal Christians…not nearly as devoted to serving as some of us." Oh, no one actually says this in so many words, but it's a well-known fact within the inner circle. I sit up straighter in my seat, adjusting my smile accordingly. After all, it does feel good to be part of the inner circle. It's a level of spirituality I have longed for.

"What can I do for you?"

Cynthia explains Pastor Glenn's new vision for outreach, his plan for expanding our church borders, increasing membership, reaching out to the community. "We're having a meeting this morning," she says in a quieter voice as if she doesn't want anyone else to hear. "By invitation only. And Pastor Glenn asked me to be sure to invite you."

My smile is feeling more genuine. "I'd love to come."

"Good. It's at ten o'clock. And if you don't mind, could you run by the bakery and pick up some goodies? I'd do it myself, but I promised Pastor Glenn that I'd make some copies for the—"

"No problem. But I better get going. I think I'm causing a traffic jam."

She nods. "See you at ten."

As I drive away, I go back and forth, trying to decide whether to stop by the bakery now and then go home and take a shower and clean up or the reverse order. I don't know why it takes me so long to make this decision. I just can't afford not to do this right, not to do it perfectly. Finally I pray, asking the Lord to guide me.

When the traffic light toward downtown is green, I take it as a sign and head for the bakery first. But as I stand before the glass case, eying the various pastries, I feel confused again. Which ones should I get? How many? I should've asked Cynthia how many people will be at this special meeting. It's probably small. Maybe a dozen people? But what if there are more? I don't want to get too few pastries. Oh, why is this so hard? I see others come in, place an order, and leave. Why can't I be like that?

"Are you ready yet?" the girl with a pierced nose asks me for the third time.

The number three comes to me. So I order three dozen. Surely there won't be more people than that. And if so, maybe not everyone will want a whole pastry. I'm surprised at the total, and I realize I'll have to write a check. Another check! My face heats up as I write it out, knowing that Rick will probably question this too. But perhaps the church will reimburse me. I will be sure to ask Cynthia.

The girl hands me a stack of three large pink boxes, and as I walk to the car, I feel certain that I bought too many pastries. Good grief, what was I thinking? Perhaps I can take the leftovers to the teachers' lounge. I'm sure they'd appreciate a treat.

I put the boxes in the backseat and cover them with a blanket. I tell myself this is to keep them from sliding onto the floor, but I know it's to prevent Rick from seeing them. Although I doubt he'll be up this early.

It feels so good to finally take a shower. And, as usual, I soap up and rinse off three times. I try to limit myself to three times, especially when I'm in a hurry like today. But sometimes, if I'm not paying attention or if I feel a desperate need for cleansing, I will stay in the shower until the hot water is all used up. And even then I won't feel totally clean.

I asked my sister about this once, back when we were teens and she was complaining about how long it took me to shower. "How many times do you soap up and rinse?"

"How many *times*?" She looked at me as if I were from another planet. "What are you talking about, Ruth?"

"Oh, nothing…"

Since then I've learned to keep my personal hygiene habits to myself. But still, I don't understand how other people can jump in and out of the shower for just a few minutes and consider themselves clean. It just doesn't make sense.

To my relief, Rick is still sleeping soundly, snoring like a chain saw, as I tiptoe into our room and into the closet to retrieve some clean clothes. I pick a nice gray skirt, white blouse, navy sweater, and my good black pumps. A respectable outfit I often wear to church, but it seems appropriate for an important meeting as well.

I don't normally use any cosmetics, not since I heard Cynthia teaching at a women's seminar a couple of years ago. She said that "according to Scripture, it's sinful to use makeup." Of course, Colleen said that was bunk. Well, not to Cynthia's face. But I'm still not so sure, and when Lynette talked me into getting a department-store makeover with her last June before a cousin's wedding, I actually caved and purchased some concealer and a few other things. I use them occasionally, like when Rick and I go out, which is very rare. I'd be tempted to put on a bit of concealer today since I'm really not looking my best, but images of sitting under bright fluorescent lights and Cynthia's intense gaze are enough to intimidate me. Better to look old and frumpy than to be considered sinful.

"Where you going, Mom?" Matthew asks when I come into the kitchen and find him making a sandwich as well as a mess. Why is it that something as simple as peanut butter and jelly can create such chaos in my kitchen?

"A meeting." I frown at the sticky countertop.

"Don't worry, I'll clean it up," he says quickly, as if reading my thoughts. "It must be a church meeting." He licks the knife.

As I put the lid back on the peanut butter jar, I look away, fearful that he'll slice his tongue in half. Why are children so careless?

"Don't have too much fun." He chuckles.

"Do you work today?" I reach for a paper towel and use it to wipe the greasy jar clean before I set it back in the cupboard.

"Yeah. But not until noon." He sits at the breakfast bar and begins to devour his sandwich, jelly dripping off the edges. "And I don't get off until closing," he says with a full mouth.

"Did you ask your boss about Sundays?" We've been going round and round about how much church he's been missing since he started this job.

Matthew just shrugs. "He said if I wanna work, I gotta stick with the schedule."

I glance at the clock. "Well, I'd better go. Have a good day."

He tells me good-bye, and I head out to the minivan and the camouflaged pastries. And for some reason the sight of those pink boxes partially covered with a plaid wool blanket fills me with guilt, and it reminds me of the three-hundred-dollar check and the deep, dark hole I seem to be climbing into.

3

We need revival!" Pastor Glenn pounds his fist on the table, causing the overloaded plate of pastries to jump. "And we need it now!"

"Amen!" says Cynthia.

Carl and Marie both echo her *amen,* and not wanting to be a misfit, I chime in as well. I continue to nod and to smile as Pastor Glenn reveals his strategic plan to our small group, drawing on the whiteboard charts and graphs that I pretend to understand as I look at the squiggles.

"We'll kick this whole thing off with a big concert. A local Christian band has agreed to perform for free if we allow them to sell their CDs in the lobby. I thought that was more than fair, and hopefully this will draw in some younger folks. The concert will be on Friday, October 21, and I want the auditorium packed."

I am curious as to why there are only five of us at this meeting. I would assume that something of this importance would be much bigger. But as Cynthia points out, "This is only the beginning." I am also a little surprised that besides Carl Schulman, no other church elders or councilmembers are present. More than anything, I'm surprised that I've been included in what seems a somewhat spiritually elite group. Nothing like this has ever happened to me before. Perhaps after nearly twenty years someone—maybe even Cynthia—has taken notice of my desire to serve at our church. Or maybe it has something to do with my unintentional donation of three hundred dollars yesterday.

Maybe what I mistook as a blunder was actually ordained by the Lord. I sit a bit straighter in my folding chair, nodding and smiling as if I completely understand Pastor Glenn's intricate plans, but I'm actually remembering Rick's negative reaction last night to my generosity. Of course, it makes complete sense now. I was simply being persecuted for doing good. There's that twenty-twenty hindsight again. I wish I had realized it sooner. Suffering for the Lord isn't the same as suffering for our own stupidity. I can handle this.

The meeting is coming to a conclusion as we're all assigned various tasks. Although I've never been very comfortable speaking on the phone, I agree to do some phoning, taking a long list Cynthia has printed out, along with a written dialogue prepared by Pastor Glenn. I console myself with the fact that I can do this in the evenings when Rick isn't around to listen, question, or make fun of me. Then we bow our heads, and Pastor Glenn wraps up the meeting with a fervent prayer.

"You certainly got plenty of doughnuts this morning," Cynthia says as we put the remains back into the pink boxes.

"I figured we could share any leftovers with the teachers."

She smiles. "Oh, that's so generous of you, Ruth. And since I'm heading that way, I'd be happy to take them over there for you. Thank you for coming today. It's so good to know that I can depend on you at times like this. There seem to be fewer and fewer women who are truly committed to serving the Lord wholeheartedly these days. Everyone is too busy or too lazy."

I smile back, but part of me wants to inquire about a possible reimbursement for the pastries. And another part of me, the selfish and sinful part, wants to deliver the goodies to the teachers myself. After all, I'm the one with children attending school here; I could afford to make some brownie points with the staff. But that's not going to happen today, so I just thank Cynthia for inviting me to the meeting and say good-bye.

As I drive through town, I'm hammered with doubts. What am I going to do about my checkbook? What will Rick say when he learns I've written another check—this one for *doughnuts for the church*? He'll be furious. He'll be indignant. Spending grocery money on doughnuts? What was I thinking? Maybe Rick is right. Maybe I should get a job. But who might be hiring? My experience of waiting tables and a couple of years of random college classes hardly seem enough to build a résumé on. But somehow I've got to start bringing in some income—and soon. I need money! I've heard of people selling their plasma, but that seems a bit extreme.

Dear Lord, help me figure this out. Help me. Help me. Help me.

I'm astonished to see that I've driven all the way across town. So focused on my monetary worries, I don't remember driving past my own intersection. And now I'm approaching the neighborhood I grew up in. I remember how I used to go to my dad for financial help in times like this. But my dad passed away four years ago, and that door is firmly closed now.

I feel a lump in my throat, wishing he were still around, blaming myself for not taking better advantage of the times we had together. Not that my dad and I ever spent much time together. He never did much with any of us kids—or my mom for that matter. She used to claim he was married to his job. Despite the fact that she nagged him for years to retire, he refused to give up his dentistry practice until he turned seventy-one. Within a year of retirement, he suffered a heart attack and died on his way to the hospital.

But I still miss him. And even though we weren't close, I always felt more comfortable with him than my mom, and occasionally he would come to my defense. I think he felt sorry for me. I think he somehow understood my plight. Maybe he'd been a misfit too. As I drive past their old neighborhood, I chastise myself for not taking the time to know him better. And I feel certain that if I could go to him now and ask him for help…I think that he, unlike my mother, would be there for me.

Suddenly I am filled with indignation. What right does my mom have to make me feel this way? Like I'm not worthy to ask her for help when I really need it, when I know that my father would've been happy to reach out and lend a hand. Is it fair, just because he is dead and gone, that I shouldn't ask for some parental assistance?

I know for a fact that both my brother and sister have gone to our mother for money over the years. Who knows how many times? Lynette "borrowed" money for the down payment on their new home a few years ago, and Jonathan went to Mom for money to start a florist business—a business that's still floundering, last I heard. And although I would never dare to inquire about my siblings or their debts, I feel fairly certain that neither Lynette or Jonathan has repaid the money or ever will.

It makes no sense that I'm afraid to go to Mother for money, especially when it was Dad who worked so hard, literally worked himself to death, to earn their income. And it was his death, or rather his life-insurance policy, that made my mother so comfortable that she could afford her fancy new house and vacations in places where Dad never had time to travel to. So why is it fair for her to just sit there like some tight-fisted queen, denying me not only her love but any financial help as well? It is wrong! I pound my fist on the steering wheel. Again and again I pound it. Wrong, wrong, wrong!

Then I realize I haven't exactly asked my mother for help. Oh, I considered it last summer after I decided to put the girls in Christian school, but I just couldn't bring myself to that humiliating place. Instead we used our savings—our nest egg, our cushion.

I turn down the street toward the expensive subdivision where Mom lives. Maybe it's time to humble myself and actually ask her for help. What could it hurt? After all this woman has already said and done to me, how could she possibly inflict any more pain on my heart? Surely I must be impervious to it by now. Her words should slide over me like…like water off a duck's back. This is what I use to assure myself as I park in front of her house. *Like water off a duck's back, like water off a duck's back.*

But my knees feel rubbery as I walk down the paved path to the oversize front door. I know she's home since her blue Cadillac is parked in the driveway. At night she keeps it safely locked in the garage, but she must've already been out this morning. Probably meeting friends for coffee or taking a golf lesson at the club.

"Ruth!" she calls from the side of the house. With a bamboo rake in hand, she waves as she walks toward me. "You're just in time." She's wearing a pale green velour jogging suit, her favorite form of leisurewear.

I study her carefully. "In time for what?"

"You can help me rake up all these leaves." She grins, then nods to where the old maple tree has already dropped what appears to be several bushels' worth of leaves.

I look down at my nice gray skirt. "But I'm not really dressed for yard—"

"You can wear something of mine. You know, I've put on a few pounds since your father died; we're probably just about the same size now."

"That's okay. I don't want to change." I take the rake from her. "I'll be just fine." And then I start raking.

"What about your shoes?"

"I'm fine."

So she goes off to retrieve another rake, and I spend the next two hours helping her rake the leaves in both the front and back yards. But I can't help but notice that while I'm raking, she's mostly talking. And whenever a neighbor passes by, she takes a break to chat, ignoring me as she discusses everything from the weather to the neighborhood association to the high-school football team's recent winning streak. Finally I am done. There doesn't seem to be another leaf in sight. But my black pumps are coated with dust and leaf debris, I have a run in my stocking, and my skirt will need to be dry-cleaned. Other than that I'm fine. *Just fine!*

"Come in and have a bite to eat." Mother sets aside her rake and heads into the house through the front door. I follow somewhat reluctantly. "But take off your shoes!"

This house has immaculate white carpeting that she keeps spotless. Respecting her wishes, I set my dusty shoes on the entryway's white marble floor and follow her to her kitchen—a kitchen I try not to envy, with its sleek granite countertops, stainless steel state-of-the-art appliances, and smooth hardwood floor. It's like a page out of *House Beautiful.*

"Have a seat," she says.

I pull an expensive-looking metal barstool out from under the island and sit down.

"I have some leftover lasagna."

"That sounds good. Your lasagna was always my favorite."

She laughs. "Well, I had Lynette and Jeff over last night. And little Sammy said it tasted like doggy-doo."

To my surprise this makes me laugh. For one thing, people don't usually criticize my mom's cooking, not to her face, but besides that, I've never heard my mom say the word *doggy-doo* before.

"I asked Sammy how he knew what doggy-doo tasted like," she continues as she places the lasagna in the microwave, "and he told me that he could *imagine* how it would taste." She shakes her head. "He could *imagine*! Only four years old and he can *imagine*. Well, I'm sure that boy must be gifted."

"Or maybe he just spends too much time around adults."

She nods. "Yes, it always did concern me that Lynette waited so long to have children. But she says little Sammy loves his Montessori school and is doing very well."

It seems strange that I'm almost enjoying myself as I eat leftover lasagna with my mom, listening to her prattle on about things that really don't interest me. And despite a little prick here and there, like when she makes the comments about my "having the girls in a *hoity-toity private Christian school*" and "how *pretty* Lynette looked with her chic new hairstyle last night" and how "Jeff's graphic design business just won a national award," I think my mother might actually be changing, softening some. I know she's been going to some kind of counseling, and it gives me hope. It also gives me courage. As I help her rinse the dishes and load the dishwasher, I bring up the subject of finances.

"Things have been pretty tight for us lately." I twist the dishtowel until it resembles a rope, wishing I'd never opened my mouth.

"This economy," she says lightly, taking the deformed dishtowel away from me, giving it a firm shake, then smoothing it out to remove the wrinkles.

"With the added expense of the girls' tuition," I continue nervously, "and trying to put away some money for Matthew's college—"

"Has Matthew decided to continue his education after all?"

"Not exactly. But we're hoping he will, in time."

"Oh."

"Anyway, we're having a hard time making ends meet this month. I mean, something sort of unexpected came up, and I—"

"Are you asking me for money, Ruth?" Suddenly her eyes get that old, hard look. The blue might be paler with age, but the intensity is just as hot.

"Well, I—"

"You know how I hate to say I told you so, but I always warned you that you and Rick got married far too young, and to make matters worse, you started your family much too soon. Remember how I told you it would be very hard to catch up?" She hangs the dishtowel on the oven handle, then turns to me. "Your father and I made certain that our finances were well in order before starting our family. Sure, it meant we had to wait a bit, but our car was paid for, and we bought a house long before Lynette was born." She sighs and shakes her head. "It's just how people did things in *our* day. We believed in stability."

"I know, Mom. And, really, we were doing okay. It's just this tuition—"

"I don't understand that either. Public schools were good enough for you kids. I don't see why they're not good enough for your children. And when I think of the school taxes I pay—"

"Just forget it," I say as I head to the door. I want to remind her that her youngest grandson—the gifted one—is in private school too, but it will do no good. What's acceptable for Lynette has always been too good for me. "Sorry I even asked," I mutter as I reach for my purse.

"You don't need to get in a huff, Ruth. After all, I *am* your mother. If I can't speak my mind to you, who can? You've always had such a stubborn streak, such a hard time respecting authority."

I turn and look at her. "When did I have a hard time respecting authority?"

"Oh, you know, the way you used to challenge me about every little thing. You were a handful as a child. There's no denying that."

Now I know it's time to bite my tongue. The Lord will not be glorified if I start screaming at my mother and acting like a complete lunatic. Even if every word from her mouth is a bald-faced lie, there's no need to fight about it. I remind myself of the familiar scripture that says to respect your parents. But more than anything I want to yell at this cruel woman. I want to lash out and remind her of how I was her whipping girl, how I got blamed for things I never did, how I was left out, picked on, and often simply ignored. I want to remind her of how Lynette, *the beautiful,* and Jonathan, *the baby,* got away with everything while I, Ruth, *the unwanted,* usually got stuck with all the crud. Somehow—maybe it's the Lord's grace—I manage to keep quiet. But I'm fuming inside, and I'm sure my face is flaming red.

"Oh, Ruthie, you should see yourself. You look just the way you did when you were a little girl. The way your mouth is all puckered up and your eyes like little black fireballs." She laughs. "It's rather cute." But the way she says this is demeaning. Clearly an insult.

"Glad I could amuse you, Mother," I say in a tightly controlled voice as I reach for my shoes.

"Don't run off in a big huff." She's relocated herself to the living room now, sitting on her pale blue velvet couch with her legs casually crossed and patting the seat beside her. "Come on over here, and tell me how much you need. Maybe we can work something out."

Feeling just like a stupid fly heading straight into a spider's web, I set my purse back on the marble-topped table and slowly walk back toward her and down the steps to the sunken living room, where I pause and consider running in the other direction.

"Good grief, Ruth, come and sit down!" She slaps the couch again.

But I choose the chair across from her instead, carefully sitting as I wait for this woman's next move.

"First I have some questions."

I press my lips together and simply nod.

"Well, as I already said, I always felt that you and Rick started your family far too soon. But there's nothing to be done about that now. So I won't say another word about it. Just the same, I'd like to know why you think it's so important for the girls to be in a private school, a school that it appears you are unable to afford. Can you answer that?"

So I launch into the same explanation I gave her during the Fourth of July picnic at my sister's house last summer, telling her how low the academic standards have gotten in public schools, how lax the morals and values are, and how the school board has even considered placing condom machines in the rest rooms. She actually nods as I speak, almost as if she can accept my rationale.

"I suppose some of that may be true. But, goodness, this is only October, Ruth. If you're struggling financially now, how will you manage to get through the rest of the year?"

"Oh, the worst of it is over." I admit to how we used our savings to cover a year's worth of tuition for both girls. "It's just made things a little tight for the time being."

Her pale blue eyes grow wide with horror. "You bankrupted your savings?"

Now I realize I've said too much. Far too much.

"Oh dear…" She shakes her head, her lips tightly pressed together in clear disapproval.

"I'm going to get a job, Mom. Soon."

"Well, that should help some."

"And, really, we'll be just fine." I stand, ready to give up, wondering why I even bothered and how I could be so stupid as to think anything had changed. Nothing ever changes between my mom and me. The sooner I figure this out, the better things will be for everyone. I didn't even pray about this impromptu visit. What was I thinking? *What was I thinking?*

I head toward the door again. "I'm sorry to bother you with—"

"How much do you need?" She's on her feet now, walking toward the big oak desk against the far wall, the same desk my dad once used for paying bills and whatnot. The roll top makes a familiar squeak as it's pushed up to reveal a neatly organized desk.

I consider her question and, without really thinking, toss out a figure. "Five hundred dollars." Now I realize that it's more than the checks I need to cover, but I figure my mother can easily afford it. "And I'll pay you back as soon as I get a job."

She sits down and slowly writes out the check. But each stroke of her pen feels like a lashing, like I am being whipped, disciplined for my foolishness. And I recall the times when this same woman made me go outside to cut a switch from the big wisteria bush in the front yard to be used against my bare legs as punishment for some real, or more likely imagined, offense. I hold back tears as she hands me the check. My whip.

"Thank you," I say in a choked voice.

"I know you'll pay me back, Ruth. And I won't charge you any interest as long as you pay it back within six months."

Interest? I know for a fact that both Jonathan and Lynette received money from her that was not only interest free but just *plain free.* Still, I keep these thoughts to myself. I am wearing my flat face again. Just like the old Etch A Sketch screen that's been shaken and shaken and shaken. And as I walk to my car, I am shaking too.

Dear Lord, forgive me for hating my mother. Dear Lord, forgive me for hating my mother. I run this sentence through my head so many times that one sentence seems to link right into the next, going around and around in a tight circle, each word merging into the next, until it feels like they are wrapping themselves like a noose around my neck.

Finally I literally smack my hand against my forehead as I attempt to mentally wipe away my nonsensical prayer by saying "amen" *seven* times. There has always been something magical about the number seven. I can't really explain it and wouldn't want to, but I know that if I say "amen" seven times it will end this nonsense.

Even so, my mother's worn-out words about how Rick and I got married too young, started our family too soon begin to taunt me. Good grief, how many times have I heard those words over the past nineteen years? Can't she get over it? But something about those words feels different today…something in me is worried that perhaps my mother was right. Maybe it was a mistake. Maybe my marriage, my whole life, has been just one great big mistake. Maybe the Lord is punishing me. Why else would I be so miserable?

I can recall only about three or four years in my life—between the ages of eighteen and twenty-one—when I felt like I was really doing okay, like my life was on track and I was somewhat content with who I was and what I was doing. Oh, things weren't perfect, but it was okay. The rest of the time, both before and after, I have felt sadly and increasingly insufficient. Always falling short of everyone's expectations, including my own. Never good enough. Never fitting in. Never really happy. Never enough. Never enough.

But I allow myself to go back. Back to when I was eighteen, shortly after graduation. The happiest day of my life was when I moved out of my parents' house. Sharing an inexpensive apartment with my best friend, Colleen, who amazingly had settled down thanks to her newfound religion, I started going to community college part-time and working in a little deli the rest of the time. And although I was struggling to make good grades as well as ends meet, I had never been more fulfilled in my life. Or more free. Finally it seemed like I was living like Mary Tyler Moore, and Colleen was my Rhoda. Or maybe it was the other way around.

Colleen tried to get me to come to her new church, Valley Bridge Fellowship, but I regularly blew her off. "I was raised in church," I told her. "And I've had more than enough of that to last a lifetime."

Ironically, this religious experience was all fresh and new to Colleen, and after a while I could see that she was actually changing. And the changes were pretty impressive. So finally, partly from curiosity and partly from being worn down by her constant pleading, I gave in and went to church with her. And Valley Bridge Fellowship was refreshingly different from the church of my childhood. So I continued to go with Colleen. But I was mostly a spectator in those days. I held myself back, refusing to take the big plunge and commit my heart to the Lord. I guess I was waiting.

I had just turned twenty when a cute guy began handling the route that made deliveries to the deli where I worked. I started flirting with him right off, and it wasn't long before he "accidentally" dropped off the wrong package at my apartment. I invited him in for a Coke and learned his name was Rick Jackson. Shortly after that we started dating, and it quickly turned serious. I wasn't even twenty-one when I married him, quit school, and quit my job, and our first child, Matthew, was born the following year.

While I was pregnant with Matthew, I started taking church and God more seriously. Rick claimed to be a Christian but was never too interested in going to church with me. Sunday was his only day to sleep in, and nothing would make him give that up. So Colleen, still single, continued to pick me up every Sunday morning while my husband snoozed. I finally committed my life to the Lord just a few months before Matthew was born. It seemed the right thing to do, and for a while I rode this kind of spiritual high, and it seemed that things were really changing for me. Plus I had this amazing peace— a peace I'd never experienced before. I knew it was real, and I knew it was from God.

Rick had wanted to name our firstborn son Taylor, but I insisted on a biblical name: Matthew, after the first gospel in the Bible, which I'd just started to read. And I secretly hoped to have three more sons, whom I would subsequently name Mark and Luke and John, after the other gospels. Rick should be thankful that we had only girls after that. But we were happy back then. Life was simpler. And we were in love.

Cheered by those old memories, I smile to myself as I drive through the business section of town. Things will be better now. My mother's check is safely zipped in my purse, and life is, once again, under control. I park in front of the bank and go inside. I don't like using the drive-up window; I worry that the teller will make a mistake or money will get lost in that strange black tube. I carefully fill out the deposit form, putting most of the check into our account, enough to cover my recent "errors." But I take the remainder out in cash, asking for fives and tens, which I hide in the zipper pocket of my purse.

I have no idea why I need small bills or why I need to hide it. But I do it anyway. Maybe it's the Holy Spirit guiding me. Just today Pastor Glenn said that the Holy Spirit often urges us to do the unexpected. I feel a huge sense of relief as I drive away from the bank. But as I get closer to home, I realize that this feeling is heavily mixed with guilt.

4

Colleen and I have grown apart these past few years. At first I thought it was because she and her husband moved to the other side of town. But when I speak to her today, I'm not so sure. I'm afraid that Colleen is falling away from the Lord.

"I heard you went to that meeting," she tells me as I wait in the parking lot for the girls to come out of school. Colleen's twin boys also attend VBF, and she parked her SUV next to my minivan and is now standing by the driver's side so that I am in essence a prisoner in my own vehicle.

"How did you hear that?" I ask in a slightly hushed tone, although no one is close enough to overhear our conversation.

"Ginger."

"Oh." I nod. Ginger has been the church secretary for nearly thirty years, which, she likes to point out, is a lot longer than Pastor Glenn has been there. Ginger is also a good friend of Colleen's. And, in my opinion, Ginger talks too much.

"So what's going on?" Colleen frantically waves at her son Kyle, yelling at him to quit hitting his brother with his backpack.

I shrug. "Just some planning."

"Ginger said that Pastor Glenn is doing something behind the backs of the elders and that they're not happy about it."

"Carl was there."

"Everyone knows Carl is Pastor Glenn's puppet."

I turn and stare at her. "That's not a very Christlike thing to say."

She just rolls her eyes, the same way she did in high school. "It's a well-known fact."

I sigh deeply, trying to think of a kind way to reprimand my old friend.

"I don't see why you're so loyal to Pastor Glenn. Can't you see he's tearing this church down with all his so-called words, which are really just false accusations? He's going too far. And it's just a matter of time before the council and elders toss him out."

"You shouldn't talk like that, Colleen. It's disrespectful."

"I'm just calling a spade a spade. Church attendance is way down. Lots of parents have removed their kids from the school. Glenn Pratt is tearing this place apart, and unless you've got your head in a hole, you know it's true."

"Just because a few people have been offended?"

"Not just a few people, Ruth. Sure, only a handful were publicly rebuked. But Glenn has torn more than a few apart in private, including my own husband!"

"Are you serious?" I study Colleen carefully. She's always been a bit of a drama queen, but I don't think she's ever lied to me.

"Dennis confronted Glenn about the harshness of his 'word of knowledge' rebukes, and Glenn got mad and really lashed into poor Dennis."

I frown. Pressing my lips tightly together, I consider reminding her that Dennis is far from perfect. I happen to know that he plays poker with his friends from work and that, even worse, beer is served. Colleen knows all about this, but she doesn't seem to care. I wouldn't be surprised if that's the reason Pastor Glenn reprimanded Dennis. Still, I don't say anything. I don't want to hurt her feelings.

"Anyway, Dennis met with some of the elders last week. He told them that either Glenn goes or we do."

"Really?" I blink. "You'd leave the church?"

"And we'd take the kids out of school too. I'm so glad we're paying tuition by the month. I can't believe you paid the year in advance, Ruth. I hope you're not sorry."

I don't know what to say. And now her twins are bouncing around their SUV, yelling and swinging their backpacks at each other like a couple of hoodlums. Maybe the apples don't fall too far from the tree.

My girls are approaching now, and I can tell by Mary's expression that it hasn't been a good day. "I better get going."

"Call me!" Colleen climbs into her SUV, loudly telling her boys to buckle up and shut up.

I feel embarrassed for my friend. Despite giving her heart to the Lord so many years ago, she still has a few rough edges. And her distrust and dislike of Pastor Glenn comes as no surprise. She was terribly upset when Pastor John retired a few years ago. She's never given poor Pastor Glenn a chance. Still, this insurrection comes as news to me. Oh, I knew that some people's noses were out of joint for the public rebukes, but I had no idea it had gone this far. As the girls get into the van, I make a mental note to call Cynthia to mention this to her.

"I hate our new school," Mary says as I exit the church parking lot.

"Me too," echoes Sarah.

"It's just going to take some time. You have to be patient. It's only been a little more than a month, and things are still new." Then I begin to quote to them from 1 Corinthians 13. "Love is patient and kind. It is not jealous or boastful...or arrogant or rude." Even as I recite these words, I feel some personal conviction. But more than that I feel offended by Colleen's unjust judgment of Pastor Glenn. What right does she have to judge him?

I call Cynthia as soon as I get home. Trying to avoid sounding like a gossipmonger, I convey my concern over some of the rumors circulating through the church. But I don't mention Colleen's name.

"Oh, trust me, I'm well aware of this problem. As is Pastor Glenn. This is part of the reason for our new outreach ministry. Pastor Glenn feels we need to bring new blood into the church. We need fresh people with fresh ideas and, most of all, open minds. We want people who are willing to let the Spirit move, even if it gets uncomfortable at times. You know, the Lord doesn't want to make us comfortable. He wants to push us onward and forward, pressing us into his glorious image, making us perfect even as our Father in heaven is perfect."

"Yes!" I say with enthusiasm. "That's just how I feel too. That's what I want in my own life."

"I know. And that's why you're part of our team, Ruth. We need you."

"And I'll get right to the phoning."

"Good for you," she says. "May the Lord bless your conversations!"

So while Mary and Sarah play outside, dressing up our golden retriever, Sadie, in some of Sarah's old baby clothes, I start making calls. And I find that if I do the same lines each time, the lines Pastor Glenn wrote out for me, I'm okay. But if I deviate in any way, I get lost and confused. When I first started, I dropped my notes one time and got so flustered that I actually had to hang up on a woman.

Thankfully, I hadn't identified myself or our church yet. After that I was much more careful.

I notice it's getting dark, so I call the girls in to do homework, and I start dinner and put a load of laundry in, but soon I'm back to phoning. Cynthia told me that the prime time is from six to eight o'clock, and I've made it my goal to get through at least a third of my list tonight. I'm curious as to where these names and numbers came from, but I trust that whoever compiled this list must know what they're doing. And it's better than going through the phone book. I assume that most of the people I'm calling are at least saved. But occasionally I am surprised.

"How'd you get my name?" one man growls at me.

"It was on the list, and I—"

"Well, take it off the list. And you can tell whoever made that stupid list that it's wrong for one church to be beating the bushes of another church just to increase their membership."

"Oh, that's not what this is—"

"I know what this is, sister. I wasn't born yesterday. And I plan to tell my clergyman just what you people at Valley Bridge Fellowship are up to. That pastor of yours is nothing but a wolf in sheep's clothing!"

"But we just wanted to invite—"

Click!

I shake my head and look at the kitchen clock. It's after eight. Time to quit anyway. Still, I feel bad about the grumpy man. I was only saying what I'd been told to say. I hope it doesn't reflect poorly on our church.

"Can we watch TV now?" Mary asks.

Television is a controlled substance in our house. At least when I'm home. Rick sometimes breaks the rules during the weekends, and

I've caught Matthew watching some things that were completely out of line. But for the most part, we only watch the acceptable shows. Mostly family sitcoms. And although they often have situations that aren't very godly, if I'm watching with the girls, I can run damage control on some of the immoral values being taught and maybe even make some good points for the Lord.

Since Mary and Sarah are done with their homework and ready for bed, I have no excuse to keep them from watching television. And to be honest, it's a relief just to sit down and focus on something relatively mindless. And I actually catch myself laughing a few times. Oh, I know that some of the jokes aren't particularly godly and Pastor Glenn might not approve, but I am, after all, only human. Besides, it's such a safe and comforting feeling to have my girls on either side of me. Everything seems under control now, and during a commercial break, which I mute, Mary makes us some microwave popcorn, and I begin to relax. It feels good.

Too soon the shows are over, it's time for bedtime prayers, and Matthew should be coming home from his job at the bookstore. I occupy myself with folding laundry and unloading the dishwasher, but finally it's after ten, and Matthew is still not here. It's times like this when I wish we had cell phones.

Rick has tried to get me into this new craze (or maybe it's an old one by now), but something about walking around, or driving around, with our heads attached to those silly little phones seems ungodly. And I've heard that they can heat up and explode in your ear. So I told Rick no. Besides, our budget wouldn't allow it. But right now, with Matthew still not home, I wish he had a cell phone.

I do a few more chores and then sit down to read my Bible, but it's nearly eleven and still no Matthew. Fearing the worst, I pace back and forth in the kitchen, praying for the Lord to send his angels to protect my only son. I don't like that Matthew rides his bike downtown to work. Oh sure, it's only a few miles, and he has a good bike light and a sturdy helmet, but it's so dark out there at night, especially since autumn has set in, and it feels so late when he gets off work at nine.

I wipe down the countertops to distract myself, scrubbing and scrubbing until it feels like I'm going to wear through the laminate finish. Then I stand at the sink, looking out the window as I wash my hands again and again. I can't help but feel that Matthew's welfare is directly related to me. If only I were a better mother, a better person, a better Christian, my son's life would be on a better track. If anything happens to him tonight, I know it'll be my fault. All my fault. All my fault.

I feel certain that some evil person has attacked my son, robbed him, mugged him… Or perhaps it was a hit-and-run driver. I read about one in the paper just last week. I go and look out the front-room window, longing to see his little light coming down the street, but all I see is darkness. Darkness that keeps getting darker.

My heart beats faster and faster as image after image assaults my mind. First I imagine my Matthew twisted and bleeding on the side of the street, crying out for help, but no one stops. And then I see my son tied up and gagged, stuffed into the trunk of a big black sedan. And it's more than I can stand. I see myself identifying his lifeless body at the morgue, a white tag attached to his toe.

"O dear Lord, please help my son! Protect Matthew, Lord. Please, please protect my son." I am on my knees now, a familiar posture, as I hunch over the couch and repeat this prayer again and again, as if these words will be the magic charm to keep all harm at bay.

I'm not sure how many times I say these words, but it's as if I'm stuck and can't stop. I will never stop praying these words until I see my son again, whole and well. And suddenly I hear the back door open, and Matthew walks into the kitchen. Make that staggers.

"Wha's up?" he says with a crooked little smile and a noticeable slur.

I stand and stare at him, then turn and point to the clock. It's after midnight now. "Where have you been?"

"Jus' hangin' wif friends…" He tries to walk past me but bumps into me, and I smell the distinct stench of alcohol on him. He tries to continue on his way, but I stop him in his tracks, firmly holding him by one arm as I stare into his watery eyes.

"You've been out drinking, haven't you?"

"Nah…" He stupidly shakes his head. "Some of my friends were drinking, but not me. I don't drink."

"Don't lie to me!" I grab him by both arms, actually shaking my six-foot son as if he were a ten-year-old.

"Stop it, Mom."

"What's going on here?"

I turn to see Rick enter. He sets his lunchbox in the sink and walks over to where I'm still holding on to Matthew, my fingers digging into his arms.

"She's outta control," Matthew says like he thinks it's funny.

"He's drunk. *Your son is drunk.*"

"*My* son?" Rick looks at me curiously.

"Our son!" I glare at both of them now. "Matthew just got home. He's obviously been out drinking, and he's had me worried sick and—"

"I don't feel so good." Matthew tries to pull away from my grasp, slowly twisting from side to side.

"Let him go!" Rick says, but I continue to hang on. "*Ruth!* Let him go! He's going to throw up!"

I reluctantly release my son, and he staggers toward the bathroom but not in time. He bends over, clutching his stomach with both hands, and vomits in the hallway, right on the carpet.

"See." Rick points to the mess. "I told you to let him go."

"Thanks." I glare at him.

"Better clean that up," he tells me. "It's gonna stink."

"Why do *I* get to clean it up?"

"You're the one who wouldn't let him go."

Matthew eventually makes it to the bathroom, and it sounds like he's throwing up again. And I'm almost glad that he's sick. It serves him right. Perhaps it's the Lord's way of warning him about his stupid choices. But Rick goes to check on him.

Turning my back on both of them, I head to the laundry room for a bucket and some disinfectant. Then as I'm cleaning up my son's vomit, I am infuriated to hear Rick gently consoling Matthew, actually using a soothing voice as if everything's going to be just fine. He even helps Matthew to bed and takes off his shoes like he's a toddler!

I've just finished cleaning up the nasty mess as best I can for tonight—although I'm certain the carpet will need to be steam-cleaned tomorrow—when Rick comes out of Matthew's room and actually chuckles.

"You think this is funny?" I stand with the bucket in one hand and a soggy rag in the other.

"It's just life, Ruth. It happens."

"Your eighteen-year-old son comes home plastered, and you act like it's *no big deal*?"

"Hey, we've all done it at some point in life. The good thing is that he—"

"I cannot believe you!"

"You're going to wake the girls, Ruth."

I am seething. How can my husband act like it's perfectly normal for our son to do something like this? As if underage drinking, or drinking at all, is perfectly acceptable—humorous even? What is happening to this family? Surely God's judgment will be rained down upon all of us before long. And perhaps it's what we deserve. I've heard Pastor Glenn preach enough about God's judgment and wrath that I don't want to be on the receiving end.

Still fuming, I take the bucket and rags to the laundry room. I refill the bucket with more hot water, then attack the carpet, scrubbing and rinsing again and again, trying to eradicate the smell as much as I want to eradicate the sin from my son's life. And from this family. It seems that we're all steeped in sin.

As I take the last bucketful back to the laundry room, I can hear Rick watching television in the family room. The Lord only knows what kind of garbage he's watching at this hour. I'm not even sure that I care. I tiptoe off to the master bathroom and take a long, hot shower, imagining that it's fire burning away the sin. I scrub until my skin is red and raw and there isn't a drop of hot water left. If Rick wants a shower, he'll have to wait or take a cold one. Perhaps an icy shower will wake him up—wake him up to the reality of our messed-up lives. When will that man become the spiritual leader that this family needs? Will he ever? In some ways my husband is just like my dad. Married to his job and checked out of his family. Maybe this is my punishment. My never-ending punishment.

As I go to bed, I realize that I didn't get a chance to tell Rick that I replaced the money I gave to the family in need. But maybe it doesn't matter. Maybe it's too late to fix this thing after all. Maybe I really am hopeless. And maybe my family is hopeless too. I feel tears coming now, the aching kind of tears that come from deep, dark places inside.

God, help me. God, help me. God, help me... I pray this again and again, hoping the soothing rhythm, similar to the sound of a train rumbling down the tracks, will lull my wounded spirit to sleep. But I fear I am heading toward a great big boulder, a train wreck just waiting to happen.

usually feel better in the morning. I think it has to do with the sunlight. But today is cloudy and gray, and my spirits seem to match. Still, I go through the paces, fixing the girls' breakfast, driving them to school. But after they're safely delivered, I don't feel ready to go home. I don't want to see Matthew, probably still green around the gills and sporting an attitude. And I really don't want to face Rick just yet, although I doubt that he's even up.

So I park the minivan on the back side of the church parking lot, take out my leather-bound Bible, and begin to read in Isaiah. It's the prophetic section of the book, and I read some parts I've heard Pastor Glenn teach on. But the words just seem to float over my head, and I fear their meaning is far beyond me—something only people like Pastor Glenn or Cynthia can understand. And yet there is something soothing about this spiritual exercise, and so I read on. It's as if something is still under my control. And I get a sense of safety here, snuggled up in my minivan, parked near the rear entrance of the church. As if the Lord's big umbrella of protection extends from the church walls and out over me. And I imagine that reading the Bible is cleansing me, washing away all the crud from the previous evening.

I nearly jump out of my seat when I hear a tapping on the driver's side window. I turn to see Cynthia standing outside in the drizzly rain that has just begun to fall.

I roll down the window and smile at her.

"Are you okay?" she asks with a concerned expression.

I nod. "Yes. I think I am now."

"I've had such a burden for you this morning."

"You're getting wet. Do you want to come inside?"

She hurries around to the other side and slides into the passenger seat.

"Sorry, it's kind of messy in here," I say quickly. "You know how it is with kids." Then, of course, I immediately regret that comment since Cynthia is single with no children.

She just smiles, albeit a bit stiffly. Then she reaches over and puts her hand on my arm. "Now, tell me, Ruth, how is it going? *Really*."

Caught off guard by the intensity of her gaze and the knowledge that she is gifted at knowing what's below the surface of things, I almost break. I almost pour out all my fears and insecurities and worries about my family and how Matthew came home drunk last night and how I got so angry at my husband. But in the nick of time, I stop myself. A lifetime of training, of covering up my real feelings, kicks itself into gear, and I put on my flat face, followed up by a smile. "The phoning went really well last night! I'm about a third of the way through the list. And there was this one woman, a single mom named Candy, who was really eager to come to the concert. She said she's been looking for a church family."

"Oh, that's wonderful!" She peers closely at me again. "So everything is really okay with you, then?"

"Yes. I just wanted a quiet place to sit and read for a bit." I hold up my well-worn Bible. "With Rick's different schedule, working swing shift, and then there's Matthew at home. He doesn't usually go to the bookstore until later in the morning… Well, having a quiet time can be kind of difficult at my house."

She smiles. "I can just imagine. But you know you can always come into the church library to read. With the cold weather coming, I'm sure it could get pretty chilly out here in the parking lot."

"That's a great idea."

"I wanted to let you know that I passed your comments along to Pastor Glenn."

"My comments?"

"Your concerns about some of the rumors circulating around in the church."

"Oh…"

She sighs deeply. "Pastor Glenn suspected that you'd been talking to your friend Colleen McKinley."

My cheeks grow warm. I should've known that he'd figure this out. Why was I so stupid?

She pats my arm. "Don't worry, Ruth. Pastor Glenn doesn't blame you for the rumors. He knows what's going on. But he did want you to know that he's got some concerns and that Colleen and Dennis have been having problems."

"Problems?"

"Yes. I can't divulge the nature of their problems, but I can tell you that it's definitely impacting their walk with the Lord."

I nod without saying anything.

"We've really been doing some spiritual warfare on behalf of their family. I'm sure that you will do the same."

"Of course." Now I feel guilty for not having spent much time with Colleen lately. "I had no idea they were having problems. I would've been praying for them all along."

"Unfortunately, I must warn you to keep your distance from Colleen. You must be careful in your friendship with her, wise as a serpent and innocent as a dove. Colleen's spiritual vision is probably impaired right now, and we wouldn't want her to lead you astray." She smiles. "Because Pastor Glenn feels you have strong leadership potential."

"Really?"

"Yes. He says you have a servant's heart and an obedient spirit— wonderful traits in a believer."

I sit up straighter, genuinely touched that my pastor has noticed these things about me.

"Now, I have a favor to ask you, Ruth, but I want you to really pray about it before you answer."

"Okay."

"Well, as you know, women's Bible studies start up next week. And I realize that you've been attending Laura Fletcher's Bible study for several years, but I would like for you to come to my study, and I would like to have you as my prayer partner."

"Your prayer partner?" I'm overwhelmed by this unexpected invitation. *Cynthia Leman's prayer partner.* That's a position only a spiritually mature person would be asked to fill.

"Yes." She sighs. "You probably heard that Susan and Jeff Saunders relocated to the East Coast last spring. I had to finish out the year without a real prayer partner."

"I remember that now. What a loss. Susan must've been a wonderful prayer partner." I'd always admired Susan. She seemed so together and so deeply spiritual.

Cynthia nods. "I miss her. But I've been praying for her replacement, and I think you could be a wonderful support to me. Would you prayerfully consider this?"

"You can count on it!"

"Thank you." Then she opens the passenger door. "And I won't take up any more of your valuable quiet time."

"Oh, that's okay."

"See you at church tonight?"

"Certainly."

"And maybe you'll know your answer by then."

I nod. But I feel sure that I already know my answer. It would be a huge honor to be Cynthia's prayer partner! And suddenly my gloom about my life and my son and my husband seems to evaporate like the drizzle that's just letting up. It feels like the Lord is opening doors for me, amazingly moving me into a position of real leadership at our church! How long I have wished for something like this to happen to me. And now it is! I am so excited that I sing praise songs all the way back home.

Rick is in the garage when I get home, changing the oil in his pickup. I go out and say a cheerful hello to him.

He smiles cautiously. "Nice to see you're not still mad at me."

I wave my hand. "No no… And I'm sorry that I sort of blamed you about Matthew last night. Will you forgive me?"

"No problem."

"Is Matthew up yet?"

He nods as he checks the level on the dipstick. "But he's not feeling too great."

"Good." I want him to suffer as much as possible. I want him to learn that drinking will only bring him trouble.

"And I did have a more serious talk with him." Rick wipes his hands on an oily blue rag.

"Did Matthew listen?"

"He seemed to. He said he definitely doesn't plan to drink again."

"Do you think he really meant it?"

Rick shrugs. "Hard to say. What would you say if you were in his shoes?"

"Well, I do know that he's not working tonight, so I think I'll make him come to church with the girls and me."

"Guess that can't hurt."

"Can't hurt?" I frown at him.

"I mean, if that's part of his punishment."

"Going to church is *not* punishment, Rick."

"Maybe not for you. But it is for some people." He sticks his head under the hood of his pickup, almost as if he wants to escape my reaction to this statement.

I stand on the step that goes to the house, and I briefly consider telling him about Cynthia's invitation. But something stops me. Perhaps that would be like casting my pearls before swine. Not that I think my husband's a pig exactly. But sometimes he just doesn't understand spiritual things.

"I replaced that three hundred dollars in the checking account," I call out to him as I open the door to the house.

"Huh?" He sticks his head out and looks at me with a curious expression, and it's clear I have his full attention now. It figures that he'll listen to me when it comes to money. Where your treasure is…

"I deposited it into our checking account. So you don't have to worry about it anymore."

"How'd you do that?"

I pause with my hand on the doorknob. "Maybe it's not important to know *how* I did it as long as you know that I *did* it."

He shrugs. "Yeah, sure, as long as you didn't rob a bank or take out a loan or anything stupid. If the money's back, I guess I don't really care."

"And I've been thinking that I should probably look for a part-time job," I say as I step inside the house.

He brightens. "Yeah, that'd be good, Ruth."

I sort of wish I hadn't said that, since I'm still not really sure, but I guess I'll just leave it at that. It's not that I don't want to look for a job. But I suppose I'm just doubtful that I could really find one—anything beyond working at McDonald's, that is. Maybe I'm just underestimating myself again. It's possible that things are changing for me. After all, Cynthia Leman and Pastor Glenn both seem to recognize my potential. Maybe I'm just too hard on myself.

I console myself with these thoughts as I turn on my favorite Christian radio station and give the house a very thorough cleaning, even rewashing the hallway carpet. Hoping to save money on steam cleaning, I scrub and scrub until I'm fairly certain that I've purged all traces of Matthew's indiscretion. With each scrubbing stroke I beg for the Lord's guidance and discipline for my wayward son. *Show him your way!* I silently repeat over and over.

I take several breaks from cleaning, locking myself in the bathroom as I get down on my knees to earnestly pray about Cynthia's invitation to be her prayer partner. And while I'm at it, I pray for the spiritual welfare of my family as well. I even take the time to ask the Lord to help me find a good part-time job, pleading with him to direct me and to open some doors. And I believe he's going to do it.

By the time I pick up the girls from school, I know it's been a good day. Things are under control again.

For the most part, Matthew keeps a low profile all day, wisely staying out of my way while I clean and then fix dinner. And after he rinses and loads the dinner dishes into the dishwasher, he doesn't even complain about going to midweek worship service with us. I'm sure that he's hoping this will wipe his slate clean, that maybe I'll forget he came home drunk last night.

The girls head off to the kids' worship service in the gym, but Matthew refuses to go to the high-school youth group that meets in the youth house next door. "I'm not in high school anymore," he points out. Still, I can tell he's dragging his heels as he and I walk toward the sanctuary together.

"Ruth!" Cynthia is playing the role of greeter tonight, and she warmly shakes my hand as we enter the sanctuary. "I was just thinking of you."

"I might as well tell you," I say with a smile. "I would be honored to be your prayer partner. I believe the Lord has given me the green light. And I've already been praying for you and the first Bible study that you'll teach next week."

"Bless you! That is really good news!" She turns to Matthew, who is just a step behind me. "And how are you tonight, Matthew?"

He sort of grunts, "Okay," and I try not to feel too embarrassed.

"Well, I won't keep you from getting your seats." She turns to greet the couple coming in behind us.

We're nearing my favorite place to sit, right in the center and near the front, when Matthew says under his breath, "I don't see how you can stand her, Mom."

"Matthew!" I stare at my son.

"She's such a fake."

I give him the look—the you-better-keep-your-mouth-shut-young-man look. And fortunately he seems to get it. Still, I'm appalled at his lack of respect for his elders, and I can't help but think he's picking up on things his father is doing, or rather *not* doing. I hope that being in church tonight will remind Matthew of what's really important.

He sits hunched over like a sack of potatoes as some announcements are made from the pulpit, including the reminder that women's Bible studies start up again next week. Then when it's time to stand and worship, my son just sits there like a lump. Even when I nudge his shoulder and give him another warning look, he refuses to stand with the rest of us. This is truly alarming. I've never seen Matthew act like this before, and I'm worried that he could draw the attention of Pastor Glenn. I can't imagine how humiliating it would be to have my own son publicly rebuked in front of God and everyone. And just when I've agreed to be Cynthia's prayer partner. *Dear Lord, forgive me, I wish I'd let Matthew stay home tonight!*

I nervously glance around the room, trying to see if anyone is looking our way, and I'm surprised to notice that the congregation is much smaller than usual tonight. I can't help but notice large sections of empty seats throughout the church. And it occurs to me that they were just as empty this past summer, but as usual that was attributed to families being off on vacation. But here it is early October, and numbers still seem to be severely down. Well, it's a good thing we're having this outreach ministry to the community this month. Pastor Glenn is absolutely right; we are in dire need of some fresh faces around here!

I don't see Colleen and her husband here tonight. Come to think of it, I can't remember seeing them at midweek services much lately. I hope their problems aren't too serious. I suspect it has to do with their marriage, and I'm aware that they've had their ups and downs over the years, but for the most part they seem fairly compatible. And the twins are only seven. What a difficult age that would be for their parents' marriage to fall apart. I'll have to remember to diligently pray for them. Maybe I should give Colleen a call. Not to gossip, of course, but to encourage her. I can invite her to Cynthia's Bible study.

As everyone sits down, my attention is drawn back to the pulpit. It's that part of the service, between the worship time and the message, when Pastor Glenn often gives a word of knowledge. And occasionally Cynthia or Carl will go forward and give one as well. This seems to be the case tonight as Pastor Glenn gives her a somber nod and steps away from the podium. I watch Cynthia's squared shoulders, her long dark braid streaked with gray trailing down her straight back as she walks up the steps to the podium. Then she turns around, and closing her eyes, she lifts her head and raises her hands and begins to speak in a dramatic tone. Cynthia isn't a beautiful woman, not by anyone's standards, but when she speaks like this, with the kind of authority that comes from the Lord, she takes on an almost regal appearance that always captures my attention.

" 'I am gathering my children,' says the Lord, 'gathering my faithful ones,' " she begins. " 'I am separating the sheep from the goats, the believers from the doubters, so that I might be lifted up and glorified. Search your spirits, my children; dig out the roots of rebellion, secretly buried in your hearts by the deceptive seeds of sin. Purge yourselves with my fire. Burn away your evil with holy flames!'" She opens her eyes and points down at the center of the congregation, and I'm afraid she's pointing at me or perhaps even Matthew. I actually hold my breath, waiting with trembling knees.

"Shauna Banks," she says in a stern voice, and I slowly exhale. "The Lord has shown me your heart. His Spirit has revealed to me your spirit."

The sanctuary grows silent as a tomb, and from the corner of my eye, I glance at Shauna, just a few seats to my right. And while I feel sorry for this young mother, a woman Colleen has mentored, I am vastly relieved that it's not me. I feel that I have missed a bullet, and consequently my compassion is shallow. However, I do notice Matthew is intently looking at Shauna. I hope that perhaps he will learn something from this. It could've been him under fire.

"You have convinced yourself that your words are righteous," continues Cynthia, "but your words are toxic and lethal, and you are poisoning others each time you open your mouth to speak. The Lord has warned you, sister, 'Do not gossip' and 'Do not succumb to gossip.' But you refuse to obey. You refuse to heed his warnings. Like a dog returning to his vomit, you return to your wicked ways again and again."

I can't help but look at Shauna now. Everyone else is staring too, and the room is deathly quiet. Shauna's eyes glisten brightly, and her cheeks are flushed, and I really expect her to confess and to repent, to make her heart right before the Lord, but her jaw remains firm, her lips pressed together, and she says absolutely nothing.

"Until you acknowledge your wicked ways and repent, you are no longer welcome in the fellowship of the saints." Cynthia's still pointing at her. "We will be travailing in prayer for you, Shauna, and we will welcome you back with wide-open arms—but only if you confess your sins and ask for the Lord's deep cleansing and forgiveness."

Without saying a word, Shauna stands up, picks up her purse and her Bible, and then walks out of the sanctuary. Pastor Glenn steps up to the podium now. He pats Cynthia on the back, then clears his throat and nods to the pianist. He begins a song about turning our hearts back to the Lord and leads us in worship. We sing several songs, and I am, not for the first time, impressed with his singing ability. I wonder why he doesn't always lead us in worship.

Then the sanctuary grows quiet again, and he gives a moving altar call, inviting us to recommit our hearts to the Lord and to repent of our sins and be made whole and clean. As usual, I go forward. How can I not? I feel the need to repent on a daily basis. Sometimes on a minute-by-minute basis. But I am a little dismayed when I notice that only a handful of people have come forward. I just don't understand what's happening to our church, but I do believe we are under some kind of spiritual attack. It seems that people's hearts are growing hard and cold, and I find it frightening.

Pastor Glenn's sermon is about spiritual darkness and how it's pressing in around us. He speaks of all sorts of demons—demons of deception, lust, selfishness, murder, idolatry, jealousy, drunkenness, debauchery, and such—and how they are lurking around every corner, ready to attack anyone who lets down his guard even for a moment. And I can't help but believe that he's right on target. I have the exact same sense of evil pressing in on us, so strongly I can almost see it. I constantly feel the need to be prepared for an attack, to be vigilant for the Evil One, who seeks to devour and destroy.

I glance over at Matthew. I hope he's absorbing some of this spiritual wisdom, particularly the bit about the demons of drunkenness, but my son's face is totally blank, and I suspect he's tuning it all out. How can he do that? Has he become spiritually blind and deaf and dumb? Sometimes I want to shake the boy, to tell him to wake up before it's too late!

People usually linger in the sanctuary after the midweek worship service, just visiting and fellowshipping, but the large room empties quickly. Even Matthew has skittered away, probably lurking in some dark corner of the parking lot where he can attempt to conceal his sinful heart. But I decide to go forward and greet our pastor. I know that his role isn't an easy one, that speaking the truth can make enemies. His wife, Kellie, is usually at his side. But right now she's standing off to the right, having what appears to be a fairly intense conversation with Cynthia. Pastor Glenn is standing alone, his palms pressed together almost as if he is in prayer, although his eyes are open. He smiles at me as I walk toward him, and he greets me warmly.

"That was a great sermon, Pastor Glenn. My spirit really resonates with your message." I'm pleased with myself that I actually used the word *resonate*.

He nods and shakes my hand. "Thank you so much, Ruth. I really appreciate the feedback. I can't always tell what people are thinking."

"Well, you really nailed it on the head." Okay, maybe that's not quite as eloquent as *resonate*, but the spirit is the same.

"It's not easy having to say the hard things. But as a shepherd, it's my role to protect my sheep from evil. Sometimes that means giving some tough warnings."

"Well, speaking as a dumb sheep, I really appreciate the warnings."

"Cynthia tells me that you're going to be her prayer partner this year."

I'm surprised that she's already informed him of this, but I'm pleased too. It makes me feel important to be noticed like this. I nod happily. "It's such an honor to serve her. I'm really looking forward to it."

"You have a good heart, Ruth. Cynthia is blessed to have you on her team." He pats me on the shoulder. "And so am I."

I know I should be humbled by this attention and praise, but it also feels very good, very satisfying. And then I begin to feel uncomfortable. What if he knows what I'm feeling? What if I'm being spiritually proud and he's about to point this out to me? "I…uh…I guess I should go find my family now."

"Rick's still on the swing shift?" he asks as he walks me toward the door.

"Yes. Unfortunately, it goes along with his promotion."

He shakes his head but makes no comment.

"Hopefully it won't last too long though," I quickly add. "Rick said there's a chance he can go back to days in a year. If another guy retires, that is."

"A year is a long time."

I nod. "I know. It's only been a couple of months, and it feels like forever."

"Well, you continue being the godly woman that you are, Ruth. Keep leaning on the Lord and obeying him, and I'm sure it will go well for you."

And that's what I tell myself as I drive my moody family toward home. Matthew is sitting way in the back, sulking, I'm sure. And Mary and Sarah got into a little snit over who could sit in the front seat by me. Sarah was certain it was her turn, but her older sister beat her to the punch, and I couldn't remember whose turn it really was. I don't like them fighting over it anyway, so I made them sit behind me in the middle seat, beside each other, until they learn to get along.

I silently pray against the demonic forces that seem to be focused on my family as I drive through the dark, wet streets of our town. Like Pastor Glenn said, I can feel them pressing in, trying to lie and cheat as they attempt to steal our peace and joy. I must learn to do better warfare!

6

Cynthia and I meet at her house on Monday morning to discuss my new role as her prayer partner. I've never been to her home before, and I am surprised that, while it's neat and clean, it's rather small, and being an older home, it seems a little run-down. The porch has a loose board, and the linoleum in the kitchen is cracked. But something else is different too. Something I can't quite put my finger on at first. Then I realize that it seems to lack personal touches.

"It's like you're my assistant," she explains to me. "Most important, you pray for me and for the word that I'm teaching. But you also pray for the women in our study. Here's a list of names." She hands me a paper. "I know it seems like a small group for now, but I expect more women to join us once we get started. And even more after we have our outreach concert."

I nod and look at the list. There are only four names on it.

"My Bible study has always been held at the church, Ruth, but the Lord has been telling me that it's time for a change." She looks around her sparse living room. "We need to meet in a private home, where women feel free to really share and minister to each other. However, I don't think this is exactly the right location."

Once again I nod. I couldn't agree more.

"How about your house?"

Now this alarms me. While my house is much warmer and friendlier than this, I've never really had the confidence to open it up much to visitors. "I…uh…I don't know. And, of course, there's Rick to consider. He works swing shift, you know, so he sleeps late in the morning."

"Then he would be asleep when we met."

"Well, I…uh…I suppose, but…" I imagine Rick walking out of the bedroom in his boxer shorts, scratching himself, while the women are prayerfully gathered in my living room. I think I would die.

"I sense the Lord is at work in you, Ruth. And although it might stretch you to open your home like this, I believe there is a blessing in store, for you and your family."

"Really?"

"Yes. Are you open to this blessing?"

And so it's settled. Friday morning at nine thirty Cynthia Leman will lead the Bible study at my house. I feel a mixture of nervousness and pleasure as I drive home. I *do* want to serve the Lord, and I *do* want his blessing, but at the same time I don't feel completely ready to open my home like this. And I have no idea how Rick is going to react to this news.

"Why can't Cynthia have Bible study at her house?" Rick scowls after I finish my little announcement. I thought it might soften him if I fixed meat loaf for lunch, since it's his favorite, but I suspect he can see right through me.

"Her house is pretty small, and she thinks the Lord is going to bless our family by having it here."

He makes a little groan and shakes his head.

"It'll be over by eleven," I promise. "And you hardly ever get up before noon anyway."

"You *really* want to do this?" He studies me closely as he takes another helping of mashed potatoes.

"I think it would be good for me," I tell him, hoping it's the truth.

"Well, then I guess it's okay. But just for the record, I don't really trust Cynthia Leman."

"Why?"

He shrugs as he digs his fork into the potatoes. "She kinda gives me the heebie-jeebies."

"Oh, that's silly."

"Don't be so sure, Ruth. All that prophecy stuff and giving words at church," he continues with his mouth full, "it just rubs against the grain. How can you believe what they say? It sounds like a bunch of phony baloney to me. And some of it's just plain mean-spirited. Besides, what about when Jesus said, 'Let he who is without sin throw the first stone'? Glenn and Cynthia seem to throw stones right and left."

I know he's referring to church yesterday. It was like pulling teeth to get him to go in the first place. And then he just sat there, frowning. I hate to admit it, but my husband is spiritually immature. More and more I feel that Rick and I are unequally yoked. He seems to be stuck in the spiritual dark ages while I am slowly but steadily moving forward, slowly but steadily being enlightened and spiritually stretched and renewed. At least he's not too opposed to having the Bible study in our house. That's a small victory. And maybe, like Cynthia promised, our family will be blessed for this. Maybe Rick will begin to take his spirituality more seriously. Maybe he'll even want to join Pastor Glenn's men's group.

Feeling spiritually strong, I call Colleen on Tuesday night. I'm all ready to be a light and an encourager to her, but I can tell she's got her hands full, fixing dinner for her family. I can hear her boys yelling in the background, and it sounds like someone's in pain. "Call me back when you're not busy," I quickly tell her.

"How about if we do coffee tomorrow morning? Like we used to do."

Before I have a chance for second thoughts, I agree to meet her at church after we drop the kids off, but I've barely hung up when I wonder if I've just made a big mistake.

The next morning I'm barely in Colleen's car when I'm certain I shouldn't have done this.

"What's with Cynthia?" she asks as she exits the church parking lot.

"Huh?"

"Why was she giving you that look right before we left?"

I shrug. "You must be imagining it." I try to redirect our conversation by telling her that I'm Cynthia's new prayer partner.

"You're kidding!"

"No, I'm serious. I was honored to be asked. Our first study is Friday at my house, and I was hoping you might want to come."

"I work on Fridays."

"Oh."

"And even if I didn't, I wouldn't come. I can't believe you want to be her prayer partner. Don't you know that Cynthia's a mess?"

"A mess?"

"She's nuts, Ruth. Everyone knows it."

I stare at Colleen like she's a stranger.

"Okay, maybe she's not nuts." Colleen sighs loudly. "But our church is in trouble. And I think it's just a matter of time before Pastor Glenn and Cynthia are both history. Carl too. He's getting way too caught up in their fun and games."

"Fun and games?"

"Oh, you know. Their spiritual charades, witch hunts—call it whatever you like. It's crazy. And Shauna told me about last week."

"Are you taking up an offense because of that?"

"Well, that was bad enough. But she's only one person. Lots of people are hurting from what's going on at church."

"Sometimes the truth hurts," I say as we arrive at the coffee shop and get out of the car. "But ultimately it is healing."

"The truth?" She turns to look at me. "Do you really believe that?"

I nod.

"Wow…"

"Pastor Glenn says it's not easy to discipline his sheep, but it's for their own good. It's so they don't get—"

"Discipline?" She shakes her head. "Is that what he calls it?"

We're standing by the door now, and I'm not sure I want to go in. I'm not sure I want to be subjected to Colleen's anger and judgment.

"He's not disciplining his sheep, Ruth." She opens the door. "He's *beating* them."

Fortunately, we stop discussing this as we order our coffees, but I feel shaken as we go and sit down. I don't know what to say to Colleen. All I can do is silently pray for the Lord to help me. *Help me to help Colleen see the light. She is trapped in darkness.*

"Maybe we shouldn't talk about this right now," she says as she blows on her mocha. "I might get so fired up that I start yelling."

I nod. "Yes. Let's not make a scene."

She laughs. "Remember that night at Denny's in high school?"

I make a face. "No, and I don't want to."

"We used to be such hellions." She sighs as if she regrets that things have changed.

"The Lord has cleansed us from all of that, Colleen." I study her. "And I'm sure you would never want to go back to that sinful lifestyle."

"Not really. But sometimes I think we, as Christians, get a little too uptight."

"We need to be on our guard," I remind her. "Satan is prowling around like a lion, waiting to devour us. We need to be ready."

She waves her hand. "Oh, that lion had his teeth pulled out, Ruth. And he's been declawed too. Remember that Jesus defeated him on the cross. Sure, we need to be aware that Satan is still around, but we don't need to be afraid."

"I'm not saying we need to be afraid. I just think we need to be prepared and equipped and on guard. We need to be wearing God's armor. We're in a spiritual battle, you know. We need to defend ourselves."

She sighs. "But that shouldn't be our only focus. Paranoid people like Pastor Glenn and Cynthia give Satan all the power when they only talk about being on the defensive. Why not be on the offensive and focus on God's power and strength instead?"

"Maybe we should talk about something else." I feel uneasy now. What if Pastor Glenn or Cynthia somehow found out what Colleen just said about them?

"So, how do your girls like school?"

I kind of shrug.

"Have they told you about morning devotions?"

I shake my head no and nervously sip my Americano.

"Well, Kyle and Jacob have told me. And Dennis and I made a formal complaint to the board last week."

"Why?"

"Because Pastor Glenn is scaring my kids to death! Jason's been having nightmares, and Kyle drew a really creepy picture of a demon."

I don't tell her that Sarah's had nightmares too. But then Sarah has such a vivid imagination. I worry that she's going to become a drama queen by the time she hits adolescence. I need to pray for her more.

"How are you and Dennis doing?" I finally remember the purpose of my phone call last night—to encourage and uplift my friend during times of trouble.

"We're fine."

"Really?"

"Yeah, why? What have you heard?" She leans forward like she expects me to tell her some juicy piece of gossip. "Did someone say we were getting divorced or that we became swingers or something?" She laughs. "Actually I did threaten to run away last night, but that's just because the twins were making me nuts, and I guess I was having PMS. Then Dennis sent me upstairs to take a bath while he cleaned the entire kitchen." She grinned. "Can't complain about that."

"That was nice of him."

"Yeah, he can be pretty nice. But how about you guys? How are you doing? You getting used to Rick's new hours yet?"

"I guess."

"Man, I think it'd be such a drag to be home alone every night. Maybe you and I should do something sometime. Have girls' night

out or something. We could take in a chick flick. Dennis is a nice
guy, but he hates chick flicks."

I glance at my watch.

"Are you in a hurry or something?"

"It's just that I promised Rick I'd start looking for a job." As we
drive back to the church, she tells me they might be hiring where she
works at the Med Center, and I act interested. But mostly I just want
her to drop me off and end this. Although she seems oblivious, acting as if we just had fun.

I force a smile as we say good-bye, but it's obvious that Colleen
doesn't take her spiritual welfare too seriously. I suspect she's the one
who'd been gossiping with poor Shauna Banks. I won't be surprised
if Colleen is publicly reprimanded before long. She's stepping way
over the line.

I glance around the church parking lot, hoping that Cynthia isn't
around to see me. I know that I owe her an explanation, and I'll have
to tell her that she's right about Colleen too. I guess I shouldn't be that
surprised. Colleen really was a wild child back in high school. Come
to think of it, she was pretty influential on me back then too. Still,
I never took things as far as she did. I've never asked her, but I sometimes wonder if her past has haunted her marriage. What would
Dennis think if he knew about her background with the guys?

As I drive home, I ask the Lord to forgive me for rubbing up
against Colleen's darkness, and I ask him to protect me from becoming critical of the church like she has. And I promise to avoid
her in the future. Colleen is dangerous, with the ability to contaminate me. And I do not want to be contaminated. As I pull into the
driveway, an invasive sense of uncleanness comes over me. I was

wrong to spend time with Colleen. I know I need cleansing. Real cleansing.

The house is quiet and empty, with no one to see me as I remove all my clothes and place them one by one in the washing machine. I wrap myself in a clean towel from the dryer, a towel that is now contaminated by me. Then I tiptoe through the house, hunched down because the blinds are open and I don't want to be seen by a neighbor. I go into the master bathroom, lock the door, then check to make sure it's really locked before I drop the unclean towel into the laundry hamper and step into the shower, where I wash and scrub, wash and scrub, over and over, until my skin is raw and red, until the water runs cold. But I continue scrubbing and washing in the cold water.

This is my punishment. I deserve it.

7

On Friday, Cynthia comes thirty minutes early so we can pray before Bible study. But after she's inside my house, instead of praying she begins to walk around. She's looking at everything, and I can't tell what she's thinking. But I'm relieved that I spent most of yesterday cleaning. The windows are gleaming, and there's not a speck of dust to be found anywhere. But even so, I feel like I'm walking on eggshells, and I'm sure that if anyone could spot something amiss, it would be Cynthia. Or my mother.

Finally she stands in the living room, where we plan to have the Bible study. But she seems to be stuck in front of a photo montage that hangs on the wall above an old chest of drawers that has been in Rick's family for generations. I have to admit that I'm somewhat proud of this arrangement. It took me the better part of a painstaking week to get those antique photos just right, and that was only after I did numerous sketches on pieces of drafting paper, carefully plotting the whole thing out to scale so it would fit exactly. I suppose I'm expecting her to compliment me on this decorating accomplishment.

"How can you bear to look at this every day?" she finally says, pointing to an old sepia-toned photograph of my great-grandparents on my mother's side.

"What?"

"Look at those eyes." She points to the man's dark and penetrating gaze. "So evil."

"Evil?" I study the antique photo more carefully, and I must admit the fellow looks a bit grim. But so does the woman. "How can you tell?"

She taps her chest. "I can just *feel* it. In here."

"Oh."

"That man definitely has a dark spirit." She turns and looks at me with concern. "Oh, it's not your fault, Ruth. So many of our ancestors were like that; it's a generational curse. But to hang this photograph right here in your house, exposing your children, your family to this dark spirit..." She shakes her head. "Well, I don't recommend it. And I don't like the idea of having it here during Bible study."

"Should I take it down?" I feel a mixture of alarm and shame as I stare at my ancestors' photo. Why hadn't I picked up on this before?

"At least for Bible study. What you do afterward is up to you."

I remove the photograph, leaving a gaping hole where it had hung. Then I look once more into those dark eyes and feel certain that she's right. They do have a sinister cast to them. I open the top drawer of the old chest and am about to put the picture in when Cynthia puts her hand on my arm.

"Not in here. Remember, this is where the Bible study group will gather. We don't want any evil spirits around to bother us, Ruth."

"What should I do with it?"

"Put it as far from this room as possible. Maybe the garage."

So I take the photograph out to the garage, and after wrapping it in one of Rick's old rags, I set it on an empty storage shelf, shoving it way in the back. But as I walk into the house, I wonder if I should've taken it out to the trash. Because even though it's wrapped and hidden, it's as if I can feel those eyes still staring at me, perhaps even bringing down a family curse from previous generations. But I push these thoughts away as I return to my living room, where Cynthia is now seated on the couch.

"Thank you," she says with a smile. "I hope I didn't offend you by my observation. It's only that my spirit is so sensitive to these sorts of things, and I just want you and your family to be safe."

"No, it's quite all right. I actually appreciate it. And I really want my spirit to become more sensitive too. Who knows what else I might have in here that's giving bad vibes."

She nods. "It can be tricky, you know. The devil is the great Deceiver." She glances around the room. "But I think we're okay for the time being. I'll let you know if I pick up on anything else. Shall we pray now?"

So we both kneel by the couch, and she starts the prayers. "O Lord," she says with genuine passion, "please reveal yourself to us today. Make your presence known to us, and please show us what you want to do in our hearts. Purge us from our iniquities, purify our spirits. We pray against the Evil One now. We know he is lurking around every corner, just waiting to catch us off balance so he can knock us down, so he can destroy us. We pray that your Spirit will bind Satan's spirit now. We pray that you will hold his powers back while we gather here to learn from your Word and to experience your bountiful gifts..." For several minutes she prays, and I do my best to agree with her, to say "amen" when it seems appropriate, and finally she collapses forward on the couch and tells me I must continue for her.

"My spirit is getting exhausted," she says breathlessly. "I need for you to go to battle for me, sister. I need you to hold back the attack of Satan and his demons. They don't want us to gather here today. I can feel it. You must pray against them with power and might."

So I pray against the demons and their evil influence. I pray against the devil and his deceptions that would lead us astray. I pray that Cynthia will be strong in the Lord and that she will remain impervious to the Enemy's fiery arrows. On and on I pray until I'm surprised that Cynthia is nudging me.

"Well done." She points to her watch. "But it's nearly time for the ladies to arrive."

"Oh!" I blink at the light in the room as I open my eyes. "I almost forgot about that."

She laughs. "You're an excellent prayer warrior, Ruth. It's no mistake that the Lord picked you to partner with me this year. We will be a great team for the Lord."

Hoping to appear humble, I nod with a solemn expression, then excuse myself to check on the coffee and tea things in the kitchen. But once I'm by myself, I feel exuberant, like I could dance and sing and praise the Lord all day. To think that I am Cynthia's partner now, that the Lord has chosen me to help this deeply spiritual woman! It's almost intoxicating.

Later on I try to conceal my disappointment when only three women show up for our Bible study. I'm embarrassed that I've put out enough coffee cups and things for at least a dozen women. But it is a consolation that at least they are three very spiritual women. Edna Bristol, Margie Morris, and Amy Johnson join us in the living room. There is no need for introductions since we've all known each other for years. But Cynthia does tell them that I am her new prayer partner, and they seem to approve.

Edna is the oldest in our group. A widow and recently retired from the post office, she is in her midsixties, I think. She's always been a pillar of faith in our church and even more so since her retirement. Margie and Amy are my age, give or take a year or two, and Cynthia is somewhere in between. I've never been sure of her age, although I'd guess she's in her mid to late fifties. She came to our church about the same time Pastor Glenn took over, and I've always assumed that she followed him here from their previous church.

Cynthia teaches from Revelation today. She focuses primarily on the section in chapter three where the Lord accuses the church of Laodicea of being lukewarm.

" 'You are neither cold nor hot,' says the Lord." She repeats this verse with emphasis. " 'Because you are…neither cold nor hot, I will spew you out of My mouth!' "

My living room is quiet now, and we're waiting for her to continue. But instead of reading or teaching, Cynthia just sits there, slowly looking at each one of us, steadily moving her intense gaze from one woman to the next as if she can see right through our clothes, past our layers of skin, and straight into our souls, which I fear she is able to do. And when she looks at me, I can't return her gaze. I look down at the Bible in my lap. I can't bear the fire of her penetrating stare. I feel certain it will melt me. Suddenly I remember that old scene from *The Wizard of Oz* where Dorothy throws water on the Wicked Witch of the West. Just like that, I will melt.

"Ruth," Cynthia says in a soft, compassionate tone, "why are you afraid?"

I look up at her and see that the other three women are looking at me now. "I…uh…I don't know."

"Are you concerned that this verse applies to you?"

I shrug. That actual thought hadn't occurred to me. More than anything I think I just didn't want to get caught in her spotlight.

"Are you worried that your love for the Lord is lukewarm?"

I consider this possibility. "Maybe so..."

"You have such a good spirit," she continues, "but something seems to be holding you back, Ruth. Can you feel it, ladies?"

They nod and seem to agree. And as unspiritual as this may sound, I briefly wonder if they aren't just relieved that her attention has been focused on me instead of them. Or perhaps I am the only one in need of Cynthia's attention right now.

"I have a strong sense that it's time for a cleansing prayer," she says to the other women. "Will you join with me for Ruth?"

Once again they nod in somber agreement.

"Are you ready for this, Ruth?" she asks.

Suddenly I remember that Rick is home. Sleeping, or maybe not, only twenty feet or so away from us. What if he is awake, listening at the door?

"Ruth?" Cynthia places her hand on my arm. "The Lord wants to cleanse and deliver you. Are you ready?"

I take in a deep breath. How can I deny the Lord? Then I nod. "Yes."

She motions to the other women, and the next thing I know, Margie has placed one of the extra dining-room chairs in the center of the living room, and I'm being escorted to sit in it. Then I am surrounded, one on each side, and all of them are placing their hands on me.

I've seen other people with hands laid on them at the front of the church, but never wanting that kind of attention, I have always managed to avoid this myself. And now the feeling of their warm palms and fingers pressing into my shoulders, my back, my head, my arms—it's unsettling, overwhelming, and slightly nauseating. And suddenly I feel too warm, and it seems the air is being sucked out of the room. I can't breathe, can't catch my breath. Perhaps I will actually pass out and Cynthia will assume that I've been slain by the Spirit and everyone will be happy and go home.

"Block all doubts from your head," Cynthia commands me. "Focus on the power of the Holy Spirit, Ruth. We are all going to agree for your deliverance now. Ladies, we are doing warfare here. I expect everyone to do her part."

They all begin to pray, just quietly to start with, sort of to themselves, and I can't really make out the words. Then Margie and Cynthia both switch over to their prayer languages, or tongues as some people call it, and yet all I can hear is a buzzing sound in my head, like cicadas on a summer night. But slowly the buzzing goes away, and some of their prayers become understandable.

"I bind the spirit of oppression," Amy says with sincerity. "Satan, you oppressor, I bind you in the name of Jesus. You are to have no part of this woman! In the name of Jesus, you must depart."

"Yes!" Cynthia agrees. "The Spirit is leading you, Amy. I also sense there is oppression in Ruth's life. But it's not just Satan alone. He is also using a *human* to oppress her. Someone close to her is being used by the devil, someone who wants to hold her down spiritually. Am I correct, Ruth?"

With my eyes still tightly closed, I consider this. "Maybe… I'm not sure…"

"Yes," continues Cynthia, "it's someone in your family… Do you think Satan has positioned this person to oppose you, to oppose the Holy Spirit?"

I open my eyes. They are all looking at me, waiting with expectation, as if I am supposed to tell them something profound, something I don't even know or understand myself. "I don't know," I say weakly.

"Show us, Lord," persists Cynthia. "Show us who this oppressor is so we may bind that person, cast that evil person out." Then they continue praying, some in tongues, some in English, and I consider who this oppressor might be. There seem two obvious possibilities. One is Rick, since I've been acutely aware of his presence in the house all morning. But the other one is my mother. If anyone has ever oppressed me, it's her. Finally I admit that I know who my oppressor is.

"Who?" demands Cynthia. "Who is it, Ruth?"

"My mother."

They all nod as if they understand, and then they fervently pray against my mother's power in my life; they bind Satan's connection to my mother and then her connection to me. They pray against generational ties that defile, and they proclaim my new freedom by the power of the Holy Spirit. Again and again they bind these evil powers of oppression in my life, and after a while I begin to cry, first softly and then eventually without any control at all. I am sobbing and blubbering and wailing so hard that by the time they all say their final "amen," my blouse is damp from my tears. I am surprised that Rick hasn't walked into the living room, maybe even in his boxer shorts, to see what is going on. But the house is quiet. Then they all hug me. They assure me they understand.

"I've been through something very similar," Amy admits. "Only it was with my grandfather. He sexually molested me as a young child. Although I didn't actually remember it happening to me." She glances at Cynthia with what seems like uncertainty, then smiles.

"But the Spirit led us," says Cynthia. "He showed us how Amy had been hurt."

"It took almost a year of deliverance prayer to get beyond it," says Amy.

"That's right." Cynthia pats Amy in a maternal way.

Amy nods, but her eyes seem sad. "Cynthia was the first one to help me to uncover and acknowledge the abuse. Without her, I'd still be in bondage today."

The others share stories of being freed from other serious things. Much of it seems related to sexual abuse of some sort—rape, incest, or promiscuity. My problem actually seems minor in comparison. But I feel a huge sense of comfort and relief as well as an amazing new sense of freedom. I know that something huge happened here today. Something spiritual and powerful—something of God! And by the time the women leave, I feel that I have joined a very special sisterhood.

"What was going on in here?" Rick demands as soon as the last car pulls out of the driveway.

"Why?" I put the unused coffee cups back in the china cabinet.

"It sounded like someone was having a fit." He narrows his eyes. "It wasn't you, was it?"

I shrug, thinking about pearls before swine again. "It was a very moving Bible study. I think we all were touched by it."

He makes a grunting sound, then fills his favorite mug with coffee and heads for the television. I suspect he really doesn't want to know the details. And that's fine with me.

As I take the dining-room chairs from the living room, I notice the gap in my photo montage. And while the arrangement now seems slightly off balance, there is no way I intend to bring that evil photograph back. Especially after the deliverance prayer over the generational curses that come through my family, my mother's side in particular. Maybe I can find something else to stick in there. And as I stand looking at the montage, I wonder about the other photos. I really don't know who all these people are, not really.

It was years ago that I began to gather old family photos, old memorabilia cast off by others. I simply thought they were interesting and part of our family history, not to mention decorative. But now as I look at these strange faces, I wonder how many other family curses might be hidden behind their sober expressions. How many other secret family sins are contaminating this generation?

I consider removing all the photos. Maybe I can box them up and stick them in the attic for the time being. But this will rouse questions from Rick. He's well aware of how long I labored over this project, how proud I was to complete it. I really don't want to have to explain this ancestral curse and oppression thing to him. For one thing, he just wouldn't get it, and he might even make fun of me. But the other thing, the thing that stops me dead in my tracks, is the nagging conviction that there might be more than one oppressor in my life. I am not ready to face that possibility yet.

've barely set down the phone, taking a moment to ask the Lord's blessing on my work, when it rings so loudly that I literally jump off the kitchen stool, causing the phone to crash to the floor. I scramble for the receiver and my wits and am relieved, at least at first, to hear Colleen's voice on the other end. But then I quickly remember Cynthia's warning to me as well as my last conversation with my old friend.

"How are you?" I ask in a somewhat stiff voice.

"Did I catch you at a bad time?"

"No, I was just finishing up calling people about next week's concert."

"Oh, that's right. I forgot all about that."

"Are you coming?"

"It actually sounds kinda fun," she says, which gives me hope. "But I've got so much to do now that I can't say for sure."

"Really? What are you doing that's so pressing?"

"That's why I called, Ruth. We're moving!"

"Again? You guys just moved into your—"

"No, I mean *really* moving. Dennis got this huge promotion at work, and it involves a transfer to Albuquerque, and we've got to be packed and ready to go in two weeks."

"Two weeks?"

"Yeah. Can you imagine?"

"No. It sounds horrible to me. Are you sure it's a good idea?"

"Of course! Dennis is ecstatic. Even the boys are excited."

"But have you prayed about it, Colleen? I've heard that New Mexico is a very dark place spiritually."

"Then maybe they need some lights down there." Colleen laughs, like this is really funny.

"Seriously, Colleen, have you guys prayed about this? I mean, you're ready to uproot your family, take the boys out of school, and go down to...to God only knows what?"

"Maybe that's how Abraham felt when he headed for the desert. Or Noah when he was building that animal yacht. Only God knew where they too were going."

"So you believe the Lord is leading you to New Mexico?"

"Dennis feels like it's the right thing. And I'm a hundred percent behind him."

"But what about church and school and—"

"To be perfectly honest, we were both getting a little fed up with the whole thing at VBF. Maybe this is God's way of rescuing us." She laughs again.

"I can't believe you think it's funny."

"Okay, it's not really funny. But Dennis and I are happy about it. The company is going to cover all moving expenses and provide us with really nice housing, and we'll just put our place up for rent. If things don't work out, we'll come back home. We see it as an adventure, Ruth. Can't you be happy for us?"

"Yeah, I guess so. I mean, if you're really happy and you're sure it's the Lord's will."

"We are!"

I guess I should be relieved. Having Colleen that far away will eliminate any possibility of my being influenced by her, which I'm sure will make Cynthia happy. Still, I feel sad. "I'm going to miss you."

"Me too! But we'll stay in touch. Have Rick teach you how to set up an e-mail account on the computer. We can e-mail each other all the time."

"Yeah..." But even as I say this, I know that I won't. Communicating with Colleen is probably not a healthy thing for me to do. Besides, the Internet isn't spiritually safe. I've heard Cynthia say this repeatedly.

"And that reminds me," she says suddenly. "I told Darlene at work that you might be interested in my job. She said to come on in and introduce yourself."

"Thanks."

"Well, I'd love to stay on the phone and gab with you, but I've got a million things to do."

So we say good-bye and hang up. And even though I know Colleen is still on the other side of town, I feel like she's already gone. I feel like the Lord has removed her from my life for a reason, and I'm flooded with a conflicting mixture of relief and sadness— and confusion.

I manage to distract myself during the next few days. We're putting up posters for the concert, taking announcements to the local Christian radio stations, and just trying to get the word out.

"We might have to hold this thing outdoors," Pastor Glenn tells us at our meeting just two days before the concert, "if the predictions for numbers are correct."

"What about the weather forecast?" asks Carl. "I heard it's supposed to rain on Friday."

"Maybe we could rent one of those big tents," suggests Edna.

"On such short notice?" says Cynthia. "We'd probably be better off to pray against the rain."

"Yes!" agrees Pastor Glenn. "Let's pray against the rain."

So we all bow our heads and fervently plead with the Lord to deliver us from the rain. We bind the spirit of storms and rain and clouds, and sometimes we even laugh at our prayers, but we mean it. God knows we mean it.

"Okay then," Pastor Glenn says with a big smile. "Let's plan on holding this thing outside in the church parking lot. Carl, you coordinate this with the sound guys, and, Edna, you let Ginger know." He claps his hands. "And everyone keep praying against the rain!"

I want to ask what the backup plan is if it should rain, but I know this would sound like a lack of faith on my part, so I keep my doubts to myself.

But when Friday comes, it is overcast and gloomy outside. As I drive the girls to school, I feel a heavy spirit coming over me. "You girls need to pray against the rain. Pray that the clouds will all blow away in time for the concert tonight."

"Do you really think the Lord will change the weather for the concert, Mom?" Mary asks.

"Why not? He sent frogs to the wicked Pharaoh. Why can't he blow away the clouds so we can have a beautiful Christian music event tonight?"

"I'll pray against the rain, Mommy," says Sarah. "I know the Lord can do it!"

"That's the spirit."

"I didn't say I *wasn't* going to pray," Mary says quickly. "I just wasn't sure the Lord would change the weather."

"The Lord can do anything," I remind them.

"That's right," echoes Sarah. "The Lord can do anything!"

We also pray against the rain at Bible study, and to my relief I'm not spotlighted in the group for any kind of special prayer or deliverance today. In fact, it's a rather ordinary Bible study, and much of our focus and energy is directed toward tonight's concert and what it might mean for our church and its growth. We pray specifically about this and for all the visitors who might show up tonight.

As the day progresses, my faith increases. It seems the Lord really is holding back the rain. When I pick up the girls, I see that the school traffic has been rerouted to the back of the church so chairs can be placed in the parking lot. And the sound stage is all set up in the front with balloons and streamers, and it really does look like something exciting is going to happen tonight. My job is to help greet new people and to give them fliers with information about our church along with a schedule of church activities.

Both girls seem excited about the concert as we fix a quick dinner for the three of us. Naturally, Rick is working and won't be able to make it. No surprises there. And Matthew is working tonight as well, but at least he promised to stop by if he can get off in time. I'm praying that will be the case. A concert like this might be just the sort of thing that my slightly prodigal son would actually respond to. At least he hasn't come home drunk lately.

We head over to the church early so the girls can get good seats while I work as a greeter. But as I drive toward the church, I am surprised at how dark it is outside, and seeing people's homes decorated for Halloween, which is only a few days away, I feel a spirit of darkness looming over our entire town. Silently I pray against it and against the rain.

I feel a wave of relief when I pull up to the church, parking far off to the left of the building where there are still a few spaces available. But as we walk through the well-lit parking lot, where Mary and a bunch of her friends helped to string scores of Christmas mini-light strands so it looks really festive, I am glad to see quite a few people are already here. Some are at work, while others are visiting and milling about the parking lot, and then the musicians start warming up. There's a feeling of energy and high expectation in the air. And all in all it appears to be a happy and inviting scene. Yet something is bothering me.

"The band wasn't too thrilled to find out that we're having this outdoors," Amy quietly tells me as she hands me a stack of fliers.

"Why's that?" I ask as Cynthia joins us.

"They're afraid it's going to rain and their equipment will be ruined."

"Pastor Glenn assured the young men that prayer warriors have been praying against rain for the last several days," Cynthia adds in an authoritative voice. "And as you can see, it hasn't rained a drop all day."

"Maybe we should pray right now." I mostly suggest this because my faith is lagging a bit. I can feel the heaviness in the air, which I know is partly spiritual opposition, but I can also feel a heaviness of rain, perhaps even a storm coming. I've always been sensitive to weather like this. My dad sometimes called me his little barometer. Of course, I don't want to tell the women this.

"That's an excellent idea," says Cynthia. "Why don't you lead us, Ruth?"

And so I do. And together we all bind the rain and the clouds and the darkness and Satan and his demons and deceptions. And then we loose the Lord's Spirit and goodness, and finally we shout out, "Amen!"

"Good for you," Pastor Glenn says as he passes by with a couple of the elders flanking him on either side.

"And pray for our pastor," Cynthia whispers to me after Amy goes over to distribute more fliers to some other greeters.

"Any special reason why?" I'm surprised I have the nerve to ask this, but it seems my confidence has been growing lately.

"The elders and the council," she says in a hushed tone. "They haven't been supportive of the outreach concert."

"Too bad."

But people are starting to arrive, so we move to our preappointed positions, ready to greet the newcomers and make them feel at home. But within a few minutes, it becomes clear that parking is going to be a challenge since we're using most of the church parking lot for the concert. Cars are forced to park in nearby neighborhoods, and people must walk several blocks to get back here. Naturally this leads to some complaining once they arrive. And then some savvy drivers start dropping off passengers closer to the church, which actually causes a bit of a traffic jam and slows things down even more. But eventually most of the people are in place, the chairs are filled, and finally, about thirty minutes later than planned, Pastor Glenn steps onto the stage and offers a warm welcome to all.

"We're so pleased you could make it tonight. And we're equally pleased that the Lord has been gracious to answer our prayers, holding back the rain so we could all enjoy a beautiful outdoor concert." He continues to tell them about his vision for reaching out to the community, opening the church up, and making everyone welcome. And as he speaks, I think, not for the first time, that Pastor Glenn has a certain kind of charm and charisma. When he's being lighthearted and happy, most people are naturally drawn to him.

"And it seemed that a concert was a wonderful way to kick things off," he says finally. "We hope you'll be blessed by the music tonight. So, let's all offer a warm welcome to our talented musicians—Recycled!"

With that, the band strikes up a lively song, and most of the audience seems caught up in the rhythm and enthusiasm, and some of the younger people, including my two daughters, even stand up and clap along. After the first song, there is long, loud applause, and then the leader of the band introduces himself and his band members. It really seems like tonight is going to be a huge success, and even the elders and council should be pleased. Then midway through the second song, a flash streaks across the sky, followed several seconds later by a loud clap of thunder. But the band keeps playing.

Sarah's hand slips into mine, and I know she's afraid, but I give it a gentle, reassuring squeeze, and then I close my eyes and fervently pray with every ounce of faith I have, begging the Lord to hold off this storm until the concert is over and everyone is safely back in their cars and heading for home. But the third song barely starts before it begins to rain. Huge, fat droplets shoot from the sky like soft bullets, but at least there aren't many of them. Then the second bolt of lightning flashes, almost directly overhead, accompanied by a thunderous boom that I can feel in my chest.

People immediately rise to their feet, but the brave band continues to play. That may be reassuring to some of the younger members of the audience, like my Mary, who seems hardly fazed, but the older ones are already skirting toward the edges of the chairs and into the church. The musicians look nervous, and the leader appears to be signaling to them that they'll quit at the end of their third song. But before the song is finished, another bolt slashes down through the sky, and it feels like God's judgment. And in the next second the music is silenced, and everything turns pitch black, and a few people actually scream in terror.

Sarah still clings to my hand, and I reach to grab hold of Mary's. Everyone seems to be running in different directions now, and I'm not even sure which way to go.

"This way, Mom," Mary says to me, and for some reason I trust my twelve-year-old and follow, pulling Sarah along behind me. Finally we make it to the far edge of the parking lot, away from the church, going the exact opposite direction of almost everyone else. Now it's really pouring, and we're getting soaked.

"Let's go," says Mary.

"Where?" I ask dumbly, thinking we should head back to the church.

"Home!"

I start to protest but then realize she's probably right. And then another flash of lightning shows us that the minivan is only a few yards away. So, holding hands, we make our way through the wet darkness to where we think we spotted our van. It's such a relief to unlock the doors and climb into the dry and well-lit interior. And then I get an idea.

"Maybe we should drive over there," I say to the girls. "Closer to the church with our headlights on so others can see to find their way to their own cars."

"Good idea, Mommy!" exclaims Sarah.

So I carefully back up and navigate my way closer, pointing my lights directly toward the church. I'm amazed at how much they illuminate the previously blackened parking lot. People seem to understand what we're trying to do, and some even wave as they dash through the rain toward their cars. And before long, other cars are doing the same thing. That's when Sarah starts singing "This Little Light of Mine." Mary and I join right in, and soon we are laughing and making jokes, and it's really not so bad. Oh sure, I feel sorry that the concert was ruined, but it's not the end of the world.

Finally, when it seems things are under control and plenty of vehicles are lighting the way for others, I decide to take my girls home. We've had enough excitement for one night. But we're all in good spirits when we get home, and I'm pleased to discover that the power outage hasn't hit our side of town.

"Can we watch a video?" pleads Mary once we're safely inside the house.

"Oh, I don't know…"

"Please," begs Sarah.

"We would've still been up if we'd stayed at the concert," rationalizes my older daughter.

"And we're too excited to sleep anyway," adds Sarah, which I know is true.

So we change out of our wet clothes into jammies, pick out an old Doris Day video, make some popcorn, and snuggle onto the family-room couch and watch the movie together. And, really, isn't this better than a concert out in the rain and cold?

Of course, I feel guilty for having this thought. I know it's wrong to rejoice over someone else's misfortune. And then I consider all the work, time, and prayers we all put into this thing tonight. And what about the band and their instruments? Well, I know I should feel much worse. Maybe I will tomorrow.

9

I ran into Dennis McKinley at the gas station yesterday," Rick tells me on Saturday. He's sitting at the kitchen table with the newspaper, but he's eying me carefully as if he's suspicious about something. "Dennis says they're moving to Albuquerque."

"Oh, didn't I tell you that?" I close the dishwasher and rinse my hands in the sink.

"No, you didn't."

"Well, Colleen called to tell me about it a few days ago. I must've forgotten to mention it."

"You forgot? I thought Colleen was your best friend, Ruth. Seems like you'd remember something as important as that."

"I've had a lot on my mind."

"Dennis also mentioned that Colleen thinks you could get her job if you wanted."

"Yes, and I told Colleen I'd probably look into it."

"Probably?" Now Rick is looking at me with one brow slightly arched, his skeptical look. And I wonder exactly what he's getting at. Why doesn't he just come out and say it? Why play these silly games?

"Like I said, it's been a busy week, Rick. There was the whole concert thing and—"

"And *that* turned out to be a colossal waste of time," he reminds me, making me wish I hadn't told him the whole story last night.

Although if I hadn't, the girls surely would've told him about it this morning anyway.

"It's not like I knew that was going to happen. No one did."

"The weatherman did. He'd been predicting rain for Friday since midweek."

"And how often is the weatherman right?"

"I'm guessing his prediction record is a whole lot better than Glenn Pratt's."

"Rick Jackson!" I narrow my eyes at him. "It's a wonder the Lord doesn't zap *you* with a lightning bolt."

Rick just laughs. "It's a wonder God missed Glenn Pratt last night since he was obviously aiming at him."

"What an evil thing to say."

"Not according to what Dennis McKinley told me today. He said—"

"If you're about to repeat gossip, I am *not* interested."

"Dennis says that your good Pastor Glenn has been having an affair, and it's—"

"Stop it! It's bad enough that you listen to such lies, but you don't have to bring them home with you." I can hear Matthew snickering behind me. I didn't realize he was in the kitchen. "See what you're doing, Rick?" I shake my finger at my husband. "The kind of example you're setting for your son?"

"He's old enough to know the truth."

I feel close to tears now. I can't believe I'm being subjected to such evil talk and in my own home too. "You used to care about the spiritual welfare of our family."

"Who says I don't care now?"

"Your words say it clearly enough."

"Not that you ever listen to me, Ruth."

"Why should I? Look at the kind of spiritual leader you've been lately."

"Seems to me like you're the one doing all the spiritual leading. And you refuse to listen to my thoughts on the subject anyway." He pulls out the sports section and begins to study it. Just then the phone rings, and relieved for the distraction, I answer it before anyone else has a chance.

"Oh, Ruth!" exclaims Cynthia. "I'm so glad I caught you. Are you busy?"

"Not really." I walk the cordless phone into the living room, where I hope to have a little more privacy.

"You're not going to believe what happened."

"What?"

"Maybe you should sit down first."

I sink into the couch and brace myself. "What is it, Cynthia? Did someone die?"

"Worse."

"Worse?" I try to imagine something worse than death.

"The council has fired Pastor Glenn."

"You're kidding!"

"How I wish I were. No, it's absolutely true. Kellie called me only a few minutes ago. She's brokenhearted. The council called Pastor Glenn into an emergency meeting early this morning, and then they let him have it. Kellie said he took off in their car, very upset and distraught, and she hasn't seen him for several hours. She's worried sick."

"Oh dear!"

"Anyway, I thought you'd want to know…so you could be

praying for him in this time of need. It's so unfair. The poor man is devastated."

"Of course. Do you think he's in any danger? Would he, well, you know…"

"Oh, I think he's just off travailing in prayer, Ruth. Probably trying to see what the Lord would have him do about this."

"What can he do?"

"I don't really know. Kellie seems to think there's no recourse. She said the council and elders have the authority to hire and fire as they please."

"Is this because of the concert last night? Because of the storm and the rain?"

"That certainly didn't help matters. But to be honest, I think they've been looking for a reason to get rid of the poor man."

"But why?"

"Why…" She seemed to be thinking about this. "Sometimes, Ruth, when a man is called to serve the Lord, and he's a godly man, and he refuses to bend to the power of other, less godly men, well, sometimes that rubs people the wrong way."

"It reminds me of some of the old prophets," I say in anger. "They were misunderstood too."

"And so was our Lord Jesus," adds Cynthia. "Look what they did to him."

We talk a bit more, and finally she tells me that Kellie asked for this matter to be kept private. "I know I can trust you, Ruth."

"Of course you can." I consider mentioning the nasty rumor that Rick just told me, but it seems like adding insult to injury now.

"I'll keep you posted," she promises.

"And I'll be praying for Pastor Glenn."

———

By now it seems that my house is overflowing with activity. Everyone is home, and due to the wet weather, everyone is inside the house. Although the living room is the least busy, I can still hear the hubbub of Sarah and Mary arguing over whose turn it is to feed the dog, and Rick is watching a football game on the family-room television. And Matthew is making one of his protein drinks in the blender.

Desperate for quiet, I slip out the front door, then go around back and into my garden shed, where I sit on the rough wooden bench. It's cold and damp in here, and I wish I'd brought along a sweater, but no matter if I get chilled. It's more important to pray than to be comfortable.

I feel brokenhearted over Pastor Glenn's firing. Oh, I might not have agreed with every single thing he ever said or did, but he was only thinking of his sheep, trying to serve the Lord, and doing his best. And to think that my own church's leadership couldn't recognize this is terribly distressing. How is it possible that I can be part of such a blind church? And how can the councilmembers and elders possibly call themselves Christians and then pull something like this? It's so wrong!

So I pray to the Lord, begging him to straighten out these so-called leaders. Make them see their blunder and admit they've made a mistake. I ask the Lord to chastise these people who are being so critical and judgmental of a man who only wanted to see our church grow both in spirit and in size. What on earth is wrong with that? And to blame poor Pastor Glenn for last night's weather? Why, that's absolutely crazy! I'm half tempted to drive over to church right now and demand a chance to be heard. But the council and elders probably aren't even there. They're probably all at home, plopped in front of their televisions just like my own husband, turning into regular couch potatoes while they watch the local college game. How very spiritual!

By the time I finish praying, I am thoroughly enraged. How dare the leaders of our church pull something like this? If they want to fire Pastor Glenn, they should put it to a vote. Let the whole congregation decide. This decision is too big to be left to a handful of narrowminded people.

I storm back into the house and call Cynthia. "Sorry to bother you," I say quickly, "but I am really getting aggravated about this situation with Pastor Glenn." And then I begin to spill all my doubts and concerns about the lack of discernment among our council and elders. I even share a few personal observations and some things I've heard through the grapevine—things that prove that some of these men aren't very godly. "What makes them think they're so much holier than the rest of us? Why do they get the final say on Pastor Glenn's fate? And the fate of our church?"

"You're not alone, Ruth. A number of us are very concerned."

"Should we try to arrange a meeting to talk to them?"

"Carl has already tried."

"And?"

"He has been officially excused as an elder."

"Oh!"

"But I do have some good news, Ruth. I'm glad you called."

I sink back down into the living-room couch again, releasing a loud sigh. "I'd like to hear some good news."

"Pastor Glenn made it safely home not long after I spoke to you. I just got off the phone with him. He's the one who told me about

Carl's dismissal. And, bless his heart, Pastor Glenn is not holding a grudge against the elders and the council. He says he thinks he can see the Lord's hand in all this and that everything is going to be just fine."

"How?"

"Well, as he was driving around town, he stopped for coffee. He said it was this little coffee shop on the edge of town that he'd never been in before. And you'll never believe what happened. Right there in that very coffee shop was an old friend of his, a woman he'd gone to Bible college with. Her name is Bronte Wellington, and it seems she had driven to our town on something of a mission."

"A *mission*?"

"Yes, she said that the Lord told her to come here to build a church."

"Really?"

"Yes. Isn't that exciting?"

"Well, yes, I suppose…" I'm still thinking about the council and elders and how I'd like to give them a piece of my mind.

"Anyway, let me cut to the chase. Pastor Glenn has asked me to call all those who may sympathize with his cause, the ones who believe that the Lord has called him to be their pastor, and he wanted me to invite them to come to a meeting tomorrow. Naturally, that includes you, Ruth."

"Tomorrow?"

"Yes. He wants to hold it at ten, the same time as church would normally be, and he wants everyone to come prepared to partake in a very exciting adventure."

"What about children?"

"Children are invited too. So, do you think you'll want to join us? Or do you plan to continue going to VBF?"

"Well, I, uh, I don't know…"

"Do you mean you'd consider remaining there? After this?"

"Actually, I'm not sure what Rick will think." I don't admit to her that I usually have to drag him to church anyway. "And I also have to consider my daughters. I'm not sure what they'd think about going to a different church."

"Oh, it's not a church yet. The meeting is just to gather and prayerfully consider this possibility. But if you think you and your daughters are better off at a place like VBF…if you believe that's acceptable, well, I can't—"

"No, I'd like to go to this meeting," I say suddenly. "I'd like to hear more about it and to meet this woman."

"Oh good. I'm thinking this is going to be like one of the early churches. One of the ones the disciples set up. It's going to be so exciting, Ruth!"

Then she tells me the location and invites me to help her with the phoning, giving me a list of ten people to call. I thank her, then take the cordless phone into the master bathroom, where I run water, hoping the background noise will camouflage my conversations since I'm not sure I want my family to overhear any of this just yet.

It takes me about an hour to complete the phoning, and I feel dismayed at how negative most of the responses were. Out of ten phone calls, only one person, Carrie Epson, expressed any desire to come. Her response didn't surprise me much since I've suspected for years that she's nurtured a secret crush on Pastor Glenn. She used to come to the same Bible study as I did, and the way she would gush about our "attractive and talented" pastor was almost embarrassing at times. But then she is single and lonely, and I suppose it's only natural that she would look up to him. With my task completed, I finally emerge from the bathroom, but I feel like I'm emerging from a battlefield.

"You okay?" Rick asks when I finally come out. He's sitting on the edge of the bed, changing his shoes.

"I'm fine." I watch him tugging on his laces. I consider telling him about Pastor Glenn's dismissal, but I'm afraid he'll be glad. He might even gloat. And I'm not ready for that. Nor am I ready to tell him about tomorrow's meeting. I'm still processing all of this myself.

"Matthew already left for work, and now the girls are trying to talk me into taking all of us to a matinée."

"What movie?" I ask absently.

"That new animated one that's been advertised for the past few weeks."

"The scary one?"

"Well, Halloween is just a few days away." He shoves his foot into the second tennis shoe. "And it's only a cartoon, Ruth. How scary can it be?"

"I don't know…"

"Well, the truth is, I already promised them we could go." He looks at me with slight exasperation as he pulls the laces tight. "You can come with us or stay home. It's your call."

I feel torn. Part of me wants to be with my family, and it's not often that Rick offers to take the girls and me to a movie. The other part of me is worried that this movie is going to be worldly and evil and that Satan will be glorified. But if I express my concerns to Rick, he'll only make fun of me.

"I don't know…"

"Well, you've got about twenty minutes to figure it out." Then he stands and leaves.

I sit on the bed and attempt to pray, asking the Lord to lead me. What is the best thing to do in this situation? What is his will for me? for my family? Why is it so hard to discern these things?

"Come on, Mom," urges Mary as she and Sarah slip into my room while my head's still bowed. "Come to the movie with us!"

"Yeah." Sarah takes one of my hands and gives it a tug. "It won't be any fun without you."

"Yeah," says Rick from behind them. "I'll even take you all out for pizza afterward."

"Come on, Mom." Mary grabs my other hand as both girls pull me to my feet. "We're supposed to be a family, aren't we?"

Well, how can I argue with that? "Okay, okay. Just let me get my coat." And before I can reconsider my decision, we are piling into the minivan and taking off. But as soon as we're driving toward the multiplex, I suspect I've made a mistake.

Once we're seated in the crowded theater, far too close to the front, I know I've made a terrible mistake. And when the movie actually starts, following several horrible trailers for films that my girls will *not* be seeing, I am absolutely certain that I am the stupidest Christian mother on earth. What was I thinking to agree to this?

This disgusting movie is nothing more than the glorification of witches and demons and evil spirits and all sorts of Satan-inspired forms of entertainment. Oh sure, some of it is highly disguised, and I almost laugh at some of the lighter scenes, but for the most part, it is horrible. And if I were alone, I would've left the theater long ago. How I long to grab my girls' hands and drag them from this vile exposure. But that would only make a big scene, and I would end up looking like the bad guy, the spoiler. So for their sakes and for Rick's, I remain planted in my seat with my fingers holding on to the arms of my chair in a death grip. But, I promise myself, I will never make this mistake again.

After the movie my stomach is in a tight knot as Rick drives us to our favorite pizza place, but the girls chatter away happily, replaying scene after scene of the horrifying movie. I'm trying to pray but not succeeding. I feel almost as if I'm not really here at all, as if the Lord has come down and swooped me away and I'm simply watching this scene from someplace above the minivan. And maybe that would be best for everyone. As it is, I'm determined to keep my mouth shut for fear that I will say something very hurtful and ruin this day for everyone.

I must pray my way through this. Then I realize we're already at the pizza place and Rick is parking the minivan. *I must keep quiet and just pray through this.* And later on when Rick is not around, I will gently explain to the girls why that film was not only unacceptable but very ungodly as well. I think if I say it right, they will understand. I think I can turn this nightmare into a learning moment for them. But first I need to really pray.

"I need to use the rest room," I tell my family as we enter the noisy building. Then I go into the ladies' room, enter a stall, and standing there with my head pressed against the cold metal door, I pray. *I pray and pray and pray.* And after a while, I realize I'm standing in a very dirty place with my head touching a very dirty door, and I find this extremely disturbing.

So I go out to the sinks, where I wash my hands and my face and then my hands again. But each time I wash my hands, I don't quite get it right. I accidentally touch something that defiles them again. It's so difficult to get clean in a public rest room. And for some reason my efforts keep getting frustrated, almost as if I'm under satanic attack, probably due to the images that were burned into my brain during that disgusting movie. For whatever reason my old system of turning on the hot water and soaping my hands, then pulling out the paper towel while my hands are still soapy, then rinsing and rinsing, then drying on the ready towel, and then using it to turn off the tap and open the door is not working. So I do it again. And again.

"Mom?" Mary pokes her head into the women's rest room. "What are you doing?"

Flustered, I throw the paper towel in the trash, and while Mary is still holding the door open, soiling her own hands with its invisible but deadly germs, I make my exit without saying a word.

"Are you okay?" she asks as we walk toward the table where Rick and Sarah are waiting with questions on their faces.

"I'm fine," I tell her. But when I see that the pizza is already at our table, which means I must've been in that filthy rest room for nearly twenty minutes, my cheeks grow hot with embarrassment.

"Sorry."

"Are you feeling okay?" Rick echoes Mary's earlier question.

"I don't know."

"Do you want some pizza?" Sarah hopefully points at the pizza that's already been partially eaten. "We ordered half-and-half with your favorite on this side."

I take a narrow slice of the mushroom, olive, and sausage pizza and pretend to nibble on it, but my stomach feels like someone poured wet concrete into it, concrete that has hardened into stone. And I know that I'm probably overreacting, but I don't know how to stop it. The best I can do for now is to remain quiet, to keep my worries and concerns to myself. But as I do this, I am enraged at

Rick. After all, this is really his fault. If he hadn't insisted on taking the girls to that vile and evil movie, none of this would've happened. And as he drives us home, I sit with my attention focused out the passenger window, silently fuming.

10

When I was about Mary's age, I discovered I had a grandma. Oh, I knew that our dad had parents—Grandma and Grandpa Reynolds—but they lived in New Jersey and were getting pretty old, and other than a random birthday card or holiday greeting, I didn't really think too much about them. Then one morning, right out of the blue, my mom told me that Grandma Clark had invited me to come visit.

"Grandma who?" I looked up from the Nancy Drew mystery I was reading.

"My mother," she said with her typical impatience. "Grandma Clark. She wants you to come visit her."

"Me?" I studied my mom closely, wondering if this was some kind of trick. I was usually the last one picked for anything special. In fact, I had been moping around for a week, feeling sorry for myself, because Lynette was off at a month-long summer camp, and Jonathan was just starting Little League. It seemed I was the only one in the family with a boring summer to look forward to. Oh, that and the extra household chores due to my siblings' extracurricular activities.

My mother nodded. "She just called and asked to see her grandchildren."

"Grandchildren," I repeated, wondering if my mother understood that this word was plural, as in not just one. Not just me.

"Obviously Lynette is gone, and Jonathan is committed to baseball. You'll have to go alone, Ruth."

I frowned up at her, trying to decide if this was a good thing or not. "By myself?"

"That's what 'going alone' means." She shook her head as if she couldn't quite fathom how she had raised such a dense child. "Go pack your things."

"Right now?"

"Of course, right now. Did you think I meant next Tuesday?"

"When am I going?" I stood and dog-eared a corner of my paperback. I actually wanted to ask whether or not I had a choice in any of this, but I suspected by the firm tilt of her chin that I didn't.

"Today. I'm driving you over just as soon as you're packed."

Well, being twelve going on thirteen, I suppose I felt I had some right to question my own destiny, especially when it concerned matters like previously unknown grandparents. "What if I don't want to go?"

My mother's brow creased as her eyes narrowed into her don't-cross-me look.

"I mean, I don't even know this person."

"She's your grandmother, Ruth."

I wanted to say, "Yeah, so what?" but her expression was getting even grimmer.

"She lives at the coast," my mother added, almost with a sweetness to her voice, as if she were offering me a bribe of candy.

"Really?" I took the bait. "Close to the beach?"

"Go pack. You'll see when we get there."

So, imagining myself wearing a bikini, which I didn't even own, and stretched out on some sunny beach, maybe even learning to surf and changing my name to Gidget, I hurried into my room and began packing all the appropriate items.

My mother acted strangely out of character as she drove us along the winding coast highway. She was actually congenial. She talked about when she was a girl and growing up in a small town on the Oregon coast and how she loved to get up early after a storm and walk down the beach, scouring the sand for treasures.

"Did you find any?" I asked, caught up in the story.

"Yes, I had a whole box full of wonderful shells and agates and things."

"Do you still have them?"

She frowned. "No."

"Why not?"

"My mother got rid of them."

"You mean she gave them away?"

The frown deepened. "Something like that."

"Oh."

That's where the happy conversation ended. But we were getting close to the ocean, and the smell of the sea air combined with the excitement of being someplace new and different from boring old home was distraction enough for me. Wait until Lynette heard about this.

Traffic in the town seemed busy—station wagons, campers, bikes, and people on foot, all of whom looked like they'd come here expressly for the purpose of fun—and my expectations soared even higher. I took note of the ice cream store, the candy shop, a place that rented surfboards and crab pots, and even a store with bright-colored bikinis hanging in the window. I wondered how much something that small might cost.

I began to imagine what this mysterious grandmother's house might be like. Would it be right on the beach? Maybe a large stone mansion with a dark, haunted past like the place Nancy Drew was currently visiting in my book, trying to solve the mystery of the missing sea captain. Or maybe it would be a modern beach house, like something from a movie, with large windows overlooking the ocean, a big rock fireplace, and clever nautical décor. Or even just a cozy cottage with faded wood siding, window boxes spilling with bright red geraniums, and a calico cat sleeping in a wicker rocker on the front porch. That was probably the favorite image playing in my mind as my mother slowly drove her Mercury through the bustling tourist town.

Then instead of turning left onto one of the streets that ran directly toward the ocean and the beach, she eventually turned right, down a gravel road where a rusty and decrepit mobile home was parked. Not a fancy double- or triple-wide either. This one was long and narrow, resembling a sausage more than a house, and where the rust hadn't yet taken over, the paint in faded tones of pink and turquoise was peeling.

"This is it?" I said, my tone dripping with disappointment.

She nodded grimly, almost as if she too was surprised. "It's gotten a little run-down."

I just sat there in the front seat, too stunned to move, thinking I had to find some way out of this. I was not going to stay in this horrible place. It probably smelled inside. What kind of a person lives in a place like this?

"Come on, Ruth." My mom opened the passenger door and handed me my suitcase.

"I don't know…"

She started to give me her look—the one that meant "Do not mess with me!"—but she stopped and her face softened. "Look, Ruth, I know this seems strange. But your grandmother isn't a bad person. She's just a little different. Mostly I think she's lonely." She reached out and actually took my hand. "Come on, I think you're going to like her."

Well, I had no idea how my mother ever got that idea, but like the proverbial lamb being led to the slaughter, I allowed my mother to lead me through the weed-infested and overgrown yard toward the questionable trailer. I slowed down in front of some rickety-looking steps, but my mother's grip tightened, tugging me up. I might've giggled when the high heel of her shoe went right through a soft spot on the lopsided porch except I was so worried about what lurked beyond that rusty door.

My mother knocked several times, louder with each try, and I fostered a teeny bit of hope that perhaps this grandmother wasn't home. Or maybe she'd died in there. Then my mother tried the door, and it was unlocked. "Mother?" she called into the dim interior of the sausage house with a strange-sounding, singsong voice. "We're here. Ruthie is here to visit."

I followed my mother into the house, fully prepared to smell something truly horrible. Maybe even something dead. Or perhaps, like our crazy neighbor lady down the street, my grandmother might be housing dozens of cats. But I was pleasantly surprised by the smell of something baking.

"Gingerbread," my mother said as if in answer to my unspoken question. "Your grandma loves gingerbread."

Of course this immediately brought to mind the story of Hansel and Gretel along with the frightening image of the wicked old witch who fattened up the children so she could eat them. Why do grownups encourage children to read such things?

"Hello?" called a fragile-sounding voice. "Is that you, Cora?"

"Yes, Mother. And I have Ruth with me."

And to my surprised relief, a petite and fairly normal-looking elderly woman emerged from a small door, which I later discovered led to her tiny little bedroom. "I was just freshening up a bit." She smiled as she came closer. "Why, little Ruth. You're as tall as me, almost a grown woman. And pretty as a picture!" She reached out, almost as if she was going to touch my face, but then she stopped, withdrew her hand, and wiped it on a white lace-trimmed hanky. "Welcome to my humble home."

I grinned at her. Maybe this wouldn't be so bad after all. Although her home was indeed humble and very tiny, it was also immaculate. Nothing like the shabby exterior. In fact, the inside of her little sausage trailer house reminded me of a dollhouse, and if I used my imagination, I could easily make myself believe that this truly was the interior of the little sea cottage with the geranium-filled flower boxes.

My mother, clearly uncomfortable, never sat down and never touched anything, not even her own mother. After some very brief small talk, she excused herself, saying she needed to get home in time to fix dinner, then left. As I recall, she didn't even mention when she'd be back to pick me up. Maybe she hoped my grandmother would keep me indefinitely. But I wasn't too worried. Oh, I sensed that this old woman was a bit strange; I also sensed something kindred in her. And during the following week, I discovered we had much in common.

The first thing Grandma Clark did after my mother left was to teach me the proper way to wash my hands. She had only one small bathroom in her sausage house, but she'd already put out a special towel and a bar of lavender soap just for me to use.

"You'll have to sleep on the sofa," she told me apologetically. "I've cleared out this cupboard for you." She opened a built-in door. "See, there are the bed linens and blankets and a shelf where you can put your things."

"Shall I put them away now?" I asked, eager to restore some order to my life.

She smiled. "Yes, please do."

I quickly discovered that Grandma Clark had a strict routine for everything—most of it in regard to hygiene and cleanliness—and it had to be done right. I did my best to comply with her wishes, but I could tell that she wasn't completely comfortable having me there. So I discovered that I could walk to the beach in less than ten minutes. And weather permitting, I spent as much time there as possible. This seemed to make us both happy. But when I got back, I knew to remove my tennis shoes or flip-flops and leave them outside, shake all traces of sand from my clothing, and then come in and properly wash up. Rinse, soap, scrub, rinse, soap, scrub, rinse, soap, scrub—three times or it was no good.

Sadly, I wore out my welcome within a week's time. Not that I did anything particularly wrong but simply because Grandma Clark could only take so much. Still, in some ways it was one of the best weeks of my life. Yet in another way it was rather disturbing. For although I now understood I wasn't the only misfit in this world, I didn't want to grow up to be like this strange woman either. It was plain to see that she was lonely and troubled. Her only link to the outside world was an elderly friend named Gladys, who brought her groceries once a week, along with mail. And as far as I can remember, her old-fashioned black telephone never rang once. The only time we used it was to call my mother, asking her to come get me.

As it turned out, my dad picked me up. It was on a Sunday, and he actually seemed glad to see me. But he wouldn't set foot into Grandma Clark's house. He merely called out a stiff greeting, asked if I was ready, and then I hopped into his car, and we drove away.

Grandma Clark died the following winter. I cried for her and begged to go to her funeral, but my mother said that there wouldn't be a funeral, that Grandma Clark had been cremated, and that a friend, I assumed Gladys, would drop her ashes into the ocean. A very tidy way to end things, I supposed.

I feel surprised now at the clarity of this memory as the water in the shower suddenly grows tepid, and I realize that I've drained the hot-water tank again. Not that anyone should notice or care since it's nearly two in the morning. But after all that's gone on tonight and after sitting in that foul-smelling movie theater followed by the greasy pizza parlor, well, I just couldn't bear to go to bed feeling unclean. Now if I could only wash the images of that vile movie from my mind.

Rick doesn't even move when my alarm goes off this morning. Not that this is so unusual since I almost always have to prod him out of bed for church anyway. But today I won't try nearly so hard. In fact, a part of me (my flesh, I'm sure) would like to remain in bed too. Why not? It's not as if any of us got a good night's sleep. I try not to remember the details of how Matthew came home slightly inebriated again last night. Not to the point of throwing up, thankfully. And although he tried to cover it up with breath mints, he'd definitely been imbibing.

Even so, I was too spiritually drained (still struggling with the aftereffects of the day) to deal with it. I left it for Rick to sort out. The two of them talked and argued rather loudly late into the night, and I managed to stay out of it. Although I did pray; over and over I begged the Lord to knock some sense into my foolish prodigal son. After the house finally got quiet, I took that long shower, then crept into bed, where I finally fell asleep, thoroughly exhausted.

Of course, it wasn't long after that, at about three in the morning, when Sarah woke up, screaming in terror from a nightmare. Why should I have been surprised? As usual, I prayed with her, fighting off the demons that were playing havoc with her sensitive spirit. I felt certain this too was the result of that movie. I almost woke Rick just so he could see the consequences of exposing our children to that kind of darkness. But I didn't. Maybe I felt a smidgen of sympathy for him since he'd already done his time with Matthew. Maybe I was just too tired.

I'm sure he thinks that gives him a good excuse to skip church this morning, which subsequently will excuse me from having to explain why I'm going to this morning's meeting with Pastor Glenn and the others—something I've been dreading telling him about since yesterday. Perhaps Matthew's drunkenness was simply the Lord's intervention. Although I hate to think that. I couldn't bear the idea of the Lord using my son in that way. I'm sure it's the work of the Enemy.

"Are you getting up for church?" I quietly ask my still-snoozing husband.

He just groans and rolls over so I can't see his face.

"Well, you did have a pretty late night with Matthew. Maybe you need a day of rest."

"Uh-huh." I can hear the relief in his deep sigh.

I pat him on the back and quietly gather some clothes from my closet, then get dressed in the bathroom. As I tiptoe out of our bedroom, I secretly hope the girls will still be asleep too, alleviating the need for me to explain why we're not going to VBF this morning. Then I can just leave a note saying that I went to a meeting. But no such luck. Mary is already up and dressed and even mixing some pancake batter. My early riser.

She smiles at me. "Want pancakes?"

"Sure." I look over her shoulder to make sure the electric griddle is at the right temperature, but she appears to have it under control. "Is Sarah up?"

Mary nods as she carefully pours her first pancake, watching as it sizzles on the hot surface. "Yep. She's in the bathroom."

My good girls. Up and dressed and ready to go to church, or rather the kids' worship service. How am I going to break the news to them? But maybe I don't have to. Why not just drop them at church like usual and then scoot over to the meeting, which is less than five minutes from the church? Really, who would be the wiser?

So after our breakfast of pancakes and applesauce, I get us out the door a few minutes earlier than usual.

"Does Matthew work today?" Sarah asks as I drive toward church.

"I think he's supposed to go in at ten." I turn on the windshield wipers to clear the drizzly rain from my fogged-up window.

"Wonder if he'll even make it," Mary says in a cynical tone as if she knows something about last night and her brother's wayward behavior.

I focus my attention on the wet road, trying to decide if I should tell my girls that I won't actually be in church this morning. Not that they would care or even notice my absence since they rarely venture out of the kids' worship area afterward.

"Why don't I drop you girls by the door," I suggest as I enter the church parking lot. "That way everyone doesn't have to get wet."

They seem to like this idea.

"See ya later," calls Mary as the two of them pop out of the mini-van and head for cover.

I wave, then slowly drive away as if in search of a parking spot, which actually could be a challenge since the parking lot is fuller than usual. Not a good sign. But when I'm sure my girls are well inside the building, I take a side exit, hoping that no one else is watching me. I feel like a kid playing hooky as I drive away from the church. Some might think this is irresponsible behavior, dropping my girls at church and then leaving, but how is this any different than the way I drop them off here for school each morning?

11

Fighting off unreasonable guilt, I drive over to the address Cynthia gave me. The street name is familiar, but it's not in a residential neighborhood. As it turns out, it's an old drugstore at the end of a strip mall about a mile from Valley Bridge Fellowship. At first I think I may have gotten it wrong, but then I see Cynthia's old white Subaru parked out front with a couple of other cars, including Pastor Glenn's. Feeling a tiny bit relieved but still nervous, I park alongside her car and then dash toward the building, dodging raindrops as I go.

"Good morning, Ruth!" Cynthia holds the door open for me. "Isn't your family with you?"

I remove my damp coat, give it a shake, then explain that Rick is tired from a late night and that Matthew is working.

"And the girls?"

A small wave of guilt washes over me as I drape my coat over my arm. "I let the girls go to the kids' worship service at the church," I say quietly, glancing over to where Pastor Glenn and Kellie and several others are chatting by a table with coffee and things. "It just seemed easier." I almost mention how full the church parking lot was but think better of it.

She nods. "Yes, I can understand that. At least for the time being."

Soon there are a couple dozen people in the room, most of them from VBF but a few new faces too. Pastor Glenn invites us to be seated in the metal folding chairs arranged in a half circle with a small wooden podium facing them.

"Welcome," he says, then chuckles. "Although I'm not totally sure exactly what I'm welcoming you to. Maybe it's just a great spiritual adventure." Then he briefly retells what happened to him yesterday, how the council and elders blindsided him, and how discouraged he was afterward.

"I felt like Job," he says sadly. "Or maybe Jesus during those last trying days. It seemed that the whole world had turned against me. I even began to question myself, to doubt the Lord's hand and call upon my life." He shakes his head and looks out over us with tear-glistened eyes. "Even the night of the concert, that unforgettable storm, the rain, the lightning, the loss of power—well, it really got me to thinking that perhaps I was more than just physically all wet."

He pauses, and I'm not sure if he means this as a joke, but then he continues. "And finally to suffer the judgment and condemnation of men I considered my brothers, my peers, my friends…well, as much as I tried to muster up my faith, as much as I wanted to believe and to trust in the Lord's goodness and mercy, I found myself standing on the edge of despair, looking down into the black abyss of failure and doubt and gloom." He holds out his hands in a hopeless gesture. "I was ready to give up."

He pauses again, and the room is so quiet you can hear traffic driving by on the wet street outside. I'm sure I'm not the only one moved by his honesty, transparency, humility. I'm so relieved that he's not holding back. We desperately need to hear his story and to feel his pain almost as if it's our own. Maybe it is. Maybe that's what being the body of Christ is all about. When one hurts, all suffer.

"And that's when I decided to get myself a cup of coffee," he says with an unexpected lightness in his voice. Several people chuckle at this, and soon we are all laughing, corporately relieved that the heaviness seems to be lifting.

"Yes, I know it must sound very shallow on my part, especially considering my dire straits and sagging spirits, but at the time I just really wanted a hot cup of joe. I suppose I thought it might help clear my head. And suddenly there appeared to me an angel of light." He chuckles as if this too is a joke. "But it was actually my old classmate Bronte Wellington from Bible-college days. You can imagine my surprise when she made herself known to me." He glances at Kellie and smiles. "Let me be perfectly clear. Although Bronte and I dated for a while in college, that is all behind me now. Mostly I'd like to tell you folks that she is one of the most spiritual women I have ever been privileged to know."

He pauses again, and I can tell that everyone is curious as to where he's going with this story. "Anyway, I want you to meet her," he says loudly as if to cue someone. "Come on up here, Bronte." He waves to a woman whom I now notice standing on the sidelines. I'd seen her in the parking lot but had assumed she was on her way to someplace else. Not that I like to judge people by appearances, but she doesn't seem like a church sort of person.

I feel slightly stunned as this tall, beautiful woman steps up to join Pastor Glenn at the podium. With her shoulder-length blond hair cut to perfection, high cheekbones, and even features, she is drop-dead gorgeous. When Cynthia told me this woman had attended college with Pastor Glenn, I naturally assumed she was about his age, which I believe is fifty-something. But this stylish woman appears to be younger than I am. Not that I look so young, but she could be in her thirties. They make a striking pair. Pastor

Glenn's dark, handsome looks contrast with her fair-haired beauty. But then I remember they're not actually a couple.

"Bronte,"—Pastor Glenn places an arm around her shoulders and smiles—"why don't you share with my friends your vision for us."

She smiles back at him and then turns to us with an even bigger smile, complete with the straightest, whitest teeth I have ever seen. Really, she could model for toothpaste. "I'd love to."

"Thanks." Pastor Glenn pats her on the back, then returns to his seat next to his wife, loudly scraping his chair on the hard floor.

"Good morning, my friends." Her voice is low pitched but feminine and maybe even what some would call sexy. "It's so wonderful to be here with you, to be in your town, and to see that the Lord is already at work in your midst. My story begins many years ago, but I will skip ahead to about two months ago when I came to…well, I came to visit some friends in a nearby town. During that time I received a vision from the Lord. He showed me your town and how it was slowly being draped in darkness, falling under the Enemy's influence, and how evil spiritual forces were at work here. In my vision I saw that Christians have been and will continue to be under fierce attack and that the suffering will be great."

Several heads are nodding now, and to be honest, I can't disagree since I've had these same feelings, even though I could never put it quite that eloquently. And yet there is something about this woman that I don't completely trust. Maybe it's simply her stunning good looks or the way she smiled at Pastor Glenn. Perhaps if she looked more like Cynthia, I would have no problem. But I know it's wrong to judge, and I confess this attitude to the Lord. I should know better than to allow physical appearances to distract me from his purposes.

"For some reason," she continues, "Satan has set his sights on your city. For some reason Satan has gathered his demons and his powers, and he is preparing for victory, for death and destruction." She pauses, closing her eyes and tilting her head back slightly as she takes in a long, deep breath. "And the spiritual warfare will be like nothing you've ever witnessed before."

The room grows very still, almost as if we're all holding our breath, literally sitting on the edges of our seats, waiting for her to continue.

"I've only been here a short while, but I have been waging warfare against Satan and his demons the whole time. I have been waging warfare during the night and all through the day. I've been praying for the Christians in this town—for you people right here in this very room—that you will unite and be strong in the Lord and able to fight back, able to hold the demons at bay! I've been praying for your deliverance, for your spiritual victory, and for the defeat of our enemy!"

"Amen!" Carl claps his hands.

"Amen!" echoes Cynthia and several others, including myself.

"We must unite." She holds up a fist. "We must arm and equip ourselves with spiritual weapons. We must prepare ourselves to take the offensive position so we can kick Satan and his demons right out of this town!

More "amens" and then we are all on our feet, clapping with unbridled enthusiasm, many with tears in their eyes.

"That's the spirit," says Pastor Glenn as he steps forward with an acoustic guitar slung over his shoulder. "Thank you, Sister Bronte!"

"I am your servant," she says to everyone.

"We appreciate that you heeded the Lord's call," says Pastor Glenn as she returns to her seat. "Don't we, friends?"

Again we all clap and say, "Amen."

Then Pastor Glenn strums his guitar. "Well, as you know, I'm not highly experienced at leading worship, but if you'll forgive me, I'd like to give it a try this morning." And despite his disclaimer, he does a wonderful job of leading worship, and we all sing with a fresh kind of fervor that I haven't experienced in ages. Maybe not ever. It is an amazing time, and I feel the Spirit is really moving.

After the worship time comes to an end, several people step forward to share a word of knowledge. For the most part they simply reaffirm and confirm what both Bronte and Pastor Glenn have already established. Then Bronte steps forward again, and the room gets very quiet as she stands with hands uplifted and eyes closed. And I can't deny that something about her has a very celestial and angelic look, and I realize with thankfulness that my earlier prejudice has completely melted away.

"The Lord says," she begins in a quiet but serious voice, " 'Friday night's storm was not merely a coincidence, my children. It was not simply a badly timed slip of the weather. No. The storm that canceled the concert, the storm that knocked out half the town's electricity, the storm that ruined some valuable sound equipment—that storm was just a tiny sample of my judgment,' says the Lord. 'A tiny portion of my condemnation, which I will rain down on everyone who stands against me, everyone who refuses to join me in this battle against my enemy. I have chosen you,' says the Lord, 'to be my soldiers, my righteous army against the spirit of darkness and the demonic powers that will crush this town unless we prevail. Join me now, my children; enter my ranks that we might reign victorious, that we might deliver this town from the blackness of sin and the power of Satan.' The Lord has spoken!"

More "amens" and then we sing more songs, and the air is charged with so much spiritual energy that I can literally feel the hairs on the back of my neck standing on end. And I'm not even surprised when Edna is prayed for and then falls to the floor, slain in the Spirit, shaking and trembling like jolts of electricity are running through her. This happens to several others who go forward, waiting for Bronte and Pastor Glenn to lay hands on them. I even consider going up there myself, but something is holding me back.

I've never been slain in the Spirit before, and I suppose I've always feared it. In fact, Colleen and I went to a Pentecostal revival once and actually made fun of some of the antics there. So to lose control like that and in front of everyone, well, it's too frightening. Yet at the same time, I want to be obedient. I want to be Spirit filled. And then, as I'm standing by my chair arguing with myself, I see Bronte approaching, looking directly at me.

"Can I pray for you, sister?" she asks with the clearest blue eyes I've ever seen, eyes that help me to trust her.

I slowly nod, and I can feel a lump in my throat and tears burning behind my closed eyelids when she places her hands on my head and begins to pray. I feel I must be perfectly still, and I am almost afraid to breathe as I listen to her speaking in another language and yet with authority. Then she goes back to English, binding demons, actually calling them by name, it seems. And yet they are strange and foreign-sounding names I've never heard before. She casts them out with incredible power and confidence.

Without any warning everything goes fuzzy, then black, and the next thing I know, I am lying on the cold concrete floor with my arms and legs shaking uncontrollably. And although I am scared and unsettled and confused, I am also relieved. Strangely relieved. It's as if I fit in now.

"The Lord is in you, sister." Bronte helps me to my feet. "But the demons are also. We must wage continuous warfare against them, for as quickly as we send them out, they run to their friends and invite them to come back in. You need our help, sister; you cannot do this on your own. You cannot keep them away without the power of the army surrounding you. Left to themselves, these demons will devour you."

I nod without speaking. I'm not sure I'm even capable of speech at the moment. Cynthia has joined us now, placing a comforting hand on my shoulder. "Ruth is a good servant of the Lord," she tells Bronte, almost as if I'm not here or as if I'm a small child, and yet I don't protest. "But you are right. Ruth still has need of great deliverance."

Bronte smiles. "You have come to the right place, Ruth. The Lord has brought you here for a reason. Will you join us again on Wednesday night?"

Without really thinking, I say yes.

"You are all invited to join us again," Bronte announces in a loud voice that causes the room to grow quiet again. "We will meet here again on Wednesday evening at seven o'clock. Pastor Glenn will preach, and we will be doing even more deliverance prayers. We will cast out more demons and wage serious spiritual warfare for this city. We invite you to bring your friends and family and anyone in need of a touch from the Lord. Together we will fight against the darkness. Together we will deliver this town from Satan's hold!"

"But before we leave here today"—Pastor Glenn has moved up to the front again—"we need your help, brothers and sisters. I know your spirits have confirmed that the Lord led Bronte to our town, to us, and to this building. She has graciously talked the owner into letting us use this building for just one week, but that was with the promise that we would come up with enough money for a year-long lease. We believe the Lord can provide for us, but we need you to believe and partner with us as well. We need you to help us by giving whatever you can. Please, ask the Lord to stretch you in your gifts today, knowing that he will bless you greatly in return. Brother Carl will be standing by the door with an offering basket." And then Pastor Glenn asks a special blessing on all of us.

Suddenly I remember the money left over from the check my mother wrote for me a few weeks ago. I took the remainder in small bills and then zipped them into the pocket of my purse, not even knowing why. And thinking of my mother reminds me of how the Bible study ladies determined that she was my oppressor and prayed for my deliverance. Suddenly I know without any shadow of doubt that I am to rid myself of that money. Giving it away will be just one more step toward my deliverance. It felt like my whipping money at the time, and now I can be free of it, giving it to the Lord to be used and blessed by him.

The realization that I can do this fills me with so much excitement that my fingers tremble as I unzip the pocket and remove the thick wad of cash. How I would love to be able to give offerings of this size every day. And perhaps the Lord will bless me now, maybe even make it possible for me to be generous like this on a regular basis. I smile to myself as I drop my impressive pile of money into the basket Carl is holding.

He looks at me with raised brows and then smiles. "Bless you, sister!"

"Yes," agrees Bronte, who is standing next to Carl. *"Bless you!"*

12

So far my family is unaware that I have joined another church. Of course, it's only been a day since I sneaked off to that meeting, and I suppose it's premature to think that means I've actually joined. It's not as if I signed a membership card. But in my heart I feel that I have joined, that I belong there. I understand their vision, their mission, and I want to be a part of it. Still, I'm not sure how to explain this to Rick or the kids. And for that reason I feel torn as I drop the girls at our old church, where they still attend school every day. It feels wrong to be here, hypocritical even. And yet what can I do about it? As much as I'd like to wipe away this part of my life completely, it's just not that simple.

"Ruth!" I hear my name being called as Sarah and Mary climb out of the minivan. Turning, I see Colleen walking toward me, waving.

I roll down my window and say hello, telling her that I should keep moving so I don't hold up the cars behind me. I've been chastised before for slowing down the caravan of drop-offs.

"I'm parked there." She points to her SUV not far away. "Come on over, and we can catch up."

I reluctantly drive around and park my minivan next to her car. I'm not sure I'm ready for Colleen just yet. However, as I slowly climb out of the car, I notice how the clouds have cleared, and the warmth of the sunshine feels good on my back and shoulders. Maybe the fresh air will help clear my head. I'm still feeling kind of fuzzy and sluggish, probably the result of another night of disturbed sleep. Sarah's nightmares again. That horrible Halloween movie seems to be haunting her.

"How's it going?" Colleen asks.

I take a deep breath, leaning against my minivan and gazing up at the blue sky overhead. "Okay, I guess. How about you? All packed and ready to go yet?"

She laughs. "Are you kidding? You should know I'm not that organized. Right now my house looks like a hurricane hit. I don't even know where to begin. I wish I was as neat and orderly as you are, Ruth." She smiles at me. "Do you still alphabetize your spices?"

I just smile, then shake my head as if this is a totally ridiculous idea. But she's absolutely right. Not only do I still alphabetize my spices but my canned goods as well.

"Seriously, I wish I were more like you, Ruth. I remember how our apartment was always shipshape with you at the helm."

I suddenly feel like she's moved and gone, and I'm missing her already. And now I wish we hadn't grown apart these past couple of years. Maybe it's not too late. "You sure you guys really want to move?"

"Actually, we almost had second thoughts, especially after we heard about the changes."

"Changes?" I ask hopefully, thinking that maybe Dennis's job offer isn't as tempting as they originally believed.

"At church."

I slowly nod in realization. How easily I fell into this. "Oh yeah…"

"Hey, I didn't see you at the morning service yesterday. Were you there?"

I fold my arms across my chest, shaking my head.

"Well, it was awesome, Ruth. Ed Chambers handled the service, and he told us the whole story of how the elders and council had gotten up really early on Saturday morning, how they met before dawn and labored in prayer for several hours, and how God really confirmed to every single one of them that it was time to let Glenn go."

"Every single one of them? What about Carl Schulman?"

"Well, of course, they had to ask Carl to leave too. I mean, he and Glenn are practically best friends."

"Of course…"

"But it was such a moving service. Ed actually cried as he told us the story. It was really amazing! And I have to hand it to him, he didn't even bring up the affair or—"

"The affair?"

"Yes." Colleen lowered her voice. "Dennis told me that the elders decided not to go public with it, not without a confession from Glenn first."

"And why would he make a confession?" I'm trying to keep my voice quiet too, but I feel like screaming.

"Because that's what a Christian would do." She shrugs. "Confess your sins and ask for—"

"How do you know he's guilty?"

Colleen holds up her hands like she's surrendering. "Okay… maybe we shouldn't talk about this. Sorry."

"Gossip is so evil. People shouldn't repeat mean things about others." I sigh loudly. "It's cruel and it's wrong…it's sinful even."

Colleen nods sadly. "Yeah, you're right, Ruth. I didn't mean to go there. Mostly I just wanted to tell you how great the service was. It was so cool to see the church packed. Apparently a lot of people heard about it by then. You know how the word gets around."

"Yes…I know." I want to remind her of the evils of gossip again.

"Anyway, the whole congregation was so happy and relieved. It's like a dark cloud was lifted. And afterward everyone hung around and talked, and there was such a good feeling in the air. It was really awesome! I wish you'd been there."

I don't say anything in response but just nod like I understand what she's saying, like I agree. But everything in me wants to shout, "This is wrong! This is so wrong!" Firing a perfectly good pastor and then being glad about it? What's the matter with these people?

"So even though Dennis and I are okay with our move to Albuquerque, we almost wish we could stick around and enjoy the changes here at VBF." Then she reminds me it's her last week at work, encouraging me to drop off my résumé at the clinic.

I tell her I will, but I'm pretty sure I won't. I'm not like Colleen. And I'm certain I could never handle something like that. It's too much responsibility for me. Not to mention the idea of being in a place where people come in sick. I can't imagine how many germs I'd be exposed to, and all the hand washing it would take to stay clean and germ free would be a nightmare. And what if I made some terrible mistake? No…it's a bad idea. And yet I know I need to bring some money into our household. I remember the promise I made to Rick.

I also remember the money I owe my mother. And as badly as I want to pay her back and be free of that weight that sits upon my shoulders, I don't have the slightest idea how I will do it. How long does it take to earn five hundred dollars, anyway?

These thoughts are blasted from my head with the blaring of a horn behind me. I jump and then realize I've been stopped at the intersection and the light is green. Flustered, I pull into the intersection way too fast, and without even looking, I make my left-hand turn.

The next thing I know I hear a loud bang, and I'm thrown sideways toward the passenger seat, where I see a pickup that is far too close. So close it appears to be inside my minivan, pressing into the scrunched seat where Sarah had been sitting only thirty minutes ago.

I'm shaking and crying as a young man in a leather jacket helps me out of the minivan. "Are you okay, ma'am?" He guides me to the nearby sidewalk.

"I...I think so."

"I'll call for help." He pulls a silver cell phone out of a pocket.

Another man is approaching us now, coming from the direction of the wreck. He looks really angry. "You pulled right out in front of me, lady!" he yells with his hands in the air. "There's no way I could stop. What was I supposed to do? My truck's paid for too, and I don't have comprehensive insurance anymore. You *better* have good insurance!"

This man looks so furious, so evil, that I actually feel I'm in real danger. I cower next to the younger man talking on the phone, hoping he's speaking to the police since I'm afraid I'm going to need some help.

"What's wrong with you, lady?" The man is staring at me now. "Don't tell me you don't have no insurance?"

"No," I say quickly, "I do have insurance. I'm just...just—" And then I really start to cry again.

"You're scaring her," says the young man, pausing on the phone. "Lighten up a little, will you?"

"That's right," says a woman about my age who has come over to join us. "Let her calm down before you start blasting her with all your insurance questions." She puts a hand on my shoulder. "Are you all right?"

"Yes." I try to stop crying. "Just upset. And the man's right. I did pull out in front of him. It's all my fault."

"That's right!" he snaps. "You people are witnesses. You saw the whole thing. She pulled out right in front of me."

The young man is still talking into his cell phone, telling someone what happened and the location. Before long we hear a siren, and soon the police and emergency vehicles are there, redirecting traffic and asking questions. The young man with the cell phone offers to call my home, and in the background I can hear him talking to Rick, saying, "Your wife has been in a wreck..."

I return to my scrunched vehicle and find my proof of insurance and other papers in the glove box and hand them to the police officer. I try to coherently answer his questions, but I'm not sure I'm making sense, even to myself. This feels like a bad dream, and I'm hoping I'll wake up soon. Then Rick arrives in his pickup. I feel a mixture of relief and dread as he parks, then darts across the street toward me.

"Are you okay, Ruth?" He takes me in his arms.

Suddenly I feel like it's going to be okay, and I lean into him and really cry. He strokes my hair as he talks to the policeman, answering more questions. And soon the tow trucks arrive to take the crumpled vehicles off to some place that Rick and the driver of the pickup must've previously agreed to.

"Is that it?" Rick says to the officer filling out the forms.

"That's all we need for now," he tells Rick. "Might as well be on your way."

It feels so good to be in Rick's pickup, to be away from the noise and the questions and the staring bystanders. I've never been in a wreck before, and after this I hope never to be in one again. I lean back into the seat and sigh deeply. "I'm so sorry. I'm not even sure *how* it happened."

"Well, one of the witnesses said the guy behind you, the one blaring on his horn, is partly to blame. She said the light had just turned green and the horn must've startled you into moving too fast."

"Really?"

"Not that it means you weren't responsible. Taking a left-hand turn against oncoming traffic was a violation."

"Did you check out the minivan?" I ask weakly. "Did it look pretty bad?"

"Well, the hood is dented, the grill and front bumper are all mashed, the right fender and passenger side door are completely smashed, and even the sliding door is pretty well mangled. I'm guessing the cost of fixing all that might be more than the minivan is actually worth. It's probably totaled."

I let out a groan. "I'm so sorry."

"Hey, I'm just glad you're okay, Ruth. That was what really had me scared earlier. The guy who called didn't say much, just that you'd been in a wreck and where it was. I didn't know what to expect as I sped over to find you."

"You sped?"

"Yeah, guess I'm lucky I didn't get in a wreck too." He laughs.

Now I'm rubbing my right wrist. It's sore and starting to swell a little.

He glances over at me. "You sure you're okay?"

"I might've banged my wrist on something when I got hit."

"You'll probably be sore all over by tomorrow. I remember the time I rolled my pickup back in high school. I thought I was just fine when it happened, but I could barely get out of bed the next day. Make sure you take some Advil when we get home."

I rub the back of my neck, which is also starting to ache. Rick continues to chat in an almost cheerful way, and I think about how I really did marry a great guy, and I wonder why I don't appreciate him more. How have we gotten so off track? so pulled apart? Is it possible to get back what we once had?

"You sure you don't want to go to the doctor?" he asks as I slowly ease myself out of the pickup at home.

"I think it's like you said, Rick. I'm just going to be pretty sore for a few days."

He's really kind and caring as he helps me into the house. Then he insists I lie down on the couch while he gets me some Advil.

I drift off to sleep for a while, but when I wake up, Rick is standing over me. "You sure you'll be okay while I go to work?"

I sit up and nod, making my neck ache. "I'll be fine."

"I called Colleen and told her what happened. She's going to bring the girls home for you after school."

And for some reason this makes me tear up again.

"I could stay home," he offers in a gentle tone. "Or maybe I should take you to see the doctor just to make sure you're all right."

"No, I'm fine. Really. Just still sort of shaken up. And I got sad when you mentioned Colleen. I was thinking of how I'm going to miss her when they move."

He nods. "Okay then. I'm putting the cordless phone right

here on the coffee table. If you need anything, just call me at work, okay?"

"Thanks." I force a smile. "I won't need to. I'm fine."

Mary and Sarah are both so sweetly concerned when Colleen drops them at home. Mary immediately goes into the kitchen and makes me a pot of my favorite tea. Sarah cuddles up with me on the couch.

"Looks like you're in good hands." Colleen frowns at her son Jacob as he chases poor Sadie through the living room. "Leave the dog alone!" she yells at him. Then she turns back to me. "Maybe we should get out of your hair. Give you some peace and quiet."

"And you've probably got a lot to do with packing and everything."

She rolls her eyes. "Don't remind me."

"Thanks for bringing the girls home."

"Oh yeah, I almost forgot. Laura Fletcher is going to bring you dinner tonight."

"She doesn't need to—"

"She *wants* to, Ruth. She also said to make sure I invited you to come back to her Bible study group. I'm sure you've already heard that Cynthia has left the church and won't be doing a study now."

I don't say anything to this. I'm not ready to tell her, or anyone for that matter, that I've left the church too. At least I *think* I have. Suddenly I'm not so sure. Not so sure about anything. It's hard to think clearly right now. I wonder if I hit my head during the wreck, although I don't feel any lumps or bumps. Perhaps my brain has been rattled. I know my spirit has been shaken.

13

I pretend to be sleeping when Laura drops off dinner tonight. I listen from beneath my blanket on the couch as Mary graciously handles everything, even writing down Laura's instructions for reheating the lasagna. Bless Mary. I think Laura is suitably impressed with the maturity of my older daughter. I know I am.

And when I finally do get up and go into the kitchen, Mary is already setting the table, and Sarah is filling our water glasses.

"How are you feeling, Mom?" Mary asks as I sit at the table and watch them.

"Better, I think. Just sore."

"Is Matthew coming home for dinner?" Mary asks.

"No, he works late tonight."

"He's going to be rich," says Sarah.

"He thinks he's almost got enough money to put a down payment on a car." Mary sets a green salad on the table. "I heard him telling Dad this weekend."

"What's going to happen to our car?" Sarah asks with a creased brow.

"I'm not sure. Dad said it might be totaled."

"What's that mean?" asks Sarah.

"It means we won't get it back." Mary sets the lasagna pan on the trivet on the table. "It'll go to the junkyard."

Sarah looks truly sad now.

"Don't worry," I tell her. "We'll get something else to drive."

"But what about Samantha?" She looks close to tears.

I totally forgot about Sarah's American Girl doll. Samantha is her favorite doll—the thing she takes everywhere, including the ride to and from school. She'd take her to class as well, but they don't allow it.

"We'll get Samantha back," I assure her.

"Is she still in the car?"

"Yes. She'll be safe there, Sarah."

"Did she get hurt in the wreck?"

"I'm sure she's just fine."

Sarah still looks worried.

"I'll have your dad get Samantha first thing tomorrow morning."

"But she'll be all alone all night long," Sarah says sadly. "She'll be scared in the dark all by herself."

"You can pray for her, sweetie. Pray that the angels keep her safe."

This seems to help a little. I bow my head and ask God to bless our food and to watch over Samantha in the car. Then we eat. We're just finishing when the phone rings. Mary jumps up to get it, then hands it to me, covering the mouthpiece with her hand as she whispers, "It's Cynthia Leman," as if that's a bad thing. I thank her and take the phone into the living room.

"I heard about your wreck," Cynthia says with concern.

"How did you hear?"

"Carrie Epson called me. She ran into Laura Fletcher at the grocery store this afternoon. Apparently Laura was bringing you *a meal*?" She says this as if it's a concern, as if there might be something wrong with the food.

"Yes, Laura did bring us dinner tonight."

"I just thought that was a little odd…"

"Why's that?"

"Well, we'd just assumed you were cutting all ties with VBF, Ruth."

I think about this but don't respond. I'm not even sure how to.

"Oh, we understand these things take time. And there are your girls and their school to consider. But we just hope you're not abandoning us. We all feel that you're an important part of this new body. Even Bronte mentioned how impressed she was with your spirit on Sunday."

"Really?"

"Yes. In fact, she and I would like to come by tomorrow. We want to see how you're doing as well as to discuss some things with you in regard to the women's ministry and the role we'd like you to play. Do you think you're feeling up to visitors?"

I glance around my slightly messy living room. "I…uh…I guess so."

"Great. What time works for you?"

"Maybe in the afternoon." I hope Rick will be at work by then, and maybe I'll be able to do some cleaning.

"Good. Shall we say two-ish?"

"That sounds fine."

Mary is standing in the doorway, watching me as I finish my phone call.

"What did she want?" Mary asks in a slightly suspicious tone.

"She just wanted to be sure I was okay. She wants to visit me tomorrow."

"Why?"

"Because she's my friend," I tell her.

"You really like her?"

I smile at her. "I know Cynthia seems a little odd at first. But she really loves the Lord, Mary, and she's a strong Christian and a good friend."

"But wasn't she good friends with Pastor Glenn?"

"Yes…" I study my daughter's expression. I can tell she's slightly perplexed about something, and I wonder how much she knows.

"But didn't he get fired?"

"Is that what you heard?"

She nods. "Everyone was talking about it at school today. And we were so glad when he didn't come in to do morning devotions."

"You didn't like his devotions?"

"I guess I liked them sometimes. But sometimes he got carried away."

"Carried away?"

"You know, Mom. He starts talking about how we have to do all this spiritual warfare and stuff. Sometimes it just gets old."

"So you don't think it's important to do spiritual warfare, Mary?"

"Yeah, I guess it is."

"What were devotions like today?"

She grins. "We didn't even have them."

I sort of blink at this. "You didn't even have them?"

"No, we all went into the gym just like usual, and then after we sang a couple of songs, Mr. Thomas announced there would be no devotions. He said we needed a break. And all the kids clapped and cheered."

"Oh."

Sarah has been hovering in the shadows, but I can tell she's been listening to her sister's tale. What does she think about this?

"Did you clap and cheer too, Sarah?" I say, and Sarah steps out where we can see her, but her face looks worried. I'm guessing she's still fretting about her missing Samantha doll.

"I felt bad," she says in a sad little voice. "I miss Pastor Glenn."

"No way," says Mary. "You must be crazy, Sarah."

But Sarah just shakes her head.

I pat the couch, motioning for her to come sit beside me. "Pastor Glenn is a good man."

"Then why did he get fired?"

Something about Mary's attitude bothers me, and I wonder if it's something she's picking up on at school. I consider how best to answer her. *Why did Pastor Glenn get fired?* I don't know that I'm totally sure myself. "Pastor Glenn was doing his very best to serve the Lord at Valley Bridge Fellowship. And sometimes when people are trying to serve the Lord, they offend others."

"Like Daniel?" Sarah says quickly. "Like when he wouldn't bow down to the golden idol, and they put him in the lions' den?"

I nod. "Yes, kind of like that."

"But no one told Pastor Glenn to worship a golden idol." Mary crosses her arms over her chest.

"No, you're right. But people did want him to worship the Lord in a different way, a way that felt dishonest to Pastor Glenn."

"How's that?" Mary sits in the chair across from me.

"Well, Pastor Glenn felt the Lord had called him to protect his sheep. He felt the Lord had told him that his sheep were going to be under attack and that we needed to be ready to defend ourselves against the Enemy."

"He told us that at devotions too," says Sarah. "He told us we have the power to beat the devil but we have to use it. He said, 'Use it or lose it.'"

"That's right. The Lord doesn't want us to get beat up by the devil. He wants us to be strong and to stand firm against the devil and sin. But some people didn't like hearing that. Some people got uncomfortable when Pastor Glenn talked about sin."

"What's going to happen to Pastor Glenn now?" asks Sarah.

I smile. "The Lord is helping him make a new church."

"Where is it?" she asks.

So I tell them a little about it and that maybe I can take them to visit it sometime. Mary doesn't seem too interested, but for some reason Sarah really wants to go. And this is encouraging.

Finally homework is done, and the girls are in bed, and I try to pick up a little around the house. Other than my neck and wrist, I don't feel too bad physically. But I still feel shaken in a spiritual sense. Why did the Lord allow that to happen to me today? And I can't help but think it was part of Satan's vicious attack. Especially as I recall the man whose truck rammed into me and the way he was so angry, so full of hatred. I feel frightened just to think of it. We are so vulnerable. One minute everything seems okay, and the next minute you could be seriously injured, maybe even killed.

What if my girls had been with me when I was hit? They could be in the hospital right now. As I think this, I begin to pace back and forth in the kitchen, replaying the incident and imagining how much worse it might have been.

"What's up, Mom?" Matthew asks as he comes in and slings his backpack onto the floor by the door.

First I study him carefully, making sure he hasn't been out drinking again. But he seems to be sober and normal. I tell him about the car accident today.

"Seriously?" He stares at me in disbelief. "Did you get hurt?"

"No. Just shaken up." I look into his eyes. "But it made me realize that we really have to be careful, Matthew. And you need to be really, really careful when you're on your bike, especially at night. Things happen so quickly. And Satan is out there just waiting for a chance to take you out."

Matthew kind of laughs.

"It's not funny. And if you go out drinking again and something bad happens, well, you'll see what I mean."

"So had you been drinking today, Mom?" His eyes twinkle. "Is that why you got into a wreck?"

"No, of course not."

"Why then?"

"I guess I let myself be distracted." I nod as it sinks in. "Yes, I was worrying about something else, something the Lord probably didn't want me to be thinking about. And I wasn't praying like I should've been. I wasn't doing warfare, and then it was too late, and I got hit."

He just shakes his head. "So the Lord zapped you?"

"Not the Lord, Matthew."

"The *devil* then?" His words are dripping with sarcasm, and I wonder how it is that both Matthew and Mary have grown so cynical. Oh, Mary isn't as bad as her brother, but she's questioning things much more than she used to do. It seems that little Sarah is the only one of my children who is truly growing up in the fear of the Lord. Hopefully I can protect her and keep her faith strong.

"He is real," I tell Matthew. "Satan is alive and well, and he prowls the streets ready to destroy and devour. Don't fool yourself."

"Yeah, Mom, I know, I know... I've heard it all before." He opens the fridge. "Anything to eat in here?"

I point out the leftover lasagna, then go to my room and close the door. I kneel before the bed and labor in prayer for my children, for their faith, and for their spiritual safety. And as I pray, I wonder if this is my fault. Perhaps I've been spiritually lax or have let down my guard. Or maybe I just haven't instructed them as I should. Haven't given them the tools they need to take on the spiritual battles facing them. But I also know that Rick is partially to blame too. He hasn't been the spiritual leader this family needs.

Finally the back of my neck is throbbing, and I lie down on the bed to continue praying. But then I feel myself drifting, and I fear I am too spiritually weak to hold this family together.

O Lord, protect us. Deliver us from evil. Protect us. Deliver us from evil. Protect us. Deliver us...

14

I've heard that hostages can be tortured into submission through sleep interruption and deprivation. Sometimes I feel that's what is happening to me. Sarah's nightmares, which happen almost nightly, seem to always wake me out of a dead sleep. And I feel I'm being tortured as I force myself to get out of bed. Not that I don't want to comfort her and pray with her and finally lull her back to sleep. I certainly do. But by the time she's peacefully slumbering, I'm usually wide awake. It must've been after four thirty when I finally got myself back to sleep last night.

And I must've slept hard too, because when I finally awaken, I see that my alarm clock, which apparently didn't go off, says it's after nine. I leap out of bed, causing a pain to shoot through my neck, and I dash out to see if the girls have gotten up yet. But they are gone. And Rick is gone too. Rick, who never gets up before ten, is not in bed!

A wave of panic surges through me. I've heard Pastor Glenn preach on the Rapture enough times to know that Jesus is coming back like a thief in the night. And as crazy as it sounds, I fear this may be what has happened. I crack open the door to Matthew's room to see that he is still in bed, sleeping soundly. And for a moment I'm reassured, but then I remember that Matthew seems to have fallen away from the Lord this past year. So, really, it's no consolation that he's still here.

"Don't be a fool," I whisper to myself as I close his door. Then I go into the kitchen, where I see breakfast dishes still in the sink and spot the note on the table, informing me that Rick has taken the girls to school and then gone to check on the condition of the minivan. I rub the back of my sore neck and remember yesterday's accident. Of course. Why was I so stupid?

It takes time, but the kitchen is finally properly cleaned, and I go to get dressed, carefully pulling a sweater over my head, trying not to stress my sore neck. I start to put on jeans but then remember that Cynthia and Bronte are coming over today. Perhaps jeans aren't appropriate. I'm sure my mother would agree. She still thinks that ladies don't wear jeans. Well, unless they're working in the yard. This thought almost makes me go for the jeans again, just to rebel against the memory of my mother's oppression. But I don't. I suppose a small part of me is worried that my mother might've been right.

I try to pace myself as I continue putting my house in order. Both my wrist and my neck still hurt, but the rest of me aches as well. In fact, I feel like I've been hit by a truck. I guess I have.

"What are you doing?" demands Rick when he finds me vacuuming the living-room carpet.

I turn off the noisy machine. "Cleaning."

"Why?"

"Because the house is dirty."

He unplugs the vacuum and coils up the cord. "First of all, the house is not dirty. It's just fine. But second of all, and more important, I took the girls to school so you could sleep in and rest this morning. Not so you could go on some crazy housecleaning binge."

"But I—"

"No buts, Ruth." He walks me over to the couch. "Just sit down and rest, okay?" He sets my favorite throw in my lap.

It's hard not to appreciate his kindness. Rick isn't usually that nurturing. Yet at the same time, it's past noon already, and I still have a lot to do. The bathroom hasn't even been touched.

"The minivan is probably totaled." He sits in the chair across from me. "The insurance adjuster already looked at it."

"What does that mean, *probably* totaled?"

He sighs. "Well, if we were to get it fixed, which might could be done, it would cost us a thousand dollars right out of our pocket."

"But what if it's totaled?"

"Then the insurance will pay off the remainder of the loan, and we'll have to get another car."

"You mean we'll have to pay for a brand-new car completely on our own? The insurance won't even cover it? The loan on the minivan was more than halfway paid off. We would've owned it free and clear in just a couple of years."

"Yeah…" He sighs. "That's called 'depreciation,' Ruth."

"That doesn't seem fair."

He laughs. "Whoever said that life was fair? Especially when it comes to insurance companies."

"So what are we going to do?"

"As soon as you feel well enough, we'll have to go car shopping."

I start to tell him that I feel well enough now, but then I remember that Cynthia and Bronte are coming over. "Maybe tomorrow?"

He brightens. "Okay. Let's make it fun, Ruth. And, you know, we don't have to get a minivan again. Especially since Matthew is eighteen and thinking about his own car. Maybe we could get something smaller, something sportier."

"Maybe something more economical."

"And you're going to look into that job?" he asks hopefully.

"Colleen said she's pretty sure you could get it, and she's bringing the girls home again today."

I rub the back of my neck, and Rick tells me to get some rest, but as I lean back on the couch, all I can think is that our debt is piling up and that it's mostly my fault. Or maybe it's Satan's attack on me, trying to kick me when I'm already down. I need to fight back. Fight back. Fight back! I close my eyes now, imagining that I am a warrior, swinging my saber like Luke Skywalker in *Star Wars,* as I slay one demon after another.

I stay on the couch, doing my spiritual warfare, until I hear Rick's pickup pulling out of the driveway and it's safe to continue cleaning the house. I work fast, knowing that Cynthia and Bronte will be here soon. But just as I finish with the guest bathroom, I find Matthew in my kitchen amid a mess of tortillas, refried beans, and shredded cheese, which looks like it must've exploded out of the shredder.

"What are you doing?"

He looks slightly indignant. "Making bean burritos. What's it look like?"

"It looks like a disaster. And I just cleaned this up, and I—" The doorbell ringing interrupts me, followed by Sadie barking in the laundry room. I glare at my son, then tell him to quiet the dog and to clean up his mess when he's done.

I invite the two women in, using my sore neck as an excuse to plant ourselves in the living room. "I'm sorry. I'm not much of a hostess today."

"Don't worry about that," Bronte says with a graceful wave of her hand. "We didn't expect you to lift a finger on our account." She smiles and holds up a small white bag. "In fact, Cynthia told me that you like Krispy Kremes."

"Oh, you shouldn't have—"

"Shall I put them in the kitchen for you?"

"*No,* no. My son's fixing burritos in there. You might as well leave them in here. That is unless you'd like some—"

"No thanks," says Bronte. "We just had lunch, and I'm stuffed. Cynthia's been showing me around town. Pointing out some of the local dark spots."

"Local dark spots?" I imagine people who forgot to pay their power bill.

"I mean *spiritually* dark."

"Oh…" I nod, sending a shot of pain through my neck. "Yes, I see what you mean."

"We started in the tavern district," explains Cynthia, "then on toward the porn shops and finally the new strip club." She shakes her head in revulsion. "Naturally, there are prostitutes all over that area too. It's really appalling what's happening to this town."

"I recently read that the ACLU is working to legalize prostitution as well as to defend the sale and distribution of child pornography." I shake my head in disgust but am pleased that I'm up-to-date.

"That's right," Cynthia says with a horrified expression. "Can you believe they are calling it a form of *artistic expression?*"

We all express our mutual disgust.

"And then we finished at the abortion clinic," says Bronte. "Very sad."

"Yes," continues Cynthia, "I told Bronte how our church protested the abortion clinic, at least to start with…and then how the council and elders wouldn't support our efforts."

I flash back to the time I took Sarah and Mary with me to one of the antiabortion protests. Mary wasn't even in school yet, and baby Sarah had to ride in her stroller. Cynthia had been pleased to see children present, but I also remember how angry Rick was when he heard what I'd done. "Our children aren't pawns to be used for public protests," he told me that night after Mary had spilled the beans at dinnertime.

"We've got our work cut out for us." Bronte brings me back to the present.

"Which is one reason we came to see you." Cynthia smiles. "And to wish you a speedy recovery."

"We have a question," says Bronte. "You don't have to answer us right now, since I'm sure you'll need to pray about it. But we'd like you to consider heading up the children's ministry at our church. Cynthia said that you used to teach Sunday school and that you're very good with kids."

"Well, I…I don't know…"

She waves her hand again. "Like I said, we don't expect an answer from you right now. We just want you to prayerfully consider this pos-sibility. To start with it'll be a volunteer position, but if we grow and increase our membership—and we feel certain that will happen—we would eventually like to put you on salary. Maybe even by the end of the year."

I know that my reaction is carnal and that it has nothing to do with faith, but the possibility of a salary, a paying job, is very tempting.

"Cynthia will be heading up our women's ministry," continues Bronte. "And I'll be an associate pastor with Glenn. And that's as far as we've gotten at this point."

"Our first staff meeting will be tomorrow morning at nine," says Cynthia.

"Mostly to pray and prepare for the midweek service," adds

Bronte. "But if you feel up to it, we'd love to have you join us."

"My car got totaled in the wreck, so I'm sort of without wheels right now. Although Rick wants to go car shopping. Maybe even tomorrow."

"I can give you a ride," offers Cynthia.

And so without really thinking about it and certainly without praying about it, I suddenly say, "I think I'd like that Sunday school position. I think it would be good for me." As I close the door after they leave, I'm fairly certain it's a real answer to prayer. Even Rick should be pleased to hear that I'm finally taking a job!

I stand and watch as the women get into Bronte's car, an impressive-looking sedan that's almost the same golden color as her hair. And as they're leaving, I see Colleen's SUV get ready to turn into my driveway. I can't believe it's already three thirty. She waits as the golden car pulls away, but I can tell she's really checking them out. Fortunately, the windows are dark, making it impossible to see who's inside. Nevertheless, I'm sure she'll have questions. I consider playing possum again, pretending to be asleep on the couch. But I suppose she'd see right through it since it's obvious I just had company.

"Who was that?" she asks as she and the girls come in through the front door.

"Just friends," I say lightly.

"Pretty impressive friends," says Colleen. "That was a brand-new Jaguar!"

"What friends?" Mary acts just as suspicious as Colleen.

"A woman named Bronte. We met recently, and she's talking to me about a job."

"What about a job at the clinic?" protests Colleen. "I already told Darlene you'd be coming in to talk to her."

"I don't—" Before I can finish, Colleen's twins burst through the front door, and she starts yelling at them, telling them they were supposed to stay in the car.

"Thanks for bringing the girls home. I think Rick and I will go car shopping tomorrow."

"Is the minivan totaled?" asks Mary.

"Did Daddy bring Samantha home?" Sarah asks with worried eyes.

"See ya!" Colleen waves over her shoulder as she herds her rambunctious boys back out my front door with a loud slam.

Relieved that I got off that easily about my curious visitors and job situation with Colleen, I produce the Samantha doll for Sarah, who shrieks in delight, and then I ask Mary to go see about Sadie, who is barking like a wild thing in the laundry room right now.

I take some Advil, and things finally settle down in our house. I begin to restore order to my kitchen, since Matthew was obviously in some great big hurry to get off to work. Mary and Sarah change from their school uniforms, take care of their household chores, and with the promise of their favorite television sitcom later tonight, they finally settle down to the dining-room table for homework. Meanwhile, I excuse myself to rest.

But instead of taking a nap, once I'm alone in my bedroom, I get down on my knees and pray. First, I ask God to guide my decision about the children's ministry job. But in the next breath I am thanking him for this wonderful opportunity, praising him for this chance both to serve him in the church and to earn some much-needed money to help out my family. I feel a huge sense of relief as I pray. I can see my heavenly Father's hand in all this. And it seems that all my recent spiritual warfare is finally beginning to pay off.

15

Rick, as promised, gets up early again on Wednesday morning. Of course, this makes me feel guilty because I know he works hard and needs his rest. Besides, I'm sure I'm perfectly capable of driving his pickup to deliver the girls to school. But he insists, and I don't argue. I am too relieved.

After he and the girls leave, I attempt to get dressed for the meeting, going through my closet in a desperate search for the perfect outfit, which seems impossible. The challenge is that I want an ensemble that will accomplish two things: one, I want to appear modest and dignified so as to please Cynthia's rather conservative tastes, but, two, I'd like to look a little bit stylish because of Bronte. It hasn't missed my attention that this woman knows how to dress.

In some ways she reminds me of Lynette, and I suspect that she and my sister would really hit it off when it comes to fashion. Although the relationship would end right there since Lynette claims to be a New Age Christian and vehemently refuses to join a church of any kind. Naturally, she blames most of this on her first marriage or, more specifically, on her first husband, who was supposedly a Christian. But that was a long time ago. Mostly I think this is just her excuse to be spiritually lazy.

This reminds me that Lynette has called a couple of times recently, leaving messages for me to return her calls, but as usual I haven't. I shove this new miniwave of guilt away, focusing instead on finding something to wear that someone like Lynette would approve of.

This eventually leads me to a nearly forgotten navy pantsuit. Lynette talked me into buying the designer blazer and slacks from a clearance rack last spring. They were marked down considerably but still out of my price range. Yet she made me try on the suit and insisted it was perfect for me. I thought I'd return it later, but time and life got in the way, and now here it hangs, price tags still attached.

I hold up the wool-blend pieces and can't help but notice they seem very well made. And although I'm fully aware that Cynthia wouldn't be caught dead in trousers of any kind, I couldn't help but notice that Bronte was actually wearing blue jeans yesterday. I'm sure they were very expensive jeans, probably some big designer name that makes Liz Claiborne look like a hick. But Bronte had combined those jeans with a leather jacket the color of honey and high-heeled boots about the same shade, and she didn't exactly look like she was ready to go pull weeds in the garden. So I'm hoping a pantsuit might be acceptable today.

To go with it, I choose a soft pink turtleneck sweater that Rick got me for my birthday last winter, along with a pastel-colored silk scarf that was a hand-me-down from my mother and something I never expected to wear. Then I put all these pieces on and stand in front of my full-length mirror. I actually look pretty good. And rather professional too. I might even look like someone who's ready to accept a position. And that's exactly what I plan to do.

I called Cynthia earlier this morning, and she should be here to pick me up soon, but I'm hoping and praying that she hurries. I want her to get here before Rick returns from dropping off the girls. I've already written him a note, explaining that I'm at a meeting and that I may even be interviewing for a job. I give him the location and ask him to pick me up at eleven, since Cynthia felt certain we would be done by then. I promise him I'll be ready to go car shopping at that time. It seems a good plan.

Despite the fact that Matthew is still home, sleeping in as usual, I go around and turn off all the lights in the house. No need to waste electricity. And then as I'm pacing, waiting for Cynthia to arrive, I check the stove to make sure I turned off the element after cooking eggs this morning. I repeat this routine several times, and finally, just when I'm about to give up on making it out the door before Rick gets back, I hear a car in the driveway. To my relief it's Cynthia's white Subaru, and I'm halfway down the driveway before she's even come to a complete stop.

"Sorry I'm late."

"No problem," I say as I buckle myself in, catching my breath.

"Traffic this morning. It just seems to get worse and worse in this town."

My hands shake as she pulls into the street. For some reason I feel like I'm running away, like I'm some sort of fugitive. That is perfectly ridiculous. I'm only going to a church meeting and looking into a potential job opportunity. But my heart is pounding with an enormous weight of guilt just the same. I look out the window and count the light poles along the street, trying to calm and distract myself as Cynthia continues to talk about the heavy traffic and how this town is growing too fast, "attracting the wrong sorts of people…turning into a modern-day Sodom and Gomorrah."

I pick a piece of lint off my sleeve, then smooth my hands over my pants, trying to wipe away this disturbing sense of guilt gnawing at me. I know I'm not doing anything wrong. I don't need to feel guilty.

Cynthia glances at me as she pauses at a stop sign. "You look different, Ruth."

"It's a new pantsuit." I brace myself. "I know you don't approve of women in pants, but I noticed Bronte wears jeans, so I thought…"

She pulls away from the stop sign a little too fast, which makes me jump in my seat, worried that she also will be hit by a truck.

"Well, surely you know what the Bible says about women wearing trousers—it's a sin for a woman to dress like a man."

"Oh…I never read that before."

"Or to cut her hair, for that matter."

"Is that why you keep yours long?"

She reaches back to touch her long, gray-streaked braid, then nods with satisfaction. "And you are not to adorn yourself with costly gold jewelry or expensive clothes or fancy hairstyles. A godly woman dresses modestly."

"So…," I venture, probably in an effort to get my thoughts off myself and my guilt, "do you think that makes most modern-day women *sinful*?"

She tosses me a sideways glance that's hard to read, and suddenly I don't know how I dared to ask her this. Goodness, I must sound arrogant. But the truth is, I'm just curious as to how she sees the rest of us. Does she really think we're a bunch of sinners?

She makes a snorting sort of laugh. "We're *all* sinful, Ruth. You should know that much by now."

"Well, of course I know that. But I guess I just wonder what you think of someone like, say, Bronte Wellington. She doesn't exactly dress in the way you described."

She shrugs. "Oh, I'm well aware that most people think I'm pretty old-fashioned and fundamental when it comes to the way I interpret Scripture and the way I dress, but we have to live by our convictions, don't we?"

"Yes."

"But just so you'll know, I do respect Bronte. I can tell in my spirit that she's a godly and deeply spiritual woman. And perhaps the Lord is bending the rules for her a little, because she is, you know, a *real* prophetess."

"What do you mean by 'a *real* prophetess'?"

"I suppose that didn't come out quite right. I don't mean to insinuate that others, even myself, aren't genuine prophets. We most definitely are. But I can see the Lord's special anointing on this woman. I've never known anyone so spiritually deep, so intimately connected with the Lord, Ruth. And I am humbled and amazed that she has chosen us." She clears her throat. "Or rather that the Lord has chosen us."

She pulls into a parking space right in front of the drugstore now and turns to look at me with an expression that I can only describe as pure rapture, and I'm slightly taken aback. "Do you feel it too?" she says with a kind of passion that I've only heard her express from the pulpit while giving a word. "Do you get the sense that Bronte Wellington is the Lord's divine gift to us, that she is going to lead us and our town to huge spiritual victory?"

I consider this as I reach for my Bible and purse. "Yes," I finally admit as we both get out of the car, "I do get that same sense."

"It's so exciting!"

We apologize for being a few minutes late, and Pastor Glenn calls our small meeting to order. "Normally we would open with prayer," he says. "But since we plan to devote most of our time to interceding this morning, we thought it would be better to cover some business things first." Then Pastor Glenn proceeds to tell us that he's invited Carl, who is seated on his left, to join the team. "Because of his background in accounting, Carl will help manage our finances." Then he nods to his wife, Kellie. "My better half here has offered to play the role of church secretary, at least for the time being. We'll see how it goes."

Kellie nods. "Since Katie went off to college this year, I think it would do me good to get out of the house. Get away from that whole empty-nest thing. We're going to set up an office in the back of the building. I've already brought some things over from home, and we're installing a phone line later this week."

"Which brings us to the subject of the building," continues Pastor Glenn. "The Lord has blessed us with the finances to cover the deposit on the lease for this property. However, we're in immediate need of enough funds to pay next month's rent. Naturally, we're trusting the Lord to meet this need, but if anyone has any ideas or a rich uncle," he chuckles, "we're more than interested to hear about them."

"We could have a bake sale," says Cynthia. "We could set up tables by the front door on Sunday mornings. And then Pastor Glenn could encourage people to buy some goodies to take home with them afterward." Suddenly she looks somewhat embarrassed by her suggestion. "I know it wouldn't bring in a lot of money, but every little bit helps."

"That's right," agrees Pastor Glenn. "Why don't you handle this, Cynthia?"

She beams at him now.

"Maybe we could have a Christmas bazaar," says Kellie. "Remember when we did that to raise money for the orphanage in Africa a couple of years ago?"

"Yes," I say. "I helped with that event, and as I recall, we raised a fair amount of money too. Wasn't it about three thousand dollars?"

Kellie nods. "Of course, that was with a very large congregation."

"But we do have a good location here," says Pastor Glenn. "Plus the event might help draw in some newcomers, folks who might be interested in joining our church."

"And I'm going to buy some radio advertising," says Bronte. "We could include the bazaar information in that."

"That's a great idea," says Pastor Glenn.

"We'll have to get right on it," says Kellie. "The best bazaars usually come right after Thanksgiving."

"Would you like to head that up?" asks Pastor Glenn.

Kellie nods. "I would be glad to, especially if Ruth is willing to help again."

"Sure," I offer. "It sounds like fun."

"Maybe you could even get the children involved. Have them make some craft projects that could be sold," Kellie suggested.

"That's assuming she takes the position." Bronte glances at me with hopeful eyes.

"Oh yes," says Pastor Glenn. "I guess we did jump the gun on that. Do you have an answer for us yet, Ruth?"

I smile at him and the group. "Yes, I do. I would be pleased to head up the children's ministry."

Everyone claps and seems genuinely pleased. And I feel very happy.

"I'm sure your girls will be a great help to you." Cynthia directs this more to Bronte than anyone else. "Did you know that Ruth has two delightful daughters who are still in school? What are their ages, Ruth?"

I tell them their names and ages, but even as I say this, it occurs to me that I haven't really considered how my girls will react to the news that we are switching churches. I suspect that Sarah will be okay, but Mary may take some convincing. However, I just continue to smile. *Have faith*, I remind myself. *Have faith*.

Pastor Glenn turns to Bronte. "Well, unless anyone else has more business or fund-raising ideas, I'll turn this over to you now."

Bronte looks around the table, taking time to peer directly at each of us. Her smile is warm, and as Cynthia said earlier, it's easy to see the Lord's special anointing on this woman. "I want to begin by saying how delighted I am to be part of your church. I know that the Lord's blessing is on us, and I expect to see wonderful things, miraculous things, glorious things in the days ahead. We are all embarking on a huge spiritual adventure together, an adventure that will touch each one of us deeply, an adventure that will change the lives of many, saving souls for the kingdom and for all eternity."

Carl says a hearty "amen," and the rest of us echo it.

"Next, I want to share that the Lord has shown me that we are all to be equals in this church. For that reason we will refer to each other as brothers and sisters. Glenn will no longer be called Pastor Glenn but simply Brother Glenn. I am Sister Bronte." She kind of laughs. "I suppose it will take some getting used to at first, but it will be a good reminder that no one is above another."

As a group we continue to talk about our vision for this new church, expressing feelings of excitement, expectations, and lots of enthusiasm. And then we pray. I am amazed at how the Spirit moves in our midst, and it seems our prayers are shooting straight up to heaven, or maybe it's more that the Lord is right here among us. But I can literally feel the energy—a spiritual pulsating that is generated throughout the entire group. And by the time we are winding down—or is it up?—we are all standing, hands raised, shouting praises to the Lord and thanking him for his powerful presence and for all he's going to do.

"Amen!" Brother Glenn shouts in finale. "Amen and amen!"

We all say, "Amen," but as I open my eyes and glance around the small group of enthusiastic worshipers, I feel a mixture of self-conscious embarrassment and childlike giddiness. Gazing at our group in the stark fluorescent lighting, we seem a somewhat motley crew. And I'm sure we might look like an odd mix of people, especially to those who only see with physical eyes. There is Glenn, an attractive, middle-aged man who's been recently fired. Next to him is soft-spoken Carl, a retired CPA with sloped shoulders, thick glasses, and a receding hairline. And next to him is the beautiful Bronte, who looks like she doesn't even belong here. But she is standing next to Cynthia, who resembles an old hippie or maybe just an old maid. And, of course, I must look like a boring middle-aged housewife, not so different than Kellie Pratt, who is standing next to me. But it's the Spirit of the Lord that makes us special; it's his Holy Spirit that unites us, transforms us, and gives us power.

"Hello?"

We all turn to see who has come in the front door, and I am slightly stunned to realize it's my husband. I had totally forgotten about my note inviting him to pick me up here at eleven. I feel a rush of panic, combined with a need to apologize and explain every-thing—both to my friends at this meeting and to Rick.

"Hello, Rick," calls Pastor—make that *Brother* Glenn as he quickly approaches the front door and grasps my husband's hand in both of his. "Good to see you!"

"Yeah," says Rick, clearly confused. "Uh, what's going on here?"

"Didn't Ruth tell you?"

"Just something about a meeting." He checks out our group. "And something about a job?" Now he looks at me with one eyebrow slightly cocked as if he thinks I might've made the whole thing up.

"Well, she's decided to accept the job," announces Brother Glenn. "And we're so pleased to have her on our team."

I am by Rick's side now, trying to act natural, but I'm sure my cheeks are flaming red, and I wish I could disappear—that we both could disappear. Why did I tell him to meet me here? What was I thinking?

"We should probably get going now," I say to Brother Glenn. "I promised Rick that we'd look for cars before he has to go to work."

"Still working swing shift?" asks Brother Glenn with a sympathetic smile.

Rick nods, but he still looks slightly dazed as well as somewhat irritated.

"I'll bring him up-to-date." I tug on Rick's arm. "Life's been so busy lately, what with his odd hours, the car wreck... We really need to catch up, don't we, honey?" I glance hopefully at Rick.

"Will we see you here on Sunday, Rick?" asks Carl. And now the others have come over, forming a little semicircle around us.

"Maybe so," I answer for him.

Then I notice something in Rick's eyes. And I can tell that he's studying Bronte now. His brows are raised with curious interest as if he can't figure out how someone like her is connected with the rest of us. And although I partially resent this and maybe even feel a little jealous, I'm also relieved for the opportunity to change gears, to deflect the attention from myself. So, hoping to appear somewhat socially adept, I formally introduce the two of them.

"Bronte has been praying for our town," I say in conclusion, hoping to make sense out of what suddenly seems a little crazy, even to me. "And the Lord brought her to us to help us start our new church."

"That's right," says Brother Glenn. "Bronte is an old friend. She and I went to Bible college together, and the Lord miraculously directed her to this church."

"Well, we really should go now." I link arms with my still slightly stunned husband, aiming us toward the plate-glass front door.

"See you at worship service tonight, Ruth," says Cynthia. "Call me if you need a ride."

The door closes behind us, and I let out a deep breath. I don't know why I feel so rattled, but as we walk toward Rick's pickup, it seems every nerve in my body is pulled taut, ready to snap at the slightest trouble.

"What is going on?" Rick opens the passenger door for me and helps me to climb into the cab.

I look straight forward and don't say anything as he closes the door. But as he walks around to the driver's side, I take another slow, deep breath, trying to calm myself as well as to think of a coherent way to explain this new-church thing to him. I doubt he'll understand or be supportive. Oh, how do I get into these messes?

I spend nearly ten minutes trying to paint a positive picture of the new church and why our town so desperately needs it and why I *must* be involved and why the position in children's ministries is absolutely perfect for me.

"That's the job?" he finally says.

"Yes."

"How much does it pay?"

I look down at my lap. Why does it always come down to this? Why is money so important? Why can't the Lord just drop it down from heaven?

"Let me guess. It's a volunteer position, right?"

"Just to start," I say quickly. "As the church grows and the budget increases, then I'll go on salary. But it's worth it. You know I don't have a lot of confidence. This will give me a chance to start slowly, to build up to something, and then when it's time to get paid, I'll feel like I deserve it. They think maybe even by the end of the year."

"You deserve it now!"

I press my lips tightly together. I know he's only saying that because he's desperate for money. He wants me to work so we can get out of debt and start building up our savings again.

"Maybe we shouldn't get a car," I say suddenly, thinking I don't deserve it. After all, I wrecked the last one. "Then we wouldn't have to waste money on a down payment. Maybe that would help make up for my not earning any money for the next couple of months."

"And how would you get the girls to school?"

"I could use your pickup in the morning. And arrange for someone to drop them off. Maybe give them gas money. Think what that would save us. On insurance, car payments, gas."

"And how would you get to this supposed job?"

"Well, I figure that a lot of the work—the planning and whatnot—can be done at home. And then on church days, I could get a ride from Cynthia. I'm sure she wouldn't mind."

He shakes his head with a look of disgust. "I just don't get this thing with you and Cynthia, Ruth. Why are you suddenly turning into best buddies?"

"There's a lot more to Cynthia than you can see."

He laughs in a mean way. "She's a freak, Ruth. Can't you see she's a freak? She used to give me the heebie-jeebies every time she went forward in church with one of her so-called words. She used to weird you out too. Don't you remember?"

"No." I look straight ahead as he turns into the car lot. "Even though we're different, I've always respected her. She is deeply committed to the Lord, and she has a good heart, Rick. You shouldn't judge her."

He scowls as he turns off the engine. "You ready to do this? I called ahead to Chuck. He's going to help us look for cars."

"You're one to be talking about freaky friends." I get out of the truck. Okay, I know that's a low blow since Chuck and Rick have been friends since high school. But of all Rick's friends, Chuck is the weirdest.

"Hey, buddy!" Chuck heads for us. He has on a shiny black shirt with a red and gold dragon embroidered along one side. As usual, the top two buttons are open, like he's stuck in the eighties, and this reveals a heavy gold chain along with a chest that looks like it could belong to an orangutan. Chuck slaps Rick on the back and gives me a wary smile. "Hear you totaled your car, Ruth. Too bad."

Now he starts trying to sell us every sporty-looking car on the lot. I can tell that Rick has given him the wrong idea.

"Look," I say to him. "We're a family. We have three kids and a dog. A two-door thing like this is not going to work."

"Too bad," says Chuck. "I could just see the two of you going out on date night together in this little beauty." He glances at me. "You do have date night, don't you?"

"Well, uh, Rick works nights, and it's—"

He turns and looks at Rick now. "You don't work every night, buddy. Don't tell me that you can't take the little woman out for a date once a week. Marla and I have been doing date nights for a couple of years now. I think it might actually be the secret to making a marriage last."

I restrain myself from rolling my eyes. This is Chuck's third or fourth marriage, and I would never admit it aloud, but I doubt it's going to stick.

Rick runs his hand over the sleek hood. "It's a great-looking car, Chuck, but I don't think it's for—"

"Hey, buddy, why not just take her for a spin? I already got the dealer plates on and everything. She's all signed out, and since I know you personally, I won't even have to go with you. Just take her out and imagine the two of you going out for a date. Better yet, imagine you're going to the coast for the weekend, you've got the sunroof open, and it's a gorgeous day." He slaps Rick on the back again and hands him the keys.

Rick looks at me with a lopsided grin. "Ya wanna?"

I shrug, feeling a little sorry for this man who's been so understanding about my wrecking the minivan. I think maybe I owe him. "Sure, why not."

So we get in, and I have to admit that it feels pretty good. "Is this leather?" I ask Chuck before I close the door.

"Yeah, this baby is loaded. Not even two years old and only twelve thousand miles on her. She's barely broken in, and yet you're getting a great deal. Like I said, I've been thinking about taking this one home myself."

Rick nods and starts the ignition. It sounds pretty good, and then I notice it's a five speed. "I don't know how to drive a stick," I say as Rick pulls the car out and heads toward the street.

"You can learn." He pulls out into traffic.

I hold my breath as he zips around in this peppy little car. I'm not used to riding this low, to feeling the car moving so quickly. It's frightening...and yet sort of exhilarating too. I can't quite describe how it makes me feel. I peer at my husband, who seems to have turned into someone else behind the wheel.

He is smiling with a very relaxed look as he leans back into the seat. "I could get used to this."

I kind of groan. "This is not a family car." Something about this car seems evil to me. Maybe it's the color or the way it smells, but it reminds me of the kind of car that is spawned from a midlife crisis or the kind that might bring one on.

He frowns. "I know it's not a family car, but..."

"The kids would be packed in like sardines back there. And what if we wanted to take Sadie somewhere?"

"My pickup."

I let out a loud sigh and lean back into the seat. This is crazy. Rick is letting his flesh rule his spirit again. How can I make him understand this is wrong? Wrong, wrong, wrong!

"I liked Chuck's idea about date nights, Ruth."

"Yeah, like that man should be giving out marriage advice."

"He made a good point."

"Well, I don't know about that, Rick, but I do know this is nuts.

We cannot buy a car like this. Not at this stage of life, anyway. Maybe when the kids are all grown and we're empty nesters."

I almost add "like Kellie and Glenn Pratt" but fortunately think better of this. That would only irritate him. Still, I have to make him understand this car would be a big mistake. For all I know, the previous owner could've been demonized. Who knows what might've gone on in here? I want out of this car, and I want out right now. I'm already gripping the door handle, ready to leap out and shake myself off.

"What if we're too old and decrepit to enjoy a car like this by then?" he asks as he turns back into the car lot.

Still gripping the door handle as I remind myself that I'll need to wash very carefully to remove whatever sort of nastiness I've been exposed to, I quickly do the mental math. "I won't even be fifty by the time Sarah graduates from high school. And you'll only be fifty-three, Rick."

"My dad died when he was fifty-three."

"Well, that doesn't mean anything." I swallow hard. "Not really."

"Maybe not to you…"

He's barely parked the car, and I practically leap out. I can't get away from this vehicle fast enough.

16

So it is that we buy not the evil red Nissan Sentra but a com-promise. Chuck somehow talked us into a brand-new Nissan Altima, a sleek silver car with four doors and all the extras you could want and more. The sticker price is way beyond what Rick told him we could afford. But Chuck explained that the payments would be less since it's new. Of course, this simply means we owe a whole lot more money for a much longer period of time, but, as Rick points out, we pretty much live by our monthly budget anyway.

"A car payment is a car payment," he says. "And you are going to get a paying job, right?"

I nod like this is a fact. Then Rick asks if I mind driving the car home so he can make it to work on time. "It'll take them about an hour to finish the paperwork and get the car ready."

"That's fine," I assure him. Then after he leaves, I hurry to the women's rest room. Relieved to see it's the kind with only one toilet and a locking door, I remove my blazer, gingerly hang it on the door's hook, and immediately scrub my hands clear up to my elbows. As I scrub, I try not to imagine my husband slaving away at work, work-ing himself to death because of my blunder of totaling our minivan and then purchasing a vehicle beyond our means. I try not to remem-ber what he said about his dad dying young. But when I finally return to the waiting room, it's all I can think about. Even though I try to pray, all I can think of is Rick's early demise. In my mind's eye I can see my husband stretched out on the floor at work, paramedics gathered around, shaking their heads as they put away their cardio equipment and pronounce him dead at the scene. Dead. Dead. Dead.

Finally I am in the new Altima, and I push these intrusive thoughts away as I very carefully drive out of the dealership lot. I haven't been behind the wheel since the day of the wreck, and I need to pay attention, not only to my own driving but to other drivers as well. Defensive driving, as my dad would say. Defensive, defensive, defensive.

I cautiously navigate my way to Valley Bridge Fellowship, taking the quieter back streets, driving like a ninety-year-old woman with cataracts. Finally I see the girls' school and feel my iron grip on the steering wheel loosen a bit. I no longer think of these buildings as "the church," as I did before, because it's not *my* church anymore. And after today, it won't be my daughters' church either. It will simply be their school. Valley Bridge Christian School. That's all.

Maybe this news of switching churches will digest more easily once they see the new car. I can just imagine their squeals of delight when they climb inside and see all the extras. This car makes our old minivan look like a dinosaur. It's a relief to know that this car has been carefully cleaned, and as far as I can see, it's spotless. And since it's new, I'm not overly worried about the bad spiritual vibes that previous owners may have left behind. Yet I realize that others may have driven it, if only briefly, and I take the time to pray over the car, to cast out any possible demons.

I'm in the midst of a particularly powerful casting-out sentence when I practically jump out of my skin at the sound of someone knocking on the window. I turn to see Colleen peering in at me. I push the button to lower the window, trying not to look too startled.

"Man, I thought that was you in here! What a cool car, Ruth!"

It's still a few minutes before school lets out, so I get out of the car to talk to her. "We just bought it."

"Look at you!" she says, checking me out. "What're you dressed up for? Let me guess. You're going in to talk to Darlene about the job, right? She's there until—"

"I, uh, I already got a job."

"Huh?" She looks at me curiously. "When did you have time to do that?"

"It was sort of in the works…"

"Did it have to do with that Jaguar in your driveway yesterday?"

"As a matter of fact, it sort of did."

She frowns. "So what kind of job is this, Ruth? Some kind of selling? Don't tell me you've fallen for one of those pyramid scams?"

I laugh. "You mean like you did?"

"That was a long time ago. And even so, you should've learned from my mistake."

"It's not a pyramid."

"Well, what then?"

I glance at my watch and see that it's straight up three o'clock now. "The kids will be getting out. I better get ready to scram."

She glances back to see the cars lining up and knows I'm right. "Okay, well, call me then. I want to hear about this job." She grins. "You look like a million bucks, Ruth, standing there by that car."

My cheeks grow warm. Part of me is flattered, but the rest of me knows it's vanity and sin. I wave and get back into my car, lowering the passenger-side window so I can yell at the girls when they come out. I'm sure they won't be expecting me to pick them up today and certainly not in something like this.

I grin like a clown when my girls come out the door. I holler their names and enjoy the looks of astonished surprise when they realize it's their mom in the fancy silver car. Mary is the first one over, jumping happily into the front passenger seat, but Sarah doesn't look too unhappy as she climbs into the back. And then they both start talking at once as I pull away, making room for the line to move up.

"Slow down and buckle up. I can't answer both your questions at once." Then I explain that, yes, this is our new car, and that Daddy and I just got it today.

"This must've been expensive." Mary turns on the radio. "It even has a CD player, Mom. Look, it can hold six CDs."

They both carefully check everything out, exclaiming over every new discovery. And just before we get home, I tell them that I've taken a job and that it will involve switching churches as well.

"We have to go to a different church?" Mary says in dismay.

"Yes. It's part of my job. Since I'm the director of kids' ministries, my kids need to go there too."

"You're the director?" Sarah sounds impressed. "Just like Mrs. Stanton?"

"Yes," I tell her as I turn down our street, "just like her."

"Does that mean we won't go to school at Valley Bridge anymore?"

I can't tell by the tone of Mary's voice whether she thinks that would be good or bad. "This church doesn't have a school. You girls will continue at VBF."

"Good!" exclaims Mary.

"So you finally decided you like it?" I ask in surprise.

"Yeah, it's pretty cool now that Pastor Glenn is gone."

"I like it too," chimes in Sarah.

"It's like you said, Mom," Mary continues in her mature tone. "It just takes time."

I swallow hard, trying to decide how much to tell them right now. "Well, that's how it will be with our new church too. It'll just take time."

Thankfully, I am pulling into the driveway. The girls will be distracted by chores and homework, and I won't have to answer any more difficult questions about our new church. Perhaps it's better just to let them find these things out for themselves.

Once they're occupied, I go to my room, and after changing from my nice suit into everyday clothes, I get down on my knees and pray.

"Some things are better left unsaid," my mother used to tell me in a stern voice, her hint that I should butt out of her business. Like the time she and Dad almost got a divorce. Lynette and Jonathan seemed fairly oblivious to the whole thing, but I knew what was going on from the start. Still, I knew better than to push too hard on such matters. It didn't take much for my mother to lower her sights onto me, and the next thing I'd know, I was doing extra chores, cutting switches, or being grounded.

As much as I resented that then, I'm beginning to think maybe she was right. The less said about our new church situation, the smoother I suspect it will go. After all, Mary and Sarah are my children. If I say it's time to change churches, what right do they have to protest?

It would be different if Rick were more involved in the spiritual welfare of this family. And as much as it pains me to admit this, I'm afraid there's little I can do to influence Matthew in this regard. It was hard enough making him go to Valley Bridge Fellowship with me. Getting him to go to this much smaller and different sort of fellowship would be nothing short of a miracle. Still, I pray for this miracle and even more as I travail for my family and our new church.

By the time I finish praying, my knees are sore, and I feel exhausted. It's not easy to hold back the forces of evil when you are only one woman. I go out to see how my daughters are faring, only to discover that they have abandoned their homework and are out in the backyard huddled around something.

"What are you doing?" I call out the patio door.

"We found a kitten." Sarah holds up a scrawny black cat that looks to be a few months old.

"She must be a Halloween cat," Mary says as they bring the cat toward me.

"Can we keep her, Mom? Isn't she sweet?" Sarah holds up the young cat for me to see better.

"She or he must belong to a neighbor," I tell them.

"She doesn't have a collar," Mary points out.

"That doesn't mean she doesn't have an owner."

"But she's hungry," says Sarah. "She was eating Sadie's food."

"Where is Sadie?"

"We put her in the laundry room. Didn't you hear her barking at the kitten?"

I consider this and realize I must've been deep in prayer then. "Well, it's time to come in. Leave the cat outside."

"We can't leave her all alone," Sarah says, close to tears. "It'll be dark soon, and she's hungry."

I feel exasperated. The last thing we need is a cat.

"Can't we just keep her for the night," suggests Mary, "then put out a Found Cat sign tomorrow with our phone number?"

"Can't we just feed her and give her a bed?" asks Sarah. "Jesus said that what we do for the least of them, we do for him. Can't we take care of her for Jesus? She needs our help, Mommy."

"How do you know the cat is a she?"

"Mary said so."

Mary grins at me. "Katy told me how you tell. You know they have cats, Mom. I called her, and she explained everything."

"Everything?" My brows lift.

"Just for the night?" pleads Sarah.

I think perhaps I see the Lord's hand in this. "Okay," I finally say, "but on one condition, girls."

"What?" they say in unison.

"You feed her and make her a bed in the laundry room, and then there is no complaining when it's time to go to church and she has to stay behind." I am surprised at how readily they agree to this plan. In fact, as we're getting in the new car to go to our new church, I wonder if I wasn't the one who was duped.

"Now remember our agreement." I start the car and carefully back out. "No complaining."

"You mean about leaving the cat at home," asks Mary, "or about going to this new church?"

"Both." I explain how the church is still small and how there isn't a kids' program yet.

"That's because you're going to do it?" asks Sarah.

"That's right. But there will be a lot of music tonight," I assure them. Brother Glenn told us at the meeting today that until the kids' program takes off, they'll try to keep the services more children friendly.

"This is a store," Mary says when I park the car out front.

"It's where our church will be meeting for the time being." I notice there are a couple dozen cars out front, which seems a good sign.

Then, just before we go inside, I tell them that Pastor Glenn is the leader here, but we call him Brother Glenn now. Mary lets out a big groan, and Sarah lets go of my hand.

"Remember your promise," I hiss at them. Someone is holding the door open for us. "I expect you girls to behave like ladies." I take Sarah's hand again. I sound just like my mom now, and that only makes me more irritated at myself. Why does this have to be so difficult? Why does the Lord allow us to live in a world with so much adversity?

Cynthia warmly greets us once we're inside. Mary is acting like a preadolescent, but Sarah actually responds to the greeting, and I feel a smidgen of hope. Brother Glenn and another man I've never seen before are up front playing music. Just a nice kind of background music, friendly and inviting. Glenn, as usual, is on the guitar, and the other man is playing the fiddle, but there's also an electronic keyboard off to one side, which seems promising.

"Are these your lovely daughters?" Sister Bronte asks as we go to find our seats.

I pause to introduce the girls, and I can't help but notice that Mary seems to be paying close attention to Bronte. I think she's rather impressed by this woman's extraordinary good looks.

"Well, I'm so pleased to meet you." Sister Bronte shakes both their hands. "I think our little church is off to a wonderful start, and I'm so glad you girls could join us. Are either of you very musical?"

They both shrug in a self-conscious way. "Mary has a lovely singing voice," I say, "and Sarah knows how to play the recorder."

"Just a little," Sarah admits. "We just started learning."

"I want to learn to play the piano," says Mary.

"Well, it must be the Lord," Bronte says with a wide open

smile. "I just happen to play the piano, and I sometimes give lessons."

"Really?" Mary looks slightly dazzled.

"Yes, really. Let's talk later."

As the girls and I find seats in the second row, I try to estimate how many people are here. It seems like more than on Sunday, and I feel somewhat amazed. How are people learning about this place so quickly?

"Is Sister Bronte someone famous?" Mary whispers to me.

"I don't know for sure. But she is well known by the Lord."

Mary nods, as if taking all this in. Meanwhile, Sarah's toes are keeping time to the music, and I'm thinking perhaps this will be easier than I expected.

Sister Bronte turns out to be the keyboardist and very talented. She also has a beautiful singing voice, and the music portion of our worship service goes for about thirty minutes. Not only is it well done, but it's incredibly moving too. Even my girls are touched by the Spirit as we stand and lift our hands and sing.

But the worship seems to end a bit abruptly, or maybe it's just me, but following a very emotional song, the room becomes quiet. Then the lights go down, and there's one spotlight shining toward the front. Sister Bronte stands and delivers a word from the Lord that is both exhilarating and slightly frightening.

" 'Take up your sword,' says the Lord!" she says in a passionate voice with hands held high. " 'Prepare for bloodshed and the breaking of bones! But remember, my children, you are not fighting against earthly flesh and blood. Your war is not against earthly bones. You are fighting against powers and principalities of the underworld!' "

She pauses, and there is a clash of cymbals and some evil-sounding background music. I'm not sure who's handling the sound system just now, but I must admit it is effective, and both Sarah and Mary take my hands. I give them a reassuring squeeze, then Sister Bronte continues.

" 'You are waging war against satanic power,' says the Lord, 'fighting against the devil's darkness and against all his legions of demonic forces. But beware, my children, for your enemy will disguise himself as an earthly being. These foul followers of Satan will masquerade themselves, pretending to become the familiar, but know that they are full of evil. Donning sheep's clothing, these ravenous wolves will claw their way into your hearts and into your lives, hoping to earn your trust in order to destroy you. The time is coming,' says the Lord, 'when my children will not only feel their spiritual attackers in the unseen world, but the time is coming when you will see these impostors with your own eyes, and you will hear their screams and lies and their vicious cries with your own ears. For Satan's fury is going to be unleashed sevenfold.' " She stops again for more sound effects and then a long, quiet pause. "But know this, my children: not all will hear and see the Enemy. For only those who are chosen by the Lord, only those who are fully surrendered to his power, only those who are truly filled with his Holy Spirit—they alone will be allowed to see such things."

"I see one now, sister," calls a voice from the back. Everyone in the congregation turns to see Brother Carl pointing toward a door off to the right. I think it leads to the storeroom, where Kellie has begun setting up the church office. The lights come up a little, not too bright, but just enough that we can see a bit more clearly.

"I see it too." Cynthia points in the same direction. I peer at the door, and while I do see some shadows, I'm not sure I actually see anything real. Although the harder I look, the more I think I can perhaps discern a shape that resembles something weird and evil.

Brother Glenn is going toward this apparition now, holding both hands out as he goes. "In the name of Jesus, we cast you out!" He is yelling, and several others join him. They call out and pray, and after a minute or two, it seems this thing—this shadow of darkness—has gone. The lights brighten a bit, and the room is very quiet.

"The Lord has shown me," says Cynthia in a strong voice, "that this building needs cleansing."

"Amen, sister," someone else calls out.

"My spirit agrees," says Brother Glenn. "We need to begin our warfare right here, right in this very building."

"Who is ready to go to battle?" asks Bronte from where she is still standing in the front. "If you are ready to go to war against the Lord's enemy, stand. Stand now and join together."

Everyone in the room stands. My heart is pounding, and I'm still holding both girls' hands in mine. I glance down at their faces, worried that they may be even more frightened than I am. And while they do look somewhat scared, I can also detect another emotion. Maybe it's simply childish excitement, or maybe it's the Holy Spirit at work in their hearts, but they seem to be with us on this.

I smile at them. "Praise the Lord." They echo my words. And soon we are joining in with all the other members of the congregation, working our way around the building as we pray against the evil inhabitants. We pray for the walls and posts and doors and windows and floors. We pray for the podium and the chairs and even the musical instruments. We continue like this for about an hour until finally it seems we are all prayed out.

Bronte is back at the front again. And once again she raises her hands and closes her eyes. " 'You have done well,' says the Lord, 'exceedingly well. You are my army, my chosen ones. You are showing yourselves to be powerful warriors against my enemy. I will pour my Spirit out among you. I will cause you to have visions and to dream dreams. Your eyes will be opened, and your ears will hear. My Spirit and my blessing are upon you.' "

This is followed by a few more songs, and then we are excused. Seeing that it's after nine and pretty late for a school night, I say some hasty good-byes and then usher the girls toward the door. I'm curious to hear their reactions to tonight's service. There were times when it seemed they were almost enjoying themselves, and yet I know it was a strange experience for them. To be honest, I found it strange myself. And yet it seemed the Lord was in our midst. It seemed, once again, that the Spirit was moving.

wait until we're in the car to ask the girls what they thought about tonight's service. "Despite my no-complaining rule, you can be free to express how you felt about church."

I take a moment to reorient myself to this new car, slipping my key into the ignition. I start the car and look every way before I slowly back out. "Just for the record, you were both very good tonight. I was proud to have you with me. So, tell me, what did you think?"

"Well, at first I wasn't so sure," begins Mary. "But I really liked the music. I didn't know Pastor Glenn played the guitar."

"Brother Glenn," I correct her, explaining why we don't call him "pastor" anymore.

"He does seem different," admits Mary. This fills me with relief.

"And Sister Bronte is a really good singer," says Sarah. "Did she used to be in a band or something?"

I kind of laugh as I pull onto the street, again looking both ways, being very careful as I slowly move along, thankful there isn't much traffic at this hour. "I don't know for sure, honey."

The car is quiet for a while, and I wonder if they're as nervous as I am about my driving ability, or rather lack of. "I really want to know what you think of the church," I say as I pick up speed, almost going the limit now.

"I got a little scared when Sister Bronte started saying all that stuff about the devil and the demons and how we were supposed to be able to see them," says Mary.

"Me too," says Sarah.

"But then I just listened, and I thought she kind of made sense."

"And I saw that demon, Mommy," says Sarah suddenly.

"You did?" Now this surprises me.

"Yes! Just like Sister Bronte said, he had big horns and sharp teeth and claws and stuff—kind of like in my dreams. I was really scared. But then we prayed, and he went away." She laughs. "That's because we do have more power, don't we, Mommy?"

"That's right, Sarah. We do. But we have to use that power."

"Do you really think there are demons all around us?" Mary asks as I drive through town. "Like on the street and everywhere?"

"I think so. It's just that we don't see them. Well, not normally anyway."

"Do you think Sister Bronte was right, then?" continues Mary. "That if we are really filled with the Holy Spirit, we will see them for real?"

"I, uh, I guess so."

"I don't know if I want to see them," Sarah says in a small voice. "I mean, not all the time. They kind of scare me."

"I know. They kind of scare me too. But we just need to remember that we have the Lord in us and that he has more power than Satan."

Finally we're home, and I'm relieved to get into the house, where we can turn on lights and focus on more normal things, like taking care of the kitty and the mess on the laundry-room floor. But Mary cleans it up, and Sarah tucks the little black cat back into the doll bed she has donated for the night. Then I tell the girls to get ready for their own beds. And after prayers are said, after I bind all the evil spirits from invading my girls' dreams, and after I tuck them in and kiss them good night, I walk around the house and consider what Bronte said at church tonight.

Her warning that demons are all around us and that we can see them for ourselves if we're truly filled with the Holy Spirit makes me wonder. What if I'm not truly filled? Then isn't it possible that the demons are right here? Right in my house? Possibly within arm's reach? I feel a shiver down my spine as I look around the living room. Only one small table lamp is on. Normally I leave this room dark in the evening since no one usually comes in here. But in my effort to brighten our home after tonight's slightly unsettling service, I turned it on. Yet as I'm standing near the door, just ready to leave, I notice my photo montage on the wall to my left, and I stare at the gaping hole where I removed the photo of my great-grandfather, the one Cynthia felt had an evil spirit. As I look at the familiar photographs, I begin to sense that they too have spirits attached to them, spirits I was previously unable to discern. Perhaps I wasn't as surrendered to the Lord then. Perhaps I was just spiritually dense. But it seems very clear to me now. There is only one thing to do.

One by one I remove these photos from my wall. Then balancing the stack in my arms and wishing I'd thought ahead to get a box since I don't like feeling them so close to me, I carry them out to the garage and set them in a dark corner by the back door. I stand and look at them for a couple of minutes, unsure as to whether I've made the right move or not.

I have mixed feelings, partly because I worked so hard matting and framing them and arranging them on the wall but also because I was so spiritually blind before. Why didn't I see what I was bringing into our home? The sins of the past generations in plain black and white, and sepia tones too. And here I was hanging them right on the living-room wall because I thought they looked attractive. And I took pride in my work. I took pride in hanging demons on our wall where they could influence all the members of my family!

The more I consider my spiritual stupidity, the more convinced I become that not long after hanging those photos, our family's spiritual problems got noticeably worse. Rick started working nights (for the money, he said), and as a result he began attending church less and less. And then instead of going to college as planned, Matthew took a job at a bookstore that, along with other things, sells books about witchcraft and Eastern religions and all sorts of evil philosophies. And not long after that, he began to rebel against the church as well as our family's values by starting to drink.

"O Lord," I say, still standing in the chilly garage. "This is my fault. I have brought these evil spirits into our home. Please forgive me and show me how to cleanse us from these demons, how to deliver us from this evil influence."

Just then I hear a scratching noise and know without the slightest doubt it is a demon. I can actually feel its icy breath down my neck, and I have a feeling that if I looked hard enough, I could see it. But instead of standing my ground, instead of waging spiritual warfare, I run into the house, and after locking the door behind me, I lean my back against it as my heart pounds like a jackhammer.

I don't know how long I stand there, too frightened to pray, too paralyzed by fear to move, a loud ringing in my ears. But as I feel the door pushing against me, I know that it's all over for me, that the demons are stronger, and that I'm helpless. I am a pathetic excuse for a soldier. The demons have won!

"Mom?" Matthew pushes the door fully open. "What's going on?"

"Oh!" I jump out of the way, allowing my son in. "I'm so glad you're home." I'm about to give him a hug when I smell that unbearable stench again. "You've been drinking!"

"Just one beer, Mom, and I didn't even finish it." He holds his hands up in defense.

"Matthew!"

"I swear. I didn't even want it. Honest, I only had it because the guys made me."

"They made you?" I am glaring at him now, almost as if he is the enemy. Sure, I realize he's not a demon, but at the same time, I wonder how much control the demons have over him, particularly when he's been drinking.

"Seriously, it was Jason's twenty-first birthday, and as a joke someone brought him a six-pack. And after the store closed, he invited us to sit out in the bed of his pickup and have a drink. He's kind of my boss, Mom. I couldn't exactly say no."

"I don't care if it's only one beer or even one sip, Matthew Jackson. You are underage, and it's against the law, and, more important, it's against the rules of this house. And if you refuse to obey those rules, you will have to find another place to live. Do you understand me?"

He looks shocked and slightly hurt. "Are you telling me to move out?"

"If you're going to keep on drinking, I am. I cannot have you coming home drunk, Matthew. I have a responsibility to protect your sisters—"

"You think I would hurt them, Mom?" He looks angry now.

"I think that a drunk might do anything. You're opening the door for Satan and all his demons by drinking. For all I know you're doing drugs too. They say alcohol is the gateway to drugs! And drugs are the open door to demons!"

"Mom!" He stares at me in disbelief. "I don't even know you anymore."

"You and me both, buddy!" I snap back at him as he throws the strap of his backpack over a shoulder and storms off to his room.

Fine. I may be a failure at spiritual warfare, but I sure know how to fight with my son! Still, this doesn't comfort me. Not at all. I only feel a deeper sense of despair. It seems I can't do anything right. How can I possibly oversee the children's ministries at our new church when I can't even manage my own family? I not only feel like a failure but a fraud. Maybe I'm demonized right now. Maybe I'm the wolf in sheep's clothing, pretending to be so spiritual when I am nothing but a fake and a hypocrite.

I sink down in front of the family-room sofa and begin to pray. I pray to escape the fiery darts of my enemy, but at the same time I really just want to escape myself. I must be my own worst enemy. How can I possibly survive me?

18

Somehow I pretend to be normal during the next few days. And yet I feel as if I'm walking around in a stupor sometimes…as if I'm not even real. I don't know how to describe it exactly, but it frightens me. I fear that my spirit is infected and that it's making me sick. I know I'm housing demons. And I know I must do something about it, but I feel so helpless. Finally, on Saturday, after I told Rick I was having bad cramps and needed to rest, he decided to take the girls on an outing.

Had I known from the onset that this outing was to get pumpkins at a nearby farm, I might've made a quick recovery from my cramps and protested. As it was, I felt too weary to fight back. I had already stated several weeks ago that I wanted no signs of Halloween in this house, that it was Satan's holiday and not something that needed to be gloried in. But once again I was outvoted, and right now they are off slogging through the mud in search of pumpkins.

It's bad enough that we still have that cat in the house. Rick fell for it right away, declaring that we needed a cat since he'd been having trouble with mice in the garage. So the very next day, despite the fact that I posted Found Cat signs throughout the neighborhood, Rick went out and got a cat box, a giant bag of litter, food, and even a flea collar. The little black beast is still sleeping in Sarah's doll bed, but I'm afraid I'll have to put my foot down about that. My dad made that doll bed for Sarah not long before he passed away. It seems wrong to allow it to be defiled by a cat. A cat that may very well be full of diseases. Especially if, like my family claims, it's a stray or the offspring of some feral cat. And vet bills aren't cheap.

I tried to put my foot down on naming this cat, but once again I was powerless. Why should that surprise me?

"She's been here four days," Rick announced just this morning as he cuddled the black kitten with Sarah and Mary looking on. "And it doesn't look like anyone is claiming her. Therefore, I'm going to name our cat. Since she arrived the week of Halloween, I'm calling her Spooky."

"Spooky!" said Mary. "That's perfect, Dad."

"Hey, Spook," Sarah cooed as she scratched the kitten's head. "Welcome to the family."

How can they be doing this to me? How can my own daughters, the ones who did spiritual warfare at church with me just a few days ago, now turn on me like this? Can't they see that they're being sucked in? Don't they know that their father has no spiritual sense about these things? Of course, I have to admit, at least to myself, that I'm no better. The way I see it, we're all headed for serious trouble. Satan is getting the upper hand in this family, and I'm a big part of the problem.

After everyone's gone and I finally have the house to myself, I take some action. First I put on a pair of heavy rubber gloves, the kind I use for cleaning toilets. Then I put the pile of framed photos, the ones I set out in the garage the other night, into the garbage can. I go through the house looking for other items, anything that has connections with ancestors, anything that might be bringing this evil curse upon us. I pray as I go, asking the Lord's Spirit to guide me.

I remove a number of foreign trinkets that my mother brought us from some of her trips abroad. I bag up a pair of black candlesticks that have been in Rick's family. I don't know their origin, but they simply feel evil to me—like something that might've been used in an occult ritual. I find lots of things, some that were gifts from questionable people. Like the stuffed unicorn Lynette gave Mary for her last birthday. I'd always felt that was spiritually wrong.

So far I have avoided Matthew's room. The door is closed, and he will have a fit if I go in there. But this is my house, and I'm the one doing the cleansing. To leave one room undone will defile everything. So I open the door and go in. I can feel a spirit of darkness in here, and it doesn't take long before I discover the source. Since he started working at the bookstore, he has started collecting more books and CDs, and I am appalled at what I find, not hidden, but lying around for anyone to see. I carefully pick up the evil-looking CDs and horror novels. I bag them up and take these things along with everything else out to the garbage can. It takes several trips.

Fortunately, the can was emptied on Thursday, so it has a fair amount of room today. But by the time I'm finished with this spiritual cleansing, it is three-fourths full. I find an old, nearly empty fertilizer bag and press it onto the top of the can to cover the contents in case anyone decides to snoop. I use a piece of lumber to pack down the contents in the can. Some of the items break as I pound against the bag with the heavy piece of wood. And I get a strong sense of relief with these crunching noises, as if I am breaking through the bondage of the evil past, breaking free from the ancestral curse. I also feel a twinge of guilt, but then I remind myself that most of the things were from my family, and nothing is terribly valuable. Not that one can compare earthly values to what these things can cost us in a spiritual sense.

They were only odds and ends. I peel off the sweaty rubber gloves and lay them on top of the fertilizer bag. The "antiques" were simply things I scavenged from my mother over the years. Things no one else wanted. Now I can see why. Oh, I know that some of the items buried in that pile of garbage were from Rick's side of the family, but they were holding deep, dark secrets, not to mention demons and curses. I can't dwell on all that now. I should simply rejoice that I have finally purged our home of evil. I close the garage door, locking it. Now if only the garbage pickup was tomorrow. But tomorrow is Sunday.

I am spiritually exhausted as I return to my room. My plan is to finish my cleansing by praying for our entire house, every square foot, perhaps even anointing the walls with oil, as Cynthia once suggested. But I am so worn out that I fall asleep.

Before I know it, Rick and the girls are back with their pumpkins. I get up and tell them that I'm still not feeling well and that I'm going to lie down, but it is simply my escape from them as they go against me by making plans to carve jack-o'-lanterns from the pumpkins they brought home. All three of them, as well as the pumpkins, are dirty and messy, and I can't bear that they are standing in my kitchen. Rick is already gathering knives, and the image of them standing there like that makes me think of satanic sacrifices, and I am forced to look away.

"Why don't you carve the pumpkins on the deck," I say over my shoulder. "It'll be easier to clean up."

"Okay."

"And when you're done, put those muddy clothes in the washing machine to soak." I head back to my room and close the door again. As I hit my knees, I realize that my earlier sense of deliverance, the spiritual elation that came with the removal of the contaminated items, has left me. I feel flat and empty and just as frustrated and frightened as before. Perhaps even more. Why is this not working?

While I made some baby steps today, I am in serious need of personal deliverance. There's no denying that I am a huge part of this problem. Perhaps I am the entire problem. I think I have purged our home, but I'm still here, and I'm still housing evil. My fingers are shaking as I dial Cynthia's phone number. And though I thoroughly expect condemnation from her and certainly the loss of my so-far-unfulfilled position as director of children's ministry, I cannot help but confess just about everything to her. To my surprise, simply saying these horrible things aloud actually makes me feel a tiny bit better. Although I am also embarrassed. It's humiliating to let others see your messes, your weaknesses. "So it seems that I am demonized," I finally tell her.

"I'm not the least bit surprised," she finally says when I'm done.

"You suspected that?" I ask weakly.

"Remember when we prayed for you at Bible study? I felt that was just the beginning."

"Then why would you ask me to help with the children's ministry?"

"Just because you are under attack doesn't make you evil, Ruth."

"I feel evil."

"Don't you know that all of us in leadership positions are highly subject to satanic attack? Think about it. If the devil can knock out a leader, he hurts more than just one. He hurts all who are beneath him."

"So what do you do, Cynthia? How do you fight back?"

"I do constant spiritual warfare, Ruth. Don't you?"

"I try…"

"Well, don't feel bad. It's only natural that you've been under such an attack."

"Really?" I feel a faint wave of hope.

"Yes. The problem is that you've isolated yourself for too long. You've kept these things to yourself. You need to be honest, to tell your brothers and sisters when you're in need so we can pray for you, for deliverance."

"Yes!" I sigh deeply. "That's what I need."

"Do you want some of us to come over and pray for you right now?"

I glance around my bedroom, my refuge. "No," I say quickly. "My family is home, and it's not—"

"Why don't you come over here then?" She sort of laughs. "It's only me, you know."

"You don't mind?"

"Not at all."

"Okay. I'll be right over."

Rick and the girls are still outside. It seems that pumpkin carving is quite an ordeal. And it irks me that they really seem to be enjoying themselves. But I suppose I should be thankful for this distraction, and at least it's not terribly cold outside, although it's starting to get dusky. I write a quick note, saying I have an unexpected church meeting, and then hurry out to the car.

I feel like a criminal as I quietly back the car out and zip away. "I am a grownup. I can come and go as I please." But even as I hear these words from my own lips, I don't believe them. Beneath the sound of my voice, my mind is saying, *I am a fraud, a fraud, a fraud, afraid, afraid, afraid…*

And I am clothed in guilt and fear as I walk up to Cynthia's little house and knock at her door.

"Bronte is on her way over." Cynthia lets me in. "She's living with Glenn and Kellie, you know."

"I didn't know..." I glance around Cynthia's sparse living room, and the barrenness of her walls reminds me of my own house. So I tell her of my recent purging, of how I am attempting to remove all traces of evil from my life.

She nods. "Yes. That's wise. I am constantly amazed at where dark spirits can pop up. Why, I was sitting here reading a library book one day, and suddenly I knew in my spirit that the book, although a good Christian book, had been defiled. I'm not sure if this was a result of the last person who had read it, or perhaps the book had brushed up against some satanic book while waiting to be reshelved in the Christian section."

"Did you throw it away?"

She almost smiles. "I nearly did, but I didn't want to be stuck with a fine. I live on a fixed income, you know. So I just wrapped it in a plastic bag, stuck it on my back porch, and returned it the next day."

Soon Bronte arrives, and the two women prepare to pray for me.

"I really appreciate this," I say nervously as I sit in the kitchen chair that Cynthia places before me.

"First of all, you need to tell us some things," says Bronte. "It might not be easy, Ruth, but you have to be honest. Otherwise, it won't work. Do you understand?"

I nod.

"Close your eyes and relax," she tells me in a soothing voice as she places her hand on my shoulder. Cynthia puts a hand on my other shoulder. "Breathe deeply…just relax…allow the Holy Spirit to wash over you…"

I sit and do as she says, breathing deeply, trying to relax.

"Now tell me, Ruth, is it true that you were sexually abused as a child?"

My eyes pop open, and I stare at her. *What?*

"Close your eyes, Ruth. Relax and be honest, or this won't work."

I close my eyes, but I am certainly not relaxed. Sexually abused? Where did she come up with that?

I hear her taking in a deep breath, then slowly exhaling. "I sense in my spirit that you have been sexually abused. And I'm very sensitive to this…because I too was molested…by my father…so I understand. You can trust me. I know that you were victimized by your father. Don't say anything. Just be quiet and think about what I'm saying." And then she goes into a very detailed description of a small girl being molested by her father. I feel repulsed and almost physically ill as I listen to the horrifying story. I want her to stop talking, but she keeps telling me to stay quiet and to just listen.

"Do you remember this?" she finally asks me. "Keep your eyes closed and allow the Spirit to guide you. Some memories get so repressed that we can only remember them in the Spirit. Is this familiar to you?"

"No."

"You're resisting the Spirit, Ruth. Don't be so quick to say no. Take a deep breath, and listen to me…let your spirit listen to me…don't resist the truth…it will set you free."

So I listen again as she goes into even more detail, and I'm shocked that she actually seems to be describing my bedroom. "Pastel blue walls…white eyelet curtains…"

"Yes," I admit, "that sounds like my room as a child. But everything else…everything else is wrong."

"You need to go back to that room, Ruth. You need to be that little girl again…you need to feel…," and she continues elaborating on her horrible tale. Her words seem to press into me, almost as if she really does know something that I've repressed and forgotten, almost as if the Lord really is revealing a deep horrible memory to her—something I have buried deep.

I leap up from the chair, holding my hand over my mouth. "I'm going to be sick." I dash toward the little hallway where I hope a bathroom is handy. Cynthia is by my side, helping me to find the toilet, where I throw up—again and again. As I'm throwing up, I can hear Bronte and Cynthia praying loudly, in the Spirit, and I can feel their hands on my back.

"Be gone, you filthy spirit!" yells Cynthia. "Out of her, you disgusting vile creature!"

"Let this woman be!" Bronte speaks with authority. "Spirit of lust and lies and condemnation, depart from her at once."

The whole thing takes less than an hour. And when they are done, I feel so weak and empty that I don't know if my legs can support me. I don't think I can even walk from the bathroom to the living room. The two women support me on both sides, helping me to the couch, where I lie down and close my eyes.

19

What the devil is going on?" Rick demands the moment I walk into the house. It's nearly midnight, and he's probably been worried.

"Sorry." I set my purse on the hall tree, then slowly remove my coat.

"Sorry?" He frowns at me. "That's all you have to say? Sorry?"

"Sorry I worried you."

"Where have you been?"

"At a meeting."

"I drove by that so-called church of yours," he tells me in a cold tone. "No one was there, Ruth."

"The meeting was at Cynthia's."

"And it lasted this late?"

"It was a prayer meeting." I walk toward the bedroom.

"You told me you weren't feeling too good earlier today." He stays right on my heels as he follows me into our bedroom. "So I take the girls and give you some time to rest, and then you run off to some stupid prayer meeting that lasts until midnight? What's going on with you, Ruth?"

"I didn't feel well earlier. But they prayed for me, and now I feel better. Just tired." I sit on the edge of the bed, slowly removing my shoes.

"You're always tired."

I know what he means by this—that I'm always tired in the bedroom. But the truth is, I really am right now, and I want to change the subject. "Did Matthew get home?"

"Yeah, that's another thing, Ruth. He called from Jason's apartment. He said that you told him to move out and that he's going to stay at Jason's place now, that he'll pick up his stuff tomorrow." Rick bends over, putting his face in front of mine, studying me so closely that it feels like he's trying to see into my head. And maybe he is. "You told our son to *move out*?"

"I told him he couldn't live here if he was going to keep drinking and disobeying our rules."

"How's this going to help him? He moves out and spends all his money on rent, and probably booze, so he'll never save up enough for college. What kind of life do you want him to have, Ruth? He's our son, for Pete's sake!"

"Yes, he is our son. But he isn't living for the Lord right now. He's fallen away from everything we've taught him. He's rebelling. We can't have that kind of influence around the girls." I'm glaring at my husband now. "The apple doesn't fall far from the tree, does it, Rick?"

He swears and then turns and leaves the room. I'm glad he's gone. I hope he falls asleep in front of the television, the way he does so many nights. I wonder how what we have can even be considered a marriage. I put on my pajamas and get into bed and turn out the light. But the darkness feels heavy, oppressive. And I know that despite my earlier purging of the house, despite tonight's purging of my spirit, the demons are still here.

I remember Cynthia saying how we must always do warfare, so I turn the light on, get down on my knees, and begin to pray. But

I keep my eyes open this time. I remember Bronte's promise that we will be able to see and to hear these spirits if we are really filled with the Lord's Spirit. And as I kneel by the bed, staring at Rick's side of the room, at the chair where he lays his clothes at night, where his brown uniform is lying right now, I see it! I see a demon crouching beside the chair, clinging to that brown uniform and smirking at me.

At first I am too frightened to pray. My mouth is dry as paper, and my hands are shaking. But I have to deal with this. I have to bind this demon and cast him out of this room.

"In the name of Jesus, depart," I say in a trembling voice. Then I say it again with more confidence. Again and again I repeat these six words, and I can feel the power in them, and finally the demon is gone. But just to be safe, I pick up Rick's clothes and tiptoe out to the laundry room and drop them into the dirty clothesbasket.

I can hear the television in the family room as I slip back through the kitchen. It's one of those violent action movies Rick is so fond of, the kind I abhor and refuse to allow the girls to watch. Although Rick has taught Matthew to love this kind of movie, which probably explains a lot.

As I tiptoe to the bedroom, it occurs to me that, of course, the television shouldn't be in this house. If anything is full of evil and demonic influence, surely it's television. And that's when I decide that it too must go. But not while Rick is around. He will throw a fit. But maybe someday he'll understand. Maybe the Lord will show him that I'm only doing what Rick has failed to do. I am protecting this family!

The next morning I wake up to find that Rick's side of the bed hasn't been slept in. Suspecting that he's asleep in his recliner, I go out to see if my hunch is right but am surprised to find him in the kitchen, actually fixing breakfast. He has sausage cooking and is cracking eggs into a bowl.

Of course, this only makes me feel guilty. First of all for worrying him last night, then for treating him so badly, and finally for making him do my work. Why am I so useless?

"The girls are getting ready for church." He glances at the kitchen clock above the stove.

"Good," I say, still feeling guilty.

"There's coffee." He nods over to the coffee maker.

I pour myself a cup. "Sorry about last night. I should've called."

"Yeah." He nods. "You should've."

"Sorry…"

"Well, if it makes you feel any better, I don't completely blame you for what's happening. I think it's partly due to those religious weirdos you've been hanging out with. They go too far, Ruth, and they take you with them."

I don't respond to this. How can I expect him to understand?

"And that's why we're going to church at VBF today."

Now I turn and glare at him. "I'm not going to church at VBF."

"Well, I am. And so are the girls. I already told them, and they were happy about it."

"They like our new church."

"No, Ruth, they think it's a freak show. And sure, kids tend to like freak shows. But not on a regular basis. No, we're going to VBF today. It's settled."

"It might be settled for you, but it's not for me." I march off to the girls' room. "Are you girls going to church with me this morning?" I ask brightly.

"Uh, Dad said we were going back to VBF." Mary sets down her hairbrush, looking uncomfortable.

"Not exactly," I say in a calm voice. "I'm still going to the new church, and anyone who wants to come with me is welcome." I glance over at Sarah, who is tugging on a stubborn pair of tights.

"Where were you last night, Mommy?" she asks as I go over and help her to straighten out the legs.

"I was at a meeting. Sister Bronte was there."

"Sister Bronte?" Sarah brightens. "Did she sing?"

"No. But she'll be singing at church today. It's going to be a special service." I know for a fact this is true. Cynthia told me that the name of our church is to be made known today.

So it is that our family is divided this morning. But I think I can see a little bit of regret in Mary's eyes as she watches Sarah and me getting into the new car and heading off to the new church. She'll come with us on Wednesday when her dad is at work and unable to negatively influence her. Rick might've won this battle, but he is not going to win this war.

I'm surprised that even more chairs are filled in church today, one more row than we had on Wednesday night. I know we had some radio ads this week, but I'm still amazed that we're growing so quickly. Sarah and I find seats near the front, next to Cynthia. She quietly explains that most of the new faces are from the Assembly church on Parker Drive.

"Did you hear they just went through a big church split?" she whispers. "Good timing, don't you think?"

I nod, then look toward the front as the music starts, and soon we are all on our feet, singing and clapping. Sarah is smiling and swaying to the music, and I'm so glad she came. By next Sunday both girls will be here. I can't imagine Rick getting up early every Sunday. Not even to spite me. He's too lazy.

After the worship time, Sister Bronte steps forward and lifts her hands. "The Lord has shown me that his Spirit is going to come upon us like a new fire. Everyone in our congregation must pass through the flames. Just as gold is put through the inferno to remove imperfections, we will be burned with new fire to remove the evil in our lives. And through us, this same fire will purge this entire town and everyone in it like a wildfire roaring down the streets, destroying evil until only the good remains. With heated flames the Spirit will cleanse. Like a new fire." Sister Bronte's arms fall to her sides, and she sighs as if exhausted—and the room is silent.

Now Brother Glenn steps up beside her. "Sister Bronte's prophecy is from the Lord," he declares as she steps down and takes a seat. "And from this prophecy, straight from the Lord's heart, we have decided upon the name of our church." He points to where a sheet is hanging over what appears to be a large board. Brother Carl is standing off to one side.

"Go ahead," says Brother Glenn. And Carl pulls off the sheet to reveal a sign. "New Fire," proclaims Brother Glenn. "The name of this church is New Fire." Then he holds his Bible like a torch and says, "Jesus' followers waited in the upper room for his Holy Spirit." He sets down the Bible and leans forward on the podium, looking out over the congregation intently. "And the Spirit blasted through that upper room," he says in a loud voice. "Like a wildfire the Spirit roared through their midst! And power came upon all who were present. Power unlike anything they'd ever seen before. And they spoke in tongues and drove out demons, and lives were changed—drastically changed. And why"—he shakes his fist in the air—"why, I ask you, should it be any different for us?"

Several "amens" ring out. And Brother Glenn continues to preach. "We live in evil times, brothers and sisters, where every form of filth and sin abounds. You can find it on the Internet, you can hear it on the airwaves, you can see it on your televisions. Our country, our culture, has been invaded by a flood of filth and smut, and that's what the demons dine on: filth and smut and sin. And, believe me, brothers and sisters, there is plenty to go around. And just like rats in a filthy city, the demons are reproducing rapidly. Where there was one yesterday, there are ten today! But the Lord is going to unleash his Spirit, like a wildfire, and he is going to burn this place clean. Beginning right here." He thumps his own chest. "Yes, that's where it starts, isn't it? Within your own heart, within your own corrupt soul. So I invite all of you to come forward right now. Come forward and ask the Lord to burn his Spirit like a new fire right through your soul. Ask him to purge your filth with his holy flames. As the music plays, come up here and let us pray for you now."

Cynthia nudges me. "Do you feel ready to pray with people, Ruth?"

"You want me to actually pray for them?"

She nods. "You are part of the church staff."

I glance at Sarah, who looks a little frightened. "They need me to pray with people. Can you wait for me?"

She nods, but I can tell she's uncomfortable.

"Come on, Ruth," urges Cynthia. "People need prayer."

So I give Sarah a quick, nervous smile and then follow Cynthia up to the front. I am relieved to find that she wants me to partner with her. So I try to imitate her as she prays, and I even come up with a few things on my own. Rather, the Lord inspires me, and together we pray, casting out demons and binding Satan's power, and we unleash the Spirit to burn with holy fire…new fire.

Finally prayer time ends, but I don't see Sarah anywhere. I check the rest room and the back office, but she seems to have vanished into thin air. My heart pounds with fear as I assume a mother's worst nightmare—my child, my precious eight-year-old has been abducted! I run across the room to where Cynthia is standing by the door, saying good-bye to some of the stragglers.

"I've lost Sarah! I can't find her anywhere."

We quickly rally a search party, some heading out back, some out to the parking lot in front, but she is nowhere to be found. I feel like my heart is breaking, like I'm going to die right here in the parking lot. How could I have lost my baby?

"Let's pray." Cynthia grabs my hands. "The Lord can show us where Sarah is." Although I want to continue searching, I bow my head.

"Mommy!" calls that familiar sweet voice, ringing like music on the air.

"Sarah!" I release Cynthia's hands and run toward my daughter. A shaggy-haired guy in a camouflage coat is walking next to her, and I'm thinking he must be part of the search party although I don't remember him. I wrap my arms around my baby girl, pulling her tightly to me.

"Thank you!" I finally say to the young man. "Thank you for finding my girl!"

"He didn't find me, Mommy." Sarah grins at this stranger. "I wasn't lost."

"Then where were you?"

"Brother Ben took me to get a treat." She holds up a brown and yellow box of Milk Duds, her favorite. "We went to the grocery store while everyone was praying."

"You what?"

"It was my idea," admits *Brother* Ben. "I didn't have any breakfast, and my stomach was starting to growl. Sarah was sitting all by herself, so I asked her if she wanted to come."

"Well, you should've asked me," I say in a controlled voice. I actually want to scream at this young idiot. What on earth does he think he's doing, taking someone's little girl off like that? But by now the rest of the search party is gathering around us. And soon Brother Ben, the hero of the moment, is being praised for finding my lost child.

"We need to go," I tell them, still holding tightly to Sarah's little hand as I lead her to the car.

We reach the car. "Ouch, Mommy. You're squeezing my fingers."

I release her hand and unlock the car and open the door for her. But first I turn and look into her eyes. "Don't ever do that again, Sarah Jane."

"What?" She climbs into the passenger seat.

"Don't ever go off with a stranger like that again!" I slam the door shut and stomp around to the other side. I am so angry at her. I can't believe that Sarah would do something like this. She knows better! I get in, buckle my seat belt, and start the car. I hear a sniffling sound next to me, and when I turn to look, she's sitting there with tears rolling down both pink cheeks. "Why are you crying?"

"Because you're mad at me."

"I was really, really worried, Sarah. And you know better than to go off with a stranger. We've talked about that before."

"Brother Ben wasn't a stranger. He was at church, Mommy. And he introduced himself and told me I was pretty. And you were busy."

"Just because someone tells you his name and acts nice doesn't mean you should trust him or go someplace with him. You know that you never go anyplace with anyone unless Daddy or I give you permission."

"But you said we're all brothers and sisters at church. I thought Brother Ben was like Matthew. And it would be okay for me to go to the store with Matthew."

Maybe back in the old days when Matthew could be trusted. "Not without our permission. Even with your own brother, you need to ask me first. Do you understand?"

She nods but doesn't say anything.

"Answer me. Do you understand?"

"Yes, Mommy."

I put the car into reverse, and as I back up, I notice Carl and another man carrying the sign out to the front of the church: New Fire. I know I should be happy to see it, but at the moment I feel slightly burned.

20

Today is Halloween, and despite my sermon to the girls that it's just another day, they seem wound up as I drive them to school. I was surprised to learn they're having a Halloween party this afternoon. Things are quickly changing at this so-called Christian school. Fortunately, it doesn't involve costumes, a relief since my girls aren't getting any this year.

"Have a good day," I say with no enthusiasm as I drop them by the front door. They happily wave and run inside. As I pull out, I hear a horn honk. I jump, thinking I'm about to hit someone or be hit. But then I see Colleen's SUV and her hand waving out the window, as if she wants me to come over and join her. So I park next to her, get out, and ask how she's doing.

"I am totally exhausted," she says, letting out a big sigh. "But we're packed and ready to go. We leave tomorrow morning, crack of dawn."

"I'm surprised you brought the boys in today."

"They wouldn't accept no for an answer. The big Halloween party, you know."

"Right."

"So what are you and the girls doing for Halloween tonight?" she asks.

"Nothing. Halloween is an evil holiday."

"It's what you make of it. If you get all wigged out and think it's evil, well, then it is evil. But if you can lighten up and just have fun, why not?"

"So are you taking the twins trick-or-treating?"

"No. Dennis said to forget it. He calls it legalized begging."

"Smart man."

"Hey, why don't you bring the girls over to our place?" she says suddenly. "I mean, it's a mess of boxes and stuff, but I've got tons of trick-or-treat candy. Dennis will probably be working on his computer all night, trying to get stuff squared away with his new job. But we can let the kids watch a DVD, and you and I can have one last night of hanging out together."

"I don't—"

"Please, Ruthie. Just this one last night?"

I smile at my old friend. "You know, that actually sounds kind of fun. And I'm sure the girls will be thrilled."

She hugs me. "All right, it's a date. We'll send out for pizza."

"How about if I bring a salad?"

She laughs. "Sure, if you insist on nutrition. Let's make it six. With the time change it'll be getting dark by then, and I'll bet the little goblins will be out early."

As it turns out, she was right. The little goblins are already hitting the streets, and it's not even five. And despite having the porch light off and the car in the garage, the trick-or-treaters keep coming.

"We're not here," I tell the girls. "Stay away from the door."

"I just wanna see," pleads Mary.

"No. And if you want to go to Colleen's tonight, you'll mind me." I hand her a carrot. "Peel this." Then Sadie, who has been sent outside because of the cat, begins to bark, probably at one of the obnoxious goblins ringing our doorbell. "Tell Sadie to be quiet," I yell at Sarah. "Give her a Milk-Bone or something." So Sarah goes out and quiets the dog. Then we finish making the salad. And even though it's only five thirty, I tell the girls it's time to go.

"We'll drive around a little," I say quietly as we sneak through the garage to get into our car and make a stealthy exit. I drive around the neighborhood for a while, allowing the girls to watch the various trick-or-treaters dashing around in the dusky light. I know they're just kids, but it looks kind of creepy, and sometimes I think maybe I'm seeing actual demons out there masquerading right along with the trick-or-treaters. And why not? This is one of the most evil nights of the year. Of course the demons would be out there too.

"It's starting to rain," Sarah says sadly. "It'll probably ruin their costumes." I turn on the wipers and hope that this sudden downpour will dampen their Halloween fun, sending these wild children home, safe and sound, where they should be. Finally we make it over to Colleen's, and I feel grateful to be inside her friendly and well-lit house. We eat, and then the girls and the twins play hide-and-seek among the boxes until they finally calm down and plant themselves in front of the big-screen television, the only piece of furniture still remaining in the family room. Not that they seem to mind as they roll around on the rug, acting like wild things themselves.

"Too much sugar," I say as Colleen and I sit at the island in her kitchen. "They'll probably never go to sleep tonight."

"Fine with me." She refills my cup with decaf. "I'd like the boys to be all worn out on the road tomorrow. The more they sleep, the happier I'll be."

"Your boys are lively," I admit, which is an understatement since they've both been diagnosed as hyperactive, although Colleen and Dennis refuse to put them on Ritalin.

"Speaking of boys, what's Matthew up to these days? Still working at the bookstore?"

So I tell her the latest about Matthew, about how he'd started getting rebellious and drinking and how he recently decided to move in with Jason. I don't mention my ultimatum; somehow I don't think she would understand that. I also don't tell how I purged his room of his sinful books and CDs a few days ago. As far as I know, he hasn't even discovered this yet himself. Maybe he'll assume those items were lost during his hasty packing yesterday.

"We were rebels too, Ruth. Don't forget about our wild days."

"I know. And it's Matthew's choice to move out. Maybe it's for the best."

"Maybe…" She frowns. "There's something I want to tell you… before we leave… It's about your new church." Then before I can stop her, she begins to slander Brother Glenn, claiming that he is still having an affair.

"How can you say that?"

"It seems to be common knowledge."

"You mean evil gossip."

"I just thought you should know."

I'm trying not to get mad, reminding myself that Colleen will be gone tomorrow. Why make a scene? I'm literally biting my tongue to keep from reacting.

"I've heard that the woman Glenn's involved with is part of your new church, Ruth."

"Please!" I stand now. "I think it's time to go."

"I'm sorry. I just couldn't leave without warning you."

"Thank you very much," I say crisply. I call the girls and tell them we're leaving. Naturally, they protest, but I firmly remind them it's a school night.

"We'll be praying for you," Sarah tells Colleen after everyone has hugged and said good-bye.

I smooth Sarah's mussed-up hair and nod. "That's right. We will."

Colleen looks directly at me. "And we'll be praying for you too."

I try not to think about Colleen's slanderous words as I focus on driving. It's dark and rainy, and the night feels evil. I'm just starting to relax as we get close to home, but that's when I notice something fairly large lying on the side of the road. First I think it's a deer. Then I think it might be a child in some kind of animal costume. Fearing that a neighborhood child has been hit by a car, I screech to a stop.

"What's wrong, Mom?" asks Mary.

"I don't know. I think a trick-or-treater's been hurt!" I jump out of the car and run over to the damp, furry body. I bend down and see that it's not a child at all. It's a dog. It's our beautiful golden retriever, Sadie, and she's not moving.

I fall to my knees on the wet pavement. Scooping the upper half of the lifeless animal into my arms, I burst into tears. Seconds later Sarah and Mary are beside me, and although I can only sob into the soggy fur, both girls are fully aware of what has happened. And illuminated by my headlights, the three of us cluster together on the edge of the shiny wet street, holding on to each other and on to the cold, damp creature that only hours ago was bursting with life.

Finally I realize that I need to move Sadie and to get my girls safely off this dark street. "Get back in the car, girls."

"What about Sadie?" sobs Sarah. "We can't just leave her here."

"We're not leaving her," I say as I get into the car. "I just want to pull the car into the driveway, and then I'll come back to get her."

I park the car and unlock the house, telling the girls to go inside. "I'll bring Sadie home."

"She's too heavy to carry," says Mary.

"Even Daddy has a hard time lifting her to go to the vet," Sarah reminds me.

"Our red wagon," says Mary. "We can put her in our wagon."

So we go around to the backyard, and we notice the normally locked gate is unlatched and open. "Did you girls leave the gate open?" I ask as we all stand, staring at it.

"I haven't come through this way in a long time," says Mary.

"Me neither," says Sarah.

"Maybe a trick-or-treater played a trick on us?" Mary's voice sounds shaky.

A chill runs through me as I consider the evil forces that are out in number tonight. As we go to find the red wagon, I sense danger. I keep my eyes wide open, preparing myself to go to battle if needed. We war not against flesh and blood but powers and principalities.

I glance over my shoulder as we dump the rainwater out of the girls' wagon, and then the three of us take it back to where Sadie is still lying. Together we lift her, loading her body into the cold metal wagon, and then like a funeral processional, with me pulling the wagon and the two girls walking directly behind, we somberly proceed down the sidewalk to our house. We go through the still-open gate and into the backyard and pull the wagon to a protected area by the back door. I unlock it, and Mary runs inside to get a big beach towel to cover Sadie. We all help to tuck her in. Sarah bends down and kisses her, and Mary follows her little sister's example.

"We love you, Sadie," says Sarah.

"She'll be okay here until tomorrow," I tell the girls. "Then Daddy will take care of her."

We're still crying when we get inside the house. But I tell the girls to go dry off and get ready for bed. I do the same, towel drying my hair and changing into warm polar-fleece sweats, but I still feel chilled underneath. I turn up the heat in the house, and when I go to check on the girls, to tuck them in and to listen to prayers, they are still very upset. We talk some more about Sadie and about why we think this happened. I try to assure them that everything's okay and that although we're sad, we will get over this. But even as I say these things, I don't believe them myself. I feel like such a phony.

"Will you stay here with us, Mommy?" pleads Sarah. "I can feel the demons all around us tonight. I could feel them outside and in our backyard, and I know that they killed our dog and that they want to kill us too."

"We need to keep praying." I get an extra blanket from the closet and lie down on the floor between their two beds. "We are going to do extra-hard warfare tonight. We will not let the demons win."

So the three of us take turns praying until first Sarah and then Mary drift off. Even as I listen to their even breathing and know that they are soundly asleep, I remain on the floor between their beds, still praying, still keeping the Enemy at bay.

21

I wake up cold and achy, wondering where I am and why, and then I remember I'm still in the girls' room—Sadie. With a tight, painful lump in my throat I get up and, wrapping myself in the blanket, go off in search of my own bed. I'm surprised that the lights are off in the house, that it's 2:47 a.m., and that Rick has already come home and gone to bed. Completely oblivious to his family's plight on this blackest of black nights, my husband is contentedly snoring. I know it's unreasonable, not to mention un-Christlike, but I have the strongest urge to beat the living daylights out of him right now. Still, I control myself, standing there next to the bed with fists clenched in rage. I tell myself to just let this go, slip into bed, and continue to travail for the Lord's protection on my seemingly defenseless family. But I cannot do it. I cannot force myself to get into bed and to lie next to that man.

In so many ways he seems a large part of our problem. It's because of him that we are so vulnerable right now. I've heard that when the head of the family slacks off, becoming spiritually lazy in the way that Rick has these past few years, it's as if the family is left wide open. They're left uncovered and unprotected, and Satan is freer than ever to take potshots at them or, as it seems to be in our case, to launch a full-scale demonic attack. It's Rick's fault that our poor Sadie is lying cold and lifeless out in the children's old red wagon. And as I walk out of our bedroom, pausing in front of Matthew's open bedroom door, I think Rick is also to blame for our missing son.

I turn on the light, then go inside Matthew's mostly stripped-down room. I'm still not sure how he got so much stuff out of here while we were at church on Sunday, but I suspect a friend, maybe Jason, must've helped him. I close the door, then sit on the bare mattress of his twin captain's bed, where I place my head in my hands and cry. What is happening to our family? How can we survive this? When will it end?

I don't actually know where Matthew is right now. Oh, I know that Jason has an apartment downtown, and Matthew has probably even mentioned the name of the complex before, but all I can remember is that it's not far from the bookstore. I don't even know Jason's last name or his phone number. For all I know, this Jason person could be a serial killer or a sexual pervert or perhaps even a Satan worshiper, and my son could be in serious danger right now.

I lie down on Matthew's bed and once again begin to pray. Sometimes I wonder how long I will have to pray like this, waging warfare and doing battle. Will it take forever? And what if I get weary or run out of words? What if I forget how to use my prayer language or how to speak at all? What if I should completely give in to the insanity that seems to press against me from every angle, especially on nights like tonight? What if I should lose my mind? Would anyone pray for me? Would Rick?

When I wake up, the sunlight is streaming in through the opened miniblinds, straight into my eyes. It takes me a few seconds before I can see well enough to get my bearings, before I can figure out where I am, as I recognize the faded clipper-ship wallpaper border that I hung in this room back when Matthew was ten and life was good. I still have the fluffy pink blanket from the girls' room wrapped around me, but I'm chilled to the bone.

I go out to see that the thermostat's been turned down, I'm sure by my penny-pinching husband. I turn it up to eighty-three just to spite him. I hope it gets so hot in the master bedroom that he gets up and comes out roaring like a grumpy bear. And then I'll tell him about Sadie and about how he's neglected the spiritual welfare of his family and about how we are going under.

But first I need to get the girls up. It's nearly eight already, and we'll have to move fast if they're to make it to school on time. I feel sorry for them as I gently shake them awake. We had such a late night, and as they sit up in bed, their eyes are still somewhat swollen and red from all the crying over Sadie. Perhaps I should just keep them home with me today.

"Oh, it's late, Mom." Mary pops out of bed and looks at the clock. "Did we forget to set the alarm?"

"Yes. That's my fault."

"We better hurry," Mary tells Sarah. And the next thing I know, they're pulling on their uniforms, not even questioning whether or not it makes sense to go to school. Such good girls.

I have milk in paper cups, bananas, and granola bars all ready to go by the time they come into the kitchen. "Maybe you can eat breakfast on the road." I balance this makeshift meal and usher them out the door. "Just try not to spill in the new car, okay?"

Miraculously, no milk is spilled in the car, and only wrappers and banana peels and empty paper cups are left to be removed after I drop off the girls. Just the same, I stop by a trash barrel in the parking lot so I can get the debris out of my car before it has a chance to leave an odor. I feel incredibly weary as I bend down to pick these things up from the car floor, where I asked the girls to set them. It's as if I'm a hundred years old. How can I go on?

"Hello, Ruth," calls a male voice. I stand up straight and see Ed Chambers walking toward me. I know from my conversation with Colleen last night (could it have been only last night?) that Ed is still *playing* the role of head pastor at VBF until they hire someone else. Since I don't go to church there anymore, there's no need to call him "Pastor Ed," which sounds slightly ridiculous anyway. I'd rather call him "Mr. Ed," which reminds me of that old silly sitcom my girls love to watch on TV Land, the one about the talking horse.

"Hi, Ed."

"How's it going?" he asks as he comes closer.

I consider telling him how it's *really* going. Expounding on how, ever since the church fired Pastor Glenn, it's been really, really hard and how this whole town is undergoing a spiritual attack right now, particularly my own family as a result of my willingness to take up arms and stand against the Lord's enemy. And how my beloved dog died last night, most assuredly as a demonic attack against our family. But most of all I want to ask Ed what he plans to do that will make any of this better. Instead I tell him, "Things are fine, thanks."

"I see you got a new car. Nice."

"Thanks."

"I saw Rick at church last week. Were you sick?"

I consider lying, saying, "Yes, as a matter of fact, I was…," and I'm pretty sure it would be believable, considering how frazzled I must look right now. But why bother? He probably already knows what's up anyway. So I tell him about New Fire and how it's already growing by leaps and bounds. "It's really wonderful. And I'm heading up the children's ministry."

He nods. "Yes, I'd heard something about this new church. Enough to be concerned, Ruth. I don't think it's going to be a healthy church."

Now this just gets me. Who is he to judge what is or is not healthy? I almost lash out at him. But somehow, maybe by the power of the Holy Spirit, I manage to control myself. "I guess that's for the Lord to determine, isn't it?" I say in a calm voice. "It's not for us to judge one another, now is it, Ed?"

He presses his lips together as if carefully weighing his response. "I'd say that's right most of the time, Ruth. Judging usually gets us in trouble. But there are times when you must use sound spiritual discernment. Especially when church leaders twist God's Word for their own purposes and when they use fear tactics to control their congregation and lead good people astray. That's why God gives us discernment, and that's why the Bible says there is wisdom in the counsel of a multitude of—"

"I couldn't agree with you more. That's probably why I feel so at home there." I open the car door. "Now, if you'll excuse me, I have to go bury a dead dog."

He blinks in surprise at this off-the-wall statement. But I just get in my car and drive away. Who cares what he thinks? But I don't want to go home. And I don't want to bury my dead dog either. So I just drive around town and try to do warfare, especially as I drive past the seamier side of town, where the adult bookstore and new strip club are located, but my prayers sound tired and flat, not to mention totally unintimidating. So I finally go home.

When I pull up to the house, Matthew's bike is out front, and Matthew and Rick come out carrying a dresser. That's when I notice that the tailgate on Rick's pickup is open, and inside is Matthew's bed.

I get out of my car. "What are you doing, Matthew?"

"Moving my stuff."

"*Your* stuff?" I put my hand on top of the maple dresser that we got before he was born. It was low enough to double as a changing table, and I used it for the girls as well, but ultimately it ended up back in Matthew's room.

"This is my bed and my dresser." Matthew looks defiantly at me. "Dad said I can take them."

"That's right," Rick says to me.

"But it's—"

"Just let me handle this," Rick says in a warning tone.

"Yeah, right. Just the way you handle everything!" I storm off into the house, which has gotten quite warm in my absence. Naturally, the thermostat's been turned down again. Well, fine!

"Just what is that supposed to mean?" Rick says as he comes in the door.

Matthew doesn't appear to be with him. "It means, why are you making this easy for him? Why are you letting him take all that furniture? I thought you wanted him to come home. We don't even know this Jason person. For all we know—"

"Look, Matthew and I just had a pretty good talk. He said that his rent is only two hundred dollars a month and that by working full-time, he's still able to save a lot. He wants to do this, Ruth. He says it will help him grow up."

I roll my eyes. "You mean it will help him get drunk every night without having his parents on his case."

"There's nothing we can do about that. He's old enough to make his own choices."

"That's right," Matthew says as he comes into the house. I suspect he's been listening by the still-open door. "And speaking of making my own choices, Mom, you don't happen to know where some of my books and CDs have suddenly disappeared to, do you?"

I feel like my back's against the wall right now, like I am facing down the enemy and am outnumbered. Rick and Matthew have joined forces, not only with each other, but probably with the darkness as well.

"I can't take this." I put my hands to my face as if to shield myself from them. "I don't see why you have to move out, Matthew. You're only eighteen, and you—"

"I'm old enough to think for myself!"

This makes me cry. I sink down onto the seat of the hall tree, still holding my hands to my face and sobbing, "I can't take any more. I just can't."

"Is she having some kind of breakdown?" asks Matthew. I can't tell if he's concerned or amused.

"Are you okay, Ruth?" asks Rick.

"She's just being a drama queen," says Matthew. "She always does this. And next she'll go into her fanatic religious routine. Crud, Mom, I know you took my stuff. You probably thought it was evil, the work of the devil. I can just—"

"Stop it!" I stand now, facing them both. "Stop it! Stop it! Stop it!"

"See," he says to Rick, "she's having a breakdown. Better call the psych ward, see if they can get her a bed."

Now I just stare at my unfeeling son with tears streaming down my face. How have I managed to spawn such an evil child?

Rick pats me on the back in a condescending way. "Just take it easy, Ruth."

I turn and glare at him. "You're telling *me* to take it easy? I was the one who was here with the girls last night. The one who found Sadie dead on the road. We had to put her in the little red wagon in the middle of—"

"What?" Rick looks truly stunned. "What are you saying?"

"Is that true, Mom?" I can tell I have Matthew's attention too.

Fresh tears fill my eyes as I remember last night. Then I tell them about how we'd been at Colleen's, how it was pretty late, and how we found her. "It was horrible," I tell them, but they're both walking through the house now, with me following. I know they're on their way to the back door. "The girls and I cried all night. I had to sleep in their room just to comfort…"

Both Matthew and Rick bend down by the red wagon. Rick slowly removes the damp beach towel, its cheerful bright stripes a contrast to the sadness it's covering. I get a small sense of satisfaction when I see their faces, father and son, both stricken by the sorrowful sight of our family dog now deceased. But then I look at poor sweet Sadie, lying there so peacefully, and I completely lose it. I run back into the house, straight for my bedroom, and fall onto the bed in tears.

By the time I wake up, I have just enough time to take a shower before I pick up the girls. Matthew's room is completely empty now, and both he and Rick are gone. Rick probably helped him move his stuff, then continued on to work, maybe in an effort to avoid me, the crazy woman. But as I stand in the kitchen, I notice a fresh mound of dark brown dirt out in a corner of the backyard. And next to it is what appears to be a handmade cross, two sticks tied together with string. Sadie's final resting place.

I sigh, making a mental note to get some flower bulbs on the way home. The girls can plant them there for Sadie. Maybe we can hold a memorial service, just the three of us. I assume that Rick and Matthew have already said their good-byes.

After I pick up the girls, we stop by the hardware store and get tulip, daffodil, and narcissus bulbs, along with a fall chrysanthemum that Mary spots. "It's almost the same color of gold as Sadie," she points out.

Then we go home, change into our grubby clothes, and go outside to plant these things. Finally we gather round with muddy hands as we share our happiest Sadie memories, then say a prayer and sing "Amazing Grace."

"Sadie was like an angel," Sarah says as we walk back to the house. "Like she was here to protect us."

"I know," echoes Mary. "You always felt safe with Sadie around."

"Maybe you should check on your cat," I suggest, hoping to distract them from their grief. Plus I'd noticed this morning that the cat box was getting smelly, and I feel sure the cat needs some food by now. Not that I care much. Something about that cat bothers me. If not for the cat, Sadie would probably still be with us. It was mostly because of the cat taking over the laundry room that Sadie had been put outside. If she'd been safe and sound in the house, like usual, she never would've been hit by a car.

Somehow we go through the normal paces of the evening, but there is a spirit of sadness in the house. A spirit of defeat. And when the girls finish their chores and homework and ask about watching television, there is also a spirit of rebellion.

"No, I don't think that television is a good influence."

At first Mary thinks I'm kidding, but then I assure her I'm serious. "Mom," she protests in that cranky, preadolescent tone, "you're being way too fanatical and fundamental now."

"Fanatical and fundamental?" I echo, curious as to where she's picked up on words like those. "What makes you say that?"

"Katy says that Pastor Glenn was way too fanatical and fundamental. She said that's why he got fired—well, that and some other things. And she said that his new church is really messed up."

"I haven't seen Katy at New Fire," I point out, trying to remain reasonable despite the fact that I'd like to give Katy's cute little red pigtails a good hard pull.

"Well, somehow she knows all about it," continues Mary. "It was embarrassing too."

"Why was it embarrassing?"

"Because she also knew that you go there and that I've gone there too."

"I thought you liked it the one time you were there." I know I'm treading on shaky ground since Mary already has her nose out of joint because I've vetoed television.

"It was weird, Mom."

"I like it there." Sarah takes my hand in hers as if to comfort me.

"Well, so do I." I give Sarah's hand a squeeze.

"Can we watch TV now?" asks Sarah.

I let out a deep sigh. "No, you cannot. But I'm willing to read, if anyone is interested."

Sarah, who loves hearing stories, jumps at my bait, but Mary seems determined to sulk. However, once Sarah and I are seated on the couch and just getting into the good part of a mystery story—I'm actually quite good at voices, and I picked out this book for Mary's sake—I notice that she's standing in the shadows listening. "Why don't you join us?" I say in my friendliest tone.

"Can I make popcorn?" she asks.

"Yes! Definitely make popcorn. We'll wait."

So we make it through our first evening without Sadie and without television. And after the girls are in bed and we've said our prayers, I go back out to the family room and stand in front of that horrid-looking black box that seems not only to intrude but to dominate, and I wonder how best to get rid of it. If I take it out, Rick will throw a fit. But to allow it to remain seems like sin.

Finally I spin the television around on the table where it sits. The solid-looking back seems to be held together with tiny Phillips screws. I go out to the garage and hunt until I find a small Phillips screwdriver that looks like it might work. Then carefully, very carefully, I remove the screws and pull off part of the back. I know this might appear rather sneaky and underhanded to some people, people who don't understand or appreciate the powers of dark spiritual forces, but desperate times call for desperate measures.

So I take a deep breath and unplug the television, so as not to get electrocuted, and then I pull apart some important-looking but well-hidden wires and things. Then I plug the set in again, turn it around, and turn it on, and voilà, nothing happens. A small step for modern technology, perhaps, but a giant step toward spiritual victory for my house. Hopefully Rick won't figure it out.

Suddenly I remember Matthew's suspicions that I took his CDs and books, and I grow worried that Rick might start nosing around, might even decide to look in the trash. Fortunately the garbage beneath the sink is full and needs to go out. Not only that, but that stinking kitty litter has not been cleaned. So first I dump the garbage bag, careful to let the contents spill open so they're splayed all over the inside of the can, and then I pour the stinking kitty litter on top. A person would have to be very determined to muck his way through that nasty mess. With satisfaction, I close the lid, then go back into the house.

The black cat is curled up in the handmade doll bed, but she looks up at me with smug yellow eyes filled with cunning. I know it would seem crazy to some, but I can't help but think it's rather ironic how this animal showed up at our door and things suddenly got worse. Bronte said that Satan and his demons masquerade and parade right in front of us wearing earthly costumes, and not for the first time, I think this "Spooky" cat is really an impostor from the underworld, and the sooner we get rid of the beast, the better off we'll be.

I am so tempted to take this animal outside, back into the darkness it came from. Maybe if I leave the back door open, she'll run away. I look at the content animal and realize this is highly unlikely. She's obviously got it made here. Instead, I refill the litter box and make sure the laundry-room door is securely closed.

If I can't get rid of the beast, at least I can confine it. Now if I can only confine its dark powers as well. As tired as I am, I know I must take a few minutes to pray, placing both hands on the laundry-room door as I bind Satan's power in this small black beast.

As I walk back to my room, it occurs to me that it might not really be the poor cat's fault. It's possible that she too is simply a victim. Perhaps she's just an innocent cat that has been defiled by a demon, simply in need of spiritual deliverance. Not so unlike myself not too long ago.

Still, I don't have the spiritual energy to cast demons out of cats tonight. All I want is to escape the madness of this never-ending spiritual turmoil and the draining battles against my relentless enemies. If only I could just sleep, sleep, sleep.

22

This is the busiest time of year in the shipping business, and Rick's hours have increased to the point where it seems he is barely home at all. I have mixed feelings about this. But as a consequence, he no longer seems overly concerned with things like the nonworking television. He did mention it a couple of times early on, suggesting that I take it in to see if it could be fixed. I told him I would if I could find the time, but I also reminded him that we've had that old television since Matthew was a toddler and it only makes sense that it would finally give out. But more and more Rick comes home so tired that he simply crashes, sometimes on the couch in the family room, sometimes in our bed. And then he sleeps until it's almost time to leave for work again. We resemble the proverbial ships in the night. Maybe it's for the best.

Spooky, the demon kitten, is still with us. I'm not sure if this is spiritual weakness on my part, since I've come to feel sorry for the helpless creature. But I perform daily exorcisms of its demonic inhabitants. Naturally I do this when no one is around because they're all starting to look at me strangely.

At first it only seemed to be Rick and Matthew who questioned my spirituality and then my mental health. But sometimes I feel that Mary is joining forces with them as well. Or perhaps it's just pre-adolescence. Still, it disturbs me that my own family doesn't seem to grasp the stress I'm under as I attempt to offer spiritual protection for their well-being and for my friends at church and finally, and perhaps most important, for the community at large. It is a daunting task.

Our church has held numerous prayer vigils during the past couple of weeks, gathering with signs on the sidewalk in front of places like the abortion clinic, the adult bookstore, the strip club, and the porn shop as we pray for the abolition of these demonic influences and publicly protest their dens of iniquity. We've even made the six o'clock news a few times. Not that this is about fame, well, other than fame in the kingdom of God. No, this is about warfare and diligence. It's about discipline and sacrifice. And it seems to be never ending.

"So how's that job at the church going?" Rick asked me again today shortly before he left for work.

"It's not a top priority right now," I told him, trying to be patient with his inability to understand spiritual things.

"That's what you keep saying, Ruth. But what I think you really mean is that it's not really a job, right?"

"We're building the church right now. It takes time to get people in the right places, doing their parts to make the body of Christ work the way it's supposed to. Children's ministry must come later." This is almost a direct quote from Sister Bronte since I recently asked her when she thought we'd be ready to do something with the children. I felt a little silly even asking, because we have so few children in our church right now. Although I have been bringing my girls somewhat regularly, thanks to Rick's busy work schedule.

It's only his demanding hours and his spiritual laziness in general that have prevented him from kidnapping the girls off to Valley Bridge Fellowship. This is a huge relief, allowing me to focus on my contributions at my church. Plus, I feel the girls are learning to appreciate their roles at New Fire. Other church members know my girls by name now and actually treat them like real partners. We all understand our responsibilities, the need to do our part, to take up arms in this ongoing spiritual battle, and to stay on guard.

Mary has gotten over her anger at the removal of her unicorn. I finally got out the encyclopedia to show her the origins of this mythical animal, explaining how it has pagan connections and how it's truly an affront to the Lord. It took time and several meaningful discussions followed by prayers for deliverance, but I think she understands now.

I think my girls are both growing in the nurture and admonition of the Lord. My goal is for them to be well prepared to face the evils of this world, as well as to defeat our spiritual foes. I want them to understand that Satan is alive and well and that he is crafty in the ways he sends his demons out to conquer and then destroy—sometimes through something as innocent looking as a stuffed unicorn or a coloring book about fairies or a videocassette with a witch in it or even a postcard from Egypt. All such items either have been or are being purged from our home.

Sarah appears to be much more spiritually sensitive than Mary. Perhaps it's because she is learning these truths at a younger age, or perhaps it's simply the way the Lord has designed her. Bronte says that she is highly gifted. Of course, Bronte says the same about Mary, although I'm sure she means more in a musical sense. Bronte has been giving Mary piano lessons for the past two weeks and is encouraging us to buy Mary a small keyboard. Perhaps for Christmas. For now, money is tight. Despite the fact that Rick is working lots of overtime during this busy holiday season, our budget is more stretched than ever. It doesn't help matters that I still owe my mother for the loan. Not that Rick is aware of this. And that's how I plan to keep it.

I know our money concerns might be partly the result of my charitable giving at church, but I also know the Lord desires me to be generous, and Brother Glenn promises that we will be repaid for giving "beyond our earthly limits." As the future director of children's ministries, I've also been stocking up on things. I have several large plastic crates filled with crayons, paper, scissors, glue, felt pens, and all sorts of various school supplies stashed in our attic. Of course, I can't explain any of this to Rick. He is so spiritually blinded right now that he definitely would not get it. But it gives me great satisfaction just knowing those things are up there. Sometimes I go to the attic, open the crates, and just admire the neat and orderly supplies.

But the sad fact is, I'm sure my husband would throw an absolute fit if he knew exactly where our money is going. This must be why the Lord says not to let your left hand know what your right hand is doing when you give your tithes and offerings. So it is that I consider Rick to be the left hand and I, of course, am the right.

I'm fairly certain I will be taking the girls out of Valley Bridge school. I'll admit this decision is partially financial, and I'm expecting the school, despite their policy, to refund the girls' tuition. I think I can make them understand the need to do this since I fear that some of the things the girls are learning at school are in direct conflict with the Bible and our beliefs. I don't know how VBF suddenly became so liberal, but I suspect it is mainly a result of the removal of Glenn Pratt from leadership. Once that good man was no longer ministering there, it seems the whole church went astray. Consequently, the school is no longer the school I thought it was.

I haven't spoken to Rick about any of this yet, but I plan to write a letter to the school this week, clearly stating my reasons for taking the girls out of the school, starting the first of December. My plan is to deliver it the day before Thanksgiving.

The rest of my plan is to begin homeschooling the girls. Three other families in our church, the only other ones with children, are homeschooling their kids, and it seems to be working very well for them. In fact, we've been discussing the possibility of partnering in this. Different mothers would teach different subjects. I've already volunteered for math since no one else particularly cares for it and I've always been fairly good with numbers. But we've all agreed to begin this after New Year's. This gives me the chance to establish some routines and become comfortable with the idea of teaching my girls. I haven't told them of this plan yet. It seems wiser to wait until it's established. No need to have them fretting over these things during their last few days at VBF.

"Aunt Lynette is on the phone," Mary tells me, interrupting me from my regular early-morning prayer time. I promised Sister Bronte I would pray for the church every day from six until seven. Normally, there are no interruptions at this hour, although I do find it a challenge to be up so early. Especially since I often have been up praying through the night before. And I must admit that since giving up coffee after Sister Bronte taught a nutrition class for the women of the church, it is even harder to keep my mind alert. Although I do believe Sister Bronte's research is correct, and she's helped me understand that not only is caffeine extremely bad for us, as bad as drugs, but Satan can use it against us as well. Still, giving it up has been hard. It's been nearly a week so far, but I still get caffeine-craving headaches by midmorning. I guess that simply proves how right she was.

"Tell her I'm busy," I whisper to Mary since she has the cordless in her hand and I'm sure my sister is listening.

"She said not to tell her that," Mary says loudly, holding the phone out to me as if it's a weapon.

I take the phone and glare at my daughter. "Hello?"

"That's right," Lynette says in a grumpy tone. "I did tell Mary not to let you claim you were busy. You always make them say that, Ruth. What on earth are you so busy with, anyway?"

"Life," I say in a flat voice. I would try to expound on my answer, but my sister is so incredibly dense when it comes to spiritual things that it hardly seems worth the effort.

"Yeah, right. Well, so am I. And I asked Mom to call you, but she says she can't get hold of you. *No one* can get hold of you. Don't you ever pick up the phone or check your message machine? It's like you live under a rock or maybe in a cave. What's up with that, Ruth?"

"Did you call just to yell at me?"

"Hmm…maybe so. But don't you understand how aggravating it is not to be able to reach someone? I've considered driving over to your house and forcing my way in just so I can talk to you, but then my schedule's pretty full too."

"And so?"

"So in case you haven't noticed, it's Thanksgiving this week. And if you'd listen to Mom's numerous phone messages or if you'd pick up when I call, you might have remembered that it's my turn to host it. And I'm really going all out this year. You haven't made any other plans, have you? Because Jeff did run into Rick a few days ago when he shipped some stuff for work, and he said that Rick said you guys could come. So I expect you to be here. And, oh yeah, could you bring that sweet potato thing you always make? The one with the walnuts and apples and stuff? Mom said you wouldn't mind."

How dare my mother answer for me! Just because these people are relatives doesn't mean they should control me. Brother Glenn said this very thing just last week. He reminded us of how Jesus challenged people to leave their families behind to follow him. In some ways that's exactly what I think I should do right now.

"Ruth? Are you still there? Did you hang up?"

"I'm still here," I say in snipped bites. "But just barely."

"Why are you acting like this?" she asks in a softer tone. "Don't you want to spend time with your family? We really want you guys to be here. Please, tell me that you're coming, okay?"

Everything in me wants to say, "No, forget it. We are not coming." But I can't quite put these words together. I'm not sure if it's because I don't want to hurt her or because I don't have the energy to wage this battle. With so many other battles going on, why would I look for another one?

"Maybe," I finally say.

Then she tells me what time to come and asks if she can borrow my turkey platter.

"You can borrow the platter, and I'll even make the sweet-potato casserole for you, but it doesn't mean I'm coming."

"You're my sister, Ruth! I've only done Thanksgiving at my house once before, and if you remember, it was a total disaster. I need you here to help me this time. Don't let me down like this."

"I can't make any promises."

"See you on Thursday," she says firmly. "Be there or be square. Later!"

Even as I hang up, I feel fairly certain we will not go to Lynette's for Thanksgiving. Hopefully, Rick will be so busy by then that he'll have forgotten his conversation with Jeff—

"Are we going to Aunt Lynette's for Thanksgiving?" Mary asks as I replace the phone in the cradle. Sarah is standing right behind her, and both of them look hopeful. It's obvious they both heard the whole conversation.

"I don't know…"

"Come on, Mom," urges Mary. "It'll be fun."

"We'll see…" I tell them to finish getting ready for school. I almost let them in on my secret—telling them that they have only a few more days to wear those silly uniforms—but I stop myself. Best to play this hand close to the vest. And then I remember that today is the day to write that letter to VBF. Perhaps it will help that I'm still riled by my sister's demands to participate in her silly Thanksgiving family gathering. I seriously doubt anyone in my heathen extended family will bother to give thanks to God.

So after dropping the girls at school, I come home and sit down at Rick's computer. I'm not really that fond of computers, but I know how to use the Word program, and if I'm going to homeschool the girls, I suppose it wouldn't hurt to get a little more comfortable with this everyday technology. Jeannie Taylor, one of the homeschool moms at church, told me she couldn't do homeschool without it.

"But don't you worry about what the kids might be exposed to online?" I asked, truly horrified that a woman as careful and conservative as Jeannie would take such risks with her own children. I may be somewhat computer ignorant, but I happen to know that all kinds of evil lurk out there on the information highway.

"Oh, we're not hooked up to the Internet," she told me with an equal amount of horror. "We wouldn't dream of doing that. And I have to admit that the computer made me nervous at first, but we've found some really good academic programs that the kids just love to do. We even use these programs as rewards for when they've completed their handwritten work. We pretend that they're games, but they are actually all about learning." She smiled knowingly. "What they don't know won't hurt them."

So I remind myself as I start up the Word program that perhaps computers not connected to the Internet aren't such a risk after all. Still, I feel odd as I type out my letter. It's hard to explain, but I feel as if I'm being watched. Maybe it's the old Big Brother thing, or maybe it's that I know Satan is hovering over me, reading over my shoulder or perhaps right through the computer screen. And why not? He can masquerade as any earthly object or being.

Even if this computer isn't actually connected to the Internet, and I know that it's not because Rick said we can't afford it, perhaps the computer has been programmed in such a way that information could be passed through it anyway. How would I know? Naturally, I find this very unsettling, causing me to nearly abandon my efforts before I've begun. But I really need to write this letter in a way that looks official. I want VBF to know I mean business!

I soon forget my computer phobias as I become absorbed in a letter that's meant not only to explain my need for the refund of the tuition but to point out the false teaching that I believe VBF is guilty of. I even quote some Bible verses as well as a few things Sister Bronte has said. When I'm done, I'm surprised to see that my letter is three pages long. And single spaced! All in all, it's quite a sermon I've created, and I'm actually fairly proud of it. Perhaps I am ready to educate my own children after all. I say a quick prayer, print it out, then carefully fold the pages and seal my epistle in a legal-size envelope and slip it into my purse. I will deliver it tomorrow.

I am amazingly energized after creating such a fine piece of work. Similar to the way I feel after a long deliverance prayer or a deep spiritual purging, I am ready to take on my spiritual foes with force and power and authority today. I walk around my house, praying out loud against spirits, the way I often do when I'm home alone. And I ask the Lord to heighten my spiritual awareness so that I might be quick to see and quick to hear and that I might be able to sniff out the Enemy's secret hiding places and uproot them and remove them from my home.

"Don't let me hold back, Lord," I pray with fervor. "Let me be diligent and disciplined as I purify my home."

I feel the Spirit leading me as I move through our home like a purging fire. I gather up all sorts of things—it seems that many items have a history attached to them—and I pile them out in the driveway. Then I call Goodwill and ask if they'd send a truck by to pick them up. The woman informs me that they're not scheduled to go out today.

"Too bad," I tell her. "I have some valuable antiques and—" Well, that seems to get her attention, and a couple of hours later a truck swings by, and a couple of guys quickly load it up. But then my doorbell rings.

"You sure that's all supposed to go, ma'am?" the short, balding man asks. "There's some awful nice stuff in there."

"It's all supposed to go." I try not to sound guilty as I look at the antique oak hall tree in the back. Rick was fond of that piece.

The man hands me what appears to be a tax receipt. "Well, thanks, and have a happy Thanksgiving!" I close the door and lean against it to steady myself. My hand shakes as I look down at the receipt. He's jotted down a value of five hundred dollars, which surprises me. Not that I care since I know it's tainted. I take the paper to the fireplace and light a match, watching the yellow paper burn with holy flames. Then only ashes remain, and the spiritual rush I'd gotten while purging the house is fading.

I look at where the hall tree once stood, but instead of feeling relieved, I see its empty spot like a friend who has suddenly left me. And then, like a slap on the face, I wonder if I've made a huge mistake. I glance into the living room, which now seems stark. Many familiar pieces are missing, including a painting from my mother and numerous large houseplants that my brother Jonathan gave me while I was still unaware of his rejection of the Lord. I see the gaping holes on the bookshelf where Rick's old books once sat, and finally I notice where the montage of old photos once hung. Rick has inquired numerous times, and I have always evaded, acting as if I've just taken them down temporarily. Isn't life on earth temporary?

I feel a severe caffeine headache coming on again. And I suspect that Satan is tempting me now, trying to make me regret my sacrifices, to take false delight in corrupt material wealth. I go to my room, get down on my knees, and repent of these evil temptations. I pray to deliver my home from all demonic influence. I promise obedience and purging my life and my home from all evil, even if I have to strip this place down to the bare walls and floors. I would gladly do this to obtain spiritual peace. The loss of material things is a small price to pay for a safe haven. That's all I really want, after all—to be safe and protected from the Evil One.

23

W here's the hall tree, Mom?" Mary asks just minutes after we're
in the house.

"I got rid of it." I rub the bridge of my nose with my thumb and
forefinger, wishing this throbbing headache would go away and longing for another shower like the one I took before picking up the girls.
Handling all those items today has left me feeling especially unclean
and defiled.

"You got rid of it?" She sounds an awful lot like her father right
now. In fact, it occurs to me that she really resembles him too. Especially when she frowns like that. Why haven't I noticed that before?

"Yes, that's what I said, isn't it?" I start to walk away.

Why?" she demands, and I turn to see her peering at me with
blatant curiosity. At first I think perhaps she's concerned about my
throbbing headache, but then I can tell by her eyes that she's questioning my state of mind.

"I didn't want it around. And it was mine to do with as I please,
Mary. I bought it, and I refinished it. And today I realized that it
wasn't good to have it in the house. It is very old and was owned by
others, and I can tell that it holds some very disturbing secrets."

"What do you mean?"

"I mean it was evil. I got rid of it. End of story."

She walks around the living room, noticing almost every other item that's missing as if she's taking inventory on all the things in her house, and she asks me again and again, why did I get rid of this, why did I get rid of that? *Why? Why? Why?*

"I've told you! It was wrong to keep those evil things, Mary. It was sinful and dangerous. If you can't understand it, it's simply because you are not spiritually mature."

I can sense Sarah lurking in the hallway now, listening to everything but too timid to question me the way Mary does. Or perhaps she really does understand.

"Look." I try to put a positive spin on this. "Forget about these things, okay? They are just things, and really, they don't matter, do they? What truly matters is that we love and serve the Lord, right?" Mary doesn't say anything, just looks at me with those big brown eyes.

"Sarah," I call out. "I know you're there. Come here and listen to Mommy, okay? You can understand that some things are evil, can't you? You understand how the Lord doesn't want us to live with evil in our midst, don't you? How we have to take the upper hand, get rid of the demons and evil spirits so they don't contaminate our lives and our hearts, right?" Sarah nods but looks uneasy.

"Okay, I have an idea, girls. You know how Sister Bronte has been saying we should get a keyboard?" Mary's eyes light up, and Sarah nods with interest. "Well, instead of waiting until Christmas, I think maybe we should go looking for one today. Then you girls can practice that song Sister Bronte wants you to share at church. Maybe you'll have it down well enough to do it for church on Sunday."

"Really?" Mary is eager now. "Can we really get a keyboard, Mom?"

"Change out of your uniforms," I tell them, suddenly convinced this is a perfect plan inspired by the Lord. "You don't need to worry about homework tonight since you don't have school again until Monday. Let's go shopping."

The girls are chattering with excitement as we get ready to go. I know I don't have enough cash to make this purchase, but that's only because I have been so generous at church. Just the same, I know it's the Lord's will that we find this keyboard today. And he has assured me, as Sister Bronte and Brother Glenn always assure us, that what we faithfully give in the offering at church, he will repay many times over. Plus I know that music is a way to bless the Lord, and Mary is definitely gifted. So purchasing a musical instrument should be, in itself, a blessing to the Lord. Besides that, the girls will be starting homeschool in just a week. Things like music will become part of our curriculum.

Rick and I keep a special credit card that is to be used only for emergencies. We've both agreed on this. But this is a spiritual emergency. We need this keyboard now! Really, I am simply taking a step of faith here. I will trust the Lord to provide for the cost of the keyboard in due time. I open the bureau drawer and dig into the back, where an envelope holds this secret card. At first I'm dismayed that the lightweight envelope feels empty, and I wonder if Rick has already taken it, perhaps even used it for himself and his own earthly pleasures. But then with a rush of relief, I realize it is still safely there. I pull it out and examine it. Still shiny and new. I don't think it's ever been used. I replace the envelope at the back of the drawer and slip this card into my purse.

I overhear Mary and Sarah talking as they change their clothes. Mary has somehow gotten the idea that I sold the hall tree and those other things and am using that money to buy the keyboard for her. I must admit, I wish I'd thought of that possibility myself. But then wouldn't the money be tainted from the transaction? And wouldn't that taint the new keyboard? No, I decide, this is better.

We drive over to Music World and go inside. The girls are excited, and I feel a little giddy myself. But as soon as a salesman approaches, I feel nervous. I wonder if this is a mistake. I wonder what Rick will say. Will he be angry?

"May I help you?" the gray-haired man asks politely.

I'm about to say, "No, we have to go," but I see my daughters' eyes, so full of hope and expectation. We hardly ever do anything like this. How can I deprive them? So I quickly explain to him that we're looking for a keyboard for Mary. "She's only started taking lessons, but her teacher says she's coming along really well."

He smiles. "How nice."

"We don't need the top of the line." I suddenly see a staggering price tag on an actual piano and worry that we're going to be in way over our heads. "Just something for her to learn on. Not too expensive."

The salesman gives us a quick tour of what's available. Mary tries out some, and I find one that's less expensive and ask him about it. But he tells me it's used, and suddenly I imagine tiny demons popping out from between the keys. "What do you have that's new?"

"New?" He looks surprised. "This is actually an excellent instrument, ma'am. Trust me, you'd pay a lot more for something of equal quality if it were new."

"I don't care. I want to buy a *new* keyboard. Can you show me something you think is appropriate for my daughter?"

His eyes light up, and before long I've purchased a brand-new keyboard that costs twice as much as the used one. But it is new. With the keyboard snug in its case and safely loaded into the trunk, the girls and I get back into the car.

"Thanks, Mom," says Mary.

I let out a sigh of relief, glad that's over. "How about if we pick up a pizza to take home?" I pull out of the parking lot. "To celebrate." Naturally, they don't argue. They also don't ask to go inside to dine. The girls know I don't like eating in public restaurants. So we order a medium pizza and wait until it's done, then head for home.

It occurs to me that this keyboard might help make up for the lack of television in our quiet house. Mary has complained numerous times, saying we should take it in to get it repaired and reminding me that "Daddy said it was okay to get it fixed." Later in the evening she and Sarah seem quite happy to entertain themselves with the keyboard. I know I made the right choice as I hear the two of them practicing music—Mary playing and Sarah singing. Really, I don't see how Rick could disagree with something as sweet and as good as this.

Yet I feel uneasy after the girls have gone to bed. I feel guilty about using the credit card and guilty for still owing my mother five hundred dollars and guilty for sneaking money from Rick. I pace around the house and wonder if perhaps I've made some mistakes. How will I explain this keyboard to him? What if he throws a fit? I can't let him see it tonight. I can't handle the stress.

24

The devil plays games, and I find I must play games too. Just to keep up. But the rules keep changing, and sometimes I'm not sure who is winning. I wake up very early the next morning. It's still dark out, and I can't see the alarm clock, so I'm not sure what time it is. I'm not even sure whether Rick has come home from work yet or, if he has, whether he's come to bed. So I just lie quietly listening, trying to hear over the pounding, pulsating sound in my ears, until I finally think I can hear him quietly breathing beside me as if he's asleep—although I can't be sure. I can't be sure of anything. My heart is pounding harder and harder as I lie here, trying to decide what to do next. But I have to do something. Somehow I have to make up for this mess I may have created.

I had meant to return the credit card to its envelope in the drawer last night before I went to bed, before Rick got home. But after taking a very long shower and praying until I finally fell asleep, I completely forgot. Now I feel certain that Rick will go straight for the drawer and take out the empty envelope and my mistake will be discovered. I have tried to think of a way to quietly get up and put it back, but I will surely bungle it, and Rick will find me, and I'll be caught red-handed. Oh, why did I do that yesterday? What could I have been thinking? What is wrong with me? Normal people don't act like this.

As I lie here, it occurs to me that today is Thanksgiving Day. Not that there is any consolation in this fact, but perhaps this is my chance. Maybe I can make it work for me, using the activities of the day as a smoke screen to cover up my recent mistakes. If they really are mistakes. And to be honest, I can't tell yet. Maybe the devil is just trying to trick me into questioning myself again. *O Lord, please show me what to do. Show me if I've done something wrong. Please help me. Help me. Help me.*

I silently slip from bed, retrieve my clothes from the closet, and go to the bathroom down the hall to dress. All this to make sure I don't wake Rick. As I dress, I quickly devise a game plan. Or, more likely, it's the Lord who is devising this plan. He's the one guiding me. I am in desperate need of guidance.

I go to the kitchen and write two notes. One is for the girls, which I leave in their room, explaining that I have to run errands this morning and that I put their new keyboard away so they wouldn't get up and start playing and disturb their dad. I remind them that he needs his rest and ask them to be quiet. The other note I leave in the kitchen, telling Rick that I have to go to the store to get some things for Thanksgiving dinner, which I also explain we will be celebrating with my family at Jeff and Lynette's house. I figure that should make everyone else happy, even if it does make me miserable. And it will also delay the inevitable of telling Rick about the keyboard. Perhaps the Lord will show me how to deal with that before then.

I hunt until I find my turkey platter, tucked deep in the back of a lower cupboard. And as I'm putting it into a brown paper bag, I wonder why I haven't gotten rid of this platter already. Of course, it was out of sight...out of mind...but even so. Even so.

I double- and then triple-bag the bulky ceramic platter. Not because it's so heavy and I'm afraid it will break, but because I don't want to handle it, to be defiled by it. After it's safely covered in layers of heavy brown paper sacks, I set it aside, then wash my hands with dish soap, over and over, scrubbing them with a scrub brush and rinsing them in scalding water from the kitchen faucet. I finally dry them with several paper towels before I realize I'll have to touch that brown package again.

I look around the kitchen, trying to think of a way out of this, and even consider just throwing it into the trash, washing my hands all over again, and being done with it. But then Lynette will ask why I didn't bring it, and I don't really want to go there with her. Finally I spy oven mitts. I put on my coat, get my purse and keys, stick my hands in the mitts, and then carefully pick up the disgusting parcel, take it out to the car, and put it in the trunk.

As I drive across town to the only grocery store that's always open, I remember the Thanksgiving when my dad gave me that turkey platter. I'd only been married a few years. Matthew was a toddler, it was my first year to host all my family at our house, and I was very nervous. I had explained to Dad earlier in the week that I was worried my dinner wouldn't be as grand as the family was used to—I knew our house wasn't as big and nice as my parents' or even Lynette's—but I also told my dad that I really wanted to do this. He said he had confidence in me, and then he stopped by our house on Thanksgiving morning to deliver a large, flat box from Williams-Sonoma, a store I had only been able to window-shop in but one that my mother and sister frequented. Inside the box was the best turkey platter I'd ever seen. I still remember how I hugged my dad, thanking him with tears in my eyes for giving me this.

"I'll treasure it forever," I promised him. But that was before I *knew.* Everything has changed now. I firmly shake my head from left to right, trying to repress or maybe even shake away the memory of that night when Bronte and Cynthia prayed for me, exorcizing the demons associated with the sexual abuse from my father—the sexual abuse I had never consciously remembered.

I know it's wrong, but part of me wishes I had never learned about it. And I don't fully understand how it was that I didn't remember something this abhorrent. How was it that I loved my father so much, that I grieved so deeply when he died? But then Satan is the Prince of Deception and the Father of Lies. So why should I be surprised that I was so easily tricked? Even so, it is frustrating to remember this now. To be so painfully aware that the defiled turkey platter is riding in my trunk, a contaminated reminder of a past that I would rather forget.

Why, why, why? I ask myself as I pull into the parking lot of a grocery store that I would normally avoid. Why is my life so complicated, so hard? Is it really all the devil's doing, or am I partially to blame? I get out of the car and shiver in the damp morning air as I stare up at this megastore. I cannot stand this godless place. It's always disturbed me that they remain open on holidays like Christmas and Easter and every other day of the year. But that's not what's making me crazy right now. *Why, why, why* am I agreeing to spend the day with the family that has hurt me so badly, the family that holds absolutely no regard for my Lord and his divine purposes?

For starters, I remind myself as I trudge across the rain-soaked parking lot, there is my mother, *my oppressor,* the woman who has always made me feel that I am worthless, hopeless, useless, inferior… And then there is my divorced sister, who claims to be a believer but lives more like a heathen. Then there's my worldly brother. Not only does he embrace every New Age trend that comes along, but he proudly claims to be an atheist. All this combines with the suppressed memory of my father's sexual abuse when I was too young to even remember. I stop in front of an oil-soaked rain puddle and consider just turning and running—escaping everyone and everything as I ask myself once again, *Why, why, why?*

Help me, dear Lord. I force myself to continue walking, entering the small glassed-in foyer, smelling the stench of stale tobacco smoke that comes from the big ashcan where customers have hastily extinguished their cigarettes before entering the store. I press through the next set of doors and pull out a grocery cart. I can't stand the greasy feeling of the infectious plastic handle beneath my grip. And the first thing I place into this filthy cart is a large bottle of hand sanitizer and a roll of paper towels—to use later. Then I hurry to the produce section, where I hope to pick out what I need to make the casserole. And even though I've made this casserole year after year, I can't remember exactly what it takes.

I stand for a long time just looking at the bins of fruits and vegetables, trying to decide where to begin and wishing I'd brought a list. I finally pick out some sweet potatoes and then pause and look at the yams. Which do I normally use? Or does it make any difference? I can't remember. Finally I decide to get both, filling two bags of each. Then I can't remember what kind of apples to use. It takes forever, but somehow the ingredients find their way into my cart. And when the cashier tells me the total, I am stunned. How could it possibly cost $69.57 for one casserole?

"Is that total right?" I feel desperate, but I can tell by her scowl that not only is she sure of the total, but she doesn't want to hear any questions as she waits for me to fork over the cash. And suddenly

I think I see a demon sitting on her shoulder. Why would that surprise me?

I silently pray as I divert my eyes to look in my wallet, where I find, as expected, only one twenty-dollar bill and some change. But this lady and the demon on her shoulder are both glaring at me as if they'd like to devour me, or perhaps she's considering whether or not to call for help. Maybe she's about to get her boss down here to deal with me, and maybe he'll call the police and they'll haul me off to jail. But what would be the charge? Stupidity?

Then I notice the credit card from yesterday and reassure myself that this too is an emergency. My hand shakes as I give her this card and then nervously wait as she runs it through the machine. Part of me wants to bolt and just leave the groceries behind, but then I would leave my card behind as well. I'm sure they'd trace it back to Rick, and he would think that I'd lost my mind. Maybe I have. Finally I sign the receipt, and pushing the grimy cart out the automatic doors, I escape that store as quickly as possible, promising myself never to shadow their doors again. What was I thinking?

I drive around town for a while, trying to decide what to do next. In my note I said I would be at Lynette's, helping with the Thanksgiving dinner, but it's not even eight yet, and I seriously doubt she'd even be out of bed on a nonworking day. So I redeem the time by engaging in spiritual warfare over this town's darkest corners. Others may be sleeping in, thinking they are safe and sound, but I know that's not the case. Satan never slumbers; he is always on the prowl, ever ready to deceive and devour and destroy. So I drive my nice new car over to the seedy side of town, cruising past the sleazy buildings and the grubby streets that are becoming more and more familiar to me. As I slowly pass each of these regular sin spots, I pray and pray and pray. And the more I pray, the better I feel. I know that I'm being a faithful prayer warrior and that the Lord will bless me for my diligent work. Considering this is a national holiday, I feel especially validated by my sacrifice—as if I am working overtime.

Finally I see it's nearly ten o'clock, and I realize I can probably make an appearance at Lynette's house without raising too much concern. But she is still surprised when she sees me at the door.

"What on earth are you doing here now?" she asks with raised brows. "The dinner isn't until two." Even though she's wearing a sweatshirt and flannel pajama bottoms and her hair is mussed, she still looks beautiful and glamorous, and I feel an old familiar twitch of envy.

I hand a grocery bag to her. "I thought I could help you. And I brought the stuff for the casserole; I'll make it here."

She frowns, and I can tell she's not too thrilled with my unexpected appearance.

"Or I can just leave and go home," I snap at her. "You made such a big deal about this Thanksgiving dinner yesterday. You were so worried, and I thought you might need help, and I just—"

"Yeah yeah." She grabs my arm and pulls me into her house. "You caught me by surprise, Ruth. But, really, it'll be good to have some help." We're in the foyer now, and I can see she's done some decorating with autumn leaves and pumpkins and things. "You could've called first, given some warning, you know." She gives me a funny smile. "Oh yeah, but I forgot, you don't know how to use a phone, do you?"

"Look, if you don't want me—"

"No no…you'll have to excuse me, but I'm just so frustrated trying to figure out how to make stuffing and get the turkey in on time and…" She suddenly looks hopeful. "Hey, you want to take care of that for me?"

I shrug. "If you want."

"Great, let me take that bag for you and your coat."

And the next thing I know she's tying a chef's apron around me and showing me her mess of ingredients, which are splayed all over her large center island like an explosion. My sister has never been too organized.

She's looking into my grocery bag now. "The only thing in here is sweet potatoes, Ruth. Didn't you bring anything else to go with this?"

"It's in the car." I begin to rearrange her ingredients, trying to create some order out of her chaos.

"I'll get it." She makes a quick exit. I can't really blame her for wanting to escape this mess, but I'm not completely sure I can figure it out myself. I take a deep breath, tell myself to focus, and then notice she does have a recipe out. So, for starters, I study it, then I go back to organizing her ingredients. I glance at the clock and wonder if it is even possible for this turkey to be ready by two.

"How many casseroles did you plan to make?" she asks as she sets a couple of bags on the counter.

"Some of that's for later," I tell her as I begin peeling an onion. I know it's a lie, but I feel a need to cover my own stupidity.

"For later?"

"Yeah, I'm going to make a casserole for church too. We're having a potluck on Sunday." Okay, that's an even bigger lie. But on the other hand, a potluck at church might be rather nice. Maybe I'll call Cynthia later today and suggest something like this. A real Thanksgiving dinner with people who actually respect and understand the holiness of holidays like this, people who know how to pray and how to give thanks from their hearts. If only I could be with them instead of my relatives today. Cynthia mentioned that she'd be sharing the holiday with the Pratts and Bronte and that my family would probably be welcome in their home too, but I knew Rick would never agree to that. And I suppose, to be honest, it would be uncomfortable to have him there with me. I'd worry that he would attempt to interrogate my friends or to put down our church. It just wouldn't be worth it.

I'm relieved that Lynette is giving me space in her kitchen. In fact, after a while I think she's abandoned me altogether. Sammy, who is wearing a fairly authentic-looking Native American headdress and running around the house like he's had too much sugar, pauses just long enough in the kitchen to stick his fingers into things or to nab small fistfuls of candy corn that Lynette thinks she placed out of his reach.

"Where's your mom?" I put the candy corn on a higher shelf.

He pauses and stares at me as if he's seeing me in his house for the first time. "She's in her room getting *all pretty.*" He smirks at me. "How come you're not?"

I feel like reprimanding the child but stop myself. He just needs prayer. Perhaps that's why I am here, to be a prayer warrior for my family. Maybe I will have an opportunity to share something meaningful and spiritual today. *O Lord, help me to be a light in this darkness.*

25

The girls showed me the new keyboard," Rick tells me shortly after the three of them get to Lynette's house. It's a little before two, and so far no one else has arrived.

My heart begins to pound now; this is not a subject I wanted to discuss just yet. But I pretend to be absorbed in putting the potatoes on the stove and getting the gas flame to just the right height.

"Mary said you sold some things so you could afford it, Ruth." He puts his hand on my shoulder. "You shouldn't have done that, sweetheart. I know how much you loved that hall tree."

"Oh, it's okay. I really wanted the girls to have a keyboard. Mary is coming along so well."

"I know." He smiles at me. "She asked to bring it. I hope that's okay. She thought she and Sarah could do a song later on."

I smile back at him. "That will be nice."

"Well, I know you're busy in here"—he bends down and gives me a kiss on the forehead—"so I won't disturb you."

"Aren't you two sweet," Lynette says from where she's attempting to whip cream on the other side of the kitchen.

Rick laughs. "Yeah, Lynette, we still got it after all these years. Are you impressed?"

Lynette makes a face at him. "Well, I'll never be able to catch up with you guys in years of marriage." She laughs. "Not even if I combined both of my marriages. But don't worry, Rick. We've still got it too. Just ask Jeff if you don't believe me."

Jeff is getting something out of the refrigerator now. "Take her word for it," he says to Rick. "And if I were you, I'd get out of the kitchen. Wanna beer"—he holds out a bottle toward Rick—"while we watch the game and wait for the turkey to get done?"

Rick tosses me an uneasy glance and then, to my utter shock, says, "Sure, why not?"

I give him a look that is meant to convey my great disappointment, but he just ignores me. "Is Matthew coming?" I ask, hoping he will catch this little hint.

"He told me he'd probably stop by." Rick takes the opened bottle from Jeff. "But it might not be until later."

"He's not working on Thanksgiving, is he?" says Lynette.

"No, but he is going to go to his roommate's parents' house first."

"Oh, that sounds serious," teases Lynette. "Meeting the parents. What's next? A ring?"

Rick laughs, but I can tell he's uncomfortable. "It's not like *that*. His roommate is a guy."

Then the men disappear, and just as I'm about to question my sister's judgment in serving beer on Thanksgiving, my mother comes in the back door.

"I could use some help," she says as she sets a covered bowl on the countertop. "I've got some more things in the car."

"I'll get them," offers Lynette. "You just take your coat off and make yourself at home. Be right back."

"It's in the trunk." Without looking my way, Mom removes a long gray coat trimmed in fur. She sighs loudly as if exhausted from this small effort.

"Hi, Mom." I try to insert some cheer into my voice.

"Oh, hello, Ruth." She lays her coat on a kitchen stool and comes over to where I'm wiping off a countertop. "I didn't see you there." I want to ask what else is new but manage to simply nod as I scrub the granite even harder.

"It's nice you could make it," she says. "Lynette wasn't sure whether your family was coming or not."

"Well, I didn't actually hear about it until yesterday."

"We called and left messages, Ruth." I can hear the irritation in her voice. Suddenly I feel like I'm about nine years old again.

"Is this everything?" Lynette deposits a couple of bags and a covered cake pan onto the counter.

"Looks like it." Mom bustles over and immediately starts unpacking the bags, chattering happily with Lynette as she explains what she's brought and why.

It feels as if I'm not even here. Or perhaps they think I'm just the hired help. But I decide not to let them get to me. Instead, I pray silently, binding the spirits of deceit and destruction as I rinse used kitchen utensils, then load them into the dishwasher. But even as I travail in prayer, I am remembering the prophetic word Cynthia gave me about my mother being my oppressor, and I cannot help but believe that, despite their deliverance prayers for me, it is still just as true today as it was more than thirty years ago.

"I think you got that clean enough," Lynette says to me as I rinse and rinse the spatula in my hand. I bend over and place it in the dishwasher, then I slowly stand up and stare at her.

"You okay?" she says in a quiet voice.

"I'm fine!"

"You don't sound fine." Lynette frowns. "You sound angry."

"I'm just irritated at some people's ideas of what Thanksgiving is all about."

"What *is* Thanksgiving all about?" demands Lynette.

"It's supposed to be about giving thanks to God, not beer and football."

"You're mad because Rick's drinking one little brewski?" Lynette laughs. "It's no big deal."

"Maybe not to you! But have you thought about how—"

"Girls, girls, girls." My mother may be speaking in plural, but she directs her reprimand at only one of us. Me. "Don't forget, Ruth, *we're family.*"

Now to my surprise, this actually makes me laugh. "We're family? *Family?*"

"Hey, we might not all be perfect," says Lynette in defense, "not like you, anyway. But Mom's right, we *are* family. And today is a day to enjoy being together and to celebrate our family—"

"Maybe it is for you," I say to her, "but I do not find this enjoyable."

"Then maybe you should take a look at yourself."

"You mean because I don't think things like football and beer and some stupid cartoon that the kids are parked in front of have anything to do with Thanksgiving?"

"It's a cartoon about Thanksgiving."

"Not the *real* Thanksgiving, Lynette. This is nothing but a worldly interpretation of Thanksgiving. The kind of celebrating that Satan wishes we'd all succumb to. Full of demonic lies and hidden sins and deep-rooted animosities."

"Why would you say that?" My mother uses her wounded tone now. "Why would you talk to your sister like that, Ruth? Look how hard she's worked to put this day together. And you, the one who never even returned our calls, would act like this? What is wrong with you?"

I glance at Lynette and see she looks hurt. But why can't they see I'm hurting even more? Why can't they see that their alignment with the Enemy pains me so deeply I can feel it in my bones? Oh, I wish I'd never come here today. Why did I come?

"I just don't understand you," Lynette finally says. "I'm actually starting to believe you have a real mental-health problem."

"That's great," I say. "It figures you would."

"No, I'm serious. I've been doing some reading, and I—"

"That's enough. I do not need to hear what you've been reading, Lynette. I have enough battles without going to war with you too."

"But Lynette might have a point," my mother continues, as if she and Lynette have been talking about me at length. "We're concerned about your emotional health, and I think you should—"

"If you want to be concerned about anything, it should be my spiritual health. And you should be praying for me, not talking behind my back. But more than that, you should be deeply concerned about your own spiritual health. And if it makes you feel any better, *I've* been praying for you. I've been doing spiritual warfare on a daily basis for this whole family, for this whole town. And I am getting weary."

"That's just it," says Lynette. "All this talk about the Enemy attacking everyone all the time, all this living in fear, Ruth. It's not what God intended—"

"How would you know what the Lord wants? Do you even go to church? Or read your Bible? Do you get on your knees and really pray against the Enemy? How can you even pretend to know what I'm talking about?"

"But what good does all that do you?" asks my mother. "You always seem overly stressed and worried. I think your religion is harmful."

"For your information it's *not* religion. It's the Lord, and it's my life. And without the Lord and his deliverance, I might as well be dead and buried."

My eyes fall on the turkey platter now. It's sitting by the stove, ready for the turkey. But it occurs to me how ridiculous this is. It's like serving your dinner in a toilet bowl. But why should this surprise me? Our family has always been messed up. But staring at the platter and knowing that it's still defiled, I also know that I cannot eat a single bite of the turkey that is served from it. In fact, no one should. "See that?" I point to the platter. "That is just one of the many things that is plaguing this family."

Lynette looks dumbfounded. *"The turkey platter?"*

I keep pointing. "Yes. It is contaminated, and yet we are using it, pretending that it is pretty and clean. And all the while it is filthy and corrupt. Like a whited sepulcher."

"That's crazy talk, Ruth." My mother scowls at me.

"No, Mother, it's the truth. But some people cannot handle the truth. Some people would rather be deceived by Satan than face reality. And I suppose if I have seemed stressed to either of you, *that* might be the reason why."

"What might be the reason why?" Lynette looks thoroughly confused.

"Because of the way we live in this family." I point to the turkey platter again. "Like *that*. I have kept that piece for years, never admitting to myself that the man who gave it to me was evil and perverted."

"*Dad* gave you that platter, Ruth." Lynette folds her arms across her chest. "You've always loved it."

"That was before *I knew.*"

"Knew what?" my mother asks, her voice filled with irritation.

I pause and stare at both of them. Then I glance to see if anyone else is around, anyone who might be listening. Not that I should care. Someday the truth will be shouted from the rooftops, and everyone will know about these abominations. "Before I knew that my father sexually abused me."

The kitchen is so quiet I can clearly hear the soundtrack from the cartoon playing in the family room and the potatoes simmering on the stove behind me.

"*What?*" My mother's hands curl into fists as if she's ready to punch me.

Her eyes are wide, and her cheeks are flushed, and I suddenly wonder if perhaps she too has been hiding this repulsive secret. Has she been a victim too? "Do you know what I'm talking about?" I ask her, feeling almost hopeful.

"I know you are certifiably crazy," Lynette says. "I cannot believe you would say something like that, Ruth. I cannot believe you would accuse Dad of something so horrible, so mean, so unthinkable. What is wrong with you?"

"*What are you saying?*" My mother's words come out slowly, dripping with venom. Her face is pale, but those blue eyes are hot with rage.

Now I want to retract my words. It's not as if I had planned this. I never dreamed I would make this confession today. But I would've thought that speaking the truth and getting this horror out into the open would bring relief. Instead I feel confused, worried, and slightly sick to my stomach.

"I told you. Dad sexually abused me."

"When?" Lynette shakes a finger at me. "When did he do something like that?"

The two stand opposite me as if they have joined forces to shut me down. "Tell us when this atrocity happened." Lynette's eyes narrow in disbelief.

My mother's forehead creases. "Yes. Tell us. When did he ever have time?"

"It happened when I was too little to remember."

"Then *how* can you remember?" demands Lynette.

So I attempt to explain to them about the deliverance prayer and Bronte's prophetic word and how I found it hard to believe—at first.

"That's because this horrid woman was making it up," says Lynette.

"But she described my bedroom to me," I protest. "How could she do that if she was making it up?"

"And how exactly did this Bronte person *describe* your bedroom?" My mother sits on one of the stools and leans into the island as if she is very tired.

Perhaps she too remembers something, something evil and hidden, something she has concealed all along. Maybe that would even explain why she has treated me so differently all these years. Why I have, in a sense, always been her whipping girl.

"Pastel blue walls and white eyelet curtains…"

"And how old were you when this happened?" My mother's brow furrows even more.

"Probably a toddler."

Lynette's eyes light up. "We *shared* a bedroom when we were little, Ruth. Don't you remember? You didn't have the blue bedroom until you went to first grade. You must've been around six then. Don't you remember the other bedroom? It was yellow. But after you moved into the blue bedroom, Mom painted my bedroom lavender. And it had white eyelet curtains too. Yours were blue."

"That's right," says Mom. "So if this atrocity that you say happened back when you were too young to remember it…well, it wouldn't have taken place in the blue bedroom. Otherwise, you would've been old enough to remember it." She lets out a big sigh. "But it's like you to put us through something like this, Ruth. You were always a difficult child. Always doing something to get attention. But to accuse your father…well, I don't know what to say."

I am angry and flustered now. I want to defend myself, but what's the use? Oh, why did I allow this to go this far? Why did I trust them with my secret? Why did I waste my breath?

"Whoever this Bronte witch is, she must be crazy too," says Lynette.

"She's not a witch, and she's not crazy. She knew what happened to me; she knew it in detail. And I know in my spirit that she was right. Maybe it did happen in the blue bedroom. Maybe, like Bronte said, I suppressed the memory and I was older. Lots of people do that. And it explains a lot of things."

"Like what?" Lynette sounds almost bored now as she turns down the flame beneath the pot of simmering potatoes.

I am about to tell them everything, to explain all about the demons I've cast out and how I've been in need of great deliverance again and again and how this family is cursed and only the Lord can deliver us, but I suddenly realize, with amazing clarity, that would be like tossing my valuable pearls down for the swine to trample upon. These two women cannot possibly understand the spiritual ramifications of all these things. They have allowed Satan to blind them and to deaden their hearing. In fact, it seems that only their mouths are able to work right now, but their tongues are full of lies and hatred and confusion. And I know without a doubt that I can't remain in this house for one more minute.

Suddenly my spiritual eyes are reopened, and I realize that this whole house is crawling with Satan's demons. Legions of them. Why didn't I notice this earlier? Why did I allow my family to distract me from doing warfare? I can see the hideous fiends hiding in the doorways, skulking behind the furnishings, creeping around corners. They rule this household, just as they rule this family. I can even see them lurking behind my mother and sister now, probably where they've been hiding all along. And their repulsive demonic expressions are reflected in the faces of these two women—two people who have beaten me down my entire life. I can't believe I set myself up for this.

Without even trying to explain anything, I leave the room. I can hear my mother and sister whispering behind me as I go. Or perhaps it's their demons talking, congratulating themselves for defeating me once again. But no one seems to notice as I gather my purse and coat and let myself out the front door. My heart is pounding with fear as I get into the car, but as I look back, no one is watching. At least no one human. I'm sure all the demons in the house are laughing and celebrating that I'm gone. There is no one left to hold them back.

I know that I am defiled now. Just like the rest of my family. We are all defiled. The sins of the fathers, the multigenerational curse—how can one ever escape it? All I want is to escape this evil, to go someplace pure and safe, a place where I can get clean. Oh, how I need to get cleansed again; I need to be purged by fire. All I want right now is to be clean. Clean and free. Free and clean. *O Lord, please help me. Deliver me from my enemies. Make me clean. Make me free.*

26

I think I was about five years old when I started watching my step out on the sidewalk in front of our house. "Step on a crack and break your mother's back," Lynette had told me one time when we were playing outside. After that I took the cracks in the concrete very seriously. Lynette, however, didn't seem to really care whether or not she broke our mother's back. At the time I couldn't see the irony in this. Lynette was the one who enjoyed our mother's favoritism; whereas I, on the other hand, was the one who usually earned her criticism. Still, I didn't want to be responsible for breaking Mom's back. That would've been too heavy a load for me to bear.

Sometimes I got careless while walking to school, and I would absent-mindedly lose track of the sidewalk cracks. Before I knew what had happened, I would accidentally step on one. The only remedy for this was to turn around and go back until I had carefully stepped over seven cracks. Because, in my mind, seven was a magical number with the power to undo things. After stepping over seven cracks, I could turn back around and head to school again. But if I stepped on a crack a second time, the penalty return trip would double—two times seven cracks would be needed to undo my mistake. Likewise it would've required three times seven for a third infraction of this rule. However, I rarely stepped on three cracks during a single trip.

But as I'm driving around town now, trying to figure out where

I should go and what I should do, I wonder how many cracks in the road I have driven over today. And although I know it's perfectly ridiculous, it's very unsettling to know that I'm driving over so many. At this rate I would probably have to drive in reverse for three days to undo what's been done.

Maybe my mother and sister are right. Maybe I am crazy. Perhaps I do need serious help. Perhaps I am the source of all this family's problems. But what about their sinful choices? What about the way they allow Satan such easy access into their lives and their homes, welcoming him and his demonic friends as if they were invited guests?

I drive past the Pratt home for the fourth time. There are a number of cars parked out front, but I imagine myself parking across the street, then walking up to the house, knocking on the front door, and telling them my whole sad story. But what if they have just sat down to dinner? What if I interrupt them as they're asking the Lord's blessings? What if they have a houseful of guests—family and friends— and what if Kellie and Glenn just stand there looking at me, embarrassed for me and wishing they didn't know me and hoping I will simply go away? No, I can't do that. As badly as I need a deliverance prayer right now and as much as I want the comfort of my fellow believers, I must attempt to cleanse myself this time.

So I drive home and am somewhat surprised to see that Rick and the girls aren't here. Of course, they're probably still having a good time at Lynette's. Don't they wonder about me? Don't they care that I'm not there? Aren't they just the least bit worried? I see the little red light flashing on the answering machine. Of course, that's not so unusual. But, like always, I ignore it.

On a mission I head straight for the bedroom and strip off my clothes. I realize with a stab of spiritual clarity that I'd been wearing the pantsuit Lynette had enticed me to purchase, but hadn't there been rumors that the designer is a known Satan worshiper? Of course my clothes are tainted. I creep through the house in my underwear, carrying the contaminated suit at arm's length out to the garage, where I put it in a large black trash bag and then stuff it into the already-full garbage can.

Back in the bathroom I continue my preparation for a meticulous cleansing shower. It takes many careful steps to successfully perform this sort of shower. Naturally, I don't normally go around telling others about these particular steps, although I have been trying to teach my girls how to be more careful with their daily hygiene habits and how to prevent contamination following a shower. For instance, there is a right way and a wrong way to towel dry. I'm amazed at how many people aren't aware of something this basic. But then I've observed many shocking practices, particularly in public rest rooms. My girls fully understand the importance of avoiding direct contact with doorknobs, handles, faucets, and such. As well as how to use paper products to protect their hands from being infected with germs. I feel that I've done a fairly good job in this regard.

Of course, I haven't taught them how to take a cleansing shower yet. I suppose it's one of my little secrets. But this is a showering technique that I devised for those times when I feel particularly unclean. Like today. For starters, I must thoroughly disinfect the shower stall. First I remove all traces of Rick's things. Then I scrub down the shower with Lysol cleanser until my nose and eyes are burning from the strong chemical smell. Then I wash my bottles of shampoo and soap in the bathroom sink, shaking them dry before I replace them in the shower, careful not to touch or bump anything. After this, I wash my hands once more so they are sanitary enough to retrieve some clean towels and washcloths—three of each for the various stages of cleaning. After one washcloth is contaminated, I'll toss it into the laundry hamper and then use another. Likewise, I use three towels to dry off with, although this seems fairly straightforward. The first one is to wrap my wet hair into. The next one is to dry the upper half of my body. After that I place it on the floor to step onto since I know the bath mat is unclean from Rick's use. The last towel is for drying the lower half of my body, feet last.

Finally I am finished and dressed, and I am ready to bow down before the Lord in an effort to be made fully clean—inside and out. But as I'm praying, I hear a noise. Thinking perhaps Rick and the girls have come home, I rise and prepare myself for what I'm sure will be an unpleasant inquisition from my husband. But when I get out into the kitchen, it doesn't seem they are here. Still I hear a noise.

It's a scratching sound that seems to be coming from the living room, and judging by the hairs standing out on the back of my neck, I feel certain this sound's origins are demonic. With my Bible, the best tool for exorcisms, in hand, I pray aloud as I slowly walk toward the source of the noise, loudly rebuking Satan and his followers just as I've been taught, using my authority to command that they leave my home at once. "In the name of Jesus! Be gone! Depart!"

That's when I see a black form scurrying across the carpet. I let out a little scream and jump, but then I realize it's actually Spooky, the kitten. Still, I know that this innocent-looking cat is really just one of the devil's pawns, and I'm getting sick and tired of having this creature continually contaminating my home like this. Especially now, seeing that it is no longer contained within the confines of the laundry room. Things are getting out of hand.

"Here, kitty, kitty," I call out in my sweetest voice. And to my surprise the foolish cat comes right to me. I carefully pick it up, knowing full well that this will require another cleansing shower on my part, but perhaps it will be worth it. Perhaps this is the source of many of our spiritual problems, this continual infection of demonic powers into our home via a feline carrier. I take my purse and the cat and proceed directly to the car. I wish I'd thought to put the beast in a cardboard box, but I feel a sense of urgency. There doesn't seem to be a moment to waste. Consequently, the cat is free to roam around the interior of my new car, defiling, I'm sure, every surface. But I can deal with that later.

"It's not really your fault," I tell the cat in what I hope is a soothing tone. Then I start driving toward town, not really sure of where I'm going or what I'm going to do. I consider the Humane Society but then realize they would be closed on a holiday. So I continue through town and out toward the country. Finally I park near a bridge where there is a fast-moving river below. I coax Spooky into my lap and then remove her collar.

"You're simply the victim in the devil's vile game. But I can't have you constantly contaminating my house and my family." I get out of the car with the cat still in my arms and walk over to where I can see the river from the road. But it appears to be a rugged hike to get down there. And with visions of both the cat and me landing in the river, I decide this is not the best way. But now I am getting extremely nervous and scared.

With shaking knees and a pounding heart, I walk out on the pedestrian path that runs alongside the two-lane bridge. This will be for the best. A fall like this will end this deed more quickly and be less painful to the cat. But once I'm in position, midway on the bridge, the kitten purrs against my sweatshirt where I have it clutched to my chest, and I know I can't do this thing. *Lord, help me. I just cannot do it!*

Feeling weak and defeated, I get back into the car and set the kitten on the passenger seat beside me. And knowing that I'm a failure, I continue driving deeper into the countryside. If this is the best I can do, if this is my way of purging the demons from my life, well, then I suppose I deserve to be tormented by Satan for the rest of my life. I am hopeless, useless, a pathetic excuse for a spiritual warrior. Perhaps someone should throw *me* into the river.

Finally I see a small farm off the side of the road. A little white house with a barn not far behind it. A perfect home for a cat. "You'll be happier here," I calmly tell the cat as I turn down the long graveled driveway. I drive a bit until I come to a spot that's just wide enough to turn around in, and desperately hoping that no one is watching, I turn my car around so it now faces the road. I don't see any other cars around, and there don't seem to be lights on in the house.

"You can catch mice in the barn." I put my car into Park and then pick up the kitten again. "You'll have lots of room to run and play." I step outside and walk about twenty feet from the car. "Have fun." I put her down onto the damp ground. She just stands there with her back slightly arched as if she too senses danger. Then I turn and hurry to my car, and without looking back, I step on the gas, spewing gravel as I quickly drive away.

I'm surprised to find that I have hot tears running down my face as I head back down the paved road toward town. "I did that for you, Lord. I know the cat was evil and defiled. I confess that I knew it all along. O Lord, please forgive me for allowing her to stay in our home so long. Forgive me for allowing my family to be exposed to Satan's influence. But it was only because of Rick and the girls; they thought she was just a normal kitten. I am sorry, Lord. So sorry. Please make our family clean now. Protect us from Satan. Please, please, please…"

It's getting dark out, but I'm afraid to go home now. Afraid that I will have to face Rick and the girls. Afraid that I will have to explain about the missing cat. I drive past the Pratt home again, and it seems that some of the cars have left, including Cynthia's little white Subaru, which gives me an idea. I hurry over to her house and am relieved to see that she's home now. So I park and walk toward the house. Suppressing feelings of intruding, I knock on her door.

"Oh, I have been praying for you, Ruth," she says as she opens the door wide. "Come in, sister. I have had such a burden for you today."

I'm surprised at how comforting her sparse little house feels to me right now. I remember how I once thought it cold and unfriendly, but suddenly it seems like a warm, safe haven, an escape from the raging storm. We both sit on her couch, and I immediately tell her about my botched-up Thanksgiving. Although I don't mention the cat. I am too humiliated to share those details just yet. I still don't know why it took me so long to figure out that Satan can use something as seemingly harmless as a cat to get the upper hand in our lives. I should've been smarter. But I do tell Cynthia about my family and about the ugly confrontation in my sister's kitchen.

She presses her lips together, then sadly shakes her head. "That's what comes from mixing darkness and light."

"I know. Even before I went to my sister's house, I knew it was wrong. I should've boycotted the whole affair. But I didn't. I just don't know why I keep making these mistakes."

She pats me on the back. "Oh, we all make mistakes, Ruth. But the Lord can use the pain to teach us, to reprimand us, and sometimes even to punish us. Like the child who puts her hand in the fire and gets burned, you surely won't want to do that again, will you?"

"No, of course not."

"You see."

"But it's frustrating, Cynthia. Sometimes it seems I make the same mistakes again and again. Like no matter how hard I try, I'm stuck in a vicious circle."

"Yes, I know. And there's a reason for that."

"I still need more deliverance prayer?"

She nods. "Yes. Sister Bronte and I were just talking about that today. And you're not alone, Ruth. Many in the congregation are being plagued with demonic intrusions. Many are in need of more deliverance. We feel that we've only scratched the surface. Our work has barely begun."

"Really?"

"Most definitely. And, as a result, we will be having special deliverance prayers throughout every service. We will do warfare until the Enemy has been thoroughly defeated and evicted from among our own. Only then can we expect to have a real impact on the outside world. Does that make sense?"

"Of course." And while this is encouraging, I still feel lost and confused, as if it will not be enough. Will it ever be enough?

"But I can tell that you're in need of deliverance right now." She looks into my eyes. "You are under attack even as we're talking. Am I right?"

I sigh and look down at the floor. "Yes."

"I should call for reinforcements," she says with authority. "This may be more than a one-woman battle. I happen to know that Bronte is meeting with some women right now. There are others who have been under siege today." She sighs. "Unfortunately, the holidays are one of Satan's favorite times to wage all-out attacks."

So I wait in her living room as she makes the phone call. And it's not long before Bronte and several other women from the church are gathered around me and praying. Fervently praying. To my relief it doesn't take quite as long to carry out the deliverance this time. Thankfully, there is no vomiting, although I do actually lose consciousness at one point. But Bronte reassures me that this is perfectly normal. "It's just another one of Satan's tactics," she tells me. "He thinks if he can knock you out, we won't be able to knock the demons out of you." She chuckles. "But we don't give up, do we, girls?" They laugh and agree with her.

"That's right," says Edna. "You should've seen one night when Sister Bronte prayed for Shauna. Shauna went to the rest room and never came back. Turned out she had passed out in there, and we didn't even know it."

"That's why we insist on accompanying people to the rest room now," says Bronte, "during an exorcism, that is. Just to ensure they are okay."

"Satan is crafty," adds Cynthia. "It's not easy to keep up with his clever tricks."

It seems we are done praying now, and I am uncomfortably aware of the time and that my family must be wondering where I have disappeared to. I'm just about to excuse myself and call it a night, but Bronte suddenly changes direction.

"Before we break it off, I must say something," Sister Bronte proclaims. "The Lord has just shown me that Melinda is also in need of deliverance tonight. Do I have confirmation with anyone else?"

"Yes," says Cynthia eagerly, "I feel it in my spirit too."

I barely know this young woman and was surprised when she showed up here tonight. I heard Bronte met her at a 7-Eleven store where Melinda works as a cashier. I've only talked to Melinda once, and that was during a church service a couple of weeks ago, but I sensed she was extremely insecure. However, I figured this might simply be due to a very bad case of acne, plus the fact that she's rather obese. It only makes sense that she might suffer from a bad self-image.

"Do you want us to pray for you?" Sister Bronte asks Melinda.

Melinda looks a little frightened, but she silently nods her consent. Then we all place our hands on her, and Sister Bronte begins to speak. "Melinda, is it true that you were sexually abused as a child?" Melinda looks surprised, but once again she nods, then looks down uncomfortably at her lap. I try not to remember my own experience now or how shocked I was when Bronte told me those horrible things—things I believe happened, despite what my mother and sister said. Instead, I try to focus on Melinda. At least this doesn't seem to be a shock to her.

"Yes," continues Bronte, "I can see that you had more than one molester in your life. Is that correct?"

Again the nod.

"But that was a long time ago, and then you became a teenager and a young woman. And now you are using what happened to you as a child as an excuse to practice promiscuity as an adult."

Melinda's head jerks up, and she looks at Bronte with confused and fear-filled eyes.

"Isn't that true, Melinda? You are having affairs with numerous men, and you are using your childhood as an—"

"No!" Melinda says suddenly. "That's not true."

But it's obvious that Sister Bronte doesn't believe Melinda. And she continues to speak, describing specific instances where Melinda has been involved in sexual relationships with all sorts of men, even some who are married and some who are part of our church. It's really quite shocking! And yet Melinda continues to deny this.

"Sister Melinda!" Cynthia sternly admonishes the girl. "You *must* be honest with us, and you must be honest before the Lord, or else you will never be free."

"But it's *not* true," she tells us, her face wet with tears. "I never did those things. I really never did—" She crumples forward, sobbing and gasping loudly. Everyone continues to pray for her, including me.

I'm feeling somewhat relieved to have this attention focused on poor Melinda just now. So many times I feel that I'm the one who's constantly messing up, the one in need of deliverance prayers. I might have things under control after all. So I continue to fervently pray and agree with the prayers being prayed, and like the others, I loudly command the demons plaguing Melinda to depart from her. We go on like this for what must be close to an hour, but it feels like we've hit a brick wall, and I can tell we are not making progress with this stubborn young woman. Melinda refuses to cooperate. Despite Sister Bronte's detailed descriptions and the spiritual confirmations being given by the rest of the group, Melinda is in complete denial.

"It's no use," Sister Bronte finally says. "If you won't acknowledge the truth, Melinda, you will never be free from the hold that Satan has placed on you."

"But I-I…" Melinda helplessly holds up her hands. Her nose is running, and her red blotchy face is soaked with tears. I don't understand why she is holding back. Doesn't she want to be clean?

"Maybe she's repressed the memory," I suddenly suggest to Bronte.

"You know, the way I had done that time when you told me about what had happened to me as a child. I had absolutely no memory of it at all. Isn't it possible that Melinda has forgotten things too?"

"I don't see how," Cynthia says as she hands her a tissue. "Melinda is an adult. You were a very young child, Ruth. It's different."

"But what about when Shauna passed out? And then I fainted too. Maybe Satan did something like that to Melinda. Maybe he caused her to black out so he could take advantage of her."

Bronte seems to be considering my words. "Perhaps..."

"Maybe Satan has her so confused," I continue as if I'm on a roll now, "that she can't see what's happening when it's happening. Maybe he's blinded her and she's doing these things without even knowing it."

"I suppose that's possible," says Sister Bronte. "I have heard some very strange stories about satanic influence." She turns back to Melinda with a compassionate expression and a softer tone of voice. "But unless you are willing to admit to some kind of involvement, to confess to some kind of sin, we cannot help you. Do you understand? You must be willing, or it won't work."

"Okay," says Melinda slowly. "I'm thinking maybe Ruth is right. Maybe Satan really does have such a hold on me. I mean, because of what happened to me as a kid, that things are happening, things I'm not even aware of..."

"That's right," urges Cynthia. "Open your spirit and your mind. Be willing to admit that Satan is at work in you and that demonic power is keeping you in bondage."

"Do you have anything to confess?" Bronte asks her once again.

Melinda looks down at her hands in her lap again. "I do confess that I've had impure thoughts." She takes a deep breath. "And I've had sexual fantasies."

"Aha!" says Bronte. "See, this might be a key. Do you know that what you are calling a fantasy might actually be a reality?"

"Yes!" I say in enthusiastic agreement. "I know what you mean, Sister Bronte. Listen to me, Melinda. There have been times in my own life when I was unable to discern what was real and what was not." I consider the way I was bluffed into allowing the cat to remain in our house all this time, telling myself she was simply an innocent kitten. "Don't you see?" I say to Melinda. "We can all be deceived. Like Cynthia said, Satan is very, very clever."

She firmly nods her head, looking at me as if she actually trusts me, and this fills me with a fresh feeling of power and hope.

"Why don't *you* pray for her deliverance?" Bronte looks directly at me. "You seem to have some connection with her spirit."

And so I pray for Melinda. I cast out the evil spirits of deception and sexual lust and finally the demons of fornication that have taken control of her life without her even knowing it. I pray with power and might, and when I'm done, everyone loudly says, "Amen," and it seems we have finally accomplished something here.

"Thank you, Ruth," Melinda tells me afterward. "The Spirit is really in you. It was your prayers that delivered me, and I'm really, really thankful."

"I'm happy to be used by the Lord. And I know how it feels to be in need of deliverance."

"We all do," says Cynthia.

Melinda turns to me just as we're starting to leave. "Can I ask you a favor?"

"Sure."

"Can I count on you to keep praying for me about this?"

"Of course."

"Because I know these things can take time. Sister Bronte explained how it's a complicated process, with lots of steps and everything."

"Yes," I tell her, "that's been the case with me. Getting Satan out of our lives seems to be an ongoing process."

"So, I can call you, then? If I need help again?"

Now the truth is, I find this prospect a little frightening. I mean, I can barely keep my own life on track these days. How can I possibly manage to help someone else? But the others are watching me now, listening for my response. How can I possibly tell Melinda no? What kind of Christian would deny help to someone like her?

So with some reluctance I agree. "Please feel free to call me whenever you're in need of help." But I'm barely to my car when I fear I've made a big mistake in agreeing to this. And yet, what choice did I have? Perhaps it's only my flesh that assumes this is a mistake. After all, isn't it the Lord's will that we lay down our lives for our friends?

Surely the Lord will help me do this. And as I drive toward home, I am assuring myself that certainly this is just what I need right now. Helping poor Melinda will become my opportunity to focus on someone else's problems for a change. Now, really, what is wrong with that? What is wrong with that?

27

I t's after eight o'clock by the time I pull up to our house. And Rick's pickup is not in the driveway. I push the remote to open the garage door, only to see that it too is empty. So I pull inside and think that perhaps I have once again dodged a bullet. Not that my husband is going to shoot me, at least I don't think so. But just the same, I am relieved to have made it home ahead of them. And yet I feel strangely uneasy. It's nearly bedtime. Are they still at Lynette and Jeff's? And if so, why are they staying so long? The idea of Rick and the girls spending so much time in that den of iniquity is very unsettling, and as I close the garage door and go into the house, I am tempted to call Lynette to find out what's going on.

Still, as I turn on some lights, I tell myself the damage is probably already done. I'm sure that by now Rick and the girls have been exposed to the worst my family has to offer. How can a few extra hours make much difference? And yet I feel the need to do some serious spiritual warfare for their sakes. And for Matthew's sake as well. I carry a great burden for my only son; I've been grieving for him these past few weeks—almost as if he has physically died. It's hard to understand, and I haven't attempted to explain these feelings to anyone, but it feels as if Matthew has been removed from my life in an almost permanent way—plucked out of my heart by the very hand of Satan, I'm afraid. But perhaps it's not too late, I tell myself as I hit my knees. Maybe the

Lord will use my prayers to deliver him. If only I can press in with the spiritual intensity that it takes to conquer such demonic foes.

The sound of the phone ringing jars me from my fervent petition. As usual, I don't answer it. But I do pause as the answering machine begins to loudly play out the monotonous monologue that Rick recorded years ago.

"Ruth?" It's Rick's voice calling out through the machine. He sounds urgent. *"Ruth, are you there?* We're at Saint John's Hospital. If you're there, will you please pick up? I've left lots of messages, and I'm starting to get worried about—"

"I'm here," I say breathlessly into the phone. "What's going on? Is it one of the girls? What happened?" My heart is pounding in my ears, and I feel certain that my girls have been hurt in a car wreck and are perhaps unconscious or even dead. And it will be my fault. My fault for abandoning them with my family. Oh, why am I so stupid?

"It's your mother."

"Oh…" I try not to sound too relieved. "What's wrong?"

"She started having chest pains around five. But she thought it was indigestion, and she didn't tell anyone about it. She just said she was tired and was going to put her feet up and have a little rest."

"And now she thinks she's having a heart attack?" I say in what I'm sure sounds like a cold and cynical tone. My mother is such an attention getter. She always has been.

"According to the doctors, she *did* have a heart attack. Actually, they called it a myocardial infarction, but I think it's the same thing."

"Oh." I must admit this does sound serious. "How is she now?"

"She's still in the ER, but she's been stabilized and is supposed to be moved upstairs pretty soon. Of course, they'll have to keep monitoring her, and the doctor says they'll keep her a couple of days for observation and run some tests on her to pinpoint the exact problem."

"So why are you still there?"

"What?"

"Why are you and the girls staying so long, Rick? If Mom's stabilized and everything's okay, it's not as if there's anything you can do for her, is there? I don't understand why you're still there."

"We're *all* still here." He sounds irritated now. "Even Matthew's here. In fact, we've all been wondering why *you* aren't here."

I don't respond to this accusation. Because that's what it is, an accusation.

"Look, Ruth, I don't know what went on with you and your mom and sister in the kitchen today, but I can guess. It was obvious that you said something terribly upsetting to both of them, and I actually overheard Lynette telling Jonathan that you might've been the reason your mom had a heart attack."

"Lynette is blaming me for Mom having a heart attack?"

"Not blaming...but whatever you said must've really upset your mother."

"What about me? What if they said things to upset me?"

"Everything upsets you," he says in a stiff voice.

I'm tempted to hang up. Instead I pray in the Spirit. *Get thee behind me, Satan!*

"So are you saying that you don't want to come over and see your mother?"

"Not particularly."

"Fine." But I can tell by his voice this is not fine. He is angry. Really angry.

"Look," I try to reason with him. "If it's true that I upset her earlier today, what good would it possibly do for me to come now? She might end up having another heart attack and die. Then everyone could accuse me of murdering her."

"And you don't want to be here with your family, Ruth? To show some support?"

I am thinking that it's those who take up their crosses and follow Jesus who are my family. But I know it would only make Rick furious if I dared to say something like this.

"The girls should be at home by now," I tell him.

"It's not a school night."

"Well, it's late. And it's past their bedtime."

"I'll be the judge of that."

"So you're not coming home, then?" I feel weak now, as if I'm losing control. Rick is usually so busy that he's not that involved. But now it seems he's taking over. I don't like it.

"Not yet."

There's a long pause. This seems a stalemate of sorts. And I'm tempted to just hang up. What's the point?

"Look, Ruth. Even though it's not easy being here under these circumstances, it's still been good having the family together like this. Lynette and Jeff have really appreciated our being here with them, and it's nice getting to know Jonathan better. But the best part has been having Matthew with us. That kid is really starting to grow up. He's said some pretty mature things. And the girls have been drawing some pictures to decorate your mom's room with and—"

"Well, that's all very nice. It sounds like you have everything under control, Rick. Tell my mother I'll be praying for her." Then I do hang up. But I'm barely off the phone when I realize what is happening over at Saint John's right now. As soon as Rick rejoins the family, they will all be asking questions and talking about me. They will tell each other that something is wrong with me, that I'm acting crazy again, and that I've always been the odd one—the outsider, the misfit, the black sheep. But that's how it was with Jesus too. People didn't understand him either. And eventually they killed him.

As I return to my knees, I feel no comfort in knowing these things. Being left out of things again hurts just as much now as it did when I was a child. Oh sure, Rick would say that this was my choice—that I'm the one who abandoned the Thanksgiving dinner and then refused to join them at the hospital tonight. But how can I do anything else? How can I compromise myself by being with people who are so totally corrupt and sinful? It particularly pains me to think of my Sarah and Mary there now, exposed to such blatant examples of immorality. Besides my divorced New Age "Christian" sister and her second husband, there's Matthew, who has turned from the Lord as he indulges an appetite for alcohol, rock music, and deviant books. Even their own father is a poor example of godliness. How can I allow my innocent girls to be exposed to such wickedness? And what about the demons?

I become so enraged by all this that I am finally unable to pray. I know what I must do. I must rescue my two daughters from this corrupt influence. Before it's too late. I drive faster than I should on my way to the hospital, and I even park in the emergency zone. But this is an emergency. I hurry to the ER waiting area, hoping they are still down here.

"Mommy!" Sarah says happily when she spies me hurrying down the hall toward them.

"You came," Rick says with what looks like relief.

"They're just moving Mom upstairs," says Jeff. "Lynette went on ahead to put some personal things in her room."

"I just came to get the girls," I say quickly, avoiding everyone's eyes. "It's getting pretty late."

The girls protest, and Rick, to my chagrin, backs them. But I insist that it's time to go home, and to my surprise my brother agrees. "It is late," he tells everyone. "And I, for one, have had a very long day."

Without further ado, I grab Sarah's hand and use my firmest mother's voice to tell Mary it's time to leave. I'm very relieved that the girls don't argue. We call out good-byes as I escort them down the corridor to the exit and outside to my car, which, thankfully, has not been towed away.

"Is Grandma going to be okay?" Sarah asks as I drive away from the hospital.

"I think so. But we should keep praying for her."

"That's what I told everyone," Sarah says. "I told them that we should be praying for Grandma. But they all wanted to pray without words." She sighs loudly. "How does the Lord hear us when we pray without words?"

Mary laughs. "He reads our minds, stupid."

"Don't call your sister 'stupid,' " I shoot back at her. But at the same time I am wondering, *Does he really read our minds?* And what does he think when he reads my mind? Oh, I know that I am evil. Corrupt and evil. How will I ever escape?

28

A week has passed since Thanksgiving, and the girls have finally accepted that Spooky ran away from home. They put up Lost Cat posters, but no one has called. And finally, with the promise that we might get another kitty but not until after the holidays, they allowed me to put away the cat things.

My mother was released from the hospital on Tuesday, but everyone in my family is still mad at me. They think I am a horrible person because I refused to visit her. And I refused to take the girls to see her. And now I refuse to answer the phone when any of them call. But I know I've made the right decision. More and more I am understanding and accepting that many of my problems are a direct result of exposing myself to the wrong people. Particularly my own family.

"Your spirit is too easily influenced," Cynthia told me the other day after a deliverance prayer session. "You need to carefully guard your heart, Ruth. It's your responsibility to protect yourself and your children. If this means cutting off all ties with your extended family, then you must do so. Remember, our Savior said that if we're not willing to leave mother and father and brother and sister behind, then we are not worthy to follow him."

And I've been trying to remember this. As well as the verse about not bringing peace but a sword. I know I am called to go to battle. And so I do. But there is one battle I'd like to forget. The day I informed Rick that I'd taken the girls out of Christian school. At first he was glad, thinking they'd be back in public school and we could save a few bucks. But I quickly set him straight.

"Homeschool?" he demanded. "Have you lost your mind?"

"It's for the best. I've given it a lot of thought and—"

"This is totally nuts. You keep telling me you hardly have time to get things done around here, and you still haven't started working yet, and now you think you can take on homeschooling the girls too? You are flipping out on me, Ruth!"

"I can *do* this, Rick," I said, trying to keep my cool. "I really believe the Lord has called me to do it. And if he calls us to do something, he empowers us to do it." I explained about the other parents at the church who wanted to work together on it, how we'd be sharing responsibilities and how it would be fun.

"I don't want a bunch of freaks educating our daughters."

"They are not freaks. If you'd come to church, you'd see that they are simply committed Christians with hearts to serve the Lord."

"Seriously, Ruth, I think you need to get your head examined. Something is wrong with you, or maybe it's the influence of that crazy church of yours. If I weren't so busy with these extra holiday hours, I'd haul you to a shrink myself. But—"

"The only thing wrong with me is that you have failed as a spiritual leader and—"

"No! You have taken over as the leader, Ruth! But you are trying to lead the girls straight to the nuthouse. And I am going to put my foot down!"

"How are you going to do that?" My voice was calm, but my heart was pounding.

"I'm going to forbid you to take the girls to the crazy church again. All Glenn Pratt does is fill people with fear. All that extreme focus on evil and demons is nonsense. I'm not a theologian, but the Jesus I know is about love and forgiveness. Your church gives more glory to Satan than it does to God."

It got ugly as I argued back, and it soon turned into a shouting match. Me shouting scriptures at him, and him finally sinking down to Satan's level as he swore at me.

"Don't use that kind of language in my home!" I glanced over to where Mary and Sarah were lurking in the hallway. "And don't ever speak like that in front of my daughters."

Rick seemed to be caught off guard by the shocked faces of the girls. But instead of apologizing, he just grabbed his lunchbox and stormed out the door. I wanted to yell, "Good riddance," but instead I bit my tongue.

"I'm sorry about that," I told the girls in a soothing voice, pulling them toward me and hugging them both. "Your dad knows better than to talk like that. But he's under a lot of stress these days. And I'm guessing he's also having some satanic attack. Your dad really needs our prayers right now, girls."

And they took this very seriously as we all got down on our knees and fervently prayed for their dad. We also prayed for Matthew and for the Lord to heal our family and to bring us back together. We were all crying by the time we finished praying.

"That's what I want, Mommy," Sarah told me as I handed her a tissue. "I want our family to be happy again."

"Me too," admitted Mary. "I don't like this."

"I know. But only the Lord can heal these wounds. We need to keep asking him to help us. And we need to keep fighting off the demonic forces too. Satan is really attacking our family, and we're the only ones who can bind him and keep him out. We have to be strong, girls."

So the girls and I have been doing regular spiritual warfare all week long. Also, we've been staying out of Rick's way. And he seems to be avoiding us too. Despite his "putting his foot down," I have taken the girls to church. I think it's more important to obey God than man. And after the midweek worship service, where hundreds of demons were bound and cast out, we have been taking this battle more seriously than ever. What really got our attention was when Mary allowed Sister Bronte to pray for her, and consequently, the demon of rebellion (which Bronte explained to Mary is as bad as witchcraft) was cast out of my older daughter. I was so thankful and relieved!

"I saw a demon in the hallway," Sarah tells me shortly before bedtime tonight. "I told him to get out of our house in the name of Jesus, but I'm afraid he's still there."

"I think you just imagined it," Mary says as she comes out of the bathroom with a toothbrush hanging out of her mouth.

"I did not. I really saw it."

"Yes," I assure Sarah as I push her overly long bangs out of her eyes. "I'm sure that you did."

"What did it look like, then?" demands Mary. "Describe it."

"It was kind of weird since it was smiling at me," says Sarah. "But not a happy kind of smile. And it was funny color for a demon, kind of a light pink."

Mary laughs. "Yeah, sure, that doesn't sound like much of a demon to me."

"Wait a minute," I tell her. "You girls know that Satan can disguise himself. He was supposed to have been the most beautiful angel in heaven before he was thrown out. There's no reason that all demons have to be scary and ugly looking. You should know that much by now."

"But the ones in my dreams are scary," Sarah admits.

"Yes. But you said yourself that you knew the one you just saw was a demon," I remind her. "How did you know that?"

"I felt it."

I nod. "See, Mary. Sarah is probably right. We need to pray right now, all three of us together. We need to cast that demon out." So we all join hands right there in the hallway, and we bind and cast out the "pink demon" as Sarah now calls it.

"A pink demon." Mary shakes her head after we're done. "That's so crazy."

"It was real," Sarah insists.

"Well, it's gone now," I point out. "Now where is *Pilgrim's Progress*?" That's the book we've been reading before bedtime lately.

"I'll get it," offers Mary.

"Finish brushing your teeth first," I tell her as Sarah and I head into the living room.

Lately we've felt safer in the living room. We leave the lights on all day and night, but something about the central location within our house and the light-colored walls makes us feel safer. And that's where we spend our evenings, reading or doing music or coloring. Of course, it's looking less and less like a living room, but that doesn't matter since I don't plan to do any entertaining. I don't want anyone uninvited coming into our home.

"Mom!" Mary screams just as Sarah and I have gotten comfortable on the couch. Certain that Mary has been seriously injured, I leap up and run to see what's wrong. Sarah is right on my heels. We find Mary still in the bathroom, but her face is pale, and she's staring into the mirror and pointing as if she's horrified.

"What is it?" I demand, relieved to see that she's not bleeding or hurt.

"Can't you see it in the mirror?" she says in a tiny voice.

"What?" I step closer to her and look into the large mirror above the sink, but all I see is her frightened reflection.

"The demon!"

"Is it the pink demon?" asks Sarah. And suddenly I wonder if my older daughter might be pulling our legs. Although her pale face is pretty convincing.

"No!" Mary steps back from the mirror and then clings to me, burying her head into my shoulder. I can feel her shaking, and I know she's not making this up.

"Let's pray," I tell them both. And for the second time tonight, we bind and cast out a demon.

Then Mary, still holding on to me, opens her eyes and gives the mirror a cautious sideways glance. "It's gone now."

"What did it look like?" asks Sarah as we return to the living room.

"It was ugly." Mary shudders. "Black and snarling and really, really scary." She hands me the book and sits down on the couch. "Mom, it was really horrible."

I put my arm around her, pulling her close. "You're safe now, Mary."

"But it was so awful. I've never seen anything so awful. His eyes—" She closes her eyes and shakes her head. "Ugh! It was like looking at Satan."

"Why do the demons keep bugging us, Mommy?" Sarah snuggles

closer to me, pulling the afghan up to her chin. "Why doesn't the Lord make them stay away and leave us alone?"

I consider this. "It's like Sister Bronte says: we're a threat to Satan's kingdom. The devil doesn't like it when Christians really try to follow the Lord. He wants to destroy us so we can't serve the Lord."

"Maybe we should pretend not to serve the Lord," suggests Sarah.

I kind of laugh. "I think the devil would figure that out."

Mary turns to her sister. "I'm sorry I make fun of you sometimes, Sarah."

"Huh?" Sarah looks confused.

"When you talk about seeing demons and stuff. I never really believed you. I thought you were just making it up."

"But now you know?" asks Sarah.

"Yeah." Mary nods solemnly. "Now I really know. I won't make fun of you again."

"Satan is real," I remind them. "And even though the Lord is stronger, we need to keep on our toes. We need to be spiritually armed and strong to win the battle."

"Maybe we should pray again," suggests Mary as she glances around the living room, almost as if she expects to see a demon in here. "Just to be safe, you know."

So we pray again. And then I read a chapter from the book. And finally I tell the girls it's time for bed. But I can tell as I walk them into their room that they're still afraid.

"Mom, will you stay with us in here?" asks Mary. "Just for a while?"

"I don't want to sleep in here," says Sarah. "I think that pink demon is still here. I think he hides in the rug and comes out at night."

I look down at the ballerina-pink carpet and remember that Sarah said the demon was light pink. "But we cast him out."

"I can still feel him," she insists.

"I think I can feel him too," says Mary.

Now I don't know what to do. Where do you go when you don't even feel safe in your own bedroom? Your own home?

"Can we sleep in your bedroom, Mommy?" asks Sarah.

Rick would probably throw a fit to find the girls in bed with me. And so far we've done fairly well in avoiding each other as well as additional conflict. "I don't think so…"

"How about the living room?" suggests Mary.

"Yes!" agrees Sarah. "The living room. I don't think demons are in there."

"But there's only one couch," I point out. "I don't think you'd both fit."

"We could sleep on the floor," says Mary. "Like a slumber party."

"Yes," says Sarah. "We could all sleep on the floor."

"Come on, Mom," Mary urges me. "It'll be fun."

So it is that we dig out sleeping bags, and we all sleep on the living-room floor. And I'm surprised that we all sleep soundly, and for a pleasant change, no one wakes up with nightmares. I'm not too surprised when Rick questions our unusual sleeping arrangements the following day, but I simply explain that it was the girls' idea and that we thought it would be fun.

He just nods in a tired way, but then he gives me *that look*—the one that tells me he still questions my judgment and perhaps even my sanity but just doesn't have the energy to take me on right now. I get a sense that he's picking his battles more carefully these days. But at least I managed to smooth things over with him regarding the homeschool decision. This was accomplished by assuring him that I felt certain VBF would refund the girls' tuition by the start of the new year. I guess it's true what they say—money talks. I just wish my husband would listen to the Lord's voice as well.

By the following week, sleeping in the living room has become a regular thing. We've even moved the girls' twin mattresses in there and pushed them next to each other, and all three of us sleep together on them. Of course, Rick questions this too, but Mary convinces him it's the only way we feel safe at night.

"Maybe if you didn't have to work all night, leaving us girls here all by ourselves," she says to him, "maybe we wouldn't be so scared then, Daddy."

"But what do you have to be afraid of?"

"Lots of things." She glances nervously at me. "Noises and things. Last night we thought we heard someone trying to break into our house."

"That's right," I say quickly. "Don't forget that since we lost Sadie, our faithful watchdog, we've felt more vulnerable than ever."

He brightens at this. "Hey, why don't you get another dog, Ruth?"

"Yes, Mommy!" exclaims Sarah. "Let's get another dog."

"We could get a watchdog like my friend Katy has," says Mary. "Their dog is specially trained to keep strangers away from the kids."

"That's a great idea," I say. "We'll look into it."

"Good." Rick glances around our living/sleeping room. "Anything to get back to normal in this house."

So as the girls do their schoolwork, I search the classified section of the newspaper for watchdogs. And after a few calls, I think I've found the perfect dog for us. The woman tells me she's a Christian and assures me that Rottweilers are the best watchdogs around. And as soon as the girls are done with their schoolwork, we drive into the country in search of the house.

It's just getting dusky when I turn down a graveled driveway that leads to a double-wide manufactured home. We can hear dogs barking frantically before we even get out of the car. I can tell by the sign on the gate and by the large dark-colored dogs that keep lunging toward the tall chain-link fence that I'm at the right address, but I feel uneasy as we walk toward the house.

"Hello," calls a stout older woman from the tacked-on front porch. "Are you the lady who just called about getting a dog?"

"Yes." I introduce myself and the girls.

"And I'm Barb." She waves us inside. "Why don't you come into the house so you can meet Buddy?"

The dogs outside continue to bark wildly as we go onto the porch, then follow this woman into a house that smells distinctly of dogs. One glance tells me that the dogs have made themselves quite comfortable in here.

"I put the other dogs outside to quiet things down. Some of the rowdier ones can get a little wound up over company." She nods to a large black dog calmly sitting by a wood stove. "This is Buddy. I wanted you to see what kind of a dog you'll be getting." She eases herself down on a kitchen chair and slaps her knee. "Come here, Buddy."

The dog obediently comes over, then goes through a set of commands, including "sit" and "lay down" and "shake." Then she has Buddy shake hands with both girls. It's obvious this dog has a sweet disposition, and the girls seem to really like him.

"So you're selling Buddy?" I ask hopefully.

She laughs. "No, of course not. He's the sire. We need him to have more dogs. But I wanted you to meet him so you would see the fine quality of dogs we breed here, so you could decide whether or not a Rottweiler is the sort of dog you're looking for. These dogs are smart and loyal, and as you see, they're great with kids."

"Can we get one?" Mary asks as she strokes Buddy's silky ear.

"Yeah, Mom," Sarah pleads as she runs her hand down his smooth back. "Can we bring one home with us tonight?"

"Well, I don't know..." I glance over at Barb. "I'm in a car, you see, and it's rather new. I hadn't really figured how to—"

"No problem." She waves her hand. "Tom can deliver a dog to you."

"But how will we decide which one?" I ask.

"Well, if you will trust me—and you know I'm a good Christian woman like you—I'd be happy to make my best recommendation for you and your girls. I know these dogs better than anyone, and I'll be sure to pick out one that I think suits you."

"Thank you. I'd really appreciate it."

"But I was thinking," she says, "these dogs are social animals, you know, and they can get lonely, especially if you keep them outdoors most of the time. If I were you, I would consider getting a pair."

"One for me and one for Sarah," says Mary.

"That's right," agrees Barb. "A dog for each girl."

"Oh, I don't know..." I glance at Buddy, trying to imagine Buddy times two.

"I'll tell you what," says Barb. "I really like you and your girls, and I'd like to make you a special offer. You buy one dog, and the second will be half price."

"Half price, Mom!" says Mary eagerly.

Well, I'm already worried that the price of just one dog might be pushing our already-tight budget, but a second one is probably too much to even consider.

"Please, Mommy," says Sarah. "Daddy wanted a dog. Why not two?"

"We used to have two pets," Sarah tells Barb. "Our dog, Sadie, who got killed on Halloween. And our cat, Spooky, just disappeared. We think she was cat-napped."

Barb laughs. "Sounds to me like you could use a couple of good dogs at your house. And I know just the pair—they're littermates—Bonnie and Clyde." She grins. "But that's because when they were pups and got into the kitchen, they stole some hamburger I was thawing. You could change their names if you like."

"Please, Mom," begs Mary. "Sarah and I will take care of them."

"And Bonnie and Clyde can keep us safe," Sarah reminds me.

"Oh why not?" I finally give in.

So I write a check that will empty what's left in our checking account, knowing full well that Rick won't get paid until the end of the week. But at least we'll be safe. That's worth more than money.

29

It's past seven o'clock when an old pickup pulls into our driveway. The girls run to the front window, shrieking with delight when they see a pair of dogs in the back. I tell the girls to wait on the porch, then open the front door in time to hear the man swearing at the dogs and telling them to shut up. Then he looks toward the house. "You the lady who bought the dogs?"

I nod. "Is everything okay?"

"Yeah, everything's just great." His tone is sarcastic. "I get home from work, and I'm dead tired, and the wife tells me I gotta deliver her dumb dogs." He hands me an envelope. "Here's their puppy registration forms. You'll have to send them in yourself." He goes to the truck, and I tentatively follow him to where two dogs are still barking like maniacs in the back of it.

"Shut up!" The tailgate comes down with a loud bang that startles the dogs, and they look at us expectantly. Then he unties one dog and hands me one end of the nylon rope; the other end is tied to a chain choke collar around the dog's neck. "This one's Bonnie." He unties the other dog, then commands both of them out of the truck. "And this here is Clyde." Once on the ground the dogs immediately start sniffing me, and while I don't feel exactly threatened, I am a little scared. "They just wanna get to know you," he says as he hands me Clyde's rope.

"Hello, Bonnie and Clyde," I calmly say, letting them sniff the top of my hand. "You're going to be our dogs now. I hope you'll be happy here."

"I gotta go," he says as he gets into his truck. "Good luck with the dogs. Make 'em mind you." Then he takes off, and I'm left standing with two dogs that I'm sure outweigh me and could easily overpower me if they chose to.

"Can we come out now?" Mary yells.

Naturally, this makes the dogs start barking all over again.

"Quiet!" I command the dogs, and I'm pleasantly surprised that they obey. Still, I'm not sure what to do. It makes sense to introduce the dogs to the girls, but at the same time, I'm a little frightened. "No," I yell back to Mary. "You girls go back inside the house. I'm going to take the dogs into the backyard first. Then we'll figure it out."

So I lead the dogs around to the side gate and let them loose in the backyard. First they stand beside me, as if waiting for a command. "Go ahead and look around." I latch the gate behind me. "See if you like your new home." Then I go inside, where Sarah and Mary are begging to go out and play with the dogs.

I turn the exterior light on and see that both dogs are on the deck now, looking into the house and at us with curious expressions. But I'm not ready to let them inside. "Go get your coats on," I tell the girls. "And when you come outside, make sure that you remain very calm. We have to let Bonnie and Clyde get used to us slowly. Okay?"

After an hour of getting acquainted, it seems that Bonnie and Clyde actually like us. Sarah and Mary have already rounded up some old doggy toys that once belonged to Sadie. And we found Sadie's old food and water dishes, as well as some leftover dog food, and Bonnie and Clyde seem to be making themselves right at home.

"Okay, girls. Time for you two to get ready for bed."

"Where are Bonnie and Clyde going to sleep?" asks Sarah.

"I think they'll be fine out here."

"But it's cold outside," says Mary.

"Can't they come in?" begs Sarah.

"They can protect us better if they're inside," Mary points out.

"Sadie used to sleep in the laundry room," Sarah reminds me.

So Bonnie and Clyde find themselves warm and snug in the laundry room, sleeping on Sadie's old bed plus a couple of beach towels. And tonight when the girls and I finally return to our campy arrangements in the living room, everyone feels much safer. I read for a while, but before long both girls are fast asleep. And as I do my regular bouts of spiritual warfare, I'm about to join them.

It seems I've barely drifted off when we're all awakened by the sound of loud, frantic barking. It takes me a moment to remember the dogs, but then my heart is pounding with fear. There's an intruder in the house. Or perhaps it's demonic. Then I hear a voice calling my name; it's only Rick.

I hurry into the kitchen and am just about to tell him what's going on when he stupidly opens the laundry-room door. Suddenly both dogs lunge at him, and I yell at the dogs, telling them, "Stop it! Sit!" Fortunately, and to my amazement, they obey. But it might be because I'm standing between them and my husband. They seem to understand I'm their new owner. Rick is still in one piece, although I can tell he's truly frightened. It's almost amusing to see my big, strong husband so completely shaken up over a couple of dogs, but I keep these thoughts to myself.

"What the heck is going on here?" he demands after I finally get the dogs back into the laundry room and close the door behind them.

I explain about the dogs and how we decided to get two, but I can tell by his tightly pressed lips and glaring eyes that he's extremely agitated. I almost expect to see two blasts of steam shooting from his nostrils.

"You're the one who said to get a dog," I calmly remind him.

"*A* dog! As in *one* dog. And I had a dog like Sadie in mind. Not those two *killers* in there."

"Bonnie and Clyde are *not* killers."

"Yeah, right. And just for the record, the names suit the gangster dogs."

"We can change their names," I say. "And just for the record, they are actually very nice dogs, and they get along well with the girls."

"You *have* to take them back, Ruth!"

"I most certainly do not."

"I refuse to come home to those beasts trying to eat me alive every night."

"They'll get used to you."

"They won't need to, because either they go or I do!"

"Rick…we need these dogs for protection."

"I don't care. They have to go back. We are not going to keep a pair of vicious attack dogs in the house!"

"Daddy," says Sarah as she and Mary walk into the kitchen, "Bonnie and Clyde are good dogs. They just don't know you yet."

"Yeah." Mary steps up and points her finger at her father. "They probably thought you were a prowler or something, coming in here in the middle of the night like that. Can't you see they were just doing their job?"

I can see him softening some, looking at the hopeful little faces of his daughters, sweet and innocent in their nighties.

"The dogs are protecting us," adds Sarah.

"See?" I fold my arms across my chest.

"Aren't they Rottweilers?" he asks meekly. "They must've cost a fortune…"

"Yes, they're registered Rottweilers, but we got the second dog for half price."

"And they already know how to fetch," says Mary.

"And we're going to take them for walks," adds Sarah.

He rolls his eyes. "Guess I'm outnumbered on this."

"That's right," says Mary.

"I'm sorry they scared you," I tell him. "But maybe it gives you an idea of how we feel sometimes. We get scared too, Rick, especially when you're not around. These dogs make us feel safer. Can't you understand that?"

He shrugs. "Guess I'll have to get used to them."

"That's right, Daddy," says Sarah. "And they'll have to get used to you too."

Soon the girls are back to sleep, and Rick has gone to our room. I do feel a little safer with the dogs in the house, but I feel extremely uneasy too. There's a nudging in my spirit that keeps telling me something is wrong. I'm not sure if it's demonic intrusion or what exactly. But I have the sneaking suspicion that it's my husband. Oh sure, he gave in on the dogs tonight, but it was only because of the girls' pleading. If I had fought that battle alone, I would've lost. And what does this mean when I am constantly pitted against my own husband? How can a family that's so spiritually split possibly survive and stay intact?

So I realize with vivid clarity that I must do serious battle for Rick's heart and soul and spirit. Because until he is living a life that's truly surrendered to the Lord, we are all in grave danger. And that's when it occurs to me that the Lord has ordained me to be Rick's salvation. I've heard Sister Bronte explain how we can take that position, and suddenly it's very clear. I am Rick's only link back to the Lord right now. That's what motivates me to get up from the mattress on the floor and quietly creep into the master bedroom, where he's sleeping.

As he softly snores, I kneel by the bed and begin to do warfare. Whispering the words, I bind Satan in Rick's life, and I cast out his demons one by one by their actual names, just as we do during deliverance vigils. But I'm surprised at some of the names. I had always considered Rick to be a faithful husband, but some of the demons I cast out are Lust and Adultery, and I am so shocked when I cast out the demon of incest that I can't pray another word. It's as if a boulder has been dropped upon my spirit. Is it possible that my own husband has been incestuous toward our daughters?

I choke back tears as I flee from the bedroom. This battle is too difficult for me to fight alone. If what the Spirit has revealed is accurate, Rick is truly evil and vile, and our marriage is not only a sham, it is over! Haunted by this shocking revelation, I am unable to sleep, so I prowl through the house praying and binding and begging the Lord to show me what must be done. What must be done…what must be done?

30

It is only the power of the Lord that keeps me going the next few days. Thankful for the distraction of the two dogs, which the girls insist on keeping in the house in order to feel safe from demonic oppression, and the keyboard, which both girls are now practicing on, I've had minimal interaction with my daughters. In the morning I give them their assignments for school, mostly just going through the curriculum that some of the other homeschooling parents have loaned me. Then I spend the rest of the day in deep, travailing prayer and Scripture reading.

On Wednesday night we attend the midweek service, and during deliverance prayer time, the plan is for me to sit "in proxy" for my husband. This was all prearranged through a phone call to Cynthia when I told her what the Spirit had revealed to me about Rick's specific demons. She even told me it would be helpful if I brought in a piece of unwashed clothing that he had recently worn. So I have his favorite sweatshirt in a grocery bag. I can barely stand to touch it.

I had hoped that Sarah and Mary might be involved in another prayer group. Both girls are getting quite good at binding and casting out demons, and many in the congregation appreciate their fresh approach, but since this was about them as well, Sister Bronte insisted that they participate in our group. So it is with some trepidation that I have agreed. And now there are about ten people, including my daughters, gathered around the chair I am seated in. And due to Cynthia's insistence, I am wearing Rick's old gray sweatshirt. And the smell of him on it is making me feel sick to my stomach.

"Remember, Ruth," Bronte instructs me in a gentle tone, "when we speak to you, we are actually addressing Rick. Concentrate on him as we pray. You are representing him, and your answers should be coming from him. Do you understand?"

I look into Bronte's pretty face and then slowly nod. Something about her clear blue eyes makes me trust her. But I try not to see the fear in my daughters' faces as they stand nearby, intently watching. This is for them as much as it is for Rick and for me. I explained all of this to them earlier today. We even spent some time praying that it would go well and that the power of the Lord would be released. And they seemed to understand; they seemed to know how much we need this deliverance. Still, I can appreciate their fear. I'm afraid as well.

I am stunned at the power of the prayers, at the strong words and the detailed descriptions of the demons being bound and cast out. Naturally, they are the same demons I addressed the other night. But as Bronte and Cynthia reprimand these demons, rebuking them in the name of Christ, I feel sickened and sad. And at one point I feel that I'm about to throw up. But instead everything goes fuzzy, then blank.

When I come to, the prayer warriors are winding down. It seems their spiritual work is done. But Mary and Sarah are both clinging to me and crying, and I've never seen such terrified expressions on their faces.

"Are you okay, Mommy?" Sarah asks in a shaky voice.

"Yes...it's just that the Lord had a lot of work to do on Daddy."

"Is it finished now?" Mary wipes her nose on the sleeve of her sweater. "Can we go home?"

"Yes, dear." Bronte puts an arm around Mary's shoulder. "It is finished now." She looks at both my daughters and smiles. "You girls did so well tonight. I am so proud of you two. You are growing up into godly young women, and I know the Lord is pleased with your hearts."

This seems to help some, and some of the fear drains from their faces.

"Are you girls going to do some music for us on Sunday?" she asks. "Perhaps that Christmas song we've been working on?"

Mary nods. "I've got it down now."

"And I know all the words," says Sarah.

Bronte claps her hands. "Oh, I can't wait to hear it!"

Once we're home, I can tell that there are bad spirits in the air. Just the same, I tell the girls to get ready for bed. And when they're settling down on the mattresses in the living room, with the dogs on either side for protection, the girls still seem very much on edge.

"I think we need to pray some more," I tell them. And they agree. So we do all the warfare sorts of things that we know how to do, but it just doesn't seem to be enough. Both Sarah and Mary feel certain that they're seeing demons hiding around corners, beneath the couch, inside the empty bookcase.

"Maybe we should turn on more lights," suggests Sarah.

So I turn on a table lamp. "There. Is that better?"

This seems to help, but we are all still uneasy. "Why don't you read to us?" says Mary.

So I pick up *Pilgrim's Progress* and begin to read.

"I mean from the Bible," says Mary.

"Yes." I set the book aside. "I think you're right." I open my well-worn Bible, my sword, in the middle, hoping to land in Psalms, which I do. Then I randomly pick Psalm 62 and begin to read. "Truly my soul silently waits for God; from Him comes my salvation. He only is my rock and my salvation; He is my defense; I shall not be greatly moved."

"Yes!" says Mary. "Read that part again."

So I read it again and again and again. And we all find great comfort in these sentences. I especially cling to the four words that say, "He is my defense." And yet, if he really is our defense, then why do we spend so much time defending ourselves?

Finally the girls seem to be soundly sleeping, and leaving the table lamp on, I stand. Bonnie and Clyde both look expectantly at me. "Stay," I quietly command as I creep from the room. It's still too early for Rick to get home, and after the deliverance prayer and the contact with his sweatshirt, which I deposited in a trash can on the way out of church, I feel the need for a long, cleansing shower. But as I shower, I continue to ask myself that same question. If what the Bible says is really true, if the Lord is truly my defense, then why am I always feeling the need to spiritually defend myself? Why do I always feel so threatened and defeated? So alone?

Then the water runs cold, and I carefully dry off and emerge from the shower, careful not to contaminate myself in the process. But as I'm pulling on my pajama bottoms, I notice a shadow in the dimly lit bedroom. And I know in my spirit that it's demonic in nature. I quickly pull on my pajama top and then peek around the corner of the doorframe to see more clearly. And, indeed, it is a demonic form. And it's hovering back and forth between Rick's chair and his side of the bed, almost as if it's dancing. As if it's celebrating. And I know that despite tonight's deliverance prayer, Rick is still very much in Satan's hand. And Satan's demons are very much a part of my husband's life.

Most of the demons that the prayer team attempted to bind and cast out were sexual in nature. And I have become more and more convinced that Rick, who pretends to be working overtime all these extra-late nights, is really having an affair. Actually, I suspect he's involved with a number of women. Perhaps some co-workers, maybe even prostitutes, as Bronte suggested in her prayers tonight. Most of all, I know with almost absolute certainty that Rick has willingly handed his soul over to the devil and that there is probably no hope for this marriage.

I knew that the proxy deliverance prayer was a long shot tonight, but it seemed worth the effort. Cynthia and Bronte had both been extremely supportive of this attempt. Unfortunately, I think our efforts were for nothing. Well, other than the fact it seems to have established that Rick Jackson is most definitely aligned with the Enemy.

I leave the master bedroom, promising myself I will never share that bed with Rick again. It's been weeks since I slept there anyway, but I am more determined than ever to end this thing—and as soon as possible. I'm just not sure what I'll do or how I'll take care of the girls without an income. But I need to trust the Lord. He will provide. Still, I feel trapped as I return to the living room. But seeing my girls sleeping, looking so vulnerable and helpless, flanked by the big dogs to guard them, I am resolved to do whatever it takes to protect them and to protect myself.

I somehow make it through the next couple of days barely seeing Rick. He continues to come in later and later and sleeps until the last possible minute, then showers and dresses and grabs his lunchbox before he makes his escape. I suspect it's guilt that makes him act this way. But on Saturday he surprises me by getting up earlier than usual.

He putters around the garage until almost noon and then comes inside wielding an ax and announces that he's going out to get a Christmas tree today. "Anyone coming with me?" He eyes the girls with a goofy grin.

They both look interested yet wary. I know they're seeing their father through new eyes now, and quite frankly the ax doesn't help his image much. But besides that, I realize that only he and the girls and the Lord know what has transpired over the years. And just the fleeting thought of this makes me feel sick. So sick I could vomit.

"We don't want a tree," I say, quickly turning away and pretending to busy myself at the already-clean kitchen sink as I silently pray for strength.

"*What?*" I can hear his anger, but I don't care.

I turn around and just stare at him. "We don't want a tree."

He gives me his look now—the one that suggests I'm totally insane. "What are you talking about, Ruth? We always get a tree."

"Putting a tree in your house is paganism. That's not how real Christians celebrate Jesus' birth, Rick." Suddenly I'm thankful for the homeschool curriculum we've been using lately. It's exposed the nature of some of these cultural traditions that we've always blindly accepted as innocent fun.

"Well, it's how I celebrate Christmas." He looks hopefully at the girls. "And it's how this family has always celebrated Christmas before. Right, girls?"

They sort of shrug and act uncomfortable but don't say anything.

"They know it's pagan too," I tell him. "We're not giving in to Satan's pressure to succumb to pagan practices that simply invite demonic attack into our home."

"*A Christmas tree invites demonic attack?*" he says with an incredulous expression, which simply reveals how much in the dark he really is.

"That's right."

"You *are* crazy, Ruth."

"That's what some people said about Jesus too."

"I'll bet Jesus would have a Christmas tree in his home," he says loudly.

"That just shows how much you don't know," I shoot back at him.

"Well, this is *my* house!" he says even louder as he waves his ax in the air. "And I plan to put up a Christmas tree! If anyone wants to come with me, I'll be leaving in about twenty minutes." Then he turns and glares at me. "And while I'm gone, you can remove the slumber party items from *my* living room. Because that's where I plan to set up *my* Christmas tree. Thank you very much!" Then he stomps out to the garage.

I go to the sink and begin washing my hands, washing them again and again as I try to figure out what to do.

"Mommy?" I hear Sarah's voice behind me, and I dry my hands on a paper towel, then turn to see her worried face.

"What?"

"I can go with Daddy to get a tree. If it makes him happy."

"No," I tell her. "That's like giving in to the devil to make him happy. You wouldn't do that, would you?"

She shakes her head.

Both Mary and Sarah are standing near me now, and they look confused and slightly disappointed, and I suspect they want a Christmas tree, but we've already discussed this. What could help make up for this? I consider offering to take them someplace, but where? It's too cold outside to do much, and although we used to go to the mall on days like this, just to kill time and look around, that place will be plastered with all sorts of pagan decorations, so that's definitely out.

I glance around the kitchen and suddenly feel trapped. If only there was some spiritually safe place to go. Some sweet godly grandmother or aunt who could take us in. I consider taking the girls to Cynthia's house, but they wouldn't like it. They tolerate Cynthia, but they still think she's weird. If Bronte wasn't living with the Pratts, I might visit her. I would consider visiting the Pratts, but they have seemed a little distant lately. Sometimes I wonder if perhaps I have offended them. Anyway, it seems clear there is no place to go.

"Do you girls need to practice your Christmas song?" I hope this will be something of a distraction from the tree dilemma. "So you can do your best at church tomorrow?"

They reluctantly agree, and while they are practicing, I ask the Lord to deliver us from our oppressors and to protect us from our enemies—mainly from Rick. As I pray, I suddenly imagine Rick's truck flying over an embankment and rolling and rolling and finally bursting into flames—cleansing flames. Am I asking the Lord to kill my husband? No, I don't think so. Am I wishing for it? Maybe. Perhaps that would put an end to all this; perhaps we would finally be free from the never-ending attack of the Enemy. I don't know. I don't know.

"Let's take the dogs for a walk," I say after I've washed my hands until they are raw and red and the girls have practiced for nearly two hours. "Bundle up, and we'll take a nice long walk."

Knowing that Rick will probably be home soon, I figure this will be a good way to avoid him and his miserable Christmas tree. So we walk and walk and walk. And finally Sarah's legs are tired, and we turn around to head back home. It's not even four o'clock, and it's already getting dusky as we finally turn down our street. It gets dark so early these days.

This time of year has always bothered me. I can remember how, as a child, I was consumed with tracking what time the sun went down as the days grew shorter and shorter, worried that the trend would continue until there was no daylight whatsoever, nothing but darkness for twenty-four hours a day. Of course, I know now that this doesn't happen. But even so, I still feel an unexplainable uncertainty. A heaviness in my spirit. Perhaps it's spiritual discernment warning me that this darkness is more than a physical thing. Maybe the Lord is trying to show me that this spiritual battle will get darker and more difficult before the days get lighter, before we come out on the other side.

The dogs begin to bark at a man walking on the other side of the street. Mary and I are holding their leads, and we both struggle to keep the dogs from pulling us across the road. "Sit!" I yell at the dogs. "Stay!" But they continue to bark and lunge, and the man looks somewhat frightened and intimidated as he hurries on his way. Finally the dogs settle down, and I'm not sure whether to scold them or to praise them.

"That was scary," says Mary as we continue to walk, now just a few blocks from our house. "What if the dogs had gotten loose, Mom?"

"We need to work with them. We need to teach them to obey better."

"They're just trying to protect us," says Sarah, whose hand isn't burning from holding on to the leash.

"I know," I admit.

"And I think that was a demon on the other side of the street," she says in a matter-of-fact voice.

"Really?" I'm surprised at this but try not to show it.

"Yes." Sarah nods somberly. "Couldn't you see that, Mommy?"

Then I remember the sense of foreboding I'd just been experiencing. "I think I felt it in my spirit. But I wasn't really paying that much attention."

"You need to pay better attention, Mommy," she says in a warning tone.

"Heel, Bonnie!" Mary yells as we get closer to the house. It's as if the dogs can sense that we're almost home.

I can see the Christmas tree as we pause on the sidewalk in front of our house. He's already got the lights on it, and the unwelcome tree is planted right before the front window, where Satan and the whole world can see it. Without talking, we put the dogs out back and then go into the house and finally into the living room, which has been cleared of the mattresses and, other than the tree, appears rather barren now.

But when Sarah and Mary look at the tree, I can tell they actually like it. And this makes me mad. Really, really mad! Why does Rick have to do this to me? Undermining my spiritual leadership, the only real leadership this family has right now. Why is he trying to appeal to the girls' sinful nature by bringing in an instrument that can be used by the Enemy? *Why? Why? Why?*

Of course, I *know* why. Rick has submitted his heart to the devil, has willingly entered the Enemy's domain. Naturally, it only makes sense that Rick should oppose me in everything. Well, he hasn't won the final battle yet. And I won't go down without a good, long fight. Even if it's a fight unto death.

Of course, I mean a spiritual death. At least I think I do. Right now I'm so angry I'm not totally sure. I stomp out of the living room and am about to head for the master bedroom so I can get down on my knees and do some real spiritual warfare, but then I stop. The master bedroom is my husband's domain. The devil's domain. And not wanting to further defile myself, I go outside into the backyard and sit on a damp lawn chair to pray. Before long, both Bonnie and Clyde are sitting next to me. *Gone to the dogs,* I think with a sad irony.

No, I'm more like Daniel when he was placed in the lions' den because he was unwilling to bow down to false gods. And I too am unwilling to bow down to false gods, including Rick's pagan tree that currently dominates the living room and consequently our entire home. Even if I am forced to live out here in the cold and dark, it will be better than giving in to Satan's control within our household.

31

Daddy is coming to church with us today," Sarah says with excitement as I help her with her hair.

"What?" I feel like someone has just jerked the floor out from under me. Church is the one place where I can be free of Rick, free of his condemnation, his evil influence, his menacing ways. How can it be that he wants to come with us?

"Daddy wants to see Mary and me do our music," she says as I fasten a barrette.

"Are you sure?"

"Yes, Mommy, he said that he's coming." She turns and smiles at me. "Isn't that great! Maybe our prayers for him are working!"

"Maybe…" I turn away. I don't want her to see the frown growing on my face. "Finish getting ready," I tell her as I leave the bathroom. "And don't forget to brush your teeth." Then I go and find Rick standing in the kitchen, and it does look like he's cleaned up a bit, as if perhaps he is considering going to church.

"Sarah said you're going to church with us." I frown at him.

"Is that a problem?" He frowns back.

"Well, it might be…"

"Are you saying I'm not welcome at your church? Is this some kind of exclusive church? Do you need to have a membership card to get in the door?"

"No, of course not. But if you're coming to judge and to gawk, well, then you're probably not welcome."

"I'm coming to see what kind of church this is." He narrows his eyes. "I want to see what you're exposing our daughters to." Then he smiles as he sees Mary coming into the kitchen, all dressed and ready for church. "And I want to hear the girls perform."

"We don't call it *performing* at church. The girls are *contributing*. The Lord has no need for performers. Besides, you could hear them *perform* at home if you like."

"That's not the same." He pats Mary on the head. "Is it, sweetheart?"

She smiles back at him. "Well, I hope I don't goof up. Playing in front of so many people does make me a little nervous."

"Don't worry," I tell her. "The Lord will help you."

So it is that the Jackson family, all except Matthew, walk into church together. But I am not happy about this. Not one bit.

"Why don't you help your dad to find seats," I say to the girls. "I need to speak to Sister Cynthia about something."

As soon as they're on their way, I find Cynthia and explain the situation. "I realize that Rick is probably bringing some very bad spirits with him. I just felt someone should be warned."

"Do you think he'll let us do deliverance prayer for him?" she asks hopefully.

I frown. "I seriously doubt it...but you never know. The Lord can do anything."

"Well, I'll tell Brother Glenn about it. And Sister Bronte. I'm sure we'll all be fervently praying against his spirits."

I thank her, then greet a few other friends, and as the music begins to play, I go over to where Rick and the girls are seated. I'm relieved to see the girls are flanking their dad, which means I don't have to sit directly next to him. However, I do feel bad for their sakes. And I have to ask myself what kind of mother allows her children to be exposed to someone like him? And how much longer will I put up with it?

I am so nervous and uncomfortable about Rick's presence here that all I can do is stare at the bright banner that hangs on the wall behind the pulpit. I helped Cynthia make it a couple of weeks ago, carefully cutting felt pieces into flamelike shapes of red, orange, and yellow to create a frame around the words—Sister Bronte's inspiration and a word from the Lord. To keep my mind off Rick, I read the lines over and over. *Go through the fire, pass through the flame, on the other side, emerge pure and clean.* Again and again I silently repeat the words, imagining myself passing through the fiery test and coming out pure and clean…on the other side. *Go through the fire, pass through the flame, on the other side, emerge pure and clean.*

Suddenly the service is ending, and I realize that I have missed not only the entire sermon but also my own daughters' musical contribution. Still, I am so eager to get Rick out of here that I rush for the exit. Thankfully, Rick and the girls follow, and soon we're out in the parking lot, and I am hugely relieved. Not because I want to escape the fellowship of brothers and sisters, but because I want to remove Rick's influence from this holy place. His presence here may have contaminated the worship. I hope I don't hear of any terrible repercussions from others, although I feel personally defiled. It's bad enough to share a house with a sinner like Rick, but it's even worse to share the house of the Lord!

"Man, was that weird," he says as soon as we're in the car.

I glance at him but don't say anything.

"Did you think so too?" There's a trace of hope in his voice.

I still don't say anything as I buckle my seat belt.

"Is it always that weird?" he asks as he starts the car.

"Oh, it can be even weirder," Mary says from the backseat. I turn around and glare at her, but she just grins.

"It's not weird, Daddy," says Sarah. "It's what the Lord wants from his children."

Rick shakes his head and drives out of the parking lot. "I don't think so, Sarah. I don't think God wants his children to be full of fear."

"We're not full of fear!" I snap at him.

He kind of laughs. "Yeah, right."

"We do have a fear of the Lord," I say. "And we also have a healthy fear of the Enemy. Satan is a liar and a thief, and he's out to destroy." I point at him. "Look at your own life, and you should see that it's true."

"What?" He looks at me with disbelief.

"You've given Satan the upper hand."

Just then we hear a horn blasting, and Rick stomps on the brakes and narrowly misses hitting the car in the other lane.

"Just pay attention to your driving, and get us home safely," I say in a brittle voice.

The drive home is very quiet, and as soon as Rick is out of the car and stomping angrily into the house, I ask the girls if they want to go do something fun with me. Of course, they are game. But now I have to think of something that will be fun. I mentally go through the list of options, remembering things we've done in the past to entertain ourselves. But now I can see how evil and corrupt all those activities really are. And I'm shocked to think of how much time and energy we wasted on such sinful foolishness.

"Where are we going, Mommy?" asks Sarah.

I try to think of something we can do that won't be sinful, something that will honor the Lord and be enjoyable too. But all I do is drive around town. Oh, we pray against the Enemy as we pass through bad neighborhoods, but soon the girls are tired of this joyless joyride, and I take us back home, driving slowly and preparing myself for whatever awaits us there. How I wish for a safe haven, a place where I could rest. But our earthly life is not meant to be a time of rest. Our earthly life is about battles and dividing lines and spiritual warfare. But oh how I long for respite.

To my enormous relief, Rick's pickup is not in the driveway. I pull into the garage and let out a deep sigh. Maybe I will get some spiritual rest after all. Although Rick won't stay away forever. And I know that my temporary peace comes at a price. But any hope of peace is extinguished when the dogs begin to wildly bark. They do this every time we enter the house, pounding themselves against the french doors as if they might crash through the double panes of glass. Seeing their eyes glowing in the light from the kitchen, I am reminded of two demons, and I feel that familiar surge of spiritual adrenaline rushing through me. I feel myself getting on my guard, getting ready for action. Ready to pray against their dark power.

But then, I reassure myself, those are just our dogs, and they are simply doing their job by barking at all who enter our home. Just the same, I open the door and yell at them to be quiet and to quit jumping. After they settle down, I bring them into the house, where they immediately begin to frantically sniff all around as if they suspect something unwelcome is here. I wonder if animals are able to detect demonic intruders.

I follow the curious dogs through the house until they finally end up in the living room. The dogs stand attentively, staring at the Christmas tree Rick has forced upon us, almost as if they understand that it is all wrong, that it doesn't belong in our home. I feel like commanding them to attack the offensive evergreen, but I doubt they would understand. Still, it is some consolation to know that, like me, they are not comfortable with this pagan symbol. Although it saddens me to think that mere dogs have more spiritual discernment than my own husband. *God help us.*

32

After the girls finish today's homeschool assignments, I give them an extra-credit project that is more of a treat than schoolwork since it involves reading, measuring, and thinking. "You girls get to make Christmas cookies." I open my favorite cookbook to the cut-cookie page. "But no Santas or reindeer. You can only use symbols that represent Jesus." Mary gives me a little flak, but Sarah gets into the spirit of the project.

"Like crosses?" she says.

"That would be Easter cookies," says Mary.

"Crosses are fine," I tell them.

"And we could make little mangers," says Sarah. "And the animals that were in the stable."

"Why don't we make all the nativity things?" says Mary triumphantly.

"That's a wonderful idea," I tell them. "And while you do that, I have some things to take care of. Mary, you're in charge of the oven. Make sure you're careful."

"I *know* how to use an oven, Mom."

So I leave them to their own devices and go into the living room, where I remove the strings of lights from the Christmas tree, then I drag the tree out the front door and dump it next to the driveway. I go back into the house and retrieve the girls' mattresses from their beds and haul them back into the living room. None of us has had a good night's sleep since Rick moved them back into their bedroom. And although I've been sleeping on the floor between them and we've been binding and casting out demons together, I feel certain that Sarah's earlier vision of that pink demon was not only accurate but that this demon might actually be the worst of the bunch. Because while lying on the carpet last night, praying against a particularly bad demonic assault that seemed to be rooted in that bedroom, I suddenly recalled how Rick and I were able to purchase that carpet about ten years ago. It is one of those memories I'd rather forget, but it hit me full force, and suddenly it all made sense.

Matthew was in grade school and Mary and Sarah were both pretty small when my sister met Jeff and decided to remarry. I must not have been a very strong Christian at the time, and Pastor Glenn hadn't come to Valley Bridge Fellowship yet. I guess I was what I would now call a *carnal* Christian—very worldly and spiritually immature. I was pleasantly surprised when Lynette invited Rick and me to accompany Jeff and her to Reno for a quick wedding and a long weekend, and I was even more surprised when my mother actually offered to watch the kids while we were gone. It shames me now to remember how excited I was about that weekend. Rick and I hadn't had many times like that, and I even went out and bought a new outfit for the occasion. We drove down there with Jeff and Lynette, and we pretty much acted like wild teenagers, drinking and partying and gambling. At the time I felt a little guilty for acting so crazy, but I just rationalized the whole thing, telling myself that I didn't want to spoil things for the others, that I didn't want to be a party pooper.

Then on our last day there, Rick and I realized we were nearly out of money. Consequently things were getting a little sour, and that night Rick and I got into a big fight. He wanted to go down and gamble what little money we had left, and I insisted that he give it to me to ensure we'd have enough money to get back home. But he wouldn't listen. Instead he went down to gamble. Naturally, I refused to join him and went to bed mad, thinking the very worst of him. But when he showed up in our room around two in the morning and dumped a bunch of money onto the bed, he became my biggest hero. We gave Lynette and Jeff a wedding present of two hundred dollars and treated everyone to a fancy lunch. Then on the way home, I talked Rick into letting me use most of the remainder of that money to fix up the girls' room, including this carpeting that we normally would not have been able to afford.

Of course, the pink carpeting must go. And until it's gone, I will not subject my girls to whatever Reno demons are lurking there. It occurred to me last night, lying sleeplessly on that corrupt carpet, that the name of the pink demon is Lust. He may think he's pretty in pink, but he is lewd and disgusting and evil.

I stand in the living room and look out at the fallen Christmas tree by the driveway. Rick will come home and see it and simply bring it back into the house. So I go out to the garage, find his ax, and begin chopping up the tree, removing limbs and annihilating it until it no longer resembles a Christmas tree.

"Mommy!" screams Sarah.

I stop in midswing and look over to where Sarah is waving at me from the garage. "What?"

"Mary burned herself!"

I drop the ax and dash through the garage, imagining Mary with flames all around, burned and mutilated. Oh, why did I let them do this without supervision? What kind of mother am I? "Mary," I cry as I run to the kitchen.

Mary's at the sink, her whole arm under the faucet. "I told Sarah that I'm okay," she says sheepishly. "It just hurt."

"Let me see," I demand. She holds up her arm, showing a long red welt just above her wrist. "Put it back in the water. I'll get some ice. How did it happen?"

"I should've used the oven mitts," she says with the water still running. "But we could smell the cookies and got worried they were burning. So I just grabbed the dishtowel, you know, the way you do sometimes? And then my arm hit the oven rack as I was pulling the cookies out."

"You should've heard her scream," adds Sarah. "I thought her arm fell off."

"Hello?" calls a female voice from the direction of the garage.

I remember with alarm that I've left all the doors open. Anyone could walk in.

"Ruth?" calls the voice. It's my sister, but I don't answer.

Sarah, who dashes off to see who's there, says, "Hi, Aunt Lynette," and then invites her into the house. When will they learn?

"What's going on?" demands Lynette when Sarah leads her into the kitchen.

"I burned my arm." Mary holds it up for her aunt to see.

"Keep it in the water." I set the ice tray down next to her. "And rub the ice on it too."

"We're making nativity cookies." Sarah shows Lynette a tray of cookies with shapes that look more like blobs than anything.

"Oh…" Lynette looks curiously at me. "What was that in the driveway?"

"Nothing," I say quickly.

"Looked like the remnants of a Christmas tree to me."

Mary turns and looks at me now. "*Our* Christmas tree?"

Before I can say anything, Mary dashes out to the living room. Lynette and Sarah follow her, with me trailing behind, a piece of dripping ice in my hand.

"What did you do, Mom?" Mary asks with wide eyes.

I hand her the ice. "Keep that burn cold."

"She chopped it up," says Sarah solemnly.

"You *chopped up* your Christmas tree?" Lynette studies me with a perplexed expression.

"It's a pagan symbol. It has nothing to do with the real Christmas."

"You really are crazy," says Lynette. Then she looks around my living room. "Are you guys moving or something?"

"No…"

"Where are all your things? It looks like you've stripped everything out of here. And why are their mattresses on the floor?"

"Just because." Now I'm glaring at her. "Why did you come here, Lynette? What do you want?"

She looks uncomfortably at the girls, and I can tell whatever she has to say, she doesn't want to say around them.

"You guys go back and turn off the oven and clean up things in there," I tell them. "Get everything ready for the frosting, okay?" They sort of nod and reluctantly leave.

"Everyone is worried about you, Ruth." Lynette's voice is quiet now.

"Everyone?"

"Yes. Your family. Your husband. Your friends."

"My friends?" I look curiously at her. "Who have you been talking to?"

"Colleen, for one. I called her last night after Rick dropped by."

"Rick went to your house last night?"

"Yes. He wanted to talk to Jeff and me. He wanted our help."

"Your help?" I am flabbergasted now. Why would Rick go to Lynette for help with anything?

"He's frustrated, Ruth. We all are. We don't understand you. And we're seriously worried about you."

"Well, don't be. I'm perfectly fine. If you want to be worried, you should worry about yourselves. You guys are the ones in danger."

"What kind of danger?"

"Spiritual danger. Danger of going to hell."

"Oh…" She just rolls her eyes. "That's what I was afraid of…"

"What do you mean?"

"It's this new weird church, isn't it? Are they brainwashing you?"

I force a little laugh. "Brainwashing me?"

"Yes. Are they filling you full of fear and controlling you?"

"Of course not!"

"Then why are you acting so weird?"

"What makes you think I'm the one who's acting weird? Has it ever occurred to you that you guys are the ones acting weird and that I'm only serving the Lord and doing his will? I mean, you call yourself a Christian, Lynette, but I don't see the Lord's influence in your life."

"I think we must serve different Lords."

I firmly nod. "Yes, I'm sure that's absolutely true." I want to add that she and Jeff and Rick all serve their lord, the devil, but that will only prolong this unnecessary conversation.

"So it's the church thing that's causing you to act so weird?"

I shrug. "Draw your own conclusions. You will anyway."

"Well, Mom and I thought maybe it was you. I mean, you've always been a little strange. And Mom's been worried that you're getting more and more like Grandma Clark."

"Grandma Clark?" I frown at my sister. "What does she have to do with this?"

"She had her hang-ups, Ruth. You know that as well as anyone."

I refuse to respond to this.

"And you know that Mom's been seeing a therapist and trying to figure things out—"

"But not a Christian therapist," I point out. And who knows what strange ideas a nonbeliever could put into my mother's head?

"I don't know if she's a Christian or not, but I do know that she's helping Mom."

"Right…" I fold my arms across my chest and wish my sister would leave.

"And Mom admits that she's blown it with us, Ruth. Particularly with you."

"She's never admitted it to me."

"You don't give her a chance. You're always so busy preaching at us, telling us that we're so evil. How can anyone get through to you?"

"I don't need to take that from you," I say, "especially not in my own home."

"You gave it to me in my own home!"

"That was different. You guys were attacking me. I was just defending myself. You and Mom have always been against me. You've all been against me." I feel tears now, and I really didn't want to lose it in front of my sister.

"We're not against you, Ruth. We're just really worried about you. We think you need help. We want to—"

"The only help I need is from the Lord! He is my helper. He is my deliverance. He is my protector, my rescuer, my—"

"Stop it!" Lynette covers her ears. "You're making me sick."

And that's when I know for sure. "Hearing the Lord's name is too much for you, isn't it, Lynette?" I say this victoriously, knowing I have her now.

"You mean hearing the Lord's name *used in vain*?"

I stare in disbelief. "Are you insinuating that I use the Lord's name in vain?"

"Colleen is the one who made me see it."

"See what?" I narrow my eyes and wonder how she can be so blind.

"Colleen said that Glenn Pratt and his followers are constantly using the Lord's name in vain."

"What are you talking about?" I hold up my hands. "You don't even make sense."

"Maybe not to you, but I think Colleen is right. She said people who go around saying 'The Lord told me to do this…' or 'God told me to do that…' are using God's name for their own purposes and vanities. That's using the Lord's name in vain, Ruth, and I think Colleen nailed it."

I just shake my head, trying to process what she is saying. "That's crazy."

"And that's the pot calling the kettle black."

"Get out of my house! Get thee behind me, Satan!"

"You need help, Ruth." Her expression hardens. "But I can't make you see it."

"That's because you can't see. You are spiritually blind, Lynette. You don't see that you're the one who is corrupt and in need of help."

I take a step toward her. "In fact, you are in need of deliverance. And if you come to my church, we can pray for you, and we can—"

"No!" She holds her hands out to keep me away from her. "I will *never* come to your church. New Fire? What kind of name is that? I wish God would send some real fire and burn it to the ground!" And then she turns and leaves my house.

"What's wrong with Aunt Lynette?" asks Sarah, and I realize that the girls have been listening.

"She needs our prayers," I say in a tired voice. "Aunt Lynette has demons, and she needs help getting them out." We talk about this in more detail as we frost the nativity cookies. And once the strange-looking cookies are frosted, we go around our house and pray against the demons that were brought here by my sister. We pray to bind them, casting them down to the fiery pits of hell.

As the girls and I get ready for bed, I wonder where Rick is. But I am relieved he is gone. I feel certain he's not working tonight, and I suspect he's with a woman. The prayer team made that clear enough. I can only hope he will leave us for good.

Soon the girls are asleep, and I am trying to nod off too. As usual the table lamp is on, and Bonnie and Clyde are in the living room with us, protecting us. All is well, but I still feel uneasy, as if I'm waiting for the next shoe to fall. I look around the living room. The walls are bare, and other than a few large pieces of furniture, the room is quite sparse. No place for demons to hide. And yet…there is something. Maybe this is just the way it is, I tell myself as I try to relax, longing for sleep. Maybe this is simply the best I can do. But why is it never enough? Why am I never good enough? Why can't I beat this thing? Why am I so afraid?

33

I wake up to something nudging my shoulder. I quickly sit up straight, bracing myself, preparing to do warfare, ready to take up my armor, to cast out and to bind. But instead of a demon, I see my husband's worried face looking down at me. However, this is not a comfort. A demon would be easier to fight.

"We need to talk," he whispers.

I glance at the girls soundly sleeping. Bonnie and Clyde are awake and alert but not barking. Apparently they've gotten used to Rick now, although I'm a little surprised that they never made a sound when he came into the room, never gave me any kind of warning at all. I must remember to train them better.

I quietly get up and follow him out of the living room. He is leading me to the master bedroom, and everything in me is saying, *Don't go,* but I hate to start an argument. I don't want to wake the girls or upset them. So I silently pray, preparing myself for the worst as he closes the door behind us. I have a horrible feeling that he plans to kill me. I glance over to the phone on the bedside table, calculating how quickly I could reach it and dial 911.

"Sit down." He points to the chair on his side of the bed.

Knowing that I will be contaminated by sitting there, that the demon is probably within arm's length, I sit down anyway. At least I am near the phone. Rick sits across from me on the bed. He still has on his shipping uniform, as well as an unhappy frown, and he looks strangely old and tired. I think sin does that to people.

"What is it?" I ask, bracing myself.

"You have a problem, Ruth," he says slowly. "A serious problem."

I simply stare at him, trying to understand what he's really saying. "*I* have a serious problem?"

He nods with what seems like relief. "Yes. And I want you to get help."

"*I* have a problem?" I say this again, a little louder this time.

"Look, I don't want this to turn into a fight. I just want you to know that I think you need professional help."

"Well, I think *you* need help too, Rick. Spiritual help."

He nods. "Yeah, I know that already. You think I need deliverance. You think I'm demonized. The girls have told me all that, Ruth. Mary even told me about taking my sweatshirt to your church and how people prayed—"

"We're doing all we can."

He holds up his hands like he is surrendering. "Right…"

"So you'll get help?" I say hopefully. "You'll let the deliverance team pray—"

"No. That's not the answer."

"What *is* the answer?"

He takes a deep breath. "For you to get help."

I take an aggravated breath. "You already said that, Rick. And I told you that I'm not the one who needs help. You are!"

"This is my plan, Ruth."

"*You* have a plan?"

"Yes. If you don't agree to get help, I will take the girls away from you."

"You will *what?*"

"You're going to wake them up."

I try to calm myself. I remind myself that this is a spiritual war. I'm not fighting flesh and blood but demons and powers and principalities. I brace myself for the battle. "How exactly did you make this plan, Rick?"

"I met with your family. They're concerned too. We think you've been brainwashed by this cult church that you've—"

"New Fire is *not* a cult church," I tell him.

"We think it is, Ruth. And both Dennis and Colleen told me that Glenn Pratt is a wolf in sheep's clothes."

I actually laugh. "Of course, they would say—"

"He's had affairs with quite a few women in the congregation—"

"Lies, lies, lies!" I shake my head. "Why does it not surprise me?"

"New Fire is dangerous, Ruth. Those people spend more time with Satan than Christ."

"How would you know?"

"I was there; I saw it for myself. That place is way off base, and it's like you've been trapped—"

"I'm trapped?" I force a laugh. "Why don't you look at yourself, Rick? You're the one who's trapped—spiritually trapped. You belong to the devil, and unless you get deliverance, you will go to hell. Do you understand that?"

He sighs. "Maybe we've said enough for tonight. I just want you to know where I stand. I have to draw the line. I want to give you a chance to get the help you need. But if you can't—"

"I'm not the one who needs help," I say again. "You are so spiritually blind that you can't even see that. You don't know that it's only the girls and me who are holding this home together. If it weren't for our constant and vigilant spiritual warfare, who knows where we'd be now?"

He holds up his hands, palms toward me, and for a moment I think he might strangle me. I quickly stand up, stepping away from him. "Look," he says, "I'm exhausted, Ruth. I need to get some sleep."

"Yes. I'm sure you *are* exhausted. Why wouldn't you be exhausted?"

He stares at me. "What's that supposed to mean?"

"It means that I *know,* Rick." I lean over him as he sits on the edge of the bed. "I know you've been pretending to be working overtime, but I *know* what you've been up to."

"What are you talking about?"

"About your affair. Or should I say 'affairs'?"

"Affairs?" He makes a good effort at looking truly affronted, but I am not falling for it. "What are you insinuating?"

"It's ironic how you try to accuse Brother Glenn of something you're guilty of. But I know how it works. I know that there have been other women, that you've been unfaithful."

"I've been unfaithful?"

"Don't bother denying it, Rick. It doesn't really matter now anyway."

"Ruth?" He reaches out as if he wants to touch me, but I pull away.

"Don't even think about it!" I turn and leave the room.

I expect him to follow me, to keep pretending that he's innocent, that I'm all wrong, and that he's the victim here, but to my relief he doesn't. If he had, I think I would have hit him with everything I know. I would have told him about the incest too. Maybe not the details. But that he's housing a demon of incest. How far it has gone or where it came from is still a mystery to me. Something I don't want to think about!

I feel a desperate need for cleansing now, but I can't use the master bathroom. Instead I go to the girls' bathroom and do the best I can under the circumstances. It's after three in the morning by the time I get back to bed. Thankfully, the girls are still asleep. I do some spiritual warfare, but I am so tired that my words seem to be jumbled, and finally I drift off to sleep. But when I wake up, it's to the sound of the phone ringing, and it is still dark out.

I don't want to answer it, but I don't want the ringing to wake the girls either, so I sprint through the kitchen to get it. It's a little after six. Who could be calling this early? I grab the phone by the third ring, answering with a breathless and somewhat irritated, "Hello?"

"Ruth?" comes an unfamiliar female voice on the other end.

"Who is this?"

"This is Melinda, you know, from church. You said I could call you. Remember?"

I let out a big sigh. "Yes. Hello, Melinda. What's going on?"

"I really need prayer right now."

I want to say, "Join the club," but I don't. "Why's that?"

"I know I'm being demonized. I can hear them and see them, and I can even smell them. Did you know that you can smell demons? I'm so scared, Ruth. I don't know what to do."

"You're right. It sounds like you do need deliverance."

"I knew you would understand. Can you please help me?"

Now I'm very tempted to toss aside everything that's going sideways in my own life to rush out and run to Melinda's side, to pray for her deliverance, binding and casting out. But somehow I just can't make myself do this.

"I can see one now, Ruth," she continues, crying. "He's so ugly, and he's making horrible faces, saying horrible things…"

"Look, Melinda, I know what you're going through. I've been through it myself. But you've caught me at a really bad time just now. I can't go into all the details, but we're having some very serious family problems, and I just—"

"That's okay," she says quickly. "I figured you wouldn't have time for me…"

"It's not that. It's just that my husband, well, he's not a believer, you know, and he's doing some things—"

"I understand—" She makes a choking sound.

"Look, I'll call Sister Cynthia and ask her to get the deliverance team ready for you. Then I'll call you back. Okay?"

"But I want you there too, Ruth."

"I'll see what I can do. Maybe I can get away."

"Thanks."

Soon it's all settled. The team will meet at Cynthia's house at nine. I will be there as soon as I can. I get the girls settled into their homeschool assignments and tell them I have to run an errand but that I'll be back in an hour or so.

"When do we get to start having Christmas vacation?" Mary looks up from her math book.

"I already told you. It's the same as everyone else. It officially begins on Friday and goes until after New Year's."

The girls make some cheering noises, and I remind them to keep it down so their dad can sleep. *Let the sleeping dog lie!*

The deliverance team is already in the thick of praying for Melinda when I arrive, but she seems genuinely glad that I've come, and I immediately jump in and fervently pray for her deliverance. But the demons are extremely stubborn today, and Melinda is still having problems with denial. Bronte is getting a little impatient with her, and even Cynthia seems somewhat put out.

"We can't help you unless you want our help," Cynthia says to Melinda for about the tenth time.

"I'm trying. It's just that I don't remember some of these things you're telling me. I get confused, and I'm not sure what to do."

But we keep praying, and although I'm getting spiritually weary, I know we must persevere. Finally I realize that it's after eleven, and I become seriously worried about the girls. I can't block out how upset Rick seemed last night, and it's possible he could be getting up by now. He might be angry that I'm not there. I also remember what he said about taking the girls away from me. And although it's totally ridiculous and I cannot imagine him ever attempting something like this, I'm dealing with a person who has submitted his spirit to the dark side. Who can know what someone like this might do? I really should be preparing myself for anything.

"I'm sorry," I suddenly tell everyone. "I know you're not finished here, but I really have to go."

"Problems at home?" guesses Bronte.

I nod. "Yes, and I would really appreciate lots of prayers for Rick today. I think we may have reached a spiritual crossroads, and I'm not sure which way he's going to choose. There's a lot at stake just now."

"We'll be praying," promises Cynthia.

"And I'll keep praying for you too, Melinda." I pat her on the shoulder. "Don't worry. You're going to beat this!"

She looks up at me with bloodshot eyes and a dripping nose. "I-I hope so."

Then I leave. And as I drive home, I pray for Melinda, but the closer I get to my house, the more convinced I am that I need to pray for my own family just now, primarily for Rick and for his deliverance. I park my car in the driveway, next to his pickup, and I continue to pray. I bind Satan's evil influence in Rick's life, and I cast out the various demons that Bronte and the others named during our deliverance prayers for him. Finally I go into the house, bracing myself for whatever battle may be awaiting me.

The girls' workbooks and things are still splayed out across the dining-room table, but they aren't doing their work. And I'm sure they couldn't have finished all their schoolwork by now since it's not quite noon. I call out for them, but they don't answer. The dogs are outside, but that's not such a concern. Feeling worried, I call out for Rick, but he doesn't answer either. Now I'm starting to get agitated.

I thoroughly search the house and finally end up in the garage, where I find Rick sitting on a wooden crate as he looks through a cardboard box. I immediately recognize it. It contains some of the things I removed from the house several weeks ago. I was performing a spiritual purge, but our garbage can had been full that day. So I stashed it away on a shelf somewhere in the garage, thinking I'd put it out the following week. Apparently I forgot. Or perhaps there was demonic interference, an attempt to preserve these contaminated pieces in order to continually pester our family.

"What is this?" Rick holds up a porcelain figurine that my mother brought home from one of her trips to Great Britain.

"I think it was a fairy or an elf."

"That's not what I mean." He holds up the box of odds and ends. "I mean, what is this? Why are these things out here in this box?"

"Because they were corrupting our home," I tell him in a weary voice. "Each one of those things carries the spirit of something vile and evil and destructive. Things that do not belong in a godly home, Rick."

He slowly exhales. "And is that what you've done with all our other things too? All the things that keep disappearing and that you make up phony excuses for? Like my old book collection that my dad left to me?"

I just shrug.

"Don't you think that's pretty weird, Ruth?"

"Only to those who lack spiritual discernment."

He just shakes his head, carefully places the figurine back into the box, then sets it aside.

"Where are the girls?" I suddenly remember why I've been searching all over the place.

"They're not here."

"I know that." I put my hands on my hips and glare at him. "Where are they?"

"I took them to a safe place."

"A safe place?" I can hear the shrillness in my voice. It sounds like someone else's voice. Maybe even my mom's back when I was little.

"I warned you, Ruth."

"What are you talking about?" I scream at him. "I should be warning you! It's your sin that has brought these demons into this home. We are constantly battling against all your evil influences. Matthew is lost because of you. Mary was starting to follow as well, but, thank the Lord, it wasn't too late. I've managed to rescue her. But you are the problem here, Rick. We pray and we pray for the Lord to deliver us from you, but you're still here. Why don't you do your family a favor and just leave? *We would be better off without you!*"

"I'm not the problem, Ruth!"

"Yes, you are!" I can tell he's getting angry, but I don't care. Let him show his true colors. Maybe he will see himself for who he really is now.

"No! It's your stupid church that's the problem. They are a freaking mess, Ruth! If you weren't so brainwashed by their warped doctrine, you would see that. For your information I've talked to clergymen too. They all agree—your church is either a cult or heading that way. Anyone connected to it is going to get hurt. The leaders there are a mess. And Glenn Pratt is seriously messed up. If you had any sense, you would—"

"Shut up!" I look at the contents of the box, wishing for something to throw at him. "Just shut up! Shut up! Shut up!" Then I begin to pray out loud in the Spirit. First I pray in tongues, and then I switch over to English, shouting out the words for Rick and the devil and the whole world to hear. "I bind Satan in Rick's life! In the name of Jesus, I cast out Rick's demons. I cast out demons of sexual lust and incest and demons of sexual perversions and—"

"What?" he yells at me. "What on earth are you saying? Are you crazy? Can you even hear yourself?"

"I bind the spirit of hatred and anger and wrath." I spit out the words as fast I can. "I bind the spirit of selfishness and pride and idolatry and—"

"Stop doing this!" He grabs me by the forearms and peers into my face with frightened eyes. "Stop acting insane, Ruth! You are scaring the crap out of me!"

"You *should* be scared! Satan has a strong hold on you, and he doesn't want to let go. That *should* scare the crap out of you, Rick!"

"No. That's not it. I'm not scared of Satan, Ruth. I'm scared of you! Everyone is right. You need help. And you need it now!"

"Let go of me!" I jerk my arms away from him. "Leave me alone, and tell me where the girls are! Tell me now before I call the police."

But he just walks away. He opens the garage door, then goes out to his pickup and drives off.

I stand there staring at his truck as it goes down the street. How can he treat me like this? He's the one with the problem. I've been doing everything I can to keep us from falling completely apart, but it doesn't seem to be working. Angry tears slip down my cheeks as I head into the house and slam the door behind me. Once I get to the kitchen, I completely break down. I throw myself over the island counter and sob uncontrollably. "Help me, Lord. Help me. Help me. Help me." I wish I were dead!

I hear the phone ringing now, and although I don't want to answer it, it might be the girls. They might be calling for help. So I answer.

"*Ruth!*" says an alarmed voice.

"Yes. Is this Cynthia?" I'm about to pour out my distressing story to her and to beg her to come over here and help me sort this out, but I never get the chance.

"*Ruth!* A horrible, horrible thing has happened!"

"*You know?*" I am stunned but immediately realize the Lord may have given her a revelation just now.

"It's Melinda. She...she went into the bathroom while we were still praying for deliverance. I went with her and was waiting outside the door, but it was taking a little too long. So I tried the door, but it was locked, and...and—" Cynthia begins to cry now.

"What? What is going on over there? What are you talking about?"

"Melinda slit her wrists!"

She what?" It feels as if the lights are all growing dim, as if the world is getting darker by the second, as if this darkness is pressing in against me, pushing from every direction with heat and oppression. I feel like I cannot even breathe.

"Melinda is dead."

My knees give out, and I lean against the wall to support myself, then slide down to a squatting position, my knees almost touching my chin. "Why is this happening?" My words come out in a hoarse whisper. "Why is Satan beating us up like this?"

"I don't know, Ruth. But Sister Bronte had some thoughts."

"It feels like we are losing the battle," I admit.

"Yes, we may have lost this battle today. But we will not lose the war."

"I'm so tired," I confess. "I feel like I can't keep fighting…like it's useless…"

"Then I might as well come out and tell you," she says.

"What?"

"That we were all very disappointed in you today."

"In me?"

"Yes. We all heard you promise Melinda that you would be her prayer partner. But you let her down. You were not there for her. And Sister Bronte is certain that Melinda would still be alive if you hadn't let her down, Ruth."

"But I—"

"Please, don't make excuses. The only way out is to confess and to repent of your sins. You know that."

"Yes, I understand—"

"You need to handle this as soon as possible. Don't waste a moment."

"Yes," I say. "I will." Then I hang up and bow my head onto my knees and just cry. I cry for Melinda, and then I cry for myself. I am hopeless and useless. I don't deserve to live, and I wish I were dead. Life is too hard, and I know that Satan is winning. I am not strong enough to stand against him. He is too big, too strong. His demons are too numerous, legion, and they are winning. Winning. Winning.

"No!" I scream in defiance. "I will not let you win, Satan!" I will go to Sister Bronte and confess my sins. I will ask her to pray for my deliverance. And I cannot wait until this evening's midweek service to do this. I must do it now. Since it's nearly noon, I suspect that Sister Bronte and some of the others will be at the church, praying and preparing for this evening.

I don't remember driving across town, but suddenly I'm pulling into the church parking lot. And I am relieved to see both Brother Glenn's and Sister Bronte's cars parked in front. I am so eager to be with my brothers and sisters, to confess my sins and be made whole, that I run up to the building. The sanctuary is dark, but I see a slit of light beneath the office door, and I hurry over and push it open. But what I see inside the office makes me stop, and my hand flies to my mouth in horror. How can this be? How is this even possible? I quietly close the door. Bronte and Glenn never saw me, but I clearly saw them—partially dressed and tangled up in each other's arms. There is no disputing what they were doing.

By the time I get home, I am in shock. My hands are shaking, and I feel like I can't quite breathe. So I call Cynthia and tell her everything.

"Oh, Ruth! How can you make up such a filthy lie?"

"It's not a—"

"I know you must be ashamed of yourself for betraying Melinda, but to make up a story like—"

So I hang up and sink to my knees and beg God for help. But my voice seems drowned out by all the demons screaming filth and accusations at me. My house is full of them now. I don't think it will ever be clean. *I* will never be clean.

The phone is ringing, adding to the noise, but I won't answer it. No good news can come from it. If I had the strength, I would rip the vile thing off the wall. But suddenly I hear Sarah's frightened voice speaking on the answering machine.

"Mommy," she says in tiny voice. "Daddy said not to call you, but Grandma is asleep, and I wanted to make sure you're okay. Mommy?"

I grab the phone. "Hi, Sarah." I force cheer into my voice.

"Mommy!"

"Are you girls okay?"

"We don't know why Daddy made us come to Grandma's. He said you weren't doing a good job being a mommy and that you were sick and you'd left us."

"I didn't leave you," I say, suddenly finding some old resolve. "I went out this morning to help a friend. Do you remember Melinda from church?"

"The fat lady?"

"We don't call her that, do we, Sarah?"

"I'm sorry."

"Melinda was having some very hard problems, and I went to pray with her. And, well, it's very, very sad. You see, Melinda died." I pause, waiting for some kind of response. Maybe even sympathy. "Do you understand what I'm telling you, Sarah?"

"Melinda died?"

"Yes! So you see, I really needed to be there. She needed my help—" And now I start to cry.

"I'm sorry, Mommy. I'm sorry I called Melinda fat."

"It's okay, sweetheart. I just wanted you to understand why I left. Then I came home, and my girls were gone, and I was already so sad. Can you can imagine how upsetting it was when you weren't here?"

"Can you come and get us now, Mommy?"

"Yes. Don't wake up Grandma. But tell Mary what I told you and that I'll be there in about fifteen minutes. You girls be ready to go. Okay?"

"Okay."

So I grab my purse and my Bible and a few things for the girls and for me. I gather a few pieces of clothing, some food, some blankets, and I load these into the car and take off, speeding to my mother's house. I know that's the grandma Rick dumped them with since his mother lives nearly a thousand miles away. Although I'm sure he will consider that too, in time. Who knows what plans he has made?

Unfortunately, my mother is awake when I slip in the back door. And suddenly I realize that I will be fighting one of the biggest battles of my life today. Standing up to my mother is never a small thing. As hard as it was to deal with Rick, this could be harder. I will need my wits about me. No "crazy" talk about spiritual things that these people cannot understand. Instead, I will be crafty like the Enemy. I explain to my mother about my friend who died today, how I had to go to her to help, but then I came home, and the girls were gone.

"How did she die?" my mother asks. And I notice how tired she looks. She's lost weight, and there are dark circles beneath her eyes.

"That's not important now," I say as I take Sarah by the hand. "What is important is that Rick is making some big mistakes. It was very wrong for him to bring the girls to you. To try to hide them from me as if he's playing some weird control game with me. Can't you see that?"

She looks as if she's considering my words, trying to decide what's best to say. But I can tell she doesn't have much fight left in her. "But we are worried about you, Ruth. We think you're having some, uh, some mental problems."

"And did Rick tell you that he's been having an affair? Did he tell you that he comes home from work several hours late every night and that he's been cheating on me? Don't you think that might give a person some problems?"

She seems slightly shocked by this, so I continue.

"Did he tell you that his influence in our lives has been very, very wrong? Or that he's the main reason I'm struggling like this? Did he? *Did he?*"

"Well, no..."

I take Mary's hand now. "I didn't think so."

"But, Ruth—"

"Good-bye, Mother." I walk toward the door, and I can hear her behind me, but I doubt she will try to stop us. She doesn't appear to be very strong. "When you're ready to hear the truth, Mother, maybe you will talk to me instead of Rick!" Then I open the front door. "Come on, girls."

No one speaks as we get into the car. I tell the girls to buckle up, and then I drive into town, where I fill the tank with gas, using my emergency credit card since this is definitely an emergency. I tuck the card back into my purse, hoping it will hold out long enough for me to get where I need to go. I expect this will be a long trip.

"Why's all this stuff in here?" asks Mary as she peers back to where Sarah is sitting amid random pieces of clothing, blankets, and other things I hastily threw into the car.

"We're taking a trip," I say brightly as I enter the freeway, heading north.

"Where are we going?" asks Mary in a voice that sounds frightened.

"The Lord will lead," I assure them.

34

The thick gray clouds make this December afternoon seem even darker than it is. Or maybe it's just demonic oppression. But after driving north for a couple of hours, it occurs to me that I am literally driving into enemy territory. How stupid could I be? Naturally, there would be even more demonic activity up north—demons love the darkness! What was I thinking?

We're already in Washington State now, but I take the next exit, deciding to do a one-eighty and go south instead. But as I do this, I feel stupid, stupid, stupid. What is wrong with me? I take the circle loop, then drive under the overpass, make a right turn, and I am back on the freeway, going the exact opposite direction. What a waste!

"Where are we going, Mom?" asks Mary in a quiet, respectful voice. I know she's being extra careful now. I'm sure this is because I've snapped at both of them for asking too many questions. Finally I had to tell them to shut up! I felt bad at first since I don't usually talk to my girls like that. But it was the only way to make them understand. I couldn't tell them that their insistent questioning was making me start to think that the demons were still with us, hidden in my girls, and that I was dragging them up the freeway with me.

"Are we going home now?" asks Sarah from the backseat.

"No! We are not going home. We don't have a home. Don't you understand? Our home has become Satan's home, and we can't go

back to it. It has been defiled and contaminated, and it should probably just be burned to the ground."

Then Sarah starts to cry, and I wish I hadn't said so much. I
glance at Mary, and she has her knees pulled up to her chest with a
frightened look in her eyes.

"Don't be afraid," I tell them. "We just need to pray. Let's all pray
together. Let's bind Satan and his demons from this car, and I'm sure
we'll all start to feel better."

So we begin to pray, and we bind and cast out, and as we're doing
this, it occurs to me that some of the items I brought from home
must be contaminated too. It's dark now, but I must get rid of these
things. We cannot keep taking the old sinful things with us. Finally I
pull into a rest stop. I encourage the girls to take a bathroom break,
reminding them to be careful not to touch anything and that I'll be
right behind them. As soon as they're nearly to the rest room, I gather
a couple of armloads of all the things in the car, and I stuff them into
the various trash barrels.

I feel better now that the car is empty. We are driving down the
freeway, going south, and it seems like a fresh start.

"Where's all the stuff that was in the car?" asks Mary after just a
few miles.

"I put it away."

"Where?" asks Mary.

I turn and glare at her in the darkness. "You can't keep questioning everything I do, Mary. That is rebellious. And don't you
remember that rebellion is like witchcraft? You don't want to be a
witch, do you?"

"I just wondered…"

"Where is Samantha?" asks Sarah.

"Didn't you hear what I just said to your sister?"

"But I—"

"No buts," I shoot back at her. "Just be quiet. Go to sleep or something."

Both girls are amazingly quiet for the next several hours. I'm sure it's because they are scared. But maybe they should be scared. Maybe it will help them respect what an enormous battle we are in, as well as the fact that I am willing to keep fighting and fighting and fighting. Even if I am all alone and fighting without assistance of any kind, I'm still willing to stand up and oppose our enemy. And I am doing this for my daughters.

They didn't say anything when I stopped in our town on our way back south. But I was nearly out of gas by then and knew I should fill up. Still, I could sense the questions in Mary's mind. She thought something was wrong, but she was afraid to say so. To help smooth things over with the girls, I allowed them to get whatever they liked from the gas station convenience store. "You can get junk food or anything." I was surprised when they only picked out a few things. And not any candy.

But now that I'm back in the car, driving south, and it's almost eleven, I realize that using this credit card might be a big mistake. For one thing it has Rick's name on it, and that means it's tainted too. Just using it to fill the tank with gas is like inviting Satan to ride along with us. But the other thing, and perhaps even more troubling, is that I'm worried Rick might try to trace us through this credit card. He might be following us right now. The set of headlights that's been tailing us the past twenty minutes may very well belong to him.

So I take the next exit, which goes out into the country, just to see if the headlights behind us turn too. They don't. And for a few minutes, I feel relieved. But at the same time I am extremely worried that the other pieces of ID I'm carrying—my bank card and whatnot—could be used to trace me as well. So I keep driving until I come to a small bridge. Then, thinking the girls are still asleep, I quietly get out and empty the contents of my purse into the river. *There, that should do it.*

"What are you doing?" Mary is out of the car and walking toward me.

"Get back in the car! I didn't say you could get out."

"But what are you doing?" she asks again, and I can tell she is crying. "What are you doing, Mom?"

"Just getting rid of all the contaminants. Don't worry about it."

"But I thought—" Her voice breaks as we return to the car. "I thought you were going to jump off that bridge."

"Why would I do that?" I put the car in gear and head back toward the freeway.

"I…I don't know."

"Go back to sleep."

"But I'm afraid, Mom. I want to go home."

"I want to go home too," says Sarah from the backseat.

"I already told you. We can't go home. We don't have a home!"

"But we do," persists Sarah. "And Daddy is there. And Bonnie and Clyde are there. And I want to go back."

"No! We can't go back. We can never go back." And now both girls are sobbing so loudly that I can hardly think. And I can't even pray.

I'm on the freeway again, still driving south, but I feel so confused. Something is wrong, and I'm sure it's demonic. And I'm afraid it's with my girls. I'm afraid that the influence of Rick, and maybe even Matthew, has been too much for them. I'm afraid they are still allowing Satan's influence in their lives.

"We need to cast out your demons," I say as I drive. "Let's ask the Lord to bind and cast out every last demon that's in you, girls. Can you do that with me?"

"I don't have any demons in me, Mommy," says Sarah.

"You don't know that. They're tricky. Remember? They pretend to be other things. We need to bind them and cast them out."

"No!" shouts Mary. "We don't. This is crazy, Mom. I want to go home. I want to see Dad and the dogs, and I want to—"

"Get thee behind me, Satan! In the name of Jesus, I bind you from my girls. In the name of Jesus, I cast you out of this car. You are not welcome here, you Father of Lies, you foul Deceiver. Leave us at once!"

Both girls are crying again. And I can tell this isn't working.

"Please, Mom," begs Mary. "Please take us home."

"Yes, Mommy," says Sarah. "Please!"

"No! We don't have a home. You have to understand that."

Then Mary unbuckles her seat belt, and for one frightening moment, I think she's going to leap out of the car onto the freeway. But instead she climbs over the front seat and goes into the back with Sarah. "Let's pray, Sarah," she says. "Let's ask the Lord to help us."

And then they begin to pray. But instead of asking the Lord to protect them from Satan and his demons, they are begging the Lord to protect them from *me*! I can't believe my ears, and I want to yell at them and tell them to stop. But somehow I can't.

"Please, dear Lord," says Mary, "please show Mom that she's acting crazy and that she needs to take us home."

"Please, dear Lord," prays Sarah, "protect us tonight. Send your angels to watch over us. Help Mommy to see that this is wrong and—"

"That's enough!" I quickly take the next exit from the freeway. The girls remain silent as I slowly drive through the business section of a small mill town. It's after midnight now, and everything seems to be closed. Except maybe the building down at the end of town. It's a tavern, but I just don't care. I know what is wrong. I know what I have to do. And feeling as if part of me is completely shut down and dead now, I do it.

"Get out," I say to the girls as I come to a stop not far from the tavern.

"What?" says Mary.

"Get out. Get out of the car."

"Why, Mommy?" says Sarah. "What are you doing?"

"Get out! Get out now! Get out! Get out! Get out!"

I hear the back door open and then close, and then I see my two girls standing on the dimly lit street, clinging to each other as they stare at the car. I punch the gas and drive away. I can hardly see the road through the tears filling my eyes and streaming down my face. And instead of getting back onto the freeway, I go beneath the underpass and start driving up an old logging road that goes east and into the hills. It isn't a well-maintained road, and there are several times when I can't tell the road from the blackness that surrounds it, but I don't really care.

Go through the fire, pass through the flame, on the other side, emerge pure and clean. Go through the fire…through the flame…the other side…pure and clean. Why can't I do this right? Why can't I be purged? Why am I never pure and clean? No matter what I do, the evil remains with me. Why? Why? Why? As I continue into the darkness, I think I am getting closer to the answer. Or perhaps I am driving straight into hell. But somehow I understand. *I know the truth now.*

It seems perfectly clear. *I am the problem.* The demons are in me. They always have been. They always will be. I have tried and tried to drive them out. I have done everything I know. Used every spiritual weapon I have. I've done everything humanly possible. But it's no use. I am hopeless, useless, a total failure. I am a total failure as a mother. A total failure as a wife. A total failure as a friend, a sister, a daughter. A total failure as a Christian. There is no hope for me.

I continue along this pitch-black mountain road with no idea where it leads, but I am certain it will take me where I need to go—to the other side of darkness, to that place where Satan greets his victims, where demons gnash their teeth, devour, and destroy. I am going there now, and once and for all, I will end this thing.

Just when I am certain that I can't last another minute, that I must find that precarious place where the steep road drops away to nothing but darkness below, the car hits something. And although I step on the accelerator, hoping that this is it, that the car will leap from this road and plunge me to the end, my car comes to a complete stop.

It is stuck diagonally across the narrow road, and I cannot make it go forward, and I cannot make it go back. I attempt to rock the car back and forth, thinking that it's lodged on a boulder and that if it can come free, it will plummet down the steep rocky mountainside.

I pound my head against the steering wheel. Over and over I pound it. *"You are hopeless!"* I scream at the top of my lungs. *"Worthless! Useless! A failure! You can't do anything right! You can't even kill yourself right! You are a complete and utter failure!"*

On and on I go, finally resorting to horrible profanity, which convinces me beyond doubt that Satan has gotten full control of me now. Or perhaps he's always been in control. All those times when I was pointing my finger at everyone and everything else, it was Satan who was ruling my heart.

It's very cold up here, probably freezing, and this gives me an idea. I open all the windows and remove my jacket. Perhaps I will get hypothermia. I've heard that victims simply fall asleep and never wake up. But as I sit here shivering for what seems like a very long time, I question whether or not I can even do this right.

"Dear Lord, please help me!" I pound my fists on the steering wheel and dashboard. Then I pound my head against the steering wheel again, very hard this time—and complete blackness follows.

35

When I come to, it is still dark, and I am very cold. It takes me a few seconds to realize where I am and what I have done. But when realization hits, I feel so tormented, so devastated that I desperately wish it were all over. Why can't it be over? Why didn't I get hypothermia and just die? Oh, how I wish I were dead or, better yet, that I'd never been born at all.

I cannot bear to think of what I have done. How could I have possibly abandoned my two beloved daughters like that? And what has become of them? This thought makes me so sick that I open the car door and lean over and retch the contents of my stomach onto the muddy road beside me. I retch and retch and retch. Why can't it kill me? I know why I made the girls get out of the car. It was to spare them. To save them from the devil—and from me. To take them any farther with me would have put them in greater danger. Oh, why am I still living? Why must I be tortured like this?

I'm still shivering, and my head is throbbing. I can feel the swollen place on my forehead, but it doesn't matter. It wasn't enough to kill me. I attempt to rock the car again, but it seems solidly stuck. Suddenly I remember a scene from a movie where a murderer stuffs a rag in the exhaust pipe and the person in the running car is asphyxiated with carbon monoxide. I turn on the engine again, raise the windows, turn on the lights, then grab my jacket and climb out of the car. I slip through the mud as I make my way to the rear bumper. Then I kneel down until I can smell the gasoline and feel the heat of the exhaust. I stick my jacket into the pipe, stuffing it hard against the fumes trying to escape. Then I hurry, slipping and sliding through the mud, and climb back into the car. I make sure the vents are closed and the windows are tight, then I lean back.

This will be it. It will all be over soon.

Dawn is coming now. A small slit of golden light breaks through the silhouettes of trees up ahead, and I realize that my car nearly made it to the crest of this hill. Although a tiny part of me is hungry to see light again, I am mostly disappointed. I wanted to die out here in the darkness. I deserve to die out here in the darkness. Why is it taking so long?

I stare at the golden strip of light growing larger as the sun steadily rises above the top of the hill. And despite myself, I think about my Lord. I am thinking that, despite all my horrible mistakes and how I am completely unworthy to live, I do not want to be separated from my Lord for all of eternity. And yet there seems no option. How could he still want me? I have failed him. Failed him in every possible way. I wanted to fight his battles, to defeat his enemies, and the only thing I have defeated is myself.

That was never me.

I sit up straight, looking around to see if someone is here in the car. Did someone actually say that? Maybe I just imagined it. Or maybe it's the carbon monoxide fumes finally doing their work. But I run these four small words through my head over and over. *That was never me. That was never me. That was never me.* And I don't know how, but I get it. God is telling me I've been wrong. Confused and misled. I have been the world's most foolish sheep, tricked by a wolf in sheep's clothing. Somehow I know this deep within me.

Just as plain as the sun that's now shining in my face, I know without a doubt that it's the Lord who said those four words. He's telling me that everything I've done—so many things in his name, telling myself I was doing them for him—*that was never him.* And it occurs to me that people tried to tell me. Rick, Colleen, my sister, even my mixed-up mother—they all warned me. But I wouldn't listen. Instead, I trusted people like Glenn and Bronte. The image of those two hits me again with full force. How could I have been so deceived?

"I am such a fool." I lean back in the seat and close my eyes. "Please forgive me, Lord. I am such a fool. Have mercy." Tears pour down my cheeks as I think of my girls—and what I have done. My heart feels like it's being wrenched from my chest. But what can I do? So I pray. Only it's not a warfare prayer. I simply ask God to gather Mary and Sarah, and even poor Matthew, into his arms and to protect them. And then I begin to drift.

I startle at the sound of pounding on glass and turn to see a bearded face peering at me through my car window. At first I think it is Satan, here to gather the remains of my life. Then he smiles, and I think maybe it is the Lord. But I am too sleepy to do anything.

"Open the door!" the man yells. "Or we'll bust it in."

But my arms feel as if they are tied to my sides, and all I can do is simply close my eyes and wait for this to end. When will it end?

The next thing I know I am being dragged from my car. I am wrapped in a smelly wool blanket and bundled into the back of a club cab, which then rattles down the mountain road. Fast enough, judging by the trees that blur together as they whiz by, that we may go flying off the edge and plunge to the final end below. But we don't. I can hear a man talking on a radio or phone or something, but the words go right over me. And it feels like I can't move. I vaguely wonder if I'm paralyzed. But I don't think I really care.

We come to a stop, and I see an ambulance waiting. As two men help me out of the truck, at first dragging, then carrying me, I can tell this is the town where I dropped off Mary and Sarah the night before. I want to ask, "What has become of my girls?" but I can't get the words out. It's as if my brain isn't functioning, as if it's finally quieted down for a change. So I don't fight it.

I don't remember blacking out, but when I open my eyes again, I am in a hospital room. And, once again, my arms feel like lead, as if they're tied down to my sides. Then I see that they actually are strapped down. As are my legs. This seems strange, but perhaps this is my punishment. It seems minor compared to all I have done. And, in fact, it's a relief. It's an even bigger relief when I learn that my girls are safe…a relief that's wrapped in layers of guilt.

It's not long before I figure out I'm in the lockdown unit of Saint John's Hospital, in the very town where I used to live, where I used to have a home, a husband, children, a life… I'm a patient in the psychiatric ward, the place where crazy people are kept out of harm's way. Not that I want to harm anyone. Well, maybe myself, although I seem to have already done a pretty adequate job of that. Though I never really did finish it.

I think I've been in here several days when I overhear someone explaining the symptoms of carbon monoxide poisoning and how it can take a couple of weeks before the patient fully recovers. "There may still be brief losses of memory and perhaps even some mood swings, but it will abate in time." He pauses. "Of course, as you know, she will still need further psychiatric treatment after that." The man continues talking to someone. Maybe it's Rick. I think he's been here a few times. Not that we've talked. We haven't. At least I haven't.

Two weeks after that night

If someone had given me a keg of dynamite and said, "Here, go ahead and blow up your life," it couldn't have been much more effective than what I've done. Maybe quicker and less painful. I am so ashamed. So very ashamed.

Dr. Doris (she likes being called by her first name) has been working with me. One of the first things she told me was that I need to start controlling my inner voice. "The one that is always condemning you," she explained after I confessed to her about the things I so often tell myself and the names I use, like "loser" and "failure" and "useless" and "hopeless."

"You cannot allow that inner voice to keep bullying you, Ruth."

Then she gave me a CD to listen to that says positive things, uplifting things, things I wish someone had said to me a long time ago. Maybe someone did. Maybe I just forgot. I imagine that it's the Lord's voice and that he might say such kind and gracious things to me. But I still find myself doubting that possibility. And I still find myself wanting to go to battle with my demonic oppressors. Although Dr. Doris says those demonic beings were not real, I find that hard to believe. I tell her they seemed very real to me. And then I tell her that I wasn't the only one to see them.

"The power of suggestion is strong," she explains. "The mind is complex, the memory can be confusing, and the imagination is a powerful force."

"Are you suggesting that I imagined all those horrors?"

"Have you ever had a nightmare, Ruth?"

"Of course. Who hasn't?"

"Did it seem real?" she asks me.

I don't know the answer.

"You are highly susceptible to these kinds of hallucinations."

"Hallucinations?" I try to make sense of this, but so much is still murky…or maybe it's the meds.

A few days ago Doris put me through a battery of psychological tests. "You display all the symptoms of someone who suffers from obsessive-compulsive disorder," she explained after determining the results. "More commonly known as OCD."

"Like that show *Monk,* about the detective?" I can barely remember seeing it once, a long time ago.

"Sort of. But every case is unique." Then she explains that my kind of OCD made me take normal things to unhealthy extremes. "An obsession is something you can't let go of. For instance, you keep thinking about the same thing or repeating the same sequence of words. It's like you get stuck on something and can't escape it. Do you understand?"

If I weren't so depressed, I would just laugh. "Yes, I understand. Trust me…I understand."

"And a compulsion is when you do something almost uncontrollably. You experience a pressing need to, say, wash your hands, and nothing and no one can stop you from doing it. In fact, you may do it over and over." She peers over her reading glasses at me. "Do you know what I mean?"

I just nod.

Then she goes on, telling me stories and case histories of other people who have suffered from OCD. My reaction to this news is mixed. On one hand, I am greatly relieved to know that I'm not alone and that this thing that's plagued me for nearly as long as I can remember actually has a name and, I'm told, a treatment. But on the other hand, I feel so incredibly stupid for not knowing about it sooner. I remember how people have said things to me in the past. My mother, my sister, even Rick pointed out that I had this tendency to obsess over small things. Why didn't we realize it was an illness? Or maybe they did…maybe it was just me in the dark? But why did it have to go so far?

Speaking of the other people in my life, Rick was here two days before Christmas. He told me that some members of my family wanted to come visit me. They wanted to bring me gifts and wish me Merry Christmas. I told him I wasn't ready for that.

"What about the girls?" he asked.

I didn't know what to say, so I simply looked away, said nothing. Oh, it's not that I don't love them. I do. I would do anything for them. And for Matthew too. But I am still so ashamed. So humiliated. How does anyone ever survive something like this?

"How about if I bring Matthew and the girls for Christmas? Just to say hello. It would be good for the girls to see you, to see that you're okay."

"Okay?" I looked at him with tears filling my eyes. "Okay?"

He sighed. "Well, you know. I think it would be good. And Dr. Doris agrees."

Christmas Day

Maybe Dr. Doris's medications are finally doing their job, because I am a bit calmer than I expected when Rick and the kids come to visit.

But it also feels like I'm in a fog, as if things aren't completely real, but I suppose this is for the best. They all take turns embracing me and telling me they love me. And although I believe them, I can feel the stiffness in their hugs, see the formality of their smiles. They, like me, would like to get this over with.

"We're having Christmas dinner at Lynette's," Rick informs me as they're getting ready to leave. I know he thinks this should cheer me up, realizing that he and the kids aren't sitting around our house feeling depressed, but the idea of everyone at my sister's only reminds me of the old days—of how I've always been an outsider, a castoff. And I fight back tears of self-pity as I tell my family good-bye.

As soon as they're gone, I berate myself for my selfishness, but then I remember what Dr. Doris said and how I need to squelch any negative ranting of my inner voice. So I put in my earphones and play my CD and pretend that God is talking to me. Speaking words of love, encouragement, hope, and kindness. It's still somewhat unfamiliar. But I like it.

I'm released from the hospital on December 29. I'm not entirely sure this is such a good idea, but Dr. Doris seems to think I'm ready. She has me scheduled for some form of therapy almost every day of the week. Family therapy, group therapy, individual therapy—it seems they have something for everyone. But Rick assures me that he and the kids are willing and that everyone wants to see me get better. I can only hope this is true. And I must admit the meds are helping more now—the fog is lifting some. And there are moments when I can almost see humor in things. Briefly.

I'm amazed at how much I continue to sleep once I'm home.

Rick, following Dr. Doris's recommendation, set up a bedroom for me in Matthew's old room. She told him I would need the space for a while. And due to the continuing struggle with my fear of demons and contamination, I appreciate it. Still, Dr. Doris warned me that the only way to conquer these things will be to face them head-on.

"What's the worst thing that will happen to you if you cannot take a shower?" she asked me one day after I told her about being disturbed because I wanted to take a cleansing shower and the nurse wouldn't let me. "Tell me, what's the worst?"

I didn't know how to answer that question.

"Really, Ruth. What's the worst thing? Will your toes curl up? Will your hair fall out? Will you smell so terrible that no one will want to be near you? What's the worst thing?"

I honestly couldn't think of one single *real* thing. Well, other than how I would feel. "It would make me feel bad."

"You say that, but taking a cleansing shower doesn't make you feel better either. You've told me yourself that the relief only lasts a short while and then you feel bad again. Not only that, but you end up with cracked and dry skin. It'll make you old before your time."

So that has become my big question. "What is the worst thing that will happen if I do or don't do certain things?" And while it doesn't work with every situation, I can tell that it's helping. Still, it seems a long and lonely road out of this place. Sometimes I wonder if it's even worth it.

I also wonder why God has allowed me to be this way. Dr. Doris said that while nothing is proven, there are reasons to think this disorder has some genetic connections. "It does seem to run in families," she told me after I described my grandma Clark to her. "And there are certain things that just seem to trigger it too." She warned both Rick and me that we'd need to keep a closer eye on our children. "In case you see them developing any symptoms. Early diagnosis and treatment could prevent them from ever getting to the place where Ruth has been."

God help anyone who ever has to go to the place where I have been. Even in group therapy, where I've heard some crazy stories, mine seems to take the cake. Not that I find any comfort in this. But as Dr. Doris says, it's good to keep nurturing a sense of humor. And somehow she thinks I have one. Although I'm sure it must be hidden pretty deep. And I'm practicing smiling. She says that when you make the effort to smile, really smile, it sends a message to your soul. And I think this may be true. Anyway, I am trying, and the girls seem to appreciate it.

Before being released from the hospital, Dr. Doris made me promise not to reconnect with any of my previous acquaintances at New Fire. She actually had me sign an agreement. Rick had filled her in on my involvement there, and she seemed fairly convinced that this was one of the major keys to my undoing.

"I don't think that's going to be much of a problem," I told her as I handed her back my contract. I don't add that I would rather be dead than go back to that church. But it's true.

Epilogue

Sometimes that night on the lonely mountain road where I tried to end my life seems like a lifetime away. Sometimes it seems like yesterday. A lot has happened in these past two years. And while it hasn't been easy, I think it's been good. And I think there's a reason.

I'm still in treatment, although I only see Dr. Doris every other week, and she's saying that monthly visits might be around the corner. Although I'm not convinced. But one of the things I discovered through my treatments and tests is that I have a very high IQ. I thought this was ironic since I've spent so much of my life telling myself that I was stupid, stupid, stupid. Back in grade school, I recall how other kids thought I was pretty smart, and maybe they were right. But somehow my intelligence just got buried beneath all my crazy OCD symptoms.

Speaking of school, both the girls are back in public school, happily reunited with their old friends. They did finish their year at the Christian school, since the school's policy made any refunding impossible. I suppose it was for the best because everyone there seemed to be fairly understanding. But both Mary and Sarah seem genuinely glad to be back in public school. And I am Sarah's room mother now, planning for the upcoming Christmas party.

Matthew still works at the bookstore (which I now frequent and which makes a pretty good mocha), and he still lives with Jason. He has also started taking some classes part-time at the community college. And despite his busy schedule, he still manages to drop by to visit his family on a fairly regular basis or when he's hungry. He hasn't decided to come back to church yet (Rick and the girls and I have been back at Valley Bridge Fellowship awhile now), but he does attend on holidays. Mostly I have come to accept that he's on his own spiritual journey now. And I pray for him.

Rick is still working for the shipping company, but now he's back to days. Unfortunately, the promotion and raise never fully materialized, but Rick decided it just wasn't worth it. Things are tight, but then what's new? And now that I'm not making those insane financial decisions, which we only recently recovered from, we seem to be doing okay. For the most part. Life's certainly not perfect.

But Rick swears that the counseling we've received (as a result of my breakdown, diagnosis, and treatment—thank God for Rick's health insurance) has been really life changing for him. And, I must confess, it has saved our marriage. Oh, we still have our disagreements from time to time, and my OCD still raises its bossy, ugly head occasionally (something Rick has learned not to point out with too much enthusiasm), but all in all, we are happier than we've ever been. And there's a lot to look forward to.

Maybe it was Matthew's enthusiasm about his college classes or my learning about my high IQ, but I'm considering furthering my education as well. I think I want to study psychology. But just a couple of classes, at least to begin with, since I started working part-time a couple of months ago.

Colleen and Dennis moved back to town after only six months. Apparently his job wasn't all they'd hoped it would be, and New

Mexico was just "too hot to handle." So now Colleen and I are job sharing at the clinic, and I have to admit that Colleen always was, and still is, some of the best medicine for me. I think God knew this from that first day he connected us way back in high school when I was looking for a friend who could teach me to let my hair down.

It was Colleen who talked me into going back to Valley Bridge Fellowship. I'll admit that it felt horribly awkward at first. I was certain that everyone was staring at me or whispering behind my back, but I got over it in time. And now I feel almost totally at home there. It's also been a huge help in reconstructing my image of God since the pastor there seems to be fairly well grounded and doesn't take himself too seriously.

I still remember those four words, the ones I heard up on that hill when I was trying to check out. *That was never me.* And I know it was God speaking, telling me that I'd been deceived, revealing to me that all that fear-driven crud and the focus on demons attacking from everywhere wasn't coming from him. It never had been. It was man-made and probably Satan inspired.

It also has given me a new respect for taking the Lord's name in vain. I inwardly cringe if I hear someone saying, "God told me to do such and such." Oh, they might not mean it the way it sounds, but I think we all need to be very careful. It's dangerous to put words in God's mouth, which most of the leadership at New Fire were doing.

It's a step-by-step process, coming back to God. Or maybe I'm finding him for the first time. But I've come to realize, and to truly appreciate, that God doesn't want us to live in fear. Where God is, there is perfect peace. That is such a relief.

I saw Cynthia the other day. She was in the grocery store, the one that's open 365 days a year and the one I swore I'd never go back to.

I bumped into her in the cereal section, and I thought my heart would leap right out of my chest. I was so scared. I know it makes no sense, not to a normal person. But just seeing her standing there, slightly hunched, with her long gray braid trailing down the back of one of her homely, homemade jumpers that reached nearly to her ankles, and all those old memories—the deliverance prayers, the lectures—well, they just seemed to flash before me, and I almost felt sick to my stomach. Her eyes were narrowed as she attempted to read the fine print on the back of a box of Smart Start, and I almost used this opportunity to turn and run the other way. But I didn't. I stopped and said, "Hi, Cynthia."

She almost dropped the box of cereal. But then she recovered and asked how I'd been, and I knew I had two options: I could say "fine" and just leave it at that, or I could tell her the truth. Or at least a shortened version. I decided on option two, and by the time I finished, Cynthia broke into tears.

She told me that their church fell completely apart. Bronte, who it turned out had fled from another questionable church, was having an affair with Glenn. They managed to keep the whole thing concealed for quite some time, but when it came to light, it was a death-blow to the church.

"Maybe you'd like to come back to VBF," I told her as I placed a box of Cheerios in my cart. "The pastor there is a really solid guy."

"Oh, I don't know…" She backed away from me almost as if she were spying a demon crouched on my shoulder, just as we'd done in the old days.

But I just smiled at her. "You know what, Cynthia? God showed me that none of that was ever him. God isn't like that, you know. He doesn't want us to be afraid."

Her brow creased as if she was considering this. Then she told me that *she'd be praying for me,* and before I could respond, she scurried away.

Now this just got me. In fact, it aggravated me more than I care to admit. Why should *I* need Cynthia to pray for me? And I have to confess that I actually started to obsess over this comment, making up responses in my head, things I could've or should've said to her. Ways I might've put her in her place.

And then I just said to myself, *Knock it off, Ruth!* That's when I recalled Dr. Doris's favorite question as I picked up a box of Froot Loops for Sarah. What's the worst thing that could happen if Cynthia *did* pray for me? And I just laughed at myself and laughed at my OCD, and I thanked God that he is so much bigger than all of it!

Readers Group
Guide

1. "It's not good enough" is a statement Ruth often hears while growing up, and later on she internalizes and repeats it. How do you react when you hear words like that?

2. Ruth, the middle child, never feels she's wanted or even loved. Do you think this is real or imagined? Why?

3. Why do you think Ruth begins to experience OCD symptoms at such an early age? What do you think could've been done to help her?

4. Were you surprised to discover that OCD sufferers are at greater risk for spiritual deception? Why or why not?

5. Why do you think Ruth was so consumed with a need to feel clean?

6. How would you react if a loved one became involved in a church like New Fire?

7. Ruth "unselfishly" donated time, energy, and money to the church, but it only seemed to get her deeper into trouble. Why do you think she continued to do this?

8. Sometimes Ruth and her daughters believed they saw actual demons (an element inspired from a real-life story). How do you explain this?

9. How did you feel about Ruth's role as a wife and mother? Explain.

10. Everyone is subject to some kind of obsession or compulsion. What are yours? And how do you keep them under control?

11. Ruth had a good friend in Colleen. What would you do if you believed a close friend or relative was experiencing a serious mental illness?

12. Ultimately, Ruth came to realize that God was not the one who had led her to such dark spiritual places. And while she welcomed that realization, she still needed psychological treatment and care. Why?

Additional Resources

healthfinder

www.healthfinder.gov

Healthfinder is a federal Web site you can use to find government and nonprofit health and human-services information on the Internet. Healthfinder links to carefully selected information and Web sites from over eighteen hundred health-related organizations.

Mental Health America

www.nmha.org

Mental Health America (formerly the National Mental Health Association) is the country's oldest and largest nonprofit organization addressing all aspects of mental health and mental illness.

Obsessive-Compulsive Foundation

www.ocfoundation.org

The mission of the OCF is to educate the public and professional communities about OCD and related disorders; to provide assistance to individuals with OCD and related disorders, their families, and their friends; and to support research into the causes and effective treatments of OCD and related disorders.

Mayo Clinic

www.mayoclinic.com

MayoClinic.com provides up-to-date health information and tools that give visitors access to the experience and knowledge of the more than two thousand physicians and scientists of the Mayo Clinic.

National Center for Complementary and Alternative Medicine
http://nccam.nih.gov
The NCCAM is one of the centers that make up the National Institutes of Health. The center's mission is to support rigorous research on complementary and alternative medicine and to disseminate information to the public and professionals on which modalities work, which do not, and why.

National Institutes of Health
http://health.nih.gov
The National Institutes of Health is one of the world's foremost medical research centers and the federal focal point for medical research in the United States. The goal of NIH research is to acquire new knowledge to help prevent, detect, diagnose, and treat disease and disability.

National Institute of Mental Health
www.nimh.nih.gov/health/publications/
This site offers information from NIMH about the symptoms, diagnosis, and treatment of mental illnesses. You can find brochures, information sheets, reports, press releases, fact sheets, and other educational materials.